THE WORLD TREASURY OF

FAIRY TALES & FOLKLORE

The World Treasury of

Fairy Tales & Folklore

A Family Heirloom of Stories to Inspire and Entertain

Professor William Gray
With Joanna Gilar & Rose Williamson

Wellfleet Press

A Global Book

First published in the United States of America in 2016 by
Wellfleet Press, a member of
Quarto Publishing Group USA Inc.
142 West 36th Street, 4th Floor
New York, New York 10018
www.quartoknows.com

10 9 8 7 6 5 4 3 2 1

ISBN-13: 978-1-57715-127-2

Printed in China

Conceived, designed, and produced by Global Book Publishing

Consultant Editor: Professor William Gray

Contributors: Dr. Joanna Gilar and Rose Williamson

Project Manager: Kate Duffy

Design and Silhouette Illustrations: Lindsey Johns

Color Illustrations: Fausto Bianchi

Contents

Introduction

Folklore and fairy tales define our culture. They are repositories for human experience, containing our wishes, fears, and dreams. Their predecessors have a history that predates printing; we told stories aloud before we wrote them down, and had begun to craft tales to pass down through generations before we had created the paper on which to record these imaginative narratives. Today, many of those that we know best have no known author; they are, as they always have been, public property. Even those with identifiable authors seem to have become part of the collective imagination. We narrate, change, unpick, and reweave them to speak to the concerns of the time. They become part of our evolving cultural history. This adaptive nature, endlessly changeable to new tastes and yet always familiar, contributes to the enduring nature of folk and fairy tales today.

This book contains both folktales and fairy tales, but it can be difficult to separate the one from the other. Some scholars might argue that folktales are oral and fairy tales come from a print tradition, but by setting that parameter, we find that many times tales cross over from oral to print and vice versa (and continue to do so today). Sometimes, folktales are described as tales of the common man, and fairy tales are a subset of this. The tale becomes a fairy tale when it contains wondrous elements. Undeniably, the two are in constant conversation, and this book encompasses both traditions.

Where do fairy tales begin? This is not an easy question to answer. Particular issues arise around the consideration of the origins of the tales, their motifs, and their plots. Some tales seem very similar to stories from Ancient Greece and Rome. Some echo the medieval romances and ballads of Europe. Many of them were first penned into the shapes we are familiar with in sixteenth-century Italy. Some scholars argue that it was this particular urban Renaissance culture which is responsible for inventing what we think of as the "fairy tale," and the genre's focus on swift transformations of fortune reflected the rapid changes of wealth and position that were key aspects to city life. Yet for other thinkers, these shapeshifting stories have roots going back far further, to before writing itself. These theorists trace the tales to a time when reality and story were believed to be far more intertwined. This line of thinking suggests that key fairy-tale tropes, such as the quest into the forest during which the child becomes an adult, were based on real rituals and folk practice. Thus, the tales we now tell for comfort and diversion were once serious practices of learning how to live with wild beings and our wild selves.

As intriguing as these ideas may be, the question of the fairy tale's origin has no answer. Because oral stories leave no record but exist only with what Diabate, a storyteller from West Africa, described as the "moisture of the breath that carries them," this is not a question that we can hope to answer definitively. Wherever they began, and however much they record our past, our fairy tales are also engraved with the desires, values, and understandings of the times in which they were placed upon the page, and the role of author, storyteller, and collector, while important to distinguish, is also very often indistinguishable.

What we do know, however, follows a printed path across Europe. We know that the stories which came to be called fairy tales were first written down in sixteenth-century Italy, specifically, in Venice and Naples. These bustling meeting places of trade and tale inspired two authors, Giovanni Francesco Straparola and later Giambattista Basile, to pen literary masterpieces by collecting together Italy's patchwork of traditional stories. The evolution of the fairy tale continued in seventeenth-century

France, where groups of influential noblewomen gathered together in salons to re-tell traditional stories. They adapted the tales to make them into subtle and witty critiques of the corruptions of the French court. It is to one of these women, Marie-Catherine D'Aulnoy, that we owe the term "fairy tale," although, of course, many of the stories that exemplify the genre contain no fairies at all. The popularity of the fairy tale continued in France with the author Charles Perrault, and, over one hundred years later, sprung up with renewed life in Germany, when two linguists named Jacob and Wilhelm Grimm decided to make a collection of German stories.

Many of the tales that first appeared in the Italian collections also appear in widely differing variants across the world. For example, instead of the common dwarfs, Snow White has also tamed dragons in Scotland and ghouls in Morocco. Versions of Cinderella range in the thousands and are found in Russia, Asia, Africa, and the Americas.

The stories alter dramatically, depending on both when and where they are told. Each era and location, not to mention individual tellers themselves, breathe individuality into constantly evolving versions of the stories. Both the Grimms and Perrault had children in mind when they reworked their tales, and thus edited the content to create stories appropriate for a young audience.

However, early versions, written for adults, tended to contain sexual and violent content that has been removed from nursery books. For example, in this collection, Rapunzel does not passively await her fate but conjures animals to defeat the ogress. An earlier version of "Sleeping Beauty" is darker than the bedtime story we know today. These earlier tales are unsettling, particularly given our association of fairy tales as innocent, bedtime communications from parent to child. Yet these variants are also reminders that fairy tales are, and always have been, distillations of the complexities, terrors, and transformations of our lives.

This collection is laid out into five sections. The first, Sixteenth- and Seventeenth-Century Tales, contains stories from the earliest days of the genre, which began to define the style of what we now consider to be fairy tales. The tales from Italy are evocative and familiar, but contain details that go against expectations set by more popular versions.

The second section on Eighteenth-Century Tales contains tales that were authored or translated amidst a great wave of popularity for fairy tales and tales of wonder. On the heels of authors such as Charles Perrault, Europe began to devour tales. *The Arabian Nights* helped to fulfill this need, offering tales of alien other lands, both magical and real.

The third section, Nineteenth-Century Folktale Collections, peeks into the folktale fever that came over scholars during this era. The tales showcase stories anthologized by collectors who sought to preserve them for the future as markers of regional and national folk culture.

The fourth section, Nineteenth-Century Literary Tales, represents the simultaneous trend of fairy-tale authorship that happened alongside folktale collecting. Inspired by tale collections, writers such as Hans Christian Andersen and Oscar Wilde began to pen their own stories, which took their place on the bookshelf next to the collections by the Brothers Grimm and Joseph Jacobs.

Finally, the section on Twentieth-Century Folktale Collections returns to tales that have been, in some sense, maintained as collectors heard them. More of these folktales originated outside Europe–from India to the United States–demonstrating a desire on the part of collectors and readers to hear global tales from all corners of the earth.

This collection celebrates the diversity of the genre, offering stories that range from the sublime to the ridiculous, the humorous to the tragic. They evoke the fantastical wonder of the marvelous quest, and, often simultaneously, celebrate and contemplate the magic that exists in the prosaic existence of daily life. They reveal that our stories are our lives, and our lives are implicitly and absolutely contained in our stories.

Sixteenth- and Seventeenth-Century Tales

The genre of the print fairy tale as we know it begins in the sixteenth and seventeenth centuries in Italy and France. Traditional fairy tales, which are still popular today, were first put into print by lesser-known Italian writers Giovanni Francesco Straparola and Giambattista Basile. Both used narratives in which characters in a primary plotline gathered together to tell one another stories. These stories had fairies, ogres, and magic—in short, they were fairy tales. By the end of the seventeenth century, fairy tales were fashionable. The French author Charles Perrault published his collection of fairy tales (with morals), which secured the place of fairy tales in Western culture.

Costantino Fortunato

Once upon a time in Bohemia, there was a woman named Soriana who lived in great poverty with her three sons, who were called Dusolino, Tesifone, and Costantino Fortunato. Soriana had nothing of any value in the way of household goods save three things, and these were a kneading trough of the kind women use in the making of bread, a board such as is used in the preparation of pastry, and a cat. Being now weighed down with a very heavy burden of years, Soriana saw that death was approaching, and therefore made her last will and testament, leaving to Dusolino, her eldest son, the kneading trough, to Tesifone, the pastry board, and to Costantino, the cat.

When the mother was dead and duly buried, the neighbors would sometimes borrow the kneading trough and sometimes the pastry board, as the need arose. And since they knew that the young men were very poor, they gave them by way of repayment a cake, which Dusolino and Tesifone ate by themselves, giving none of it to Costantino, the youngest brother. And if Costantino happened to ask them to give him some, they would answer by telling him to go to his cat, who would surely let him have what he wanted. So, poor Costantino and his cat underwent much suffering.

Now it so happened that Costantino's cat was a fairy in disguise, and the cat, feeling very sorry for him and very angry at his two brothers because of their cruel treatment of him, one day said, "Costantino, don't be downhearted, for I'll look after you and get enough provisions for both of us."

Thereupon the cat left the house and went into the fields, where he lay down and pretended to be asleep so cleverly that an unsuspecting young hare came close to where it was lying, and was immediately seized and killed.

Then, carrying the hare, the cat went to the king's palace, and, having met some of the courtiers, who were standing around, said that it wanted to speak to the king. When the king heard that a cat had begged an audience with him, he bade them bring it into his presence, and, having asked it what his business was, the cat replied that Costantino, his master, had sent a hare as a present to the king, and begged him to accept it. And with these words it presented the hare to the king, who was pleased to accept it, asking at the same time who this Costantino might be. The cat replied that he was a young man who for virtue and good looks had no superior, and the king, on hearing this report, gave the cat a kindly welcome, and ordered them to set before it meat and drink of the best. The cat, when it had eaten and drunk enough, adroitly filled the bag in which it had brought the hare with all sorts of good provisions, when no one was looking that way, and, having taken leave of the king, carried the spoils back to Costantino.

The two brothers, when they saw Costantino enjoying the food, asked him to let them have a share, but he paid them back in their own coin, and refused to give them a morsel. Therefore, the brothers were tormented with gnawing envy of Costantino's good fortune. Now Costantino, though he was a good-looking youth, had suffered so much privation and distress that his face was rough and covered with blotches, which caused him much discomfort.

So the cat, having taken him one day down to the river, washed him and licked him carefully with its tongue from head to foot, and tended him so well that in a few days he was quite freed from his ailment. The cat still went on carrying presents to the royal palace in the fashion already described, and by this means was able to provide for Costantino.

But after a time the cat began to find these trips to and from the palace rather irksome, and feared moreover that the king's courtiers might become impatient; so it said to Costantino, "My master, if you will only do what I shall tell you, in a short time you will find yourself a rich man."

"And how will you manage this?" asked Costantino.

Then the cat answered, "Come with me, and do not trouble yourself about anything, for I have a plan for making a rich man of you which cannot fail."

Thereupon the cat and Costantino went to a place on the riverbank, close to the king's palace. Without delay, the cat told his master to strip off all his clothes and to throw himself into the river. Then it began to cry and shout in a loud voice, "Help, help, run, run, my lord Costantino is drowning!"

It happened that the king heard what the cat was shouting, and, bearing in mind what great benefits he had received from Costantino, he immediately sent some of his household to the rescue. When Costantino had been dragged out of the water and dressed by the attendants in handsome garments, he was led into the presence of the

"'My master, if you will only do what I shall tell you,

in a short time you will find yourself a rich man.'"

king, who gave him a hearty welcome, and inquired of him how it was that he found himself in the water. But Costantino, on account of his agitation, knew not what reply to make. So the cat, who always kept by his side, answered in his stead: "I must tell you, O King, that some robbers, who had learned through a spy that my master was taking a great store of jewels to offer to you as a present, lay in wait for him and robbed him of his treasure. Then they tried to murder him by throwing him into the river, but thanks to these gentlemen he has escaped death."

When he heard this, the king gave orders that Costantino should enjoy the best of treatment, and, seeing that he was well-built and handsome, and believing him to be very rich, he made up his mind to give him his daughter Elisetta as his wife, and to endow her with a rich dowry of gold and jewels and sumptuous clothes.

When the marriage ceremonies were completed and the festivities at an end, the king ordered ten mules to be loaded with gold, and five with the richest garments, and sent the bride, accompanied by a great entourage of people, to her husband's house. When he saw himself so highly honored and loaded with riches, Costantino was greatly perplexed as to where he should take his bride; so he sought advice from the cat, who replied, "Don't be troubled over this business, master; I will provide for everything."

So, as they were all riding along merrily together, the cat left the others and rode on rapidly ahead.

After it had left the company a long way behind, it came upon some cavaliers whom it addressed as follows: "Alas, you poor fellows, what are you doing here? Get away as quickly as you can, for a great body of armed men is coming along this road and will surely attack and destroy you. See, they are now quite near; listen to the noise of the neighing horses."

At this the horsemen were overcome with fear and said to the cat, "What shall we do?"

The cat replied, "It will be best for you to act as I tell you. If they should ask you whose men you are, you must answer boldly that you serve Lord Costantino, and then no one will harm you."

Then the cat left them, and, having ridden on still farther, came upon great flocks of sheep and herds of cattle, and it told the same story and gave the same advice to the shepherds and drovers who were in charge of them. Then going on still farther, the cat spoke in the same way to whomever it happened to meet.

As the cavalcade of the princess passed on, the gentlemen who were accompanying her asked the horsemen whom they met the name of their lord; and they asked the herdsmen who the owner of all these sheep and oxen was. The answer given by all was that they served Lord Costantino.

Then the gentlemen of the escort said to the bridegroom, "So, Lord Costantino, it appears we are now entering your dominions?" Costantino nodded his head in agreement, and he answered all their interrogations in the same way, so that all the company judged him to be enormously rich. In the meantime, the cat had ridden on and had come to a fair and stately castle, which was guarded by a very weak garrison, which the cat addressed in the following words: "My good men, what is it you do? Surely you must be aware of the destruction which is about to overwhelm you?"

"What is this destruction you speak of?" demanded the guards.

"Why, before another hour passes," replied the cat, "your place will be attacked by a great company of soldiers, who will cut you to pieces. Don't you already hear the neighing of the horses and see the dust in the air? So, unless you want to die, listen to my advice, which will get you safely out of all danger. When anyone asks you who owns this castle, say that it belongs to Lord Costantino Fortunato."

Thus, when the time came, the guards answered as the cat had directed; for when the noble escort of the bride had arrived at the stately castle, and certain gentlemen had inquired of the guards the name of the lord of the castle, they were answered that it was Lord Costantino Fortunato. And when the whole company had entered the castle they were honorably lodged there.

Now the lord of this castle was a certain Signor Valentino, a very brave soldier, who only a few days ago had left his castle to bring back the wife he had recently married. But as luck would have it, he met with an accident on the road, some way before he came to the place where his beloved wife was residing, and he died immediately. So Costantino Fortunato retained the lordship of Valentino's castle.

Not long after this Morando, King of Bohemia, died, and the people by acclamation chose Costantino Fortunato for their king, seeing that he had married Elisetta, the late king's daughter, to whom the kingdom belonged by right of succession. And by these means, Costantino rose from being very poor to become a powerful king, and lived long with Elisetta his wife, leaving their children to inherit his kingdom.

Giovanni Francesco Straparola

Notes on the Story

Costantino Fortunato

Very little is known about Giovanni Francesco Straparola (c. 1480–1558), an Italian writer and fairy-tale collector from Caravaggio, who later settled in Venice, then at the heart of the burgeoning printing industry. While his given name is likely to have been Giovanni Francesco, "Straparola" is not a typical family name of that time and place; its literal meaning of "babbler" makes it a likely nickname. Straparola has been called the originator of the literary form of the fairy tale. Stories from Straparola and his Italian successor Giambattista Basile later appeared in the collections of Charles Perrault and the Brothers Grimm.

Straparola's main work is the collection *Le piacevoli notti* (*The Pleasant* or *Facetious Nights*), with seventy-five stories. Within a frame narrative modeled on Giovanni Boccaccio's fourteenth-century *Decameron*, the participants of a thirteen-night party on the island of Murano, near Venice, tell each other stories ranging from the bawdy to the fantastic. It is the first European narrative of its kind to contain folktales and fairy tales, including the earliest known written versions of famous fairy tales such as "Costantino Fortunato," which reappears as Basile's "Cagliuso" and Perrault's "Puss-in-Boots."

The Pig King

Galeotto, King of Anglia, was greatly blessed with worldly riches. His wife Ersilia, the daughter of Matthias, King of Hungary, was a princess who outshone all the other ladies of the time in virtue and beauty. Moreover, Galeotto was a wise king, ruling his land so that no one ever heard a complaint against him. Though they had been married several years, they were childless, which made them both unhappy.

One day, while Ersilia was walking in her garden, she felt suddenly weary, and noticing a nearby place covered with fresh green turf, she went over and sat down upon it. Overcome with weariness and soothed by the sweet singing of the birds in the green foliage, she fell asleep.

And it chanced that while she slept, three superior fairies passed by. When they saw the sleeping queen, they stopped and, gazing upon her beauty, took counsel together as to how they might cast a spell to protect her. When they were agreed, the first cried out, "I wish that no man shall be able to harm her, and that, the next time she lies with her husband, she may be with child and bear a son who shall not have his equal in all the world for beauty."

Then the second declared, "I wish that no one shall ever have power to offend her, and that the prince who shall be born of her shall be gifted with every virtue under the sun."

And the third fairy, who was very mischievous, said, "And I wish that she shall be the wisest among women, but that the son whom she shall conceive shall be born in the skin of a pig, with a pig's ways and manners, and in this state he shall be obliged to remain till he shall have three times taken a woman to wife."

As soon as the three fairies had flown away Ersilia awoke, and immediately arose and went back to the palace, taking with her the flowers she had plucked. Not many days had passed before she knew herself to be pregnant, and when the time of her delivery came, she gave birth to a son with limbs like those of a pig and not of a human being. When news of this prodigy came to the ears of the king and queen, they lamented greatly, and the king, bearing in mind how good and wise his queen was, often felt moved to put this offspring of hers to death and cast him into the sea, in order that she might be spared the shame of having given birth to him. But, when he debated this in his mind and considered that this son, however he might be, was of his own blood, he put aside the cruel plan which he had been contemplating, and, seized with pity and grief, he made up his mind that the son should be brought up and nurtured like a rational being and not as a brute beast.

The child, therefore, being nursed with the greatest care, would often be brought to the queen and would put his little snout and his little paws in his mother's lap, and she, moved by natural affection, would caress him by stroking his bristly back with her hand, and embracing and kissing him as if he had been of human form. Then he would wag his tail and give other signs to show that he was conscious of his mother's affection.

The piglet, when he grew older, began to talk like a human being, and to wander about in the city, but whenever he came near to any mud or muck he would always wallow in it, like a pig, and come home all covered with dirt. Then, when he approached the king and queen, he would rub his sides against their fair garments, defiling them with all manner of grime, but because he was indeed their own son they put up with it all.

"The child . . . would often be brought to the queen and

would put his little paws and his little snout in his mother's lap . . ."

One day he returned all covered with mud and muck, as usual, and lay down on his mother's rich robe, and said in a grunting tone, "Mother, I wish to get married."

When the queen heard this, she replied, "Do not talk so foolishly. What maid would ever take you for a husband, and do you think that any noble or knight would give his daughter to someone so dirty and foul-smelling as you?" But he kept on grunting that he must have a wife of one sort or another.

The queen, not knowing how to manage him in this matter, asked the king what they should do: "Our son wishes to marry, but where shall we find anyone who will take him as a husband?"

Every day the pig would come back to his mother with the same demand: "I must have a wife, and I will never leave you in peace until you procure for me a maiden I have seen today, who pleases me greatly."

It happened that this maiden was a daughter of a poor woman who had three daughters, each one of them being very lovely. When the queen heard this, she had the poor woman and her eldest daughter brought before her, and said, "Good mother, you are poor and burdened with children. If you will agree to what I say, you will be rich. I have this son who is, as you see, in form a pig, and I wish to marry him to your eldest daughter. Do not consider him, but think of the king and of me, and remember that your daughter will inherit this whole kingdom when the king and I shall be dead."

When the young girl listened to the words of the queen she was greatly disturbed in her mind and blushed red for shame, and then said that on no account would she listen to the queen's proposition. But the poor mother begged her so pressingly that at last she yielded.

When the pig came home one day, all covered with dirt as usual, his mother said to him, "My son, we have found for you the wife you desire." And then she caused to be brought in the bride, who by this time had been robed in sumptuous regal attire, and presented her to the pig prince. When he saw how lovely and desirable she was, he was filled with joy, and, all foul and dirty as he was, jumped round about her, endeavoring by his pawing and nuzzling to show some sign of his affection. But she, when she found he was soiling her beautiful dress, thrust him aside; whereupon the pig said to her, "Why do you push me thus? Have I not had these garments made for you myself?"

Then she answered disdainfully, "No, neither you nor any other of the whole kingdom of hogs has done this thing." And when the time for going to bed was come, the young girl said to herself, "What am I to do with this foul beast? This very night, while he lies in his first sleep, I will kill him."

The pig prince, who was not far off, heard these words, but said nothing, and when the two retired to their chamber he got into the bed, stinking and dirty as he was, and spoiled the sumptuous bed with his filthy paws and snout. He lay down by his spouse, and when she was asleep, he struck her with his sharp hoofs, so she would not awaken and be able to kill him.

The next morning the queen went to visit her daughter-in-law, and to her great grief found that she was dead. When the pig prince came back from wandering about the city he said, in reply to the queen's bitter reproaches, that he had only dealt with his wife as she intended to deal with him; and then he withdrew in indignation.

Not many days had passed before the pig prince again began to beseech the queen to allow him to marry one of the other sisters, and because the queen at first would not listen to his petition he persisted in his purpose, and threatened to ruin everything in the kingdom if he could not have her as his wife. The queen, when she heard this, went to the king and told him everything, and he answered that perhaps it would be wiser to kill their ill-fated offspring before he might work some fatal mischief in the city. But the queen felt all the tenderness of a mother toward him, and loved him very dearly in spite of his brutal person, and could not endure the thought of being parted from him. So, she summoned once more to the palace the poor woman, together with her second daughter, and held a long discourse with her, begging her to give her daughter in marriage. At last the girl assented to take the pig prince for a husband; but her fate was no happier than her sister's, for the bridegroom killed her, as he had killed his other bride, and then fled headlong from the palace.

When he came back, dirty as usual and smelling so foully that no one could approach him, the king and queen censured him gravely for the outrage he had committed; but again he cried out boldly that if he had not killed her she would have killed him.

As it had happened before, the pig, after a very short time, began to beg his mother again to let him marry the youngest sister, who was much more beautiful than either of the others. When this request of his was refused steadily, he became more insistent than ever, and in the end began to threaten the queen's life in violent and bloodthirsty words, if she would not give him the young girl for his wife.

The queen, when she heard this shameful and unnatural speech, was well-nigh broken-hearted and near to going out of her mind; but, putting all other considerations aside, she called for the poor woman and her third daughter, who was named Meldina, and thus addressed her: "Meldina, my child, I should be greatly pleased if you would take the pig prince for a husband. Pay no regard to him, but to his father and to me; then, if you will be prudent and bear patiently with him, you may be the happiest woman in the world."

To this speech Meldina answered, with a grateful smile upon her face, that she was quite content to do as the queen bade her, and thanked her humbly for deigning to choose her as a daughter-in-law. For, seeing that she herself had nothing in the world, it was indeed great good fortune that she, a poor girl, should become the daughter-in-law of a potent sovereign. The queen, when she heard this modest and amiable reply, could not keep back her tears for the happiness she felt; but she feared all the time that the same fate might be in store for Meldina as her sisters.

When the new bride had been clothed in rich attire and decked with jewels, and was awaiting the bridegroom, the pig prince came in, dirtier and more muddy than ever; but she spread out her rich gown and besought him to lie down by her side. Whereupon the queen told her to thrust him away, but to this she would not consent, and spoke thus to the queen: "There are three wise sayings, gracious lady, which I remember to have heard. The first is that it is folly to waste time in searching for something that cannot be found. The second is that we should believe nothing we may hear, except those things that bear the marks of sense and reason. The third is that, when once you have got possession of some rare and precious treasure, prize it well and keep a firm hold upon it."

When the maiden had finished speaking, the pig prince, who had been wide-awake and had heard all that she had said, got up and kissed her, and the couple embraced. As soon as the time for retiring for the night had come, the bride went to bed and awaited her spouse. As soon as he came, she raised the coverlet and bade him lie near to her and put his head upon the pillow, covering him carefully with the bedclothes and drawing the curtains so that he might feel no cold. When morning had come, the pig got up and ranged abroad to pasture, as was his wont, and very soon after the queen went to the bride's chamber, expecting to find that she had met with the same fate as her sisters. But when she saw Meldina lying in the bed looking pleased and contented, she thanked God for this favor, that her son had at last found a spouse according to his liking.

One day, soon after this, when the pig prince was conversing pleasantly with his wife, he said to her: "Meldina, my beloved wife, if I could be fully sure that you could keep a secret, I would now tell you one of mine; something I have kept hidden for many years. I know you to be very prudent and wise, and that you love me truly; so I wish to make you the sharer of my secret."

"You may safely tell it to me, if you will," said Meldina, "for I promise never to reveal it to anyone without your consent."

Whereupon, being now sure of his wife's discretion and fidelity, he straightaway shook off from his body the foul and dirty skin of the pig, and stood revealed as a handsome and well-shaped young man, and all that night rested closely folded in the arms of his beloved wife. But he charged her solemnly to keep silence about this wonder she had seen, for the time had not yet come for his complete delivery from this misery. So when he left the bed he donned the dirty pig's hide once more.

I leave you to imagine for yourselves how great was the joy of Meldina when she discovered that, instead of a pig, she had gained a handsome and gallant young prince for a husband. Not long after this she fell pregnant, and when the time of her delivery came she gave birth to a handsome boy. The joy of the king and queen was unbounded, especially when they found that the newborn child had the form of a human being and not that of a beast.

But the burden of the strange and weighty secret which her husband had confided to her pressed heavily upon Meldina, and one day she went to her mother-in-law and said, "Gracious queen, when first I married your son I believed I was married to a beast, but now I find that you have given me the comeliest, the worthiest, and the most gallant young man ever born into the world to be my husband. For know that when he comes into my chamber, he casts off his dirty hide and leaves it on the ground, and is changed into a graceful handsome youth. No one could believe this marvel save they saw it with their own eyes." When the queen heard these words, she deemed that her daughter-in-law must be jesting with her, but Meldina still persisted that what she said was true. And when the queen demanded to know how she might witness with her own eyes the truth of this thing, Meldina replied: "Come to my chamber tonight, when we shall be in our first sleep. The door will be open, and you will find that what I tell you is the truth."

That same night, when the appointed time had come, and all were gone to rest, the queen let some torches be kindled and went, accompanied by the king, to the chamber of her son. When she had entered she saw the pig's skin lying on the floor in the corner of the room, and having gone to the bedside, found therein a handsome young man in whose arms Meldina was lying. And when they saw this, the delight of the king and queen was very great, and the king gave orders that, before anyone should leave the chamber, the pig's hide should be torn to shreds. So great was their joy over the recovery of their son that they nearly died of it.

King Galeotto, when he saw that he had so fine a son, and a grandchild likewise, laid aside his crown and his royal robes, and elevated his son, whom he had crowned with the greatest pomp, and who was ever afterward known as King Pig. Thus, to the contentment of all the people, the young king began his reign, and he lived long and happily with Meldina, his beloved wife.

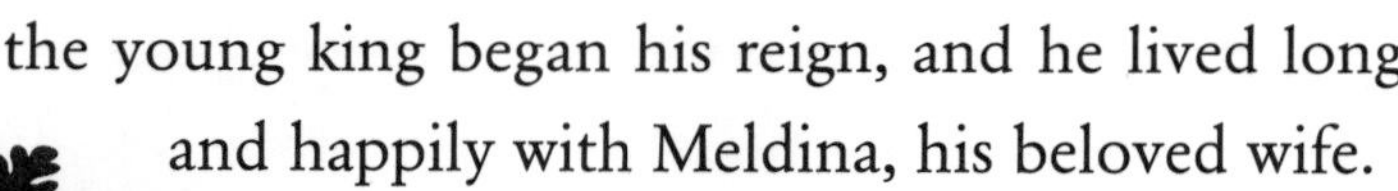

Giovanni Francesco Straparola

Notes on the Story

The Pig King

The theme in Straparola's "The Pig King" of the beastly bridegroom is a common type of folktale. It goes back to the ancient world, most famously in the story of "Cupid and Psyche" in Apuleius' second-century Latin novel *The Golden Ass* (which has been much retold, including by C. S. Lewis in *Till We Have Faces*). "Beauty and the Beast" is another version. Culturally, pigs are seen as disgusting and brutish, making a pig the perfect beastly bridegroom.

Other similar fairy tales that feature a pig (or a hedgehog) are Mme D'Aulnoy's "Prince Marcassin" and the Grimms' "Hans-My-Hedgehog." In an obvious way the tale concerns the plight of young women forced into arranged marriages; in this case the mother forces her three daughters in turn to marry the filthy, homicidal pig for money and social position. The compliance of the youngest daughter is a familiar theme in fairy tales, offering rewards to obedient women and punishing those who disobey.

Parsley

Once upon a time there was a pregnant woman named Pascadozzia, and one day, when she was standing at her window, which looked into the garden of an ogress, she saw such a fine bed of parsley that she almost fainted away with desire for some. So when the ogress went out she could not restrain herself any longer, but plucked a handful of it. The ogress came home and was going to cook her soup when she found that someone had been stealing the parsley, and said, "Ill luck to me, but I'll catch this long-fingered rogue and make him repent it. I'll teach him to his cost that every one should eat off his own platter and not meddle with other folks' cups."

The poor woman went again and again down into the garden, until one morning the ogress met her, and in a furious rage exclaimed, "Have I caught you at last, you thief, you rogue? Tell me please, do you pay the rent of the garden that you enter in this impudent way and steal my plants? By my faith, I'll make you do penance!"

Poor Pascadozzia, in a terrible fright, began to make excuses, saying that neither from gluttony nor the craving of hunger had she been tempted by the devil to commit this fault, but from her fear lest her child should be born with a crop of parsley on its face.

"Words are but wind," answered the ogress. "I am not to be caught with such prattle. You have closed the balance-sheet of life, unless you promise to give me the child, girl or boy, whichever it may be." The poor woman, in order to escape the peril in which she found herself, swore, with one hand upon the other, to keep the promise, and so the ogress let her go free. But when the baby came it was a little girl, so beautiful that she was a joy to look upon; she was named Parsley. The little girl grew from day to day until, when she was seven years old, her mother sent her to school, and every time she went along the street and met the ogress the old woman said to her, "Tell your mother to remember her promise." And she went on repeating this message so often that the poor mother, having no longer patience to listen to the refrain, said one day to Parsley, "If you meet the old woman as usual, and she reminds you of the hateful promise, answer her, 'Take it.'"

When Parsley, who dreamt of no ill, met the ogress again, and heard her repeat the same words, she answered innocently as her mother had told her, whereupon the ogress, seizing her by her hair, carried her off to a wood, which the horses of the Sun never entered, not having paid the toll to the pastures of those Shades. Then she put the poor girl into a tower, which she caused to arise by her art, having neither gate nor ladder, but only a little window through which she ascended and descended by means of Parsley's hair, which was very long, just as sailors climb up and down the mast of a ship.

Now it happened one day, when the ogress had left the tower, that Parsley put her head out of the little window and let loose her long hair in the sun, and the son of a prince passing by saw those golden tresses which invited all souls to enlist under the standard of Beauty. And, beholding with amazement, in the midst of those gleaming waves, a face that enchanted all hearts, he fell desperately in love with such wonderful beauty; and, sending her a memorial of sighs, she decreed to receive him into favor. She told him her troubles, and implored him to rescue her. But a gossip of the ogress, who was for ever prying into things that did not concern her, and poking her nose into every corner, overheard the secret, and told the wicked woman to be on the lookout, for Parsley had been seen talking with a certain youth, and she had her suspicions. The ogress thanked the gossip for the information, and said that she would take good care to stop up the road. As to Parsley, it was, moreover, impossible for her to escape, as she had laid a spell upon her, so that unless she had in her hand the three gallnuts which were in a rafter in the kitchen it would be labor lost to attempt to get away.

While they were thus talking together, Parsley, who stood with her ears wide open and had some suspicion of the gossip, overheard all that had passed. And when Night had spread out her black garments to keep them from the moth, and the prince had come as they had appointed, she let fall her hair; he seized it with both hands, and cried, "Draw up."

When he was drawn up she made him first climb on to the rafters and find the gallnuts, knowing well what effect they would have, as she had been enchanted by the ogress. Then, having made a rope ladder, they both descended to the ground, took to their heels, and ran off toward the city.

But the gossip, happening to see them come out, set up a loud "Halloo," and began to shout and make such a noise that the ogress awoke. She, seeing that Parsley had run away, descended by the same ladder, which was still fastened to the window, and set off after the couple, who, when they saw the ogress coming at their heels faster than a horse let loose, gave themselves up for lost. But Parsley, recollecting the gallnuts, quickly threw one on the ground, and lo, instantly a Corsican bulldog started up. O, mother, such a terrible beast! And with open jaws and barking loudly, it flew at the ogress as if to swallow her in one mouthful. But the old woman, who was more cunning and spiteful than ever, put her hand into her pocket and pulled out a piece of bread and gave it to the dog, which made it hang its tail and calmed its fury.

Then she turned to run after the fugitives again, but Parsley, seeing her approach, threw the second gallnut on the ground, and lo, a fierce

"She told him her troubles,

and implored him to rescue her."

lion arose, who, lashing the earth with his tail, and shaking his mane and opening wide his jaws a yard apart, was just preparing to make a slaughter of the ogress, when, turning quickly back, she stripped the skin off an ass which was grazing in the middle of a meadow and ran at the lion, who, fancying it a real jackass, was so frightened that he bounded away as fast as he could.

The ogress, having leaped over this second ditch, turned again to pursue the poor lovers, who, hearing the clatter of her heels, and seeing clouds of dust that rose up to the sky, knew that she was coming again. But the old woman, who was every moment in dread lest the lion should pursue her, had not taken off the ass's skin, and when Parsley now threw down the third gallnut there sprang up a wolf, who, without giving the ogress time to play any new trick, gobbled her up just as she was in the shape of a jackass. So Parsley and the prince, now freed from danger, went their way leisurely and quietly to the prince's kingdom, where, with his father's free consent, they were married. Thus, after all these storms of fate, they experienced the truth that–

One hour in port, the sailor, freed from fears,
Forgets the tempests of a hundred years.

Giambattista Basile

Notes on the Story

PARSLEY

Born in Naples, Giambattista Basile (1566–1632) was a soldier, courtier, poet, and collector of fairy tales. He lived for a time in Venice but returned to his native city, where he published various poetic works. He is now chiefly remembered for his collection of Neapolitan fairy tales entitled *Lo cunto de li cunti overo lo trattenemiento de peccerille* (Neapolitan for *The Tale of Tales, or Entertainment for Little Ones*), also known as *Il Pentamerone*, published posthumously in two volumes by his sister in Naples in 1634 and 1636.

These tales were written in Basile's own highly flamboyant style in the distinctive Neapolitan dialect. The Grimms rated Basile's collection highly, and it has been argued that Perrault and other French fairy-tale writers had access to his work.

Some of Basile's fairy tales are the oldest known variants in existence, including "Cinderella," "Sleeping Beauty," and "Rapunzel" (see page 153). The heroine of the latter is feistier than in some later versions.

Sun, Moon, and Talia

There was once a great lord, who, having a daughter born to him named Talia, commanded the seers and wise men of his kingdom to come and tell him her fortune. And after various discussions they came to the conclusion that a great peril awaited her from a piece of stalk in some flax. Thereupon he issued a command, prohibiting any flax or hemp, or suchlike thing, to be brought into his house, hoping thus to avoid the danger.

When Talia was grown up, and was standing one day at the window, she saw an old woman pass by, who was spinning. She had never seen a distaff or a spindle, and being vastly pleased with the twisting and twirling of the thread, her curiosity was so great that she made the old woman come upstairs. Then, taking the distaff in her hand, Talia began to draw out the thread, when, by mischance, a piece of stalk in the flax getting under her fingernail, she fell dead upon the ground; at which sight the old woman hobbled downstairs as quickly as she could.

When the unhappy father heard of the disaster that had befallen Talia, after weeping bitterly, he placed her in a palace in the country, upon a velvet seat under a canopy of brocade. And fastening the doors, he quitted forever the place which had been the cause of such misfortune to him, in order to drive all remembrance of it from his mind.

Now, a certain king happened to go hunting one day, and a falcon escaping from him flew in at the window of that palace. When the king found that the bird did not return at his call, he ordered his attendants to knock at the door, thinking that the palace was inhabited; and after knocking for some time, the king ordered them to fetch a ladder, wishing himself to scale the house and see what was inside. Then he mounted the ladder, and searching through the whole palace, he was astonished at not finding there any living person. At last he came to the room where Talia was lying, as if enchanted; and when the king saw her, he called to her, thinking that she was asleep, but in vain, for she still slept on, however loud he called. Beholding her beauty, he lifted her in his arms, and carried her to a bed, where he lay down with her. Leaving her on the bed, he returned to his own kingdom, where, in the pressing business of his realm, he for a time thought no more about this incident.

Now after nine months Talia delivered two beautiful children, one a boy and the other a girl. In them could be seen two rare jewels, and they were attended by two fairies, who came to that palace, and put them at their mother's breasts. Once, however, they were hungry, and began to suck on Talia's fingers, and they sucked so much that the splinter of flax came out. Thereupon she seemed to awake as from a deep sleep; and when she saw those little jewels at her side, she took them to her heart, and loved them more than her life. But she wondered greatly at seeing herself quite alone in the palace with two children, and food and refreshment brought to her by unseen hands.

After a time the king, recalling Talia, took the opportunity one day when he was hunting to go and see her; and when he found her awakened, and with two beautiful little children by her side, he was struck dumb with rapture. Then the king told Talia who he was, and they formed a great bond and friendship, and he remained there for several days, promising, as he took leave, to return and fetch her.

When the king went back to his own kingdom he was forever repeating the names of Talia and the little ones, so much so that, when he was eating he had Talia in his mouth, and Sun and Moon (for so

"The king, recalling Talia . . . found her awakened,

and with two beautiful little children by her side . . ."

he named the children); even when he went to bed he did not leave off calling on them, first one and then the other.

Now the king's wife had grown suspicious of his long absence while hunting, and when she heard him calling thus on Talia, Sun, and Moon, she got very upset, and said to the king's secretary, "Listen, my friend, you stand in great danger, between a rock and a hard place; tell me who my husband is in love with, and I will make you rich. But if you conceal the truth from me, I'll make you regret it."

The man, moved on the one side by fear, and on the other pricked by greed, which bandages the eyes of honor, makes justice blind, and destroys loyalty, told the queen the whole truth. Whereupon she sent the secretary in the king's name to Talia, saying that he wished to see the children. Then Talia sent them with great joy to be with their father. But the queen wanted to punish her husband and commanded the cook to kill them, and serve them up in various ways for her wretched husband to eat.

Now the cook, who had a tender heart, seeing the two pretty little golden pippins, took compassion on them, and gave them to his wife, bidding her keep them concealed. Then he killed and prepared two little goats in a hundred different ways.

When the king came, the queen quickly ordered the dishes served up; and the king fell to eating with great delight, exclaiming, "How good this is! Oh, how excellent, by the soul of my grandfather!"

And the queen all the while kept saying, "Eat away, for you're eating of your own."

At first the king paid no attention to what she said; but at last, hearing this refrain go on and

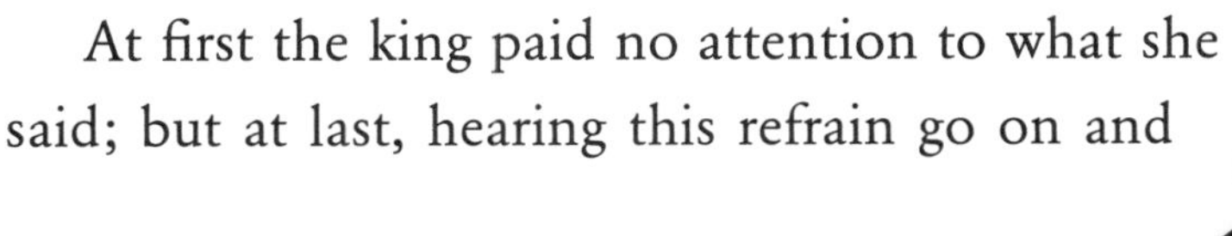

on, he replied, "Yes, I know well enough what I eat, since you have brought nothing to the house."

Meanwhile the queen, not satisfied with what she had done, called the secretary again, and sent him to fetch Talia, pretending that the king wished to see her. At this summons Talia went that very instant, longing to see the light of her eyes.

But when she came before the queen, the latter said to her, with the face of a Nero, and as full of poison as a viper, "Welcome, Mrs. Busybody! Are you indeed the pretty mischief-maker? Are you the noxious weed that has caught my husband's eye and given me all this trouble? So, you are the bitch that has caused my head to spin. Welcome to purgatory, where I will pay you back you for all the damage you have done to me."

When Talia heard this she began to excuse herself, saying that it was not her fault because the king her husband had taken possession of her territory when she was fast asleep. But the queen would not listen to a word; and having a large fire lighted in the courtyard, she commanded that Talia should be thrown into the flames.

Poor Talia, seeing that matters had taken a turn for the worse, fell on her knees before the queen, and begged her at least to grant her time to take the clothes from off her back.

Whereupon the queen, who wanted possession of her dress, said to her, "Undress yourself–I allow you."

Then Talia began to undress, and as she took off each garment she uttered a cry of grief; and when she had stripped off her cloak, her gown, and her jacket, and was proceeding to take off her petticoat, they seized her and began to drag her away.

At that moment, the king arrived, and seeing the spectacle he demanded to know the whole truth; and when he asked also for the children, and heard that his wife had ordered them to be killed, the unhappy king gave himself up to despair, saying, "Alas! Then I, myself, am the wolf of my own sweet lambs. You renegade witch, what evil deed is this that you have done? Begone, you shall get your desert!"

He then ordered her to be thrown into the same fire that had been lighted for Talia, and the secretary with her, who was the handle of this cruel game and the weaver of this wicked web.

Then he was going to do the same with the cook, thinking that he had killed the children. But the cook threw himself at the king's feet and said, "Truly, sire, I would desire no other reward for the service I have done you than to be thrown into a furnace full of live coals; I would desire no other privilege than to have the ashes of the cook mingled with those of a queen. But I look for no such great reward for having saved the children, and brought them back to you in spite of that wicked creature who wished to kill them."

When the king heard these words he was quite beside himself; he thought he was dreaming, and could not believe what his ears had heard. Then he said to the cook, "If it is true that you have saved the children, be assured I will take you from turning the spit, and reward you so that you shall call yourself the happiest man in the world."

As the king was speaking these words, the wife of the cook, seeing the dilemma her husband was in, brought Sun and Moon before the king, who, playing at the game of three with Talia and the other children, went round and round kissing first one and then another. Then, giving the cook a large reward, he made him his chamberlain. And he took Talia to be his wife, she enjoyed a long life with her husband and the children, acknowledging that–

Those who have luck may go to bed,
And bliss will rain upon their head.

Giambattista Basile

Notes on the Story

Sun, Moon, and Talia

The "Sun, Moon, and Talia" is an earlier rendition by Giambattista Basile (and the likely origin) of Charles Perrault's famous version, "The Beauty in the Sleeping Wood" (*La belle au bois dormant*), published in 1697. Like the latter, it is in two parts: the story of the heroine put into a deathlike sleep by pricking her finger; and the story of the jealous wife or evil mother-in-law who wants the children of the prince and the heroine murdered, cooked, and served up as a meal.

In Basile's version of the "Sleeping Beauty" story, the heroine becomes pregnant during her enchanted sleep when she is visited by a passing king. She then gives birth to twins who live with her in the palace. They are cared for by fairies, who ensure the survival of the three characters by supplying them with food and refreshment.

The Brothers Grimm published quite a different version in *Grimms' Children's and Household Tales;* this is called "Briar Rose," and can be found on page 147.

CENERENTOLA

There once lived a prince, who was a widower. He had an only daughter, so dear to him that he saw with no other eyes than hers; and he kept a governess for her, who taught her chain-work and knitting, and to make point-lace, and showed her such affection as no words can tell. But she was very lonely, and many a time she said to the governess, "Oh, would that you had been my mother, you who show me such kindness and love." She said this so often that, at last, the governess, having a bee put into her bonnet, said to her one day, "If you will do as this foolish head of mine advises, I shall be mother to you, and you will be as dear to me as the apple of my eye."

She was going to say more, when Zezolla, for that was the name of the princess, said, "Pardon me if I stop the word upon your tongue. I know you wish me well, therefore, hush–enough. Only show me the way. Do you write and I will subscribe."

"Well, then," answered the governess, "open your ears and listen, and you will get bread as white as the flowers. You know well enough that your father would even coin false money to please you, so do you entreat him when he is caressing you to marry me and make me princess. Then, bless your stars! You shall be the mistress of my life."

When Zezolla heard this, every hour seemed to her a thousand years until she had done all that her governess had advised; and, as soon as the mourning for her mother's death was ended, she began to feel her father's pulse, and beg him to marry the governess. At first the prince took it as a joke, but Zezolla went on shooting so long past the mark that at length she hit it, and he gave way to her entreaties. So he married the governess, and gave a great feast at the wedding.

Now, while the young folks were dancing, and Zezolla was standing at the window of her house, a dove came flying and perched upon a wall, and said to her, "Whenever you need anything, send the request to the Dove of the Fairies in the Island of Sardinia, and you will instantly have what you wish."

For five or six days the new stepmother overwhelmed Zezolla with affection, seating her at the best place at table, giving her the choicest morsels to eat, and clothing her in the richest apparel. But before long, forgetting entirely the good service she had received (woe to him who has a bad master!), she began to bring forward six daughters of her own, for she had never before told anyone that she was a widow with a bunch of girls. She praised them so much, and talked her husband over in such a fashion, that at last the stepdaughters had all his favor, and the thought of his own child went entirely from his heart.

In short, it fared so ill with the poor girl, bad today and worse tomorrow, that she was at last brought down from the royal chamber to the kitchen, from the canopy of state to the hearth, from splendid apparel of silks and gold to dishcloths, from the scepter to the spit. And not only was her condition changed, but even her name, for, instead of Zezolla, she was now called Cenerentola.

It happened that the prince had occasion to go to Sardinia upon affairs of state, and, calling the six stepdaughters, he asked them, one by one, what they would like him to bring them on his return. Then one wished for splendid dresses, another to have head-ornaments, another rouge for the face, another toys and trinkets: one wished for this and one for that. At last the prince said to his own daughter, as if in mockery, "And what would you have, child?"

"Nothing, father," she replied, "but that you commend me to the Dove of the Fairies, and bid her send me something; and if you forget my request, may you be unable to stir backward or forward. So remember what I tell you, for it will fare with you accordingly."

Then the prince went on his way and did his business in Sardinia, and procured all the things that his stepdaughters had asked for; but poor Zezolla was quite out of his thoughts. And going on board a ship he set sail to return, but the ship could not get out of the harbor; there it stuck fast just as if held by a sea-lamprey. The captain of the ship, who was almost in despair and quite exhausted, laid himself down to sleep, and in his dream he saw a fairy, who said to him, "Know you the reason why you cannot work the ship out of port? It is because the prince who is on board with you has broken his promise to his daughter, remembering everyone except his own child."

Then the captain awoke and told his dream to the prince, who, in shame and confusion at the breach of his promise, went to the Grotto of the Fairies, and, commending his daughter to them, asked them to send her something. And behold, there stepped forth from the grotto a beautiful maiden, who told him that she thanked his daughter for her kind remembrances, and bade him tell her to be merry and of good heart out of love to her. And thereupon she gave him a date tree, a hoe, and a little bucket all of gold, and a silken napkin, adding that the one was to hoe with and the other to water the plant.

The prince, marveling at this present, took leave of the fairy, and returned to his own country. And when he had given his stepdaughters all the things they had desired, he at last gave his own daughter the gift that the fairy had sent her. Then Zezolla, out of her wits with joy, took the date tree and planted it in a pretty flowerpot, hoed the earth round it, watered it, and wiped its leaves morning and evening with the silken napkin. In a few days it had grown as tall as a woman, and out of it came a fairy, who said to Zezolla, "What do you wish for?" And Zezolla replied that she wished sometimes to leave the house without her sisters' knowledge. The fairy answered, "Whenever you desire this, come to the flowerpot and say:

'My little date tree, my golden tree,
With a golden hoe I have hoed you,
With a golden can I have watered you,
With a silken cloth I have wiped you dry,
Now strip yourself and dress me speedily.'

And when you wish to undress, change the last words and say, 'Strip me and dress yourself.'"

When the time for the feast was come, and the stepmother's daughters appeared, dressed out so fine, all ribbons and flowers, and slippers and shoes, sweet smells and bells, and roses and posies, Zezolla ran quickly to the flowerpot, and no sooner had she repeated the words, as the fairy had told her, than she saw herself dressed like a queen, seated upon a horse, and attended by twelve pages, all in their best clothes. Then she went to the ball, and made the sisters envious of this unknown beauty.

Even the young king himself was there, and as soon as he saw her he was amazed and enchanted, and ordered a trusty servant to find out who this beautiful maiden was, and where she lived. So the servant followed in her footsteps; but when Zezolla noticed the trick she threw on the ground a handful of gold coins, which she had made the date tree give her for this purpose. Then the servant lit his lantern, and was so busy picking up all the coins that he forgot to follow the horse; and Zezolla came home quite safely, and had changed her clothes, as the fairy told her, before the wicked sisters arrived, and,

"'What do you wish for?'

. . . to leave the house without her sisters' knowledge."

to vex her and make her envious, told her of all the fine things they had seen. But the king was very angry with the servant, and warned him not to miss finding out next time who this beautiful maiden was, and where she lived.

Soon there was another feast, and again the sisters all went to it, leaving poor Zezolla at home on the kitchen hearth. Then she ran quickly to the date tree, and repeated the spell, and instantly there appeared a number of damsels, one with a looking glass, another with a bottle of rose water, another with curling tongs, another with combs, another with pins, another with dresses, and another with capes and collars. And they made her as glorious as the sun, and put her in a coach drawn by six white horses, and attended by footmen and pages in livery. And no sooner did she appear in the ballroom than the hearts of the sisters were filled with amazement, and the king was overcome with love.

When Zezolla went home the servant followed her again, but so that she should not be caught she threw down a handful of pearls and jewels, and the good fellow, seeing that they were not things to lose, stayed to pick them up. So she had time to slip away and take off her fine dress as before.

Meanwhile the servant had returned slowly to the king, who cried out when he saw him, "By the souls of my ancestors, if you do not find out who she is you shall have such a thrashing as was never before heard of, and as many kicks as you have hairs in your beard!"

When the next feast was held, and the sisters were safely out of the house, Zezolla went to the date tree, and once again repeated the spell. In an instant she found herself splendidly arrayed and seated in a coach of gold, and with so many servants around her that she looked just like a queen. Again the sisters were beside themselves with envy; but this time, when she left the ballroom, the king's servant kept close to the coach. Zezolla, seeing that the man was ever running by her side, cried, "Coachman, drive on quickly!" And in a trice the coach set off at such a rattling pace that she lost one of her slippers, the prettiest thing that ever was seen. The servant, being unable to catch the coach, which flew like a bird, picked up the slipper, and carrying it to the king told him all that happened.

Whereupon the king, taking it in his hand, said, "If the basement, indeed, is so beautiful, what must the building be? You who until now were the prison of a white foot are now the fetter of an unhappy heart!"

Then he made a proclamation that all the women in the country should come to a banquet, for which the most splendid provision was made of pies and pastries, and stews and ragouts, macaroni and sweetmeats–enough to feed a whole army. And when all the women were assembled, noble and ignoble, rich and poor, beautiful and ugly, the king tried the slipper on each one of the guests to see whom it should fit to a hair, and thus be able to discover by the help of the slipper the maiden of whom he was in search, but not one foot could he find to fit it. So, the king examined them closely whether indeed every one was there; and the prince confessed that he had left one daughter behind.

"But," said the prince, "she is always on the hearth, and is such a graceless simpleton that she is unworthy to sit and eat at your table."

But the king said, "Let her be the very first on the list, for so I will."

So all the guests departed–the very next day they assembled again, and with the wicked sisters came Zezolla. When the king saw her he had his suspicions, but said nothing. And after the feast came the trial of the slipper, which, as soon as ever it approached Zezolla's foot, it darted on to it of its own accord, like iron flies to the magnet. Seeing this, the king ran to her and took her in his arms, and, seating her under the royal canopy, he set the crown upon her head, whereupon all made their obeisance and homage to her as their queen.

When the wicked sisters saw this they were full of venom and rage, and, not having patience to look upon the object of their hatred, they slipped quietly away on tiptoe, and went home to their mother, confessing, in spite of themselves, that–

He is a madman who resists the Stars.

Giambattista Basile

Notes on the Story

CENERENTOLA

"Cenerentola" is Basile's variation of the well-known tale of "Cinderella." One of the oldest fairy tales, the most ancient Cinderella is a ninth-century Chinese tale called "Yeh-hsien." Although the heroine in this version is named Zezolla, the nickname "Cenerentola," or "little ashes," is the inspiration for subsequent popular versions such as Perrault's "Cendrillon" and the Grimms' "Aschenputtel." The Perrault version is the most recognizable, being the basis for the 1950 Disney film. Cinderella tales often contain a magic helper such as the classic fairy godmother. Basile gives Zezolla the Dove of the Fairies and the date tree, but other similar tales contain a magic hazel tree at Cinderella's mother's grave, a red calf, or a fish.

✣

Basile's moral to this story, "He is a madman who resists the Stars," implies that Zezolla's charmed fate was always set. This differs greatly from the end of Perrault's tale, which stresses the importance of grace and godparents for a life to have "great events."

"She told the messenger that she thanked the king,

but that she had no desire to marry."

Fair Goldilocks

There was once a king's daughter who was so beautiful that nothing in the whole world could be compared with her. And because she was so beautiful they called her Princess Goldilocks; for her hair was finer than gold, wonderfully fair, and it fell in ringlets to her feet. Her only covering for her head was her curly hair and a garland of flowers; her dresses were embroidered with diamonds and pearls; and no one could look on her without loving her.

In a neighboring country there lived a young king who was not married, and who was very handsome and very rich. When the fame of fair Goldilocks reached him, before he had ever set eyes on her, he was already so much in love that he could neither eat nor drink for thinking of her. He determined to send an ambassador to ask her hand in marriage. He had a magnificent coach made for the occasion; and, giving the ambassador more than a hundred horses and lackeys, he charged him well to bring the princess home with him.

When the ambassador had taken leave of the king and had gone away, nothing was spoken of at the court but his mission; and the king, who felt assured of Goldilocks' consent, had beautiful dresses made for her, and wonderful fittings for the palace. While the workmen were making preparations for her coming, the ambassador reached her court and delivered his message. But whether she was not in a good humor that day, or whether the offer was not to her liking, she told the messenger that she thanked the king, but that she had no desire to marry.

The ambassador left the princess's court very downhearted at not being able to bring her home with him. He took back all the gifts the king had sent her; for she had been well brought up, and knew that girls should not accept presents from boys. So she would not take the fine diamonds and all the rest of the things; but, so as not to give offence, she accepted a little packet of English pins.

When the ambassador reached the king's capital, where he was waited for with the greatest impatience, everybody was in deep distress because fair Goldilocks was not with him. The king began to cry like a child, and it was in vain they tried to comfort him. Now at the court was a young lad, who was fair as the day, and indeed in the whole kingdom there was no one so handsome. He was charming and witty, and he was called Avenant. Everybody liked him except those who were jealous that the king showed him favor and made him his confidant.

Avenant, hearing them speak of the ambassador's return and of how his embassy had been in vain, said, without thinking very much about what he was saying: "If the king had sent me to Princess Goldilocks I am sure she would have come back with me."

Then the mischief-makers hastened to the king and said to him: "Your majesty, what do you think Avenant has been saying? That if you had sent him to the princess he would have brought her back! Who ever heard of such impudence? He thinks he is handsomer than you, and that she would have fallen so much in love with him that she would have followed him anywhere."

And now the king flew into such a furious passion that he lost all control of himself. "Ha! Ha!" said he. "This spoilt monkey laughs at my misfortune! He thinks he is the better man! Go, shut him up in my great tower, and let him die of hunger."

The king's guards went to fetch Avenant, who by this time had forgotten entirely what he had said, and dragged him to prison with all kinds of violence. The poor boy had only a miserable heap of straw for a bed; and he would have died had it not been for a little stream that flowed along through the bottom of the tower, and of which he drank a little to cool his mouth, which was parched by hunger.

One day, when Avenant was sighing in despair, and was saying, "What does the king blame me for? He has not a more loyal subject than myself, and I have never done him any harm," the king passed by the tower.

Hearing the voice of him whom he had loved so much, he stopped to listen, in spite of the efforts of those who were with him, who, hating Avenant, said: 'Why does your majesty waste your time? Do you not know he is a rascal?"

But the king answered: "Let me alone. I want to listen." At the sound of his laments, tears filled the king's eyes, and he opened the door of the tower and called him.

Avenant came forward in deep distress, and, throwing himself on his knees and kissing the king's feet, he said: "What have I done that your majesty should treat me so cruelly?"

"You laughed at me and at my ambassador," said the king. "You said that if I had sent you to the Princess Goldilocks you would have brought her back."

"It is true, your majesty," replied Avenant, "that I should have made her so thoroughly realize your good qualities that I feel sure she would not have refused her consent, and in saying that I said nothing that should have displeased you."

The king saw that, after all, Avenant was in the right, and, looking with contempt on those who had slandered his favorite, took him away with him, deeply repenting all he had made him suffer.

After having regaled him with a fine supper, he called him into his private room, and said: "Avenant, I am still in love with fair Goldilocks, but I don't know what to do to gain her consent. I should like to send you to see if you could succeed." Avenant replied that he was ready to obey him in everything, and that he would set out next day.

"Ah," said the king, "but I wish to have a fine entourage prepared for you."

"That is not needful," he answered. "I want only a good horse and letters from you." The king embraced him, so delighted was he with his eagerness to set out.

It was on a Monday morning he took leave of the king and of his friends to go on his mission, all by himself, quite simply and quietly. He did nothing but think of the means he would use to persuade Goldilocks to marry the king. In his pocket he carried a writing tablet, and when a pretty thought occurred to him for his speech, he got off his horse and sat down under the trees to write, so that it might not go out of his head.

One morning he had set out at the first streak of day. While he was crossing a wide plain, a charming idea came into his head. So he dismounted, and leaned up against the willow trees and poplars on the banks of the little spring that flowed by the side of the meadow. After he had written down his thought, he was looking all round, delighted at being in such a beautiful spot, when he saw on the grass a great golden carp, panting, and at the last gasp. While trying to catch the little flies, it had jumped so far out of the water that it had fallen on the grass, and now it lay there dying. Avenant was sorry for it; and though it was a fast day when he could only eat fish, and he might well have taken it for his dinner, instead of doing so he put it back gently into the stream. As soon as the carp touched the cool water, she recovered her spirits. She let herself be carried down to the bottom. And then, coming gaily up to the surface again, she said: "Avenant, I thank you for the kindness you have just shown me. But for you I should have died. You have saved my life, and I shall do as much for you one day." With these few words of good omen she plunged into the water, leaving Avenant in great astonishment at such intelligence and such politeness in a carp.

Another day, when he was going on his way, he saw a crow in great distress. A huge eagle was pursuing the poor bird. Now, eagles feed greedily on crows, and this one was just on the point of seizing his victim, whom he would have swallowed like a lentil, had not Avenant taken pity on the bird's distress.

"There," said he, "see how the strong oppress the weak. What right has the eagle to eat the crow?" With his bow and arrow, which he always carried with him, he took good aim at the eagle–and then, crack! He shot the arrow into its body and pierced it through. It fell dead; and the crow, in great glee, perched itself on a tree, saying: "Avenant, it was most generous of you to come to the aid of a poor crow like me. But I shall not be ungrateful. I'll do as much for you one day."

Avenant, in some surprise at the gratitude of the crow, went on his way. Entering a large wood, while it was still so early that he could hardly see his way, he heard despairing cries from an owl.

"Dear me," he said, "here is an owl in distress. It must have got caught in some nets." Looking round on every side, at length he saw great nets that the fowlers had spread during the night to catch little birds. "How sad," said he, "that men are only made to torment each other, or to persecute poor animals that do them no harm or injury of any kind!"

So saying, he took out his knife and cut the cords. The owl sprang up, but came down again quickly to say: "Avenant, there is no need for many words on my part to make you understand the obligation I am under to you. It speaks for itself. The fowlers would have come and caught me, and without your aid I should have died. I have a grateful heart, and I shall do as much for you one day."

Such were the three adventures of any importance that happened to Avenant on his journey. He was so eager to reach his destination that he did not loiter on his way to the palace of fair Goldilocks. Everything there was wonderful to look at. There were diamonds lying in heaps as if they had been but stones. The dresses, the silver, and the sweetmeats—everything was marvelous. And he thought to himself that if she left it all to come with him, his master, the king, would be very lucky. He put on a doublet of brocade, with pink and white feathers in his hat. He dressed and powdered his hair, and washed his face. Round his neck was tied an embroidered scarf, with a little basket attached, and in it a pretty little dog he had bought while passing through Boulogne. Avenant was so handsome, so beautiful to look on, all his movements were so full of grace, that when he presented himself at the palace gate the guards saluted him humbly, and sent in haste to announce to Princess Goldilocks that Avenant, ambassador from the king, her nearest neighbor, requested to see her.

At the name of Avenant the princess said: "That name has a pleasant sound. I feel sure he is handsome, and that everybody likes him."

"You say truly, madam," said all the maids-of-honor. "We saw him from the loft when we were arranging your flax, and all the time he was standing under the windows we couldn't do anything but look at him."

"Well, that is a fine occupation," replied fair Goldilocks, "to amuse yourselves by gazing at boys! Now then, I want my best-embroidered blue satin gown. My fair hair must be curled. Let me have garlands of fresh flowers, and fetch my high-heeled shoes and my fan. And tell them to sweep out my room and my throne; for it is my desire that he shall tell everywhere that I am in truth fair Goldilocks."

Now all her maids made speed to dress her like a queen. They were in such a hurry that they knocked against each other and made but little progress. At last the princess passed into her gallery, with the great mirrors, to see if nothing were lacking in her appearance. Then she ascended her throne, made of gold and ivory and ebony, the scent of which was like balm, and she told her damsels to take instruments and to sing quite softly so that the sound might jar on no one's ears.

Avenant was led to the audience chamber, where he stood so dazzled with admiration that, as he has often said since then, he could hardly speak. Nevertheless he plucked up courage and delivered his speech beautifully, begging the princess that he might not have the disappointment of returning without her.

"Gentle Avenant," she said, "all the reasons which you have just given me are excellent, and I assure you I would most willingly do more for you than for another. But you must know that a month ago I was in a boat on the river with all my ladies, when, as they were serving me with luncheon, in taking off my glove, I slipped a ring from my finger, which unluckily fell into the river. It was more precious to me than my kingdom, and I leave you to judge what sorrow its loss caused me. I vowed never to listen to any proposal of marriage till the ambassador who brings it restores my ring. And now think what you have before you, for, were you to speak to me for fifteen days and fifteen nights, you could not persuade me to change my mind."

Avenant was much surprised at this answer. Making her a profound bow, he begged her to accept the little dog, the basket, and the scarf. But she said she wished for no gifts, and charged him to think of what she had just told him.

Returning to his own dwelling, he went supperless to bed, and his little dog, Cabriole, would not eat anything either, and came and lay down beside him. All through the night Avenant never ceased his sighs. "How could I find a ring that fell into a great river a month ago?" he said. "It is nothing but folly to make the attempt. The princess only spoke of it to me to make it impossible for me to obey her." And he sighed in deep distress.

Cabriole, listening all the while, said: "My dear master, I beg you not to be downhearted about your luck. You are too good not to be happy. Let us go as soon as it is day to the riverside." Avenant stretched out his hand to pat him once or twice and returned no other answer. At last, quite overcome with his sorrow, he fell asleep.

When daylight came, Cabriole began to cut capers as soon as he awoke. "My master," he said, "get dressed and come out."

Avenant had no objection. Getting up, he dressed and went down into the garden, and from the garden he turned his steps unconsciously to the riverside, where he walked along with his hat over his eyes and his arms crossed. All at once he heard a voice calling: "Avenant, Avenant!" Looking all round, and seeing no one, he thought he must have been dreaming. He went on walking, and again the voice called: "Avenant, Avenant!"

"Who is calling me?" he said.

Cabriole, who was very little and who was peering into the water, answered him: "Never again believe what I say if it is not a golden carp I see". Then the big carp appeared and said to him: "You saved my life in the meadow, where I should have remained a captive but for you. I promised to do as much for you one day. Well then, dear Avenant, here is fair Goldilocks' ring." And Avenant, stooping down, took it out of the carp's gullet, thanking her over and over again.

Instead of going home he went straight to the palace with little Cabriole, who was very glad he had brought his master to the riverside. The princess was told he wished to see her.

"Alas!" she said. "Poor boy! He is coming to bid me farewell. He thinks that what I ask is an impossibility, and he is going home to tell his master so."

Avenant, on being announced, presented the ring to her, saying: "Princess, I have fulfilled your command. Will it please you to accept the king, my master, as your husband?" When she saw the ring, the very ring she had lost, she was astonished, so astonished that she thought she must be dreaming.

"In truth," she said, "dear Avenant, you must be some fairy's favorite, for by yourself it would have been impossible."

"Madam," he answered, "I know no fairy, but I had a great wish to obey you."

"Then, since you are so willing," she went on, "you must do me another service; otherwise, I shall never marry. Not far from here there is a prince called Galifron, who has taken it into his head that he wants to marry me. He announced his intention to me with fearful threats that, should I refuse, he would lay waste my kingdom. But could I accept him, do you think? He is a giant, taller than a high tower, and thinks no more of eating a man than a monkey would think of eating a chestnut. When he goes to the country he carries little cannons in his pockets, which he uses instead of pistols, and when he speaks very loud those that are near him are struck deaf. I told him I did not wish to marry, and asked to be excused; yet, he has never left off persecuting me, and he kills all my subjects. The first thing to be done, therefore, is for you to fight him and to bring me his head."

Avenant was somewhat stunned by this proposal. He turned it over in his mind for a little while, and then said: "Well, madam, I shall fight against Galifron. I think I shall be beaten, but I shall die like a brave man." The princess was much surprised, and told him all kinds of things to prevent his undertaking the enterprise, but in vain; so he withdrew in order to fetch his armor and all that should be necessary. When he had found all he wanted, he put little Cabriole in his basket, mounted his good horse, and set out for the country of Galifron. He questioned those he met on the way about the prince, and everybody told him he was a real demon, and no one dared go near him. The more he heard this, the more frightened he became.

Cabriole reassured him, saying: "Dear master, while you are fighting, I shall bite his legs. Then he will bend his head to chase me away, and you will kill him." Avenant admired the little dog's spirit, though he knew his help would not avail.

At last he arrived near Galifron's castle. All the roads were covered with the bones and the carcasses of the men he had eaten or torn to pieces. He did not have long to wait for him, for he saw him coming through a wood, his head overtopping the tallest trees, and heard him singing in a terrible voice:

"Ho, bring me for lunch
Fat babies to crunch;
Not few and not lean,
Or my appetite keen
You will not satisfy,
So hungry am I!"

Avenant immediately began to sing to the same air:

"Here see Avenant stand
With his spear in his hand,
In humor defiant
Though he isn't a giant,
For there's never a doubt
That he'll tear your teeth out."

The rhymes were not very regular, but then he had made up the song in a great hurry, and it is a wonder it was not even worse, so terribly afraid was he. When Galifron heard these words he looked all round and saw Avenant with his spear in his hand calling him names, one after the other, to make him angry. This was hardly necessary, as he flew into a terrible passion, and, taking a heavy bar of iron, would have felled Avenant with one stroke had not the crow perched itself on the top of the giant's head, and, making a dart at his eyes, torn them out with its beak. The blood flowed down his face, and like a madman he struck out on all sides. Avenant parried the blows, and with great force he plunged his spear into the giant again and again up to the hilt, wounding him terribly, and causing him to fall from the blood he lost. Then he hacked off Galifron's head, in great spirits at his good fortune, while the crow, who was perched on a tree, spoke thus: "I have not forgotten the service you did me in killing the eagle that pursued me. I promised to pay my debt, and I think I have done so today."

"It is I who am the debtor, Mr. Crow," replied Avenant, "and I remain your servant." Then, putting the horrible head of Galifron on the horse, he rode away.

When he reached the town everybody ran after him, crying: "Here comes brave Avenant, the monster-slayer!" So that the princess, who heard the uproar, and who trembled lest they should come to tell her of the death of Avenant, did not dare to ask what had happened. But Avenant came in bearing the giant's head, which still struck terror into her, although there was no longer cause for fear.

"Madam," he said, "your enemy is dead. I hope you will no longer refuse the king, my master."

"Yes, indeed, I will," said fair Goldilocks. " I still refuse him, unless you are able to fetch me some water from the Dark Grotto. Near here there is a deep cavern fully six miles in circumference. The entrance is barred by two dragons with fire coming out of their eyes and mouths. Once inside you have to go down into a great pit, full of toads and adders and serpents. At the bottom of this pit is a little cave through which there flows the stream of Beauty and of Health. A miracle happens to whoever washes with this water. If you are beautiful, you will always be so; if you are ugly, you grow fair. If you are young, you never grow any older; if you are old, you grow young. You can understand, Avenant, that I could not leave my kingdom without taking a supply of this water with me."

"Madam," he answered, "you are already so beautiful that this water is altogether useless to you. But I am an unlucky ambassador, whose death you seek. I will go to search for what you desire, certain that I shall return no more."

Fair Goldilocks did not change her mind, and Avenant set out with his little dog Cabriole for the Dark Grotto to search for the water of Beauty. All who met him on the way said what a pity it was to see so fair a youth going recklessly to his death. "He goes to the grotto by himself, but were he to go a hundred strong he would never succeed. Why does the princess ask such impossible things?" Avenant went on his way, without saying a word, but he was sad at heart.

When he had climbed nearly to the top of a mountain he sat down to rest for a little, letting his horse graze and Cabriole run after the flies. He knew the Dark Grotto was not far off, and he looked to see if it were not in sight. At last he saw, first a hideous rock, black as ink, out of which a thick smoke was coming, and after a moment one of the dragons that shot fire from their mouths and eyes. Its body was yellow and green. It had great claws, and a long tail curled into hundreds of twists. When Cabriole saw all this he was so terrified that he did not know where to hide.

Avenant, quite resigned to death, drew his spear, and went down with a phial, which the Princess Goldilocks had given him to fill with

"'You freed me from the fowlers' nets . . . and you saved my life.

I promised to do as much for you one day.'"

the water of Beauty. To his little dog Cabriole he said: "My end is near! I can never get that water which is guarded by the dragons. When I am dead fill this bottle with my blood, and take it to the princess that she may see what her errand has cost me. Then repair to the king, my master, and tell him of my unhappy fate." While he was saying these words he heard a voice calling him: "Avenant, Avenant!"

"Who is calling me?" he asked.

He saw in the hollow of an old tree an owl, who said to him: "You freed me from the fowlers' nets in which I was caught, and you saved my life. I promised to do as much for you one day. Now the time has come. Give me your phial. I know all the paths through the Dark Grotto, and I will fetch the water of Beauty for you."

Here was good news for Avenant, as you may imagine, and he hastily gave him the phial. The owl entered the grotto without hindrance, and in less than a quarter of an hour he came back carrying the bottle well corked. Avenant, delighted, thanked him with all his heart, and, climbing the hill, again took the way to the town with a glad heart.

Going straight to the palace, he presented the phial to fair Goldilocks, who had nothing more to say. She thanked Avenant, gave all the necessary orders for her departure, and then set out on her journey with him. He seemed to her very charming, and she would sometimes say: "If you had been willing, I should have made you king, and need never have left my kingdom."

But he answered: "I would not do such a wrong to my master for all the kingdoms of the earth, though I think you lovelier than the sun."

At last they reached the capital, where the king, knowing that the Princess Goldilocks was coming, came to meet her with the fairest gifts in the world. Such great rejoicing was there at their wedding that nothing else was spoken of. But fair Goldilocks, who at the bottom of her heart loved Avenant, was never happy but when she saw him, and his praises were ever on her tongue.

"I should never have been here had it not been for Avenant," she said to the king. "He had to perform impossible feats for me, and you owe him a great deal. He gave me the water of Beauty, so I shall never grow old, and I shall be beautiful for ever."

Envious people, listening to the queen's words, said to the king: "You are not jealous, but you have good reason to be. The queen is so much in love with Avenant that she can neither eat nor drink. She does nothing but speak of him and of the obligations you are under to him, as if anyone else whom you might have sent would not have done as much."

"I believe you are right," said the king. "Let him be cast into the tower, and irons put on his feet and hands." There Avenant saw no one but the jailer, who used to throw him a bit of black bread through a hole, and give him some water in an earthen dish, but his little dog Cabriole stayed with him to comfort him, and brought him all the news.

When fair Goldilocks heard of Avenant's disgrace she threw herself at the king's feet, and, weeping bitterly, begged him to let Avenant go free. But the more she pleaded the angrier grew the king, thinking that she loved Avenant. He would not relent, so she stopped speaking of the matter, but her heart was very sad.

It occurred to the king that perhaps the queen did not think him handsome enough, and he had a strong desire to rub his face with the water of Beauty, in order that she might love him more. This water stood in the bottle on the edge of the mantelshelf in the queen's room. She had put it there so that she might the oftener look at it. But one of the housemaids, when killing a spider with a broom, unfortunately knocked down the bottle, which was broken and all the water spilt.

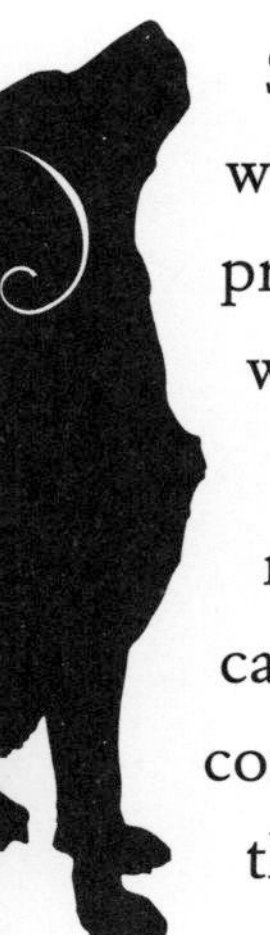

She swept away the traces quickly, and, at her wits' end of what to do, she remembered that she had seen in the king's private room a bottle just like it, full of a clear liquid like the water of Beauty. Without saying a word to anybody, she managed to get hold of it, and placed it on the queen's mantelshelf. Now the water in the king's room was for causing the death of princes and great lords when they had committed crimes. Instead of beheading or hanging them, their faces were rubbed with this water, and they fell asleep and woke no more. One evening, therefore, the king took the bottle and rubbed his face well with the contents. Then he fell asleep, and he died.

The little dog Cabriole was the first to learn of what had happened, and did not fail to go and tell Avenant, who asked him to go to Princess Goldilocks and beg her to take thought of the poor prisoner. Cabriole slipped quietly through the crowd, for there was great confusion at the court owing to the king's death.

"Madam," he said to the queen, "do not forget poor Avenant." She remembered the sufferings he had undergone on her account, and of his great faithfulness. Without saying a word to anyone, she went out and made straight for the tower, where, with her own hands, she took off the irons from Avenant's hands and feet. Then, placing a golden crown on his head and the royal robes on his shoulders, she said: "Come, dear Avenant, I make you king, and take you for my husband."

Throwing himself at her feet, he poured out his gratitude. Everyone was delighted to own him for their master. Never was there such a wedding feast, and the Princess Goldilocks and fair Avenant lived long together in peace and happiness.

Mme D'Aulnoy

Notes on the Story

Fair Goldilocks

Marie-Catherine D'Aulnoy (1650/51–1705) created the term "fairy tale" with the publication of her multivolume collection *Les contes des fees* in 1697/98. She was a prolific author, and one of the most famous of the seventeenth-century salon writers, fashionable members of the French aristocracy who held gatherings in the salons of their homes. Here, traditional folktales were refashioned for civilized entertainment—often as barely veiled criticisms of repressive French society.

✣

Written in D'Aulnoy's ornate literary style, this "Goldilocks"—a very different tale to the Goldilocks of bear and porridge fame—is an example of the "grateful animal" tale in which a hero assists animals and is in turn given help. Recent scholarship has cited it as one of the oldest tale types to be found in Europe. The kindness of the young man to the animals, and their subsequent loyalty, throws into sharp relief the cruelty of the capricious and ungrateful king.

Little Red Riding Hood

Once upon a time there was a little village girl, the prettiest that had ever been seen. Her mother doted on her. Her grandmother was even fonder, and made her a little red hood, which became her so well that everywhere she went she was called Little Red Riding Hood. One day her mother, who had just made and baked some cakes, said to her: "Go and see how your grandmother is, for I have been told that she is ill. Take her a cake and this little pot of butter."

Little Red Riding Hood set off at once for the house of her grandmother, who lived in another village. On her way through a wood she met old Brother Wolf. He would have very much liked to eat her, but dared not do so on account of some woodcutters who were in the forest. He asked her where she was going. The poor child, not knowing that it was dangerous to stop and listen to a wolf, said: "I am going to see my grandmother, and am taking her a cake and a pot of butter which my mother has sent to her."

"Does she live far away?" asked the wolf.

"Oh yes," replied Little Red Riding Hood, "it is yonder by the mill which you can see right over there, and it is the first house in the village."

"Well now," said the wolf, "I think I shall go and see her too. I will go by this path, and you by that path, and we will see who gets there first."

The wolf set off running with all his might by the shorter road, and the little girl continued on her way by the longer road. As she went she amused herself by gathering nuts, running after the butterflies, and making bouquets of the wild flowers that she found.

The wolf was not long in reaching the grandmother's house. He knocked—knock, knock.

"Who's there?" asked the grandmother.

"It is your little granddaughter, Red Riding Hood," said the wolf, disguising his voice, "and I bring you a cake and a little pot of butter as a present from my mother."

The worthy grandmother was in bed, not being very well, and cried out to him: "Pull out the peg and the latch will fall."

The wolf drew out the peg and the door flew open. Then he sprang upon the poor old lady and ate her up in less than no time, for he had been more than three days without food. After that he shut the door, lay down in the grandmother's bed, and waited for Little Red Riding Hood.

Presently she came and knocked—knock, knock.

"Who's there?"

Now Little Red Riding Hood on hearing the wolf's gruff voice was at first frightened, but thinking that her grandmother had a bad cold, she replied: "It is your little granddaughter, Red Riding Hood, and I bring you a cake and a little pot of butter from my mother."

Softening his voice, the wolf called out to her: "Pull out the peg and the latch will fall."

Little Red Riding Hood drew out the peg and the door flew open. When he saw her enter, the wolf hid himself in the bed beneath the bedcover.

"Put the cake and the little pot of butter on the bread bin," he said, "and come on the bed with me."

Little Red Riding Hood took off her clothes, but when she climbed up on the bed she was astonished to see how her grandmother looked in her nightgown.

"Grandmother dear," she exclaimed, "what big arms you have!"

"The better to embrace you, my child!"

"Grandmother dear, what big legs you have!"

"The better to run with, my child!"

"Grandmother dear, what big ears you have!"

"The better to hear with, my child!"

"Grandmother dear, what big eyes you have!"

"The better to see with, my child!"

"Grandmother dear, what big teeth you have!"

"The better to eat you with!"

With these words, the wicked wolf leapt upon Little Red Riding Hood and gobbled her up.

Moral

Little girls, this seems to say,
Never stop upon your way.
Never trust a stranger-friend;
No one knows how it will end.
As you're pretty, so be wise;
Wolves may lurk in every guise.
Handsome they may be, and kind,
Gay or charming, never mind!
Now, as then, 'tis simple truth—
Sweetest tongue has sharpest tooth!

Charles Perrault

Notes on the Story

Little Red Riding Hood

A contemporary of Mme D'Aulnoy, French civil servant Charles Perrault (1628–1703) gained widespread fame for his fairy-tale collections, published in plain language and suitable for children and adults. In his most popular collection, *Stories of Tales of Times Past, with Morals*, he rewrote tales to explore the social and cultural issues of contemporary France.

"Little Red Riding Hood" is a fascinating example of the transformations of the fairy tale. While Perrault's tale extols the virtues of modesty and timidity, and the Brothers Grimm focus their version on the moral of obedience, an earlier French version, "The Grandmother," tells a tale in which a girl outwits a were-wolf with little trouble and then dispatches him with the help of local laundrywomen. Modern versions, including Roald Dahl's poem "Little Red Riding Hood and the Wolf," and the more adult retellings, such as those found in *The Bloody Chamber* (1979) by the English novelist Angela Carter, celebrate the historical complexity of this multifaceted story.

The Fairies

Once upon a time there lived a widow with two daughters. The elder was often mistaken for her mother, so like her was she both in nature and in looks; parent and child being so disagreeable and arrogant that no one could live with them.

The younger girl, who took after her father in the gentleness and sweetness of her disposition, was also one of the prettiest girls imaginable. The mother doted on the elder daughter naturally enough, since she resembled her so closely–and disliked the younger one as intensely. She made the latter live in the kitchen and work hard from morning till night.

One of the poor child's many duties was to go twice a day and draw water from a spring a good half-mile away, bringing it back in a large pitcher. One day when she was at the spring an old woman came up and begged for a drink.

"Why, certainly, good mother," the pretty lass replied. Rinsing her pitcher, she drew some water from the cleanest part of the spring and handed it to the dame, lifting up the jug so that she might drink more easily.

Now this old woman was a fairy, who had taken the form of a poor village dame to see just how far the girl's good nature would go. "You are so pretty," she said, when she had finished drinking, "and so polite, that I am determined to bestow a gift upon you. This is the boon I grant you: with every word that you utter there shall fall from your mouth either a flower or a precious stone."

When the girl reached home she was scolded by her mother for being so long in coming back from the spring.

"I am sorry to have been so long, mother," said the poor child. As she spoke these words, there fell from her mouth three roses, three pearls, and three diamonds.

"What's this?" cried her mother. "Did I see pearls and diamonds dropping out of your mouth? What does this mean, dear daughter?" (This was the first time she had ever addressed her daughter affectionately.) The poor child told a simple tale of what had happened, and in speaking scattered diamonds right and left.

"Really," said her mother, "I must send my own child there. Come here, Fanchon; look what comes out of your sister's mouth whenever she speaks! Wouldn't you like to be able to do the same? All you have to do is to go and draw some water at the spring, and when a poor woman asks you for a drink, give it to her very nicely."

"'What's this?' cried her mother.

'Did I see pearls and diamonds dropping out of your mouth?'"

"Oh, indeed not!" replied the ill-mannered girl, "you'll not catch me going there!"

"I tell you that you are to go there," said her mother, "and to go this very instant."

Very sulkily the girl went off, taking with her the best silver flagon in the house. No sooner had she reached the spring than she saw a lady, magnificently attired, who came towards her from the forest, and asked for a drink. This was the same fairy who had appeared to her sister, masquerading now as a princess in order to see how far this girl's ill nature would carry her.

"Do you think I have come here just to get you a drink?" said the loutish damsel, arrogantly. "I suppose you think I brought a silver flagon here specially to get Madam a drink! What I think is: if you want a drink, get it yourself."

"You are not very polite," said the fairy, displaying no sign of anger. "Well, in return for your lack of courtesy I decree that for every word you utter a snake or a toad shall drop out of your mouth."

The moment her mother caught sight of her coming back she cried out, "Well, daughter?"

"Well, mother?" replied the rude girl. As she spoke a viper and a toad were spat out of her mouth.

"Gracious heavens!" cried her mother. "What do I see? Her sister is the cause of this, and I will make her pay for it!" Off she ran to thrash the poor child, but the latter fled away and hid in the forest nearby. The king's son met her on his way home from hunting, and, noticing how pretty she was, inquired what she was doing all alone, and what she was weeping about.

"Alas, sir," she cried, "my mother has driven me from home!" As she spoke, the prince saw four or five pearls and as many diamonds fall from her mouth. He begged her to tell him how this came about, and she told him the whole story.

The king's son fell in love with her, and reflecting that such a gift as had been bestowed upon her was worth more than any dowry that another maiden might bring him, he took her to the palace of his father the king, and there he married her.

As for the sister, she made herself so hateful that even her mother drove her out of the house. Nowhere could the wretched girl find anyone who would take her in, and at last she lay down in a corner of the forest and died.

Moral

Diamonds and rubies may
Work some wonders in their way;
But a gentle word is worth
More than all the gems on earth.

Another moral

Though—when otherwise inclined—
It's a trouble to be kind,
Often it will bring you good
When you'd scarce believe it could.

Charles Perrault

Notes on the Story

THE FAIRIES

Sometimes known as "Diamonds and Toads," this tale of virtuous and slovenly sisters appears in widespread variants across the globe. It is often considered to be a rite-of-passage story, in which a young woman is tested and proves her virtues in the traditional arts of domesticity. From a more feminist perspective, she discovers a deeper and more potent image of female power than that represented by her repressive mother or stepmother.

✣

Perrault helpfully provides us with two morals here, as he does in many of his tales. The question of Perrault's moral verses has been much discussed. While some have interpreted them as illustrating the rigidity of his values, others, including Angela Carter, have pointed out their humor. They are now most widely accepted as ironic commentaries in which he uses the stories to comment wryly on the morality and civility of French society.

Eighteenth-Century Tales

Falling between the fairy-tale frenzy of seventeenth-century France, and the era of passionate folklore collecting of the nineteenth century, the eighteenth century still saw important developments of the genre. In France, the enthusiasm for fashionably rewritten tales of magic continued, as is reflected in the work of Mme de Beaumont, as well as Antoine Galland, who brought the exotic tales of *The Arabian Nights* to Europe for the first time. With the Romantic movement exploding across Europe at the end of the century, this period also saw the inception of the Romantic literary fairy tale, which was to develop throughout the nineteenth century and profoundly affect fantasy writing up to the present day.

Aladdin and the Wonderful Lamp

There once lived a poor tailor, who had a son called Aladdin, a careless, idle boy who would do nothing but play all day long in the streets with little idle boys like himself. This so grieved the father that he died; yet, in spite of his mother's tears and prayers, Aladdin did not mend his ways. One day, when he was playing in the streets as usual, a stranger asked him his age, and if he were not the son of Mustapha the tailor.

"I am, sir," replied Aladdin, "but he died a long while ago."

On this, the stranger, who was a famous African magician, embraced and kissed him, saying: "I am your uncle, and knew you from your likeness to my brother. Go to your mother and tell her I am coming."

Aladdin ran home, and told his mother of his newly found uncle.

"Indeed, child," she said, "your father had a brother, but I always thought he was dead."

However, she prepared supper, and bade Aladdin seek his uncle, who came laden with wine and fruit. He presently fell down and kissed the place where Mustapha used to sit, bidding Aladdin's mother not to be surprised at not having seen him before, as he had been forty years out of the country. He then turned to Aladdin, and asked him his trade, at which the boy hung his head, while his mother burst into tears. On learning that Aladdin was idle and would learn no trade, he offered to take a shop for him and stock it with merchandise. Next day he bought

Aladdin a fine suit of clothes, and took him all over the city, showing him the sights, and brought him home at nightfall to his mother, who was overjoyed to see her son so fine.

Next day the magician led Aladdin into some beautiful gardens a long way outside the city gates. They sat down by a fountain, and the magician pulled a cake from his girdle, which he divided between them. They then journeyed onward till they almost reached the mountains. Aladdin was so tired that he begged to go back, but the magician beguiled him with pleasant stories, and led him on in spite of himself.

At last they came to two mountains divided by a narrow valley.

"We will go no farther," said the false uncle. "I will show you something wonderful; only do you gather up sticks while I kindle a fire."

When it was lit, the magician threw on it a powder he had about him, at the same time saying some magical words. The earth trembled a little and opened in front of them, disclosing a square flat stone with a brass ring in the middle to raise it by. Aladdin tried to run away, but the magician caught him and gave him a blow that knocked him down.

"What have I done, uncle?" he said, piteously; whereupon the magician said more kindly: "Fear nothing, but obey me. Beneath this stone lies a treasure which is to be yours, and no one else may touch it, so you must do exactly as I tell you."

At the word "treasure," Aladdin forgot his fears, and grasped the ring as he was told, saying the names of his father and grandfather. The stone came up quite easily and some steps appeared.

"Go down," said the magician, "at the foot of those steps you will find an open door leading into three large halls. Tuck up your gown and go through them without touching anything, or you will die instantly. These halls lead into a garden of fine fruit trees. Walk on till you come to a niche in a terrace where stands a lighted lamp. Pour out the oil it contains and bring it to me."

He drew a ring from his finger and gave it to Aladdin, bidding him prosper.

Aladdin found everything as the magician had said, gathered some fruit off the trees, and, having got the lamp, arrived at the mouth of the cave. The magician cried out in a great hurry: "Make haste and give me the lamp." This Aladdin refused to do until he was out of the cave. The magician flew into a terrible passion, and throwing some more powder on the fire, he said something, and the stone rolled back into its place.

The magician left China forever, which plainly showed that he was no uncle of Aladdin's, but a cunning magician who had read in his magic books of a wonderful lamp, which would make him the most powerful man in the world. Though he alone knew where to find it, he could only receive it from the hand of another. He had picked out the foolish Aladdin for this purpose, intending to get the lamp and to kill the boy afterward.

For two days Aladdin remained in the dark, crying and lamenting. At last he clasped his hands in prayer, and in so doing rubbed the ring, which the magician had forgotten to take from him. Immediately an enormous and frightful genie rose out of the earth, saying: "What wouldst thou do with me? I am the Slave of the Ring, and will obey thee in all things."

Aladdin fearlessly replied: "Deliver me from this place!" whereupon the earth opened, and he found himself outside. As soon as his eyes could bear the light he went home, but fainted on the threshold. When he came to himself he told his mother what had passed, and showed

"'What wouldst thou do with me?'

'I am the Slave of the Ring, and will obey thee in all things.'"

her the lamp and the fruits he had gathered in the garden, which were in reality precious stones. He then asked for some food.

"Alas! Child," she said, "I have nothing in the house, but I have spun a little cotton and will go and sell it."

Aladdin bade her keep her cotton, for he would sell the lamp instead. As it was very dirty she began to rub it, that it might fetch a higher price. Instantly a hideous genie appeared, and asked what she would have. She fainted away, but Aladdin, snatching the lamp, said boldly: "Fetch me something to eat!"

The genie returned with a silver bowl, twelve silver plates containing rich meats, two silver cups, and two bottles of wine. Aladdin's mother, when she came to herself, said: "Whence comes this splendid feast?"

"Ask not, but eat," replied Aladdin.

So they sat at breakfast till it was dinnertime, and Aladdin told his mother about the lamp. She begged him to sell it, and have nothing to do with devils.

"No," said Aladdin, "since chance has made us aware of its virtues, we will use it and the ring likewise, which I shall always wear on my finger." When they had eaten all the genie had brought, Aladdin sold one of the silver plates, and so on till none were left. He then had recourse to the genie, who gave him another set of plates, and thus they lived for many years.

One day Aladdin heard an order from the sultan proclaiming that everyone was to stay at home and close his shutters while the princess, his daughter, went to and from the bath. Aladdin was seized by a desire to see her face, which was very difficult, as she always went veiled. He hid himself behind the door of the bath, and peeped through a chink. The princess lifted her veil as she went in, and looked so beautiful that Aladdin fell in love with her at first sight. He went home so changed that his mother was frightened. He told her he loved the princess so deeply that he could not live without her, and meant to ask her in marriage of her father. His mother, on hearing this, burst out laughing, but Aladdin at last prevailed upon her to go before the sultan and carry his request. She fetched a napkin and laid in it the magic fruits from the enchanted garden, which sparkled and shone like the most beautiful jewels. She took these with her to please the sultan, and set out, trusting in the lamp. The grand-vizir and the lords of council had just gone in as she entered the hall and placed herself in front of the sultan. He, however, took no notice of her. She went every day for a week, and stood in the same place.

When the council broke up on the sixth day, the sultan said to his vizir: "I see a certain woman in the audience chamber every day carrying something in a napkin. Call her next time, so that I may find out what she wants."

Next day, at a sign from the vizir, she went up to the foot of the throne, and remained kneeling until the sultan said to her: "Rise, good woman, and tell me what you want."

She hesitated; so the sultan sent away all but the vizir, and bade her speak freely, promising to forgive her beforehand for anything she might say. She then told him of her son's violent love for the princess.

"I prayed him to forget her," she said, "but in vain; he threatened to do some desperate deed if I refused to go and ask your Majesty for the hand of the princess. Now I pray you to forgive not me alone, but my son Aladdin."

The sultan asked her kindly what she had in the napkin, whereupon she unfolded the jewels and presented them.

He was thunderstruck, and turning to the vizir said: "What sayest thou? Ought I not to bestow the princess on one who values her at such a price?"

The vizir, who wanted her for his own son, begged the sultan to withhold her for three months, in the course of which he hoped his son would contrive to make him a richer present. The sultan granted this, and told Aladdin's mother that, though he consented to the marriage, she must not appear before him again for three months.

Aladdin waited patiently for nearly three months, but after two had elapsed his mother, going into the city to buy oil, found everyone rejoicing, and asked what was going on.

"Do you not know," was the answer, "that the son of the grand-vizir is to marry the sultan's daughter tonight?"

Breathless, she ran and told Aladdin, who was overwhelmed at first, but presently bethought him of the lamp. He rubbed it, and the genie appeared, saying: "What is thy will?"

Aladdin replied: "The sultan, as thou knowest, has broken his promise to me, and the vizir's son is to have the princess. My command is that tonight you bring hither the bride and bridegroom."

"Master, I obey," said the genie.

Aladdin then went to his chamber, where, sure enough, at midnight, the genie transported the bed containing the vizir's son and the princess.

"Take this new-married man," he said, "and put him outside in the cold, and return at daybreak."

Whereupon the genie took the vizir's son out of bed, leaving Aladdin with the princess.

"Fear nothing," Aladdin said to her; "you are my wife, promised to me by your unjust father, and no harm shall come to you."

The princess was too frightened to speak, and passed the most miserable night of her life, while Aladdin lay down beside her and slept soundly. At the appointed hour, the genie fetched in the shivering bridegroom, laid him in his place, and transported the bed back to the palace.

Presently the sultan came to wish his daughter good morning. The unhappy vizir's son jumped up and hid himself, while the princess would not say a word, and was very sorrowful.

The sultan sent her mother to her, who said: "How comes it, child, that you will not speak to your father? What has happened?"

The princess sighed deeply, and at last told her mother how, during the night, the bed had been carried into some strange house, and what had passed there. Her mother did not believe her in the least, but bade her rise and consider it an idle dream.

The following night exactly the same thing happened, and next morning, on the princess's refusing to speak, the sultan threatened to cut off her head. She then confessed all, bidding him ask the vizir's son if it were not so. The sultan told the vizir to ask his son, who owned the truth, adding that, dearly as he loved the princess, he had rather die than go through another such fearful night, and wished to be separated from her. His wish was granted, and there was an end of feasting and rejoicing.

When the three months were over, Aladdin sent his mother to remind the sultan of his promise. She stood in the same place as before, and the sultan, who had forgotten Aladdin, at once remembered him, and sent for her. On seeing her poverty the sultan felt less inclined than ever to keep his word, and asked the vizir's advice, who counseled him to set so high a value on the princess that no man living could come up to it.

The sultan then turned to Aladdin's mother, saying: "Good woman, a sultan must remember his promises, and I will remember mine, but your son must first send me forty basins of gold brimful of jewels, carried by forty black slaves, led by as many white ones, splendidly dressed. Tell him that I await his answer." The mother of Aladdin bowed low and went home, thinking all was lost.

She gave Aladdin the message, adding: "He may wait long enough for your answer!"

"Not so long, mother, as you think," her son replied. "I would do a great deal more than that for the princess."

He summoned the genie, and in a few moments the eighty slaves arrived, and filled up the small house and garden.

Aladdin made them set out to the palace, two and two, followed by his mother. They were so richly dressed, with such splendid jewels in their girdles, that everyone crowded to see them and the basins of gold they carried on their heads.

They entered the palace, and, after kneeling before the sultan, stood in a half-circle round the throne with their arms crossed, while Aladdin's mother presented them to the sultan.

He hesitated no longer, but said: "Good woman, return, and tell your son that I wait for him with open arms."

She lost no time in telling Aladdin, bidding him make haste. But Aladdin first called the genie.

"I want a scented bath," he said, "a richly embroidered habit, a horse surpassing the sultan's, and twenty slaves to attend me. Besides this, six slaves, beautifully dressed, to wait on my mother; and lastly, ten thousand pieces of gold in ten purses."

No sooner said than done. Aladdin mounted his horse and passed through the streets, the slaves strewing gold as they went. Those who had played with him in his childhood knew him not, for he had grown so handsome.

When the sultan saw him, he came down from his throne, embraced him, and led him into a hall where a feast was spread, intending to marry him to the princess that very day.

But Aladdin refused, saying, "I must build a palace fit for her," and took his leave.

Once home he said to the genie: "Build me a palace of the finest marble, set with jasper, agate, and other precious stones. In the middle you shall build me a large hall with a dome, its four walls of gold and silver, each side having six windows, whose lattices, all except one, which is to be left unfinished, must be set with diamonds and rubies.

There must be stables and horses and grooms and slaves; go and see about it!"

The palace was finished by next day, and the genie carried him there and showed him all his orders faithfully carried out, even to the laying of a velvet carpet from Aladdin's palace to the sultan's. Aladdin's mother then dressed herself carefully, and walked to the palace with her slaves, while he followed her on horseback. The sultan sent musicians with trumpets and cymbals to meet them, so that the air resounded with music and cheers. She was taken to the princess, who saluted her and treated her with great honor. At night the princess said goodbye to her father, and set out on the carpet for Aladdin's palace, with his mother at her side, and followed by the hundred slaves. She was charmed at the sight of Aladdin, who ran to receive her.

"Princess," he said, "blame your beauty for my boldness if I have displeased you."

She told him that, having seen him, she willingly obeyed her father in this matter. After the wedding had taken place, Aladdin led her into the hall, where a feast was spread, and she supped with him, after which they danced till midnight.

Next day, Aladdin invited the sultan to see the palace. On entering the hall with the four-and-twenty windows, with their rubies, diamonds, and emeralds, he cried: "It is a world's wonder! There is only one thing that surprises me. Was it by accident that one window was left unfinished?"

"No, sir, by design," returned Aladdin. "I wished your Majesty to have the glory of finishing this palace."

The sultan was pleased, and sent for the best jewelers in the city. He showed them the unfinished window, and bade them fit it up like the others.

"Sir," replied their spokesman, "we cannot find jewels enough."

The sultan had his own fetched, which they soon used, but to no purpose, for in a month's time the work was not half done. Aladdin, knowing that their task was in vain, bade them undo their work and carry the jewels back, and the genie finished the window at his command. The sultan was surprised to receive his jewels again and visited Aladdin, who showed him the window finished. The sultan embraced him, the envious vizir meanwhile hinting that it was the work of enchantment.

Aladdin had won the hearts of the people by his gentle bearing. He was made captain of the sultan's armies, and won several battles for him, but remained modest and courteous as before, and lived thus in peace and content for several years.

But far away in Africa, the magician remembered Aladdin, and by his magic arts discovered that Aladdin, instead of perishing miserably in the cave, had escaped, and had married a princess, with whom he was living in great honor and wealth. He knew that the poor tailor's son could only have accomplished this by means of the lamp, and traveled night and day until he reached the capital of China, bent on Aladdin's ruin. As he passed through the town he heard people talking everywhere about a marvelous palace.

"Forgive my ignorance," he said. "What is this palace you speak of?"

"Have you not heard of Prince Aladdin's palace," was the reply, "the greatest wonder of the world? I will direct you if you have a mind to see it."

The magician thanked him who spoke, and having seen the palace, he knew that it had been raised by the genie of the lamp, and became half mad with rage. He determined to get hold of the lamp, and again plunge Aladdin into the deepest poverty.

Unluckily, Aladdin had gone hunting for eight days, which gave the magician plenty of time. He bought a dozen copper lamps, put them into a basket, and went to the palace, crying: "New lamps for old!" followed by a jeering crowd.

The princess, sitting in the hall of four-and-twenty windows, sent a slave to find out what the noise was about, who came back laughing, so that the princess scolded her.

"Madam," replied the slave, "who can help laughing to see an old fool offering to exchange fine new lamps for old ones?"

Another slave, hearing this, said: "There is an old one on the cornice there which he can have."

Now this was the magic lamp, which Aladdin had left there, as he could not take it out hunting with him. The princess, not knowing its value, laughingly bade the slave take it and make the exchange.

She went and said to the magician: "Give me a new lamp for this."

He snatched it and bade the slave take her choice, amid the jeers of the crowd. Little he cared, but left off crying his lamps, and went out of the city gates to a lonely place, where he remained until nightfall, when he pulled out the lamp and rubbed it. The genie appeared, and at the magician's command carried him, together with the palace and the princess in it, to a lonely place in Africa.

Next morning the sultan looked out of the window towards Aladdin's palace and rubbed his eyes, for it was gone. He sent for the vizir, and asked what had become of the palace. The vizir looked out too, and was lost in astonishment. He again put it down to enchantment, and this time the sultan believed him, and sent thirty men on horseback to fetch Aladdin in chains. They met him riding home, bound him, and forced him to go with them on foot. The people, however, who loved him, followed, armed, to see that he came to no harm. He was carried before the sultan, who ordered the executioner to cut off his head. The executioner made Aladdin kneel down, bandaged his eyes, and raised his scimitar to strike.

At that instant the vizir, who saw that the crowd had forced their way into the courtyard and were scaling the walls to rescue Aladdin, called to the executioner to stay his hand. The people, indeed, looked so threatening that the sultan gave way and ordered Aladdin to be unbound, and pardoned him in the sight of the crowd.

Aladdin now begged to know what he had done.

"False wretch!" said the sultan. "Come hither," and showed him from the window the place where his palace had stood.

Aladdin was so amazed that he could not say a word.

"Where is my palace and my daughter?" demanded the sultan. "For the first I am not so deeply concerned, but my daughter I must have, and you must find her or lose your head."

Aladdin begged for forty days in which to find her, promising if he failed to return and suffer death at the sultan's pleasure. His prayer was granted, and he went forth sadly from the sultan's presence. For three days he wandered about like a madman, asking everyone what had become of his palace, but they only laughed and pitied him. He came to the banks of a river, and knelt down to say his prayers before throwing himself in. In so doing he rubbed the magic ring he still wore.

The genie he had seen in the cave appeared, and asked his will.

"Save my life, genie," said Aladdin, "and bring my palace back."

"That is not in my power," said the genie. "I am only the slave of the ring; you must ask the slave of the lamp."

"Even so," said Aladdin, "but you can take me to the palace, and set me down under my dear wife's window." He at once found himself in Africa, under the window of the princess, and he was so tired that he fell asleep out of sheer weariness.

He was awakened by the birds singing, and his heart was lighter. He saw plainly that all his misfortunes were owing to the loss of the lamp, and vainly wondered who had robbed him of it.

That morning the princess rose earlier than she had done since she had been carried into Africa by the magician, whose company she was forced to endure once a day. She, however, treated him so harshly that he dared not live there altogether. As she was dressing, one of her women looked out and saw Aladdin. The princess ran and opened the window, and at the noise she made Aladdin looked up. She called to him to come to her, and great was the joy of these lovers at seeing each other again.

After he had kissed her Aladdin said: "I beg of you, Princess, in God's name, before we speak of anything else, for your own sake and mine, tell me what has become of an old lamp I left on the cornice in the hall of four-and-twenty windows, when I went a-hunting."

"Alas!" she said, "I am the innocent cause of our sorrows," and told him of the exchange of the lamp.

"Now I know," cried Aladdin, "that we have to thank the African magician for this! Where is the lamp?"

"He carries it about with him," said the princess. "I know, for he pulled it out of his vest to show me. He wishes me to break my faith with you and marry him, saying that you were beheaded by my father's command. He is forever speaking ill of you, but I only reply by my tears. If I persist, I doubt not that he will use violence."

Aladdin comforted her, and left her for a while. He changed clothes with the first person he met in the town, and having bought a certain powder returned to the princess, who let him in by a little side door.

"Put on your most beautiful dress," he said to her, "and receive the magician with smiles, leading him to believe that you have forgotten me. Invite him to sup with you, and say you wish to taste the wine of his country. He will go for some, and while he is gone, I will tell you what to do."

She listened carefully to Aladdin, and when he left, she arrayed herself gaily for the first time since she left China. She put on a girdle and a headdress of diamonds, and seeing in a glass that she looked more beautiful than ever, received the magician, saying to his great amazement: "I have made up my mind that Aladdin is dead, and that all my tears will not bring him back to me, so I am resolved to mourn no more, and have therefore invited you to sup with me. But I am tired of the wines of China, and would fain taste those of Africa."

The magician flew to his cellar, and the princess put the powder Aladdin had given her in her cup. When he returned she asked him to drink her health in the wine of Africa, handing him her cup in exchange for his as a sign she was reconciled to him.

Before drinking, the magician made her a speech in praise of her beauty, but the princess cut him short, saying: "Let me drink first, and you shall say what you will afterward." She set her cup to her lips and kept it there, while the magician drained his to the dregs and fell back lifeless.

The princess then opened the door to Aladdin, and flung her arms round his neck, but Aladdin put her away, bidding her to leave him, as he had more to do. He then went to the dead magician, took the lamp out of his vest, and bade the genie carry the palace and all in it back to China. This was done, and the princess in her chamber only felt two little shocks, and little thought she was at home again.

The sultan, who was sitting in his closet, mourning for his lost daughter, happened to look up, and rubbed his eyes, for there stood the palace as before! He hastened there, and Aladdin received him in the hall of the four-and-twenty windows, with the princess at his side. Aladdin told him what had happened, and showed him the dead body of the magician, that he might believe. A ten days' feast was proclaimed, and it seemed as if Aladdin might now live the rest of his life in peace; but it was not to be.

The African magician had a younger brother, who was, if possible, more wicked and more cunning than himself. He traveled to China to avenge his brother's death, and went to visit a pious woman called Fatima, thinking she might be of use to him. He entered her cell and clapped a dagger to her breast, telling her to rise and do his bidding on pain of death. He changed clothes with her, colored his face like hers, put on her veil, and murdered her, that she might tell no tales. Then he went toward the palace of Aladdin, and all the people, thinking he was the holy woman, gathered round him, kissing his hands and begging his blessing.

When he got to the palace there was such a noise going on round him that the princess bade her slave look out of the window and ask what was the matter. The slave said it was the holy woman, curing people by her touch of their ailments, whereupon the princess, who had long desired to see Fatima, sent for her. On coming to the princess, the magician offered up a prayer for her health and prosperity. When he had done, the princess made him sit by her, and begged him to stay with her always. The false Fatima, who wished for nothing better, consented, but kept his veil down for fear of discovery. The princess showed him the hall, and asked him what he thought of it.

"It is truly beautiful," said the false Fatima. "In my mind it wants but one thing."

"And what is that?" said the princess.

"If only a roc's egg," replied he, "were hung up from the middle of this dome, it would be the wonder of the world."

After this the princess could think of nothing but a roc's egg, and when Aladdin returned from hunting he found her in a very ill humor. He begged to know what was amiss, and she told him that all her pleasure in the hall was spoilt for the want of a roc's egg hanging from the dome.

"If that is all," replied Aladdin, "you shall soon be happy."

He left her and rubbed the lamp, and when the genie appeared commanded him to bring a roc's egg. The genie gave such a loud and terrible shriek that the hall shook.

"Wretch!" he cried. "Is it not enough that I have done everything for you, but you must command me to bring my master and hang him up in the midst of this dome? You and your wife and your palace deserve to be burnt to ashes; but this request does not come from you, but from the brother of the African magician whom you destroyed. He is now in your palace disguised as the holy woman, whom he murdered. It was he who put that wish into your wife's head. Take care of yourself, for he means to kill you." So saying, the genie disappeared.

Aladdin went back to the princess, saying his head ached, and requesting that the holy Fatima should be fetched to lay her hands on it. But when the magician came near, Aladdin, seizing his dagger, pierced him to the heart.

"What have you done?" cried the princess. "You have killed the holy woman!"

"Not so," replied Aladdin, "but a wicked magician," and told her of how she had been deceived.

After this Aladdin and his wife lived in peace. He succeeded the sultan when he died, and reigned for many years, leaving behind him a long line of kings.

Antoine Galland

Notes on the Story

Aladdin and the Wonderful Lamp

Possibly the most famous tale from *The Arabian Nights*, it is ironic that this story was not part of the original *Arabian Nights*, but added by the European translator Antoine Galland (1646–1715). Galland was a French orientalist who heard "Aladdin" from a Syrian monk in 1709. He rewrote it and included it in his version of *The Arabian Nights*, the first Western translation, which he published in multiple volumes from 1704–1717. Although Arabic manuscripts of "Aladdin" were later found, these were proved fake, and Galland's is the earliest version that can be traced (giving the tale a history nearly as full of intrigue as the story itself).

Galland, influenced by D'Aulnoy and Perrault, published *The Arabian Nights* at the peak of French fairy-tale fever. The collection was well received and spread like lightning across Europe. The same can be said for "Aladdin," which was disseminated via chapbooks (booklets), literature, and theater to become one of the world's most celebrated tales.

Beauty and the Beast

There was once a very rich merchant, who had six children, three sons, and three daughters; being a man of sense, he spared no cost for their education, but gave them all kinds of masters. His daughters were extremely handsome, especially the youngest. When she was little, everybody admired her, and called her "Little Beauty," so that, as she grew up, she still went by the name of "Beauty," which made her sisters very jealous. The youngest was not only more beautiful than her sisters, but also better. The two eldest had a great deal of pride, because they were rich. They gave themselves ridiculous airs, and would not visit other merchants' daughters, nor keep company with any but persons of quality. They went out every day upon parties of pleasure, balls, plays, and concerts, and laughed at their youngest sister, because she spent the greatest part of her time in reading good books.

As it was known that they were to have great fortunes, several eminent merchants sought their hand in marriage; but the two eldest said they would never marry, unless they could meet with a duke, or an earl at least. Beauty very civilly thanked them that courted her, and told them she was too young yet to marry, but chose to stay with her father a few years longer.

All at once the merchant lost his whole fortune, excepting a small country house at a great distance from town, and told his children, with tears in his eyes, they must go there and work for their living. The two eldest answered that they would not leave the town, for they had several lovers, who they were sure would be glad to have them, though they had no fortune; but in this they were mistaken, for their lovers slighted and forsook them in their poverty. As they were not beloved on account of their pride, everybody said, "They do not deserve to be pitied. We are glad to see their pride humbled, let them go and give themselves quality airs in milking the cows and minding their dairy. But," added they, "we are extremely concerned for Beauty. She was such a charming, sweet-tempered creature, spoke so kindly to poor people, and was of such an affable, obliging disposition."

Nay, several gentlemen would have married her, though they knew she had not a penny. But she told them she could not think of leaving her poor father in his misfortunes, but was determined to go along with him into the country to comfort and attend him. Poor Beauty at first was sadly grieved at the loss of her fortune: "But," she said to herself, "were I to cry ever so much, that would not make things better, I must try to make myself happy without a fortune."

When they came to their country-house, the merchant and his three sons applied themselves to farming. And Beauty rose at four in the morning, and made haste to have the house clean, and breakfast ready for the family. In the beginning she found it very difficult, for she had not been used to work as a servant; but in less than two months she grew stronger and healthier than ever.

After she had done her work, she read, played on the harpsichord, or else sung while she spun. On the contrary, her two sisters did not know how to spend their time; they got up at ten, and did nothing but saunter about the whole day, lamenting the loss of their fine clothes and acquaintances.

"Do but see our youngest sister," said they one to the other. "What a poor, stupid, mean-spirited creature she is, to be contented with such an unhappy situation." The good merchant was of a quite different opinion; he knew very well that Beauty outshone her sisters, in her person as well as her mind, and admired her humility, industry, and patience; for her sisters not only left her all the work of the house to do, but insulted her every moment.

The family had lived about a year in this retirement, when the merchant received a letter, with an account that a vessel, on board of which he had effects, was safely arrived. This news had liked to have turned the heads of the two eldest daughters, who immediately flattered themselves with the hopes of returning to town; for they were quite weary of a country life. And when they saw their father ready to set out, they begged of him to buy them new gowns, caps, rings, and all manner of trifles; but Beauty asked for nothing, for she thought to herself, that all the money her father was going to receive would scarce be sufficient to purchase everything her sisters wanted.

"What will you have, Beauty?" said her father.

"Since you are so kind as to think of me," answered she, "be so kind as to bring me a rose, for as none grow hereabouts, they are a kind of rarity." Not that Beauty cared for a rose, but she asked for something, lest she should seem by her example to condemn her sisters' conduct, who would have said she did it only to look particular.

The good man went on his journey; but when he came there, they went to law with him about the merchandise, and after a great deal of trouble and pains to no purpose, he came back as poor as before.

He was within thirty miles of his own house, thinking on the pleasure he should have in seeing his children again, when, going through a large forest, he lost himself. It rained and snowed terribly,

besides, the wind was so high, that it threw him twice off his horse. With night coming on, he began to apprehend being either starved to death with cold and hunger, or else devoured by the wolves, whom he heard howling all around him, when, on a sudden, looking through a long walk of trees, he saw a light at some distance, and going on a little farther, perceived it came from a palace illuminated from top to bottom. The merchant returned God thanks for this happy discovery, and hasted to the palace, but was greatly surprised at not meeting with anyone in the out-courts. His horse followed him, and seeing a large stable open, went in, and finding both hay and oats, the poor beast, who was almost famished, fell to eating very heartily. The merchant tied him up to the manger, and walked towards the house, where he saw no one, but entering into a large hall, he found a good fire, and a table plentifully set out, with but one cover laid. As he was wet quite through with the rain and snow, he drew near the fire to dry himself.

"I hope," said he, "the master of the house, or his servants, will excuse the liberty I take. I suppose it will not be long before some of them appear."

He waited a considerable time, till it struck eleven, and still nobody came. At last he was so hungry that he could stay no longer, but took a chicken and ate it in two mouthfuls, trembling all the while. After this, he drank a few glasses of wine, and growing more courageous, he went out of the hall, and crossed through several grand apartments with magnificent furniture, till he came into a chamber, which had an exceedingly good bed in it. And as he was very much fatigued, and it was past midnight, he concluded it was best to shut the door, and go to bed.

It was ten the next morning before the merchant waked, and as he was going to rise, he was astonished to see a good suit of clothes in place of his own, which were quite spoiled.

"Certainly," said he, "this palace belongs to some kind fairy, who has seen and pitied my distress." He looked through a window, but instead of snow saw the most delightful arbors, interwoven with the most beautiful flowers that ever were beheld. He then returned to the great hall, where he had supped the night before, and found some chocolate ready made on a little table.

"Thank you, good Madam Fairy," said he aloud, "for being so careful as to provide me a breakfast. I am extremely obliged to you for all your favors."

The good man drank his chocolate, and then went to look for his horse; but passing through an arbor of roses, he remembered Beauty's request to him, and gathered a branch on which were several. Immediately he heard a great noise, and saw such a frightful beast coming towards him, that he was ready to faint away.

"You are very ungrateful," said the beast to him, in a terrible voice. "I have saved your life by receiving you into my castle, and, in return, you steal my roses, which I value beyond any thing in the universe; but you shall die for it. I give you but a quarter of an hour to prepare yourself, to say your prayers."

The merchant fell on his knees, and lifted up both his hands: "My Lord," said he, "I beseech you to forgive me, indeed, I had no intention to offend in gathering a rose for one of my daughters, who desired me to bring her one."

"My name is not My Lord," replied the monster, "but Beast. I do not love compliments. I like people who speak as they think. So do not imagine I am moved by any of your flattering speeches. But, you say that you have daughters. I will forgive you as long as one of them comes willingly to me, and suffers for you. Let me have no words, but go about your business, and swear that if your daughter refuses to die in your stead, you will return within three months."

"'You are very ungrateful . . . I have saved your life

. . . and, in return, you steal my roses . . .'"

The merchant had no mind to sacrifice his daughters to the ugly monster, but he thought, in obtaining this respite, he should have the satisfaction of seeing them once more. So he promised upon oath, he would return, and the Beast told him he might set out when he pleased.

"But," added he, "you shall not depart empty-handed. Go back to the room where you lay, and you will see a great empty chest; fill it with whatever you like best, and I will send it to your home," and at the same time Beast withdrew.

"Well," said the good man to himself, "if I must die, I shall have the comfort, at least, of leaving something to my poor children."

He returned to the bedchamber, and finding a great quantity of broad pieces of gold, he filled the great chest the Beast had mentioned, locked it, and afterward took his horse out of the stable, leaving the palace with as much grief as he had entered it with joy. The horse, of his own accord, took one of the roads of the forest; and in a few hours the good man was at home. His children came around him, but, instead of receiving their embraces with pleasure, he looked on them, and, holding up the branch he had in his hands, he burst into tears.

"Here, Beauty," said he, "take these roses; but little do you think how dear they are like to cost your unhappy father." And then he related his fatal adventure. Immediately the two eldest set up lamentable outcries, and said all manner of ill-natured things to Beauty, who did not cry at all.

"Do but see the pride of that little wretch," said they. "She would not ask for fine clothes, as we did. But no, truly, Miss wanted to distinguish herself. So now she will be the death of our poor father, and yet she does not so much as shed a tear."

"Why should I?" answered Beauty. "It would be very needless, for my father shall not suffer upon my account. Since the monster will accept one of his daughters, I will deliver myself up to all his fury, and I am very happy in thinking that my death will save my father's life, and be a proof of my tender love for him."

"No, sister," said her three brothers. "That shall not be. We will go find the monster, and either kill him, or perish in the attempt."

"Do not imagine any such thing, my sons," said the merchant. "Beast's power is so great, that I have no hopes of your overcoming him; I am charmed with Beauty's kind and generous offer, but I cannot yield to it. I am old, and have not long to live, so can only lose a few years, which I regret for your sakes alone, my dear children."

"Indeed, father," said Beauty, "you shall not go to the palace without me, you cannot hinder me from following you." It was to no purpose all they could say, Beauty still insisted on setting out for the fine palace; and her sisters were delighted at it, for her virtue and amiable qualities made them envious and jealous.

The merchant was so afflicted at the thoughts of losing his daughter, that he had quite forgotten the chest full of gold; but at night, when he retired to rest, no sooner had he shut his chamber door, than, to his great astonishment, he found it by his bedside. He was determined, however, not to tell his children that he had grown rich, because they would have wanted to return to town, and he was resolved not to leave the country; but he trusted Beauty with the secret. She informed him, that two gentlemen came in his absence, and courted her sisters. She begged her father to consent to their marriage, and give them fortunes; for she was so good, that she loved them, and forgave them heartily all their ill-usage. These wicked creatures rubbed their eyes with an onion, to force some tears when they parted with their sister; but her brothers were really concerned. Beauty was the only one who did not shed tears at parting, because she would not increase their uneasiness.

The horse took the direct road to the palace; and toward evening they saw it all lit up. The horse went of himself into the stable, and the good man and his daughter came into the great hall, where they found a table splendidly served up, and two covers. The merchant had no heart to eat; but Beauty endeavored to appear cheerful, sat down at the table, and helped him.

Afterward, thought she to herself, "Beast surely has a mind to fatten me before he eats me, since he provides such a plentiful entertainment." When they had supped, they heard a great noise, and the merchant, all in tears, bid his poor child farewell, for he thought Beast was coming.

Beauty was sadly terrified at his horrid form, but she took courage as well as she could, and the monster having asked her if she came willingly, "Y–e–s," she said, trembling.

"You are very good, and I am greatly obliged to you; honest man, go your ways tomorrow morning, but never think of returning here again. Farewell, Beauty."

"Farewell, Beast," answered she; and the monster withdrew.

"Oh, daughter," said the merchant, embracing Beauty, "I am almost frightened to death. Believe me, you had better go back, and let me stay here."

"No, father," said Beauty, in a resolute tone. "You shall set out tomorrow morning, and leave me to the care and protection of Providence."

They went to bed, and thought they should not close their eyes all night; but scarce were they laid down, than they fell fast asleep. And Beauty dreamed a fine lady came, and spoke to her, "I am content, Beauty, with your good will. This good action of yours, in giving up your own life to save your father's, shall not go unrewarded." Beauty waked, and told her father about her dream, and though it helped to comfort him a little, yet he could not help crying bitterly, when he took leave of his dear child.

As soon as he was gone, Beauty sat down in the great hall, and fell to crying likewise. But as she was mistress of a great deal of resolution, she recommended herself to God, and resolved not to be uneasy the little time she had to live; for she firmly believed Beast would eat her up that night.

However, she thought she might as well walk about till then, and view this fine castle, which she could not help admiring. It was a delightful, pleasant place, and she was extremely surprised at seeing a door, over which was written, *Beauty's Apartment*. She opened it hastily, and was quite dazzled with the magnificence that reigned throughout; but what chiefly took up her attention was a large library, a harpsichord, and several music books.

"Well," said she to herself, "I see they will not let my time hang heavy on my hands for want of amusement." Then she reflected, "Were I but to stay here a day, there would not have been all these preparations." This consideration inspired her with fresh courage; and opening the library, she took a book, and read these words in letters of gold–

Welcome, Beauty, banish fear,
You are queen and mistress here;
Speak your wishes, speak your will,
Swift obedience meets them still.

"Alas," said she, with a sigh, "there is nothing I desire so much as to see my poor father, and to know what he is doing." She had no sooner said this, when casting her eyes on a huge looking glass, to her great amazement she saw her own home, where her father arrived with a very dejected countenance. Her sisters went to meet him, and, notwithstanding their endeavors to appear sorrowful, their joy, felt for having got rid of their sister, was visible in every feature. A moment after, everything disappeared, as did Beauty's apprehensions when she had this proof that the Beast was ready to grant her wishes.

At noon she found dinner ready, and while at table, was entertained with an excellent concert of music, though without seeing anybody. But at night, as she was going to sit down to supper, she heard the noise Beast made, and could not help being sadly terrified.

"Beauty," said the monster, "will you give me leave to see you sup?"

"That is as you please," answered Beauty, trembling.

"No," replied the Beast, "you alone are mistress here. You need only bid me be gone, if my presence is troublesome, and I will immediately withdraw. But tell me, do not you think me very ugly?"

"That is true," said Beauty, "for I cannot tell a lie. But I believe you are very good-natured."

"So I am," said the monster, "but then, besides my ugliness, I have no sense. I know very well that I am a poor, silly, stupid creature."

"'Tis no sign of folly to think so," replied Beauty, "for never did fool know this, or had so humble a conceit of his own understanding."

"Eat then, Beauty," said the monster, "and endeavor to amuse yourself in your palace; for everything here is yours, and I should be very uneasy if you were not happy."

"You are very obliging," answered Beauty. "I own I am pleased with your kindness, and when I consider that, your deformity scarce appears."

"Yes, yes," said the Beast, "my heart is good, but still I am a monster."

"Among mankind," says Beauty, "there are many that deserve that name more than you, and I prefer you, just as you are, to those, who, under a human form, hide a treacherous, corrupt, and ungrateful heart."

"If I had sense enough," replied the Beast, "I would make a fine compliment to thank you, but I am so dull, that I can only say, I am greatly obliged to you."

Beauty ate a hearty supper, and had almost conquered her dread of the monster; but she had liked to have fainted away, when he said to her, "Beauty, will you be my wife?" She was some time before she dared answer; for she was afraid of making him angry, if she refused. At last, however, she said, trembling, "No, Beast."

Immediately the poor monster began to sigh, and hissed so frightfully, that the whole palace echoed. But Beauty soon recovered her fright, for Beast having said, in a mournful voice, "then farewell, Beauty," left the room; and only turned back, now and then, to look at her as he went out.

When Beauty was alone, she felt a great deal of compassion for poor Beast. "Alas," said she, "it is a thousand pities anybody so good-natured should be so ugly."

Beauty spent three months very contentedly in the palace. Every evening Beast paid her a visit, and talked to her during supper, very rationally, with plain good common sense, but never with what the world calls wit. And Beauty daily discovered some valuable qualifications in the monster; and seeing him often, had so accustomed her to his deformity, that, far from dreading the time of his visit, she would often look on her watch to see when it would be nine, for the Beast never missed coming at that hour. There was but one thing that gave Beauty any concern, which was, that every night, before she went to bed, the monster always asked her if she would be his wife.

"'Beauty, will you be my wife?' . . .

At last, however, she said, trembling, 'No, Beast.'"

One day she said to him, "Beast, you make me very uneasy. I wish I could consent to marry you, but I am too sincere to make you believe that will ever happen. I shall always esteem you as a friend; endeavor to be satisfied with this."

"I must," said the Beast, "for, alas! I know too well my own misfortune; but then I love you with the tenderest affection. However, I ought to think myself happy that you will stay here. Promise me never to leave me."

Beauty blushed at these words; she had seen in her glass, that her father had pined himself sick for the loss of her, and she longed to see him again. "I could," answered she, "indeed promise never to leave you entirely, but I have so great a desire to see my father, that I shall fret to death, if you refuse me that satisfaction."

"I would rather die myself," said the monster, "than give you the least uneasiness. I will send you to your father, you shall remain with him, and poor Beast will die with grief."

"No," said Beauty, weeping, "I love you too well to be the cause of your death. I give you my promise to return in a week. You have shown me that my sisters are married, and my brothers gone to the army. Only let me stay a week with my father, as he is alone."

"You shall be there tomorrow morning, but remember your promise: you need only lay your ring on the table before you go to bed, when you have a mind to come back. Farewell, Beauty."

Beast sighed as usual, bidding her good night; and Beauty went to bed very sad at seeing him so afflicted.

When she waked the next morning, she found herself at her father's, and having rang a little bell, that was by her bedside, she saw the maid come; who, the moment she saw her, gave a loud shriek; at which the good man ran up stairs, and thought he should have died with joy to see his dear daughter again. He held her fast locked in his arms above a quarter of an hour. As soon as the first transports were over, Beauty began to think of rising, and was afraid she had no clothes to put on; but the maid told her, that she had just found, in the next room, a large trunk full of gowns, covered with gold and diamonds. Beauty thanked good Beast for his kind care, and taking one of the plainest of them, she intended to make a present of the others to her sisters. She scarce had said so, when the trunk disappeared. Her father told her, that Beast insisted on her keeping them herself; and immediately both gowns and trunk came back again.

Beauty dressed herself; and in the meantime they sent for her sisters, who hasted there with their husbands. They were both of them very unhappy. The eldest had married a gentleman, extremely handsome indeed, but so fond of his own person, that he was full of nothing but his own dear self, and neglected his wife. The second had married a man of wit, but he only made use of it to plague and torment everybody, and his wife most of all. Beauty's sisters sickened with envy when they saw her dressed like a princess, and more beautiful than ever; nor could all her obliging affectionate behavior stifle their jealousy, which was ready to burst when she told them how happy she was. They went down into the garden to vent it in tears.

And said one to the other, "In what is this little creature better than us, that she should be so much happier?"

"Sister," said the eldest, "a thought just strikes my mind. Let us endeavor to detain her above a week, and perhaps the silly monster will be so enraged at her for breaking her word, that he will devour her."

"Right, sister," answered the other, "therefore we must show her as much kindness as possible."

After they had taken this resolution, they went up, and behaved so affectionately to their sister, that poor Beauty wept for joy. When the week was expired, they cried and tore their hair, and seemed so sorry to part with her, that she promised to stay a week longer.

In the meantime, Beauty could not help reflecting on herself for the uneasiness she was likely to cause poor Beast, whom she sincerely loved, and really longed to see again. The tenth night she spent at her father's, she dreamed she was in the palace garden, and that she saw Beast extended on the grass-plot, who seemed just expiring, and, in a dying voice, reproached her for her ingratitude.

Beauty started out of her sleep and burst into tears. "Am not I very wicked," said she, "to act so unkindly to Beast, that has studied so much to please me in every thing? Is it his fault that he is so ugly, and has so little sense? He is kind and good, and that is sufficient. Why did I refuse to marry him? I should be happier with the monster than my sisters are with their husbands. It is neither wit nor a fine person in a husband that makes a woman happy, but virtue, sweetness of temper, and complaisance: and Beast has all these valuable qualifications. It is true, I do not feel the tenderness of affection for him, but I find I have the highest gratitude, esteem, and friendship; and I will not make him miserable; were I to be so ungrateful, I should never forgive myself."

Beauty, having said this, rose, put her ring on the table, and then laid down again; scarce was she in bed before she fell asleep. And when she waked the next morning, she was overjoyed to find herself in the Beast's palace. She put on one of her richest suits to please him, and waited for evening with the utmost impatience. At last the wished-for hour came, the clock struck nine, yet no Beast appeared.

Beauty then feared she had been the cause of his death; she ran crying and wringing her hands all about the palace, like one in despair. After having sought for him everywhere, she recollected her dream, and flew to the canal in the garden, where she dreamed she saw him. There she found poor Beast stretched out, quite senseless, and, as she imagined, dead. She threw herself upon him without any dread, and finding his heart beat still, she fetched some water from the canal, and poured it on his head.

Beast opened his eyes, and said to Beauty, "You forgot your promise, and I was so afflicted for having lost you, that I resolved to starve myself; but since I have the happiness of seeing you once more, I will die satisfied."

"No, dear Beast," said Beauty, "you must not die; live to be my husband; from this moment I give you my hand, and swear to be none but yours. Alas! I thought I had only a friendship for you, but the grief I now feel convinces me that I cannot live without you." Beauty scarcely had pronounced these words, when she saw the palace sparkle with light; and fireworks, instruments of music, everything, seemed to give notice of some great event. But nothing could fix her attention; she turned to her dear Beast, for whom she trembled with fear, but how great was her surprise! Beast had disappeared, and she saw, at her feet, one of the loveliest princes that her eyes had ever beheld, who returned her thanks for having put an end to the charm, under which he had so long resembled a Beast. Though this prince was worthy of all her attention, she could not forbear asking where Beast was.

"You see him at your feet," said the prince. "A wicked fairy had condemned me to remain under that shape till a beautiful virgin should consent to marry me. The fairy likewise enjoined me to conceal my understanding. There was only you in the world generous enough to be won by the goodness of my temper; and in offering you my crown, I can't discharge the obligations I have to you."

Beauty, agreeably surprised, gave the charming prince her hand to rise. They went together into the castle, and Beauty was overjoyed to find, in the great hall, her father and his whole family, whom the beautiful lady, that appeared to her in her dream, had conveyed there.

"Beauty," said this lady, "come and receive the reward of your judicious choice. You have preferred virtue before either wit or beauty, and deserve to find a person in whom all these qualifications are united: you are going to be a great queen. I hope the throne will not lessen your virtue, or make you forget yourself. As to you, ladies," said the Fairy to Beauty's two sisters, "I know your hearts, and all the malice they contain: become two statues. But, under this transformation, still retain your reason. You shall stand before your sister's palace gate, and be it your punishment to behold her happiness. And it will not be in your power to return to your former state till you own your faults; but I am very much afraid that you will always remain statues. Pride, anger, gluttony, and idleness, are sometimes conquered, but the conversion of a malicious and envious mind is a kind of miracle."

Immediately the fairy gave a stroke with her wand, and in a moment all that were in the hall were transported into the prince's palace. His subjects received him with joy. He married Beauty, and lived with her for many years; and their happiness, as it was founded on virtue, was complete.

Mme de Beaumont

Notes on the Story

BEAUTY AND THE BEAST

"Beauty and the Beast" is the most well known of the animal bridegroom tale type, which also appears in this collection in "The Pig King" (page 22), "The Frog King" (page 131), and others. It is an ancient tale pattern, which may be related to the myths of indigenous cultures in which marriage to an animal was fundamental to the protection of the tribe.

Appearing very differently in the West, here the quest is often to restore a suitor, cursed into beastliness, to his human form. This particular version of the story was first published as a novel by Gabrielle-Suzanne Barbot de Villeneuve in 1740. In the wake of the French salon culture, Villeneuve's tale was a celebration of the possibilities of love—and of female autonomy—in a patriarchal society. It was adapted by the governess Jeanne-Marie Laprince de Beaumont in 1756, who simplified and rewrote it for children; this version is the one we are most familiar with today.

The Story of Hyacinth and Roseblossom

Long ago in the far west there lived a youth. He was very good, but at the same time peculiar beyond measure. He constantly grieved over nothing at all, always went about alone and silent, sat down by himself whenever the others played and were happy, and was always thinking about strange things. Woods and caves were his favorite haunts, and there he talked constantly with birds and animals, with rocks and trees—naturally not a word of sense, nothing but stuff silly enough to make one die laughing. Yet he continued to remain morose and grave in spite of the fact that the squirrel, the long-tailed monkey, the parrot, and the bullfinch took great pains to distract him and lead him into the right path. The goose would tell fairy tales, and in the midst of them the brook would tinkle a ballad; a great heavy stone would caper about ludicrously; the rose stealing up affectionately behind him would creep through his locks, and the ivy stroke his careworn forehead. But his melancholy and his gravity were obstinate.

His parents were greatly troubled; they did not know what to do. He was healthy and ate well. His parents had never done anything to hurt him, and until a few years ago no one had been more cheerful and lively. He had always taken the lead in every game, and was well liked by all the girls. He was very handsome indeed, and danced like a dream.

Among the girls there was one sweet and very pretty child. She looked as though she were made of wax, with hair like silk spun of gold, lips as red as cherries, a figure like a little doll, eyes black as the raven. Such was her charm that whoever saw her might have pined away with love.

At that time Roseblossom, for that was her name, was devoted to the handsome Hyacinth (for that was his name) and he loved her to death. The other children did not know it. A little violet had been the first to tell them; the house cats had noticed it, to be sure, for their parents' homes stood near each other.

When, therefore, Hyacinth was standing at night at his window and Roseblossom at hers, and the cats ran by on a mouse hunt, they would see both standing, and would often laugh and titter so loudly that the children would hear them and grow angry. The violet had confided it to the strawberry, she told it to her friend, the gooseberry, and she never stopped taunting when Hyacinth passed; so that very soon the whole garden and the gods heard the news, and whenever Hyacinth went out they called on every side: "Little Roseblossom is my sweetheart!"

Now Hyacinth was vexed, but he could not help laughing from the bottom of his heart when the lizard would come sliding up, seat himself on a warm stone, wag his little tail, and sing:

"Little Roseblossom, good and kind,
Suddenly was stricken blind.
Her mother Hyacinth she thought
And to embrace him forthwith sought.
But when she felt the face was strange,
Just think, no terror made her change!
But on his cheek pressed she her kiss,
And she had noted naught amiss."

Alas, how soon did all this bliss pass away! There came along a man from foreign lands; he had traveled everywhere, had a long beard, deep-set eyes, terrible eyebrows, a strange cloak with many folds and queer figures woven in it. He seated himself in front of the house that belonged to Hyacinth's parents. Now Hyacinth was very curious and sat down beside him and fetched him bread and wine. Then the man parted his white beard and told stories until late at night, and Hyacinth did not stir nor did he tire of listening. As far as one could learn afterward the man had related much about foreign lands, unknown regions, and astonishingly wondrous things, staying there three days and creeping down into deep caverns with Hyacinth.

Roseblossom cursed the old sorcerer enough, for Hyacinth was all eagerness for his tales and cared for nothing, scarcely even eating a little food. Finally the man took his departure, not, however, without leaving Hyacinth a little book that not a soul could read. The youth had even given him fruit, bread, and wine to take along and had accompanied him a long way. Then he came back melancholy and began an entirely new mode of life. Roseblossom grieved for him very pitifully, for from that time on he paid little attention to her and always kept to himself.

Now it came about that he returned home one day and seemed reborn. He fell on his parents' neck and wept.

"I must depart for foreign lands," he said. "The strange old woman in the forest told me that I must get well again. She threw the book into the fire and urged me to come to you and ask for your blessing. Perhaps I shall be back soon, perhaps nevermore. Say goodbye to Roseblossom for me. I should have liked to speak to her, I do not know what is the matter, something drives me away; whenever I want to think of old times, mightier thoughts rush in immediately; my peace is gone, my courage and love with it, I must go in quest of them. I should like to tell you whither, but I do not know myself; thither where dwells the mother of all things, the veiled virgin. For her my heart burns. Farewell!"

He tore himself away and departed. His parents lamented and shed tears. Roseblossom kept in her chamber and wept bitterly. Hyacinth now hastened as fast as he could through valleys and wildernesses, across mountains and streams, toward the mysterious country. Everywhere he asked men and animals, rocks and trees, for the sacred goddess Isis. Some laughed, some were silent, nowhere did he receive an answer. At first, he passed through wild, uninhabited regions, mist and clouds obstructed his path, it was always stormy. Later, he found unbounded deserts of glowing hot sand, and as he wandered his mood changed, time seemed to grow longer, and his inner unrest was calmed. He became more tranquil and the violent excitement within him was gradually transformed to a gentle but strong impulse, which took possession of his whole nature. It seemed as though many years lay behind him.

Now, too, the region again became richer and more varied, the air warm and blue, the path more level; green bushes attracted him with their pleasant shade but he did not understand their language, nor did they seem to speak, and yet they filled his heart with verdant colors, with quiet and freshness. Mightier and mightier grew within him that sweet longing, broader and softer the leaves, noisier and happier the birds and animals, balmier the fruits, darker the heavens, warmer the air and more fiery his love. Time passed faster and faster, as though it knew that it was approaching the goal.

One day he came upon a crystal spring and a throng of flowers that were going down to a valley between black columns reaching to the sky. With familiar words they greeted him kindly.

"My dear countrymen," he said, "pray, where am I to find the sacred abode of Isis? It must be somewhere in this vicinity, and you are probably better acquainted here than I."

"We, too, are only passing through this region," the flowers answered. "A family of spirits is traveling and we are making ready the road and preparing lodgings for them; but we came through a region lately where

"The man parted his white beard and told stories until late at night,

and Hyacinth did not stir nor did he tire of listening."

we heard her name called. Just walk upward in the direction from which we are coming and you will be sure to learn more."

The flowers and the spring smiled as they said this, offered him a drink of fresh water, and went on. Hyacinth followed their advice, asked and asked, and finally reached that long-sought dwelling concealed behind palms and other choice plants. His heart beat with infinite longing and the most delicious yearning thrilled him in this abode of the eternal seasons. Amid heavenly fragrance he fell into slumber, since only dreams might lead him to the most sacred place. To the tune of charming melodies and in changing harmonies did his dream guide him mysteriously through endless apartments filled with curious things. Everything seemed so familiar to him and yet amid a splendor that he had never seen; then even the last tinge of earthliness vanished as though dissipated in the air, and he stood before the celestial virgin. He lifted the filmy, shimmering veil and Roseblossom fell into his arms.

From afar, a strain of music accompanied the mystery of the loving reunion, the outpourings of their longing, and excluded all that was alien from this delightful spot. After that Hyacinth lived many years with Roseblossom near his happy parents and companions, and innumerable grandchildren who thanked the mysterious old woman for her advice and her fire; for at that time people had as many children as they wanted.

Novalis

Notes on the Story

The Story of Hyacinth and Roseblossom

Novalis, born Friedrich von Hardenburg (1772–1801), was a German Romantic poet and philosopher, who worked closely with other German poets and philosophers, Schiller, Schlegel, and Fichte. Novalis held the fairy tale in high esteem, and believed it to be that to which all art, and life itself, should aspire. Although he penned few fairy tales himself, his writings in and around the genre significantly influenced later authors of the literary tale, including George MacDonald and Hermann Hesse.

✣

Novalis, whose pseudonym means "one who opens up new land," believed that the fairy tale must be "miraculous, mysterious, incoherent," yet, at the same time, saw all fairy tales as "only dreams of that familiar world of home." This contradiction between the strange and the familiar, in fact, strikes at the heart of the mystical message of both "Hyacinth and Roseblossom" and much of Novalis's thought: the idea that a journey outward is also, always, a journey that leads one home.

Nineteenth-Century Folktale Collections

In the nineteenth century, fairy-tale writing branched into two forms: the collecting of traditional folk or fairy tales, and the creation of "literary" fairy tales influenced by older stories. The former, tales collected by nineteenth-century folklorists, is the focus of this section. With increased industrialization and the changes it precipitated, the nineteenth century saw a corresponding passion for the preservation of traditional arts. One way this manifested was in an appetite for old stories. As well as the Brothers Grimm in Germany, collectors wishing to preserve traditional tales appeared across Europe, including Norway, France, England, and Russia. It is thanks to these tireless individuals that many stories have come down to us today.

"'I promise you all you wish,

. . . if you will but bring me my ball back again.'"

The Frog King

Once upon a time, when wishing still helped, there lived a king whose daughters were all beautiful, but the youngest was so beautiful that the sun was astonished whenever it shone on her face. Close by the king's castle lay a great forest, and under an old lime tree was a well, and when the day was warm, the princess went out into the forest and sat down by the side of the cool fountain, and played with her golden ball, and threw it high and caught it, and this ball was her favorite plaything.

Now it so happened that on one occasion the princess's golden ball did not fall into the little hand, which she was holding up for it, but on to the ground beyond, and rolled straight into the water. The princess followed it with her eyes, but it vanished, and the well was deep, so deep that the bottom could not be seen. On this she began to cry, and cried louder and louder, and could not be comforted. And as she thus lamented someone said to her, "What ails you, Princess? You weep so that even a stone would show pity."

She looked round to the side from whence the voice came, and saw a frog stretching forth its thick, ugly head from the water.

"Ah! Old water-splasher, is it you?" said she. "I am weeping for my golden ball, which has fallen into the well."

"Be quiet, and do not weep," answered the frog. "I can help you, but what will you give me if I bring your plaything up again?"

"Whatever you want, dear frog," said she. "My clothes, my pearls and jewels, and even the golden crown which I am wearing."

The frog answered, "I do not care for your clothes, your pearls and jewels, or your golden crown, but if you will love me and let me be your companion and playfellow, and sit by you at your little table, and eat off your little golden plate, and drink out of your little cup, and sleep in your little bed–if you will promise me this I will go down below, and bring you your golden ball up again."

"Oh yes," said she, "I promise you all you wish, if you will but bring me my ball back again." She, however, thought, "How the silly frog does talk! He lives in the water with the other frogs, and croaks, and can be no companion to any human being!"

But the frog, when he had received this promise, sank down into the water, and came swimming up again with the ball in his mouth, and threw it on the grass. The princess was delighted to see her pretty plaything once more, and picked it up, and ran away with it.

"Wait, wait," said the frog. "Take me with you. I can't run as you can." But what did it avail him to shout his "croak, croak" after her, as loudly as he could? She did not listen to it, but ran home and soon forgot the poor frog, who was forced to go back into his well again.

The next day when she had seated herself at the table with the king and all the courtiers, and was eating from her little golden plate, something came creeping splish splash, splish splash, up the marble staircase, and when it had got to the top, it knocked at the door and cried, "Princess, youngest princess, open the door for me." She ran to open the door, and there sat the frog. She slammed the door in great haste, and sat down to dinner again, and was quite frightened. The king saw that her heart was beating violently, and said, "My child, what are you so afraid of? Is there a giant outside who wants to carry you away?"

"Ah, no," replied she. "It is no giant but a disgusting frog."

"What does a frog want with you?"

"Ah, dear father, yesterday as I was in the forest sitting by the well, playing, my golden ball fell into the water. And because I cried so, the frog found it for me, and because he insisted, I promised him he should be my companion, but I never thought he would be able to come out of his water! And now he is outside there, and wants to come in to me."

In the meantime it knocked a second time, and cried,

"Princess! Youngest princess!
Open the door for me!
Do you not know what you said to me
Yesterday by the cool waters of the fountain?
Princess, youngest princess!
Open the door for me!"

Then said the king, "That which you have promised, you must perform. Go and let him in." She went and opened the door, and the frog hopped in and followed her, step by step, to her chair.

There he sat and cried, "Lift me up beside you." She delayed, until at last the king commanded her to do it. When the frog was on the chair he wanted to be on the table, and once there he said,"Now, push your little golden plate nearer to me that we may eat together." She did this, but it was easy to see that she did not do it willingly. The frog enjoyed what he ate, but almost every mouthful she took choked her.

At length he said, "I have eaten and am satisfied; now I am tired, carry me into your little room and make your little silken bed ready, and we will both lie down and go to sleep."

The princess began to cry, for she was afraid of the cold, slimy frog, which was now to sleep in her clean bed.

But the king grew angry and said, "He who helped you when you were in trouble ought not afterward to be despised by you." So she took hold of the frog with two fingers, carried him upstairs, and put him in a corner. But when she was in bed he crept to her and said, "I am tired, lift me up or I will tell your father."

Then she was terribly angry, and took him up and threw him with all her might against the wall. "Now, you will be quiet, odious frog," said she. But when he fell down he was no frog but a prince with beautiful kind eyes. He, by her father's will, was now her dear husband.

Then he told her how he had been bewitched by a wicked witch, and how no one could have delivered him from the well but herself, and that tomorrow they would go together into his kingdom. Then they went to sleep, and next morning a carriage came driving up with eight white horses, which had white ostrich feathers on their heads, and behind stood the young prince's servant Faithful Henry.

Faithful Henry had been so unhappy when his master was changed into a frog, that he had caused three iron bands to be laid round his heart, lest it should burst with grief and sadness. The carriage was to conduct the young prince into his kingdom. Faithful Henry helped them both in, and placed himself behind again, and was full of joy because of this deliverance. And when they had driven a part of the way the prince heard a cracking behind him as if something had broken. So he turned round and cried, "Henry, the carriage is breaking."

"No, master, it is not the carriage. It is a band from my heart, which was put there in my great pain when you were a frog and imprisoned."

Again and once again while they were on their way something cracked, and each time the prince thought the carriage was breaking; but it was only the bands which were springing from the heart of Faithful Henry because his master was set free and was happy.

Brothers Grimm

Notes on the Story

The Frog King

Possibly the two greatest collectors of folktales, the German linguists and folklorists Jacob (1785–1863) and his brother Wilhelm (1786–1859) Grimm transformed the world of folklore, and captured the nineteenth-century imagination with their publication *Children's and Household Tales* in Kassel in 1812. Collected both from oral and written sources and created in celebration of German nationality, language, and identity, the Grimms expanded and edited their stories in multiple editions that were published up until 1857. The tales have now been translated into over 160 languages worldwide.

✣

"The Frog King" or "Iron Henry" always remained the first story in the Grimms' collection. The Grimms always refer to the "Frog King," rather than the "Frog Prince"; the latter was introduced in Edgar Taylor's English translation *German Popular Stories* (1823). A fact that surprises many is that in the Grimms' version the transformation of the frog is not caused by kissing it, but by splatting it against a wall!

HANSEL AND GRETEL

Hard by a great forest dwelt a poor woodcutter with his wife and his two children. The boy was called Hansel and the girl Gretel. He had little to eat, and once when great scarcity fell on the land, he could no longer provide daily bread. Now when he thought over this by night in his bed, and tossed about in his anxiety, he groaned and said to his wife, "What is to become of us? How are we to feed our poor children, when we no longer have anything even for ourselves?"

"I'll tell you what, husband," answered the woman. "Early to-morrow morning we will take the children out into the forest to where it is the thickest, there we will light a fire for them, and give each of them one piece of bread more, and then we will go to our work and leave them alone. They will not find the way home again, and we shall be rid of them."

"No, wife," said the man, "I will not do that; how can I bear to leave my children alone in the forest? The wild animals would soon come and tear them to pieces."

"O, you fool!" said she. "Then we must all four die of hunger, you may as well plane the planks for our coffins," and she left him no peace until he consented.

"But I feel very sorry for the poor children, all the same," said her husband sadly.

The two children had also not been able to sleep for hunger, and had heard what their stepmother had said to their father. Gretel wept bitter tears, and said to Hansel, "Now all is over with us."

"Be quiet, Gretel," said Hansel. "Don't worry, I'll soon find a way to help us."

And when the old folks had fallen asleep, he got up, put on his little coat, opened the door below, and crept outside. The moon shone brightly, and the white pebbles which lay in front of the house glittered like real silver pennies. Hansel stooped and put as many of them in the little pocket of his coat as he could possibly get in. Then he went back and said to Gretel, "Take comfort, dear little sister, and sleep in peace, God will not forsake us," and he lay down again in his bed.

When day dawned, but before the sun had risen, the woman came and awoke the two children, saying, "Get up, you sluggards! We are going into the forest to fetch wood." She gave each a little piece of bread, and said, "There is something for your dinner, but do not eat it up before then, for you will get nothing else."

Gretel took the bread under her apron, as Hansel had the stones in his pocket. Then they all set out together on the way to the forest. When they had walked a short time, Hansel stood still and peeped back at the house, and did so again and again.

His father said, "Hansel, what are you looking at there and lagging behind for? Mind what you are about and stop dawdling, and don't forget how to use your legs."

"Ah, father," said Hansel, "I am looking at my little white cat, which is sitting up on the roof, and wants to say goodbye to me."

The wife said, "Fool, that is not your little cat, that is the morning sun which is shining on the chimneys." Hansel, however, had not been looking back at the cat, but had been constantly throwing one of the white pebbles out of his pocket on the road.

When they had reached the middle of the forest, the father said, "Now, children, pile up some wood, and I will light a fire so that you will not be cold."

Hansel and Gretel gathered brushwood together, as high as a little hill. The brushwood was lit, and when the flames were burning very high, the woman said, "Now, children, lay yourselves down by the fire and rest. We will go into the forest and cut some wood. When we have done, we will come back and fetch you away."

Hansel and Gretel sat by the fire, and when noon came, each ate a little piece of bread, and as they heard the strokes of the wood-ax they believed that their father was near. It was not, however, the ax; it was a branch that he had fastened to a withered tree, which the wind was blowing backward and forward. And as they had been sitting such a long time, their eyes shut with fatigue, and they fell fast asleep.

When at last they awoke, it was already dark. Gretel began to cry and said, "How are we to get out of the forest now?"

But Hansel comforted her and said, "Just wait a little, until the moon has risen, and then we will soon find the way." And when the full moon had risen, Hansel took his little sister by the hand, and followed the pebbles, which shone like newly coined silver pieces, and showed them the way.

They walked the whole night long, and by break of day came once more to their father's house. They knocked at the door, and when the woman opened it and saw that it was Hansel and Gretel, she said, "You naughty children, why have you slept so long in the forest? We thought you were never coming back at all!" The father, however, rejoiced, for it had cut him to the heart to leave them behind alone.

Not long afterward, there was once more great scarcity in all parts, and the children heard their mother saying at night to their father, "Everything is eaten again, we have one half loaf left, and after that there is an end. The children must go, we will take them farther into the wood, so that they will not find their way out again; there is no other means of saving ourselves!"

"'Just wait a little, until the moon has risen,

and then we will soon find the way.'"

The man's heart was heavy, and he thought, "It would be better for you to share the last mouthful with your children." The woman, however, would listen to nothing that he had to say, but scolded and reproached him. Once you've said A, you have to say B, and so, as he had given in the first time, he had to do so a second time also.

The children were, however, still awake and had heard the conversation. When the old folks were asleep, Hansel again got up, and wanted to go out and pick up pebbles as he had done before, but the woman had locked the door, and Hansel could not get out. Nevertheless he comforted his little sister, and said, "Do not cry, Gretel, go to sleep quietly, the good God will help us."

Early in the morning came the woman, and took the children out of their beds. Their bit of bread was given to them, but it was still smaller than the time before. On the way into the forest Hansel crumbled his in his pocket, and often stood still and threw a morsel on the ground.

"Hansel, why are you stopping and looking round?" asked the father. "Go on."

"I am looking back at my little pigeon which is sitting on the roof, and wants to say goodbye to me," answered Hansel.

"Fool!" said the woman. "That is not your little pigeon, that is the morning sun that is shining on the chimney." Hansel, however, little by little, threw all the crumbs on the path.

The woman led the children still deeper into the forest, where they had never in their lives been before. Then a great fire was again made, and the mother said, "Just sit there, you children, and when you are tired you may sleep a little; we are going into the forest to cut wood, and in the evening when we are done, we will come and fetch you away."

When it was noon, Gretel shared her piece of bread with Hansel, who had scattered his by the way. Then they fell asleep and evening came and went, but no one came to the poor children. They did not awake until it was dark night, and Hansel comforted his little sister and said, "Just wait, Gretel, until the moon rises, and then we shall see the crumbs of bread which I have strewn about, they will show us our way home again."

When the moon came they set out, but they found no crumbs, for the many thousands of birds, which fly about in the woods and fields, had picked them all up. Hansel said to Gretel, "We shall soon find the way," but they did not find it. They walked the whole night and all the next day too from morning till evening, but they did not get out of the forest, and were very hungry, for they had nothing to eat but two or three berries, which grew on the ground. And as they were so weary that their legs would carry them no longer, they lay down beneath a tree and fell asleep.

On the third morning after they had left their father's house, they began to walk again, but they always got deeper into the forest, and if help did not come soon, they must die of hunger and weariness. When it was midday, they saw a beautiful snow-white bird sitting on a bough, which sang so delightfully that they stood still and listened to it. And when it had finished its song, it spread its wings and flew away before them, and they followed it until they reached a little house, on the roof of which it alighted. And when they came quite up to the little house they saw that it was built of bread and covered with cakes, but that the windows were of clear sugar.

"We'll set to work on that," said Hansel, "and have a good meal. I'll eat a bit of the roof, and you, Gretel, can eat some of the window, it will taste sweet."

Hansel reached up above, and broke off a little of the roof to try how it tasted, and Gretel leant against the window and nibbled at the panes. Then a soft voice cried from the room,

"Nibble, nibble, little mouse,
Who's nibbling my house?"

The children answered,

"The wind, the wind,
The heaven-born wind,"

and went on eating without disturbing themselves. Hansel, who thought the roof tasted very nice, tore down a great piece of it, and Gretel pushed out the whole of one round windowpane, sat down, and enjoyed herself with it. Suddenly the door opened, and a very, very old woman, who supported herself on crutches, came creeping out. Hansel and Gretel were so terribly frightened that they let fall what they had in their hands.

The old woman, however, nodded her head, and said, "Oh, you dear children, who has brought you here? Do come in, and stay with me. No harm shall happen to you." She took them both by the hand, and led them into her little house. Then good food was set before them, milk and pancakes, with sugar, apples, and nuts. Afterward two pretty little beds were covered with clean white linen, and Hansel and Gretel lay down in them, and thought they were in heaven.

The old woman had only pretended to be so kind; she was in reality a wicked witch, who lay in wait for children, and had only built the little house of bread in order to entice them there. When a child fell into her power, she killed it, cooked, and ate it, and that was a feast day with her. Witches have red eyes, and cannot see far, but they have a keen scent like the beasts, and are aware when human beings draw near. When Hansel and Gretel came into her neighborhood, she laughed maliciously, and said mockingly, "I have them, they shall not escape me again!"

Early in the morning before the children were awake, she was already up, and when she saw both of them sleeping and looking so pretty, with their plump red cheeks, she muttered to herself, "That will be a dainty mouthful!" Then she seized Hansel with her shriveled hand, carried him into a little stable, and shut him in with a grated door. He might scream as much as he liked, it was of no use.

Then she went to Gretel, shook her till she awoke, and cried, "Get up, lazy thing, fetch some water, and cook something good for your brother, he is in the stable outside, and is to be made fat. When he is fat, I will eat him." Gretel began to weep bitterly, but it was all in vain, she was forced to do what the wicked witch ordered her.

And now the best food was cooked for poor Hansel, but Gretel got nothing but crab shells. Every morning the woman crept to the little stable, and cried, "Hansel, stretch out your finger so that I may feel if you will soon be fat." Hansel, however, stretched out a little bone to her, and the old woman, who had dim eyes, could not see it, and thought it was Hansel's finger, and was astonished that there was no way of fattening him.

When four weeks had gone by, and Hansel still continued thin, she was seized with impatience and would not wait any longer. "Hey, Gretel," she cried to the girl, "get a move on, and bring some water. Let Hansel be fat or lean, tomorrow I will kill him, and cook him."

Ah, how the poor little sister wailed when she had to fetch the water, and how her tears flowed down over her cheeks! "Dear God, do help us," she cried. "If the wild beasts in the forest had but devoured us, we should at any rate have died together."

"Just keep your noise to yourself," said the old woman. "All that won't help you at all."

Early in the morning, Gretel had to go out and hang up the cauldron with the water, and light the fire. "We will bake first," said the old woman, "I have already heated the oven, and kneaded the dough." She pushed poor Gretel out to the oven, from which flames of fire were already leaping. "Creep in," said the witch, "and see if it is properly heated, so that we can shut the bread in." And when once Gretel was inside, she intended to shut the oven and let her bake in it, and then she would eat her, too.

But Gretel saw what she had in her mind, and said, "I do not know how I am to do it; how do you get in?"

"Silly goose," said the old woman. "The door is big enough; just look, I can get in myself!" and she crept up and thrust her head into the oven. Then Gretel gave her a push that drove her far into it, and shut the iron door, and fastened the bolt. Oh! Then she began to howl quite horribly, but Gretel ran away, and the godless witch was miserably burnt to death.

Gretel, however, ran like lightning to Hansel, opened his little stable, and cried, "Hansel, we are saved! The old witch is dead!"

Then Hansel sprang out like a bird from its cage when the door is opened for it. How they rejoiced and embraced each other, and danced about and kissed each other! And as they had no longer any need to fear her, they went into the witch's house, and in every corner there stood chests full of pearls and jewels. "These are far better than pebbles!" said Hansel, and thrust into his pockets whatever could be got in, and Gretel said, "I, too, will take something home with me," and filled her pinafore full. "But now let's get away," said Hansel, "so that we can escape from the witch's forest."

When they had walked for two hours, they came to a great piece of water. "We cannot get over," said Hansel, "I see no foot-plank, and no bridge."

"And no boat crosses either," answered Gretel, "but a white duck is swimming there; if I ask her, she will help us over." Then she cried,

"Little duck, little duck, yoo-hoo!
Hansel and Gretel are waiting for you.
There's not a plank, or bridge in sight,
Take us across on your back so white."

The duck came to them, and Hansel seated himself on its back, and told his sister to sit by him.

"No," replied Gretel, "that will be too heavy for the little duck; she shall take us across, one after the other." The good little duck did so, and when they were once safely across and had walked for a short time, the forest seemed to be more and more familiar to them, and at length they saw from afar their father's house.

Then they began to run, rushed into the parlor, and threw themselves into their father's arms. The man had not known one happy hour since he had left the children in the forest; the woman, however, was dead. Gretel emptied her pinafore until pearls and precious stones ran about the room, and Hansel threw one handful after another out of his pocket to add to them. Then all anxiety was at an end, and they lived together in perfect happiness.

My tale is done, there runs a mouse, whosoever catches it, may make himself a big fur cap out of it.

Brothers Grimm

Notes on the Story

Hansel and Gretel

A story told to the Grimms by Dortchen Wild, the woman who later became Wilhelm Grimm's wife, "Hansel and Gretel" was part of the Grimms' earliest collection, found in the prepublication manuscripts of 1810. In this version, the birth parents decide together to abandon their children. When publishing, the Grimms softened the ferocity of this to an evil stepmother persuading a loving father to do the deed.

Like many popular fairy tales, "Hansel and Gretel" has a complex history of interpretation. From a psychological perspective, the wicked stepmother and devouring witch have been seen as symbolic projections, a child's method of dealing with a mother who is not all providing. Historical critics, however, have pointed out that during times of famine in Europe, child abandonment was a reality. Thus, as well as being symbolic, this is a fantasy which creates a happily-ever-after solution to what must have been the appalling decisions made by families struggling to survive in great poverty.

Briar Rose

A long time ago there were a king and queen who said every day, "Ah, if only we had a child!" But they never had one. But it happened that once when the queen was bathing, a frog crept out of the water on to the land, and said to her, "Your wish shall be fulfilled; before a year has gone by, you shall have a daughter."

What the frog had said came true, and the queen had a little girl who was so pretty that the king could not contain himself for joy, and ordered a great feast. He invited not only his kindred, friends, and acquaintances, but also the Wise Women, in order that they might be kind and well-disposed toward the child. There were thirteen of them in his kingdom, but, as he had only twelve golden plates for them to eat out of, one of them had to be left at home.

The feast was held with all manner of splendor and when it came to an end the Wise Women bestowed their magic gifts upon the baby: one gave virtue, another beauty, a third riches, and so on, with everything in the world that one can wish for.

When eleven of them had made their promises, suddenly the thirteenth came in. She wished to avenge herself for not having been invited, and without greeting, or even looking at any one, she cried with a loud voice, "The Princess shall in her fifteenth year prick herself with a spindle, and fall down dead." And, without saying a word more, she turned round and left the room.

They were all shocked; but the twelfth, whose good wish still remained unspoken, came forward, and as she could not undo the evil

"'Good day, old dame . . . what are you doing there?'

'I am spinning,' said the old woman . . ."

sentence, but only soften it, she said, "It shall not be death, but a deep sleep of a hundred years, into which the princess shall fall."

The king, who wanted to protect his dear child from misfortune, gave orders that every spindle in the whole kingdom should be burnt. Meanwhile the gifts of the Wise Women were plenteously fulfilled on the young girl, for she was so beautiful, modest, good-natured, and wise, that everyone who saw her was bound to love her.

It happened that on the very day when she was fifteen years old, the king and queen were not at home, and the maiden was left in the palace quite alone. So she went round into all sorts of places, looked into rooms and bedchambers just as she liked, and at last came to an old tower. She climbed up the narrow spiral staircase, and reached a little door. A rusty key was in the lock, and when she turned it the door sprang open, and there in a little room sat an old woman with a spindle, busily spinning her flax.

"Good day, old dame," said the girl, "what are you doing there?"

"I am spinning," said the old woman, and nodded her head.

"What sort of thing is that, that rattles round so merrily?" said the princess, and she took the spindle and wanted to spin too. But scarcely had she touched the spindle when the magic decree was fulfilled, and she pricked her finger with it.

And, in the very moment when she felt the prick, she fell down upon the bed that stood there, and lay in a deep sleep. And this sleep extended over the whole palace.

The king and queen who had just come home, and had entered the great hall, began to go to sleep, and the whole of the court with them. The horses, too, went to sleep in the stable, the dogs in the yard, the pigeons upon the roof, the flies on the wall. Even the fire that was flaming on the hearth became quiet and slept, the roast meat left off frizzling, and the cook, who was just going to pull the hair of the scullery boy, because he had forgotten something, let him go, and went to sleep. And the wind fell, and on the trees before the castle not a leaf moved again.

But round about the castle there began to grow a hedge of thorns, which every year became higher, and at last grew close up round the castle and all over it, so that there was nothing of it to be seen, not even the flag upon the roof. But the story of the beautiful sleeping "Briar Rose," for so the princess was named, went about the country, so that from time to time princes came and tried to get through the thorny hedge into the castle.

But they found it impossible, for the thorns held fast together, as if they had hands, and the youths were caught in them, could not get loose again, and died a miserable death.

After long, long years a prince came again to that country, and heard an old man talking about the thorn-hedge, and that a castle was said to stand behind it in which a wonderfully beautiful princess, named Briar Rose, had been asleep for a hundred years; and that the king and queen and the whole court were asleep likewise. He had heard, too, from his grandfather, that many princes had already come, and had tried to get through the thorny hedge, but they had remained sticking fast in it, and had died a pitiful death.

Then the youth said, "I am not afraid, I will go and see the lovely Briar Rose." Try as the good old man might to dissuade him, he did not listen to his words.

By this time the hundred years had just passed, and the day had come when Briar Rose was to awake again. When the prince came near to the thorn-hedge, it was nothing but large and beautiful flowers, which parted from each other of their own accord, and let him pass unhurt, then they closed again behind him like a hedge. In the castle yard he saw the horses and the spotted hounds lying asleep; on the roof sat the pigeons with their heads under their wings. And when he entered the house, the flies were asleep upon the wall, the cook in the kitchen was still holding out his hand to seize the boy, and the maid was sitting by the black hen that she was going to pluck.

He went on farther, and in the great hall he saw the whole of the court lying asleep, and up by the throne lay the king and queen.

Then he went on still farther, and all was so quiet that a breath could be heard, and at last he came to the tower, and opened the door into the little room where Briar Rose was sleeping. There she lay, so beautiful that he could not turn his eyes away; and he stooped down and gave her a kiss. But as soon as he kissed her, Briar Rose opened her eyes and awoke, and looked at him very sweetly.

Then they went down together, and the king awoke, and the queen, and the whole court, and looked at each other in great astonishment. And the horses in the courtyard stood up and shook themselves. The hounds jumped up and wagged their tails. The pigeons upon the roof pulled out their heads from under their wings, looked round, and flew into the open country. The flies on the wall crept again. The fire in the kitchen burned up and flickered and cooked the meat; the joint began to turn and frizzle again, and the cook gave the boy such a box on the ear that he shouted, and the maid plucked the fowl ready for the spit.

And then the marriage of the prince with Briar Rose was celebrated with all splendor, and they lived happily to the end of their days.

Brothers Grimm

Notes on the Story

Briar Rose

"Briar Rose" presents a striking contrast to both Perrault's "Sleeping Beauty" and Basile's "Sun, Moon, and Talia" (page 38), both of which include a detailed second half in which the princess becomes pregnant and an ogre, either mother or wife of the prince, threatens to devour her children (see Notes on the Story, page 44). This simpler tale for children, concluding with a magical kiss and marriage, is the version that is better known today.

The Grimms, who probably knew the tale from Perrault, may have kept it in their collection, while excising other French tales, because of the similar tale of Brynhild in the Germanic *Völsunga Saga*. Brynhild was imprisoned sleeping in a castle surrounded by a ring of flames. Given that much modern discussion has focused on the passivity of the princess, Brynhild the warrior-maiden and Valkyrie, who battled enemies and lovers alike, is a dramatic predecessor to the gentle Briar Rose.

Rapunzel

There were once a man and a woman who had long vainly wished for a child. At length the woman hoped that God was about to grant her desire. These people had a little window at the back of their house from which a splendid garden could be seen, which was full of the most beautiful flowers and herbs. It was, however, surrounded by a high wall, and no one dared to go into it because it belonged to an enchantress, who had great power and was universally feared.

One day the woman was standing by this window and looking down into the garden, when she saw a bed, which was planted with the most beautiful rampion (rapunzel), and it looked so fresh and green that she longed for it, and had the greatest desire to eat some. This desire increased every day, and as she knew that she could not get any of it, she quite pined away, and looked pale and miserable.

Then her husband was alarmed, and asked, "What ails you, wife?"

"Ah," she replied, "if I can't eat some of the rampion, which is in the garden behind our house, I shall die."

The man, who loved her, thought, "Sooner than let your wife die, bring her some of the rampion yourself, let it cost you what it will." In the twilight of the evening, he clambered down over the wall into the garden of the enchantress, hastily clutched a handful of rampion, and took it to his wife. She at once made herself a salad of it, and ate it with much relish.

She, however, liked it so much—so very much—that the next day she longed for it three times as much as before. If he was to have any rest, her husband must once more descend into the garden. In the gloom of evening, therefore, he let himself down again; but when he had clambered down the wall he was terribly afraid, for he saw the enchantress standing before him.

"How can you dare," said she with angry look, "to descend into my garden and steal my rampion like a thief? You shall suffer for it!"

"Ah," answered he, "let mercy take the place of justice, I only made up my mind to do it out of necessity. My wife saw your rampion from the window, and felt such a longing for it that she would have died if she had not got some to eat."

Then the enchantress allowed her anger to be softened, and said to him, "If the case be as you say, I will allow you to take away with you as much rampion as you will, only I make one condition, you must give me the child which your wife will bring into the world; it shall be well treated, and I will care for it like a mother."

The man in his terror consented to everything, and when the woman was brought to bed, the enchantress appeared at once, gave the child the name of Rapunzel, and took it away with her.

Rapunzel grew into the most beautiful child beneath the sun. When she was twelve years old, the enchantress shut her into a tower, which lay in a forest, and had neither stairs nor door, but quite at the top was a little window. When the enchantress wanted to go in, she placed herself beneath it and cried,

"Rapunzel, Rapunzel,
Let down your hair to me."

Rapunzel had magnificent long hair, fine as spun gold, and when she heard the voice of the enchantress she unfastened her braided tresses, wound them round one of the hooks of the window above, and then the hair fell twenty yards down, and the enchantress climbed up by it.

After a year or two, it came to pass that the prince rode through the forest and went by the tower. Then he heard a song, which was so charming that he stood still and listened. This was Rapunzel, who in her solitude passed her time in letting her sweet voice resound. The prince wanted to climb up to her, and looked for the door of the tower, but none was to be found. He rode home, but the singing had so deeply touched his heart, that every day he went out into the forest and listened to it. Once when he was thus standing behind a tree, he saw that an enchantress came there, and he heard how she cried,

"Rapunzel, Rapunzel,
Let down your hair."

Then Rapunzel let down the braids of her hair, and the enchantress climbed up to her. "If that is the ladder by which one mounts, I will for once try my fortune," said he, and the next day, when it began to grow dark, he went to the tower and cried,

"Rapunzel, Rapunzel,
Let down your hair."

Immediately the hair fell down and the prince climbed up.

At first Rapunzel was terribly frightened when a man such as her eyes had never yet beheld, came to her; but the prince began to talk to her quite like a friend, and told her that his heart had been so stirred that it had let him have no rest, and he had been forced to see her.

Then Rapunzel lost her fear, and when he asked her if she would take him for her husband, and she saw that he was young and handsome, she thought, "He will love me more than old Dame Gothel does," and she said yes, and laid her hand in his. She said, "I will willingly go away with you, but I do not know how to get down. Bring with you a skein of silk every time that you comest, and I will weave a ladder with it, and when that is ready I will descend, and you will take me on your horse."

They agreed that until that time he should come to her every evening, for the old woman came by day. The enchantress remarked nothing of this, until once Rapunzel said to her, "Tell me, Dame Gothel, how it happens that you are so much heavier for me to draw up than the young prince—he is with me in a moment."

"Ah! You wicked child," cried the enchantress "What do I hear you say! I thought I had separated you from all the world, and yet you have deceived me." In her anger she clutched Rapunzel's beautiful tresses, wrapped them twice round her left hand, seized a pair of scissors with the right, and snip, snap, they were cut off, and the lovely braids lay on the ground. And she was so pitiless that she took poor Rapunzel into a desert where she had to live in great grief and misery.

On the same day, however, that she cast out Rapunzel, the enchantress in the evening fastened the braids of hair which she had cut off, to the hook of the window, and when the prince came and cried,

"In her anger she clutched Rapunzel's beautiful tresses . . .

and snip, snap, they were cut off . . ."

"Rapunzel, Rapunzel,
Let down your hair,"

she let the hair down. The prince ascended, but he did not find his dearest Rapunzel above, but the enchantress, who gazed at him with wicked and venomous looks.

"Aha!" she cried mockingly. "You wouldst fetch your dearest, but the beautiful bird sits no longer singing in the nest; the cat has got it, and will scratch out your eyes as well. Rapunzel is lost to you–you will never see her more."

The prince was beside himself with pain, and in his despair he leapt down from the tower. He escaped with his life, but the thorns into which he fell, pierced his eyes. Then he wandered quite blind about the forest, ate nothing but roots and berries, and did nothing but lament and weep over the loss of his dearest wife.

Thus he roamed about in misery for some years, and at length came to the desert where Rapunzel, with the twins to which she had given birth, a boy and a girl, lived in wretchedness. He heard a voice, and it seemed so familiar to him that he went toward it, and when he approached, Rapunzel knew him and fell on his neck and wept. Two of her tears wetted his eyes and they grew clear again, and he could see with them as before. He led her to his kingdom where he was joyfully received, and they lived for a long time afterward, happy and contented.

Brothers Grimm

Notes on the Story

Rapunzel

The much-celebrated story "Rapunzel" reflects a folk belief that pregnant women must eat the food they crave or risk death; a superstition perhaps not far from the truth, in places where fresh vegetables and necessary vitamins were hard to come by. The earliest version known is Basile's, published here as "Parsley" (page 32). In contrast to the character Parsley, the Grimms' Rapunzel does not plan her escape for herself, but rather is rescued by fate in a chance meeting with her lost prince.

"Rapunzel" caused controversy when published in 1812, for in the first version, Rapunzel asks not why the witch herself is so heavy, but why her own skirts are so tight. The implicit pregnancy was deemed so unsuitable for young readers that one critic condemned the collection as "utter junk." The Grimms took this to heart, and changed the text so that Rapunzel's children appear more subtly later in the tale.

"'Preserve the egg carefully for me . . .

a great misfortune would arise from the loss of it.'"

FITCHER'S BIRD

There was once a wizard who took the form of a poor man, and went to houses and begged, and caught pretty girls. No one knew where he carried them, for they were never seen again. One day he appeared before the door of a man who had three pretty daughters; he looked like a poor beggar, and carried a basket, as if he meant to collect gifts in it. He begged for a little food, and when the eldest daughter came out and gave him a piece of bread, he touched her, and she was forced to jump into his basket.

Thereupon he hurried away with long strides, and carried her away into a dark forest to his house, which stood in the midst of it. Everything in the house was magnificent. He gave her whatsoever she could possibly desire, and said, "My darling, you will certainly be happy with me, for you have everything your heart can wish for." This lasted a few days, and then he said, "I must journey forth, and leave you alone for a short time. There are the keys of the house; you may go everywhere and look at everything except into one room, which this little key here opens, and there I forbid you to go on pain of death." He likewise gave her an egg and said, "Preserve the egg carefully for me, and carry it continually about with you, for a great misfortune would arise from the loss of it."

She took the keys and the egg, and promised to obey him in everything. When he was gone, she went all round the house and examined everything. The rooms shone with silver and gold, and she had never seen such splendor. At last she came to the forbidden door;

she wished to pass it by, but curiosity let her have no rest. She examined the key; she put it in the keyhole and turned it a little, and the door sprang open. A great bloody basin stood in the middle of the room, and therein lay human beings, dead and hewn to pieces, and hard by was a block of wood, and a gleaming ax lay upon it. She was so terribly alarmed that the egg, which she held in her hand, fell into the basin. She got it out and washed the blood off, but it appeared again in a moment. She washed and scrubbed, but she could not get it out.

It was not long before the man came back from his journey, and the first things that he asked for were the key and the egg. She gave them to him, but she trembled as she did so, and he saw at once by the red spots that she had been in the bloody chamber. "Since you have gone into the room against my will," said he, "you shall go back into it against your own. Your life is ended." He threw her down, dragged her thither by her hair, cut her head off on the block, and hewed her in pieces so that her blood ran on the ground. Then he threw her into the basin with the rest.

"Now I will fetch myself the second," said the wizard, and again he went to the house in the shape of a poor man, and begged. Then the second daughter brought him a piece of bread; he caught her like the first, by simply touching her, and carried her away. She did not fare better than her sister. She allowed herself to be led away by her curiosity, opened the door of the bloody chamber, looked in, and had to atone for it with her life on the wizard's return.

Then he went and brought the third sister, but she was clever and crafty. When he had given her the keys and the egg, and had left her, she put the egg away with great care, and examined the house, and at last went into the forbidden room.

Alas, what did she behold! Both her sisters lay there in the basin, cruelly murdered, and cut in pieces. But she began to gather their limbs together and put them in order, head, body, arms, and legs. And then the limbs began to move and unite themselves together, and both the maidens opened their eyes and were once more alive. Then they rejoiced and kissed each other.

On his arrival, the man at once demanded the keys and the egg, and as he could perceive no trace of any blood on it, he said, "You have stood the test, you shall be my bride." He now had no longer any power over her, and was forced to do whatsoever she desired.

"Oh, very well," said she, "you shall first take a basketful of gold to my father and mother, and carry it yourself on your back. In the meantime I will prepare for the wedding."

Then she ran to her sisters, whom she had hidden in a little chamber, and said, "The moment has come when I can save you. The wretch shall himself carry you home again, but as soon as you are at home send help to me." She put both of them in a basket and covered them quite over with gold, so that nothing of them was to be seen, then she called in the wizard and said to him, "Now carry the basket away, but I shall look through my little window and watch to see if you stop on the way to stand or to rest."

The wizard raised the basket on his back and went away with it, but it weighed him down so heavily that the perspiration streamed from his face. Then he sat down and wanted to rest awhile, but immediately one of the girls in the basket cried, "I am looking through my little window, and I see that you are resting. Will you go on at once?" He thought it was his bride who was calling that to him, and got up on his legs again.

Once more he was going to sit down, but instantly she cried, "I am looking through my little window, and I see that you are resting. Will you go on directly?" And whenever he stood still, she cried this, and then he was forced to go onward, until at last, groaning, he took the basket with the gold and the two maidens into their parents' house.

At home, however, the bride prepared the marriage feast, and sent invitations to the friends of the wizard. Then she took a skull with grinning teeth, put some ornaments on it and a wreath of flowers, carried it upstairs to the garret window, and let it look out from thence. When all was ready, she got into a barrel of honey, and then cut the featherbed open and rolled herself in it, until she looked like a wondrous bird, and no one could recognize her. Then she went out of the house, and on her way she met some of the wedding guests, who asked,

"O, Fitcher's bird, how come you here?"
"I come from Fitcher's house quite near."
"And what may the young bride be doing?"
"From cellar to garret she's swept all clean,
And now from the window she's peeping, I ween."

At last she met the bridegroom, who was coming slowly back. He, like the others, asked,

"O, Fitcher's bird, how come you here?"
"I come from Fitcher's house quite near."
"And what may the young bride be doing?
"From cellar to garret she's swept all clean,
And now from the window she's peeping, I ween."

The bridegroom looked up, saw the decked-out skull, thought it was his bride, and nodded to her, greeting her kindly. But when he and his guests had all gone into the house, the brothers and kinsmen of the bride, who had been sent to rescue her, arrived. They locked all the doors of the house, that no one might escape, set fire to it, and the wizard and all his crew had to burn.

Brothers Grimm

Notes on the Story

Fitcher's Bird

A story of a serial-killer husband, "Fitcher's Bird" resembles the more commonly known "Bluebeard," with remarkable differences. The Grimms included two stories of this type: "The Robber Bridegroom" and "Fitcher's Bird." Neither has entered the cultural consciousness so much as Perrault's "Bluebeard," which is unfortunate, as this is a fascinating and invigorating version of the story. Here, curiosity is paired with wit and courage, and to open the chamber is not sin but necessity. Not only is the final sister able to save herself "with nothing but wits and guts and a talent for improvised costumes," as the Canadian writer Margaret Atwood has put it, she is also quite capable of saving her sisters as well.

✣

The history of the word "fitcher" is unclear; the Grimms traced it to *fitgular*, an Icelandic waterbird, but later interpreters suggest it derives from the German for feather (*feder*) or wings (*fittich*).

Snow White

Once upon a time in the middle of winter, when the flakes of snow were falling like feathers from the sky, a queen sat at a window sewing, and the frame of the window was made of black ebony. And while she was sewing and looking out of the window at the snow, she pricked her finger with the needle, and three drops of blood fell upon the snow. And the red looked pretty upon the white snow, and she thought to herself, "Would that I had a child as white as snow, as red as blood, and as black as the wood of the window-frame."

Soon after that she had a daughter, who was as white as snow, and as red as blood, and her hair was as black as ebony; and she was therefore called Snow White. And when the child was born, the queen died.

After a year had passed the king took to himself another wife. She was a beautiful woman, but proud and haughty, and she could not bear that anyone else should surpass her in beauty. She had a wonderful looking glass, and when she stood in front of it and looked at herself in it, and said–

"Looking glass, Looking glass, on the wall,
Who in this land is the fairest of all?"

The looking glass answered–

"You, O Queen, are the fairest of all!"

Then she was satisfied, for she knew that the looking glass spoke the truth.

But Snow White was growing up, and grew more and more beautiful; and when she was seven years old she was as beautiful as the day, and more beautiful than the queen herself. And once when the queen asked her looking glass–

"Looking glass, Looking glass, on the wall,
Who in this land is the fairest of all?"

It answered–

"You are fairer than all who are here, Lady Queen."
But more beautiful still is Snow White, as I ween."

Then the queen was shocked, and turned yellow and green with envy. From that hour, whenever she looked at Snow White, her heart heaved in her breast, she hated the girl so much.

And envy and pride grew higher and higher in her heart like a weed, so that she had no peace day or night. She called a huntsman, and said, "Take the child away into the forest; I will no longer have her in my sight. Kill her, and bring me back her heart as a token."

The huntsman obeyed, and took her away; but when he had drawn his knife, and was about to pierce Snow White's innocent heart, she began to weep, and said, "Ah dear huntsman, leave me my life! I will run away into the wild forest, and never come home again."

And as she was so beautiful the huntsman had pity on her and said, "Run away, then, you poor child."

"The wild beasts will soon have devoured you," thought he, and yet it seemed as if a stone had been rolled from his heart since it was no longer needful for him to kill her. And as a young boar just then came running by he stabbed it, and cut out its heart and took it to the queen as proof that the child was dead. The cook had to salt this, and the wicked queen ate it, and thought she had eaten the heart of Snow White.

But now the poor child was all alone in the great forest, and so terrified that she looked at every leaf of every tree, and did not know what to do. Then she began to run, and ran over sharp stones and through thorns, and the wild beasts ran past her, but did her no harm.

She ran as long as her feet would go until it was almost evening; then she saw a little cottage and went into it to rest herself. Everything in the cottage was small, but neater and cleaner than can be told. There was a table on which was a white cover, and seven little plates, and on each plate a little spoon; moreover, there were seven little knives and forks, and seven little mugs. Against the wall stood seven little beds side by side, and covered with snow-white counterpanes.

Snow White was so hungry and thirsty that she ate some vegetables and bread from each plate and drank a drop of wine out of each mug,

for she did not wish to take all from one only. Then, as she was so tired, she laid herself down on one of the little beds, but none of them suited her; one was too long, another too short. At last she found that the seventh one was right, and so she said a prayer and went to sleep.

When it was quite dark the owners of the cottage came back; they were seven dwarfs who dug and delved in the mountains for ore. They lit their seven candles, and as it was now light within the cottage they saw that someone had been there, for everything was not in the same order in which they had left it.

The first said, "Who has been sitting on my chair?"

The second, "Who has been eating off my plate?"

The third, "Who has been taking some of my bread?"

The fourth, "Who has been eating my vegetables?"

The fifth, "Who has been using my fork?"

The sixth, "Who has been cutting with my knife?"

The seventh, "Who has been drinking out of my mug?"

Then the first looked round and saw that there was a little hole on his bed, and he said, "Who has been getting into my bed?" The others came up and each called out, "Somebody has been lying in my bed too." But the seventh, when he looked at his bed, saw Snow White, who was lying asleep therein. And he called the others, who came running up, and they cried out with astonishment, and brought their seven little candles and let the light fall on Snow White.

"Oh, heavens! Oh, heavens!" cried they, "what a lovely child!" And they were so glad that they did not wake her up, but let her sleep on in the bed. And the seventh dwarf slept with his companions, one hour with each, and so got through the night.

When it was morning Snow White awoke, and was frightened when she saw the seven dwarfs. But they were friendly and asked her what her name was.

"My name is Snow White," she answered.

"How have you come to our house?" said the dwarfs. Then she told them that her stepmother had wished to have her killed, but that the huntsman had spared her life, and that she had run for the whole day, until at last she had found their dwelling.

The dwarfs said, "If you will take care of our house, cook, make the beds, wash, sew, and knit, and if you will keep everything neat and clean, you can stay with us and you shall want for nothing."

"Yes," said Snow White, "with all my heart," and she stayed with them. She kept the house in order for them; in the mornings they went to the mountains and looked for copper and gold, in the evenings they came back, and then their supper had to be ready. The girl was alone the whole day, so the good dwarfs warned her and said, "Beware of your stepmother, she will soon know that you are here; be sure to let no one come in."

But the queen, believing that she had eaten Snow White's heart, could not but think that she was again the first and most beautiful of all; and she went to her looking glass and said–

"Looking glass, Looking glass, on the wall,
Who in this land is the fairest of all?"

And the glass answered–

"Oh, Queen, you are fairest of all I see,
But over the hills, where the seven dwarfs dwell,
Snow White is still alive and well,
And none is so fair as she."

Then she was astounded, for she knew that the looking glass never spoke falsely, and she knew that the huntsman had betrayed her, and that Snow White was still alive.

"'Oh, heavens! Oh, heavens!' cried they,

'what a lovely child!'"

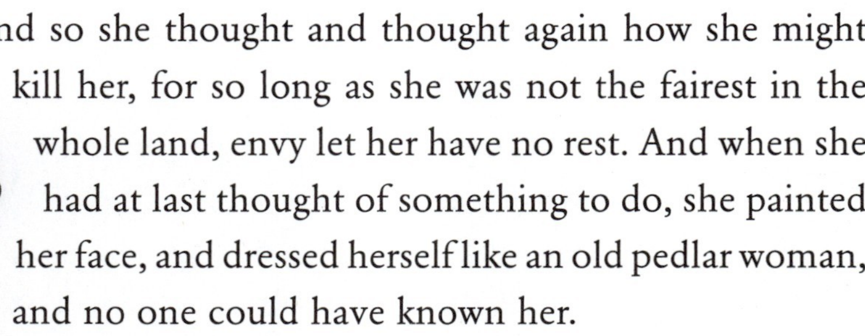

And so she thought and thought again how she might kill her, for so long as she was not the fairest in the whole land, envy let her have no rest. And when she had at last thought of something to do, she painted her face, and dressed herself like an old pedlar woman, and no one could have known her.

In this disguise she went over the seven mountains to the seven dwarfs, and knocked at the door and cried, "Pretty things to sell, very cheap, very cheap."

Snow White looked out of the window and called out, "Good day my good woman, what have you to sell?"

"Good things, pretty things," she answered, "stay-laces of all colors," and she pulled out one which was woven of bright-colored silk.

"I may let the worthy old woman in," thought Snow White, and she unbolted the door and bought the pretty laces.

"Child," said the old woman, "what a fright you look; come, I will lace you properly for once." Snow White had no suspicion, but stood before her, and let herself be laced with the new laces. But the old woman laced so quickly and so tightly that Snow White lost her breath and fell down as if dead. "Now I am the most beautiful," said the queen to herself, and ran away.

Not long afterward, in the evening, the seven dwarfs came home, but how shocked they were when they saw their dear Snow White lying on the ground, and that she neither stirred nor moved, and seemed to be dead. They lifted her up, and, as they saw that she was laced too tightly, they cut the laces; then she began to breathe a little, and after a while came to life again.

When the dwarfs heard what had happened they said, "The old pedlar woman was no one else than the wicked queen; take care and let no one come in when we are not with you."

But the wicked woman when she had reached home went in front of the glass and asked—

"Looking glass, Looking glass, on the wall,
Who in this land is the fairest of all?"

And it answered as before—

"Oh, Queen, you are fairest of all I see,
But over the hills, where the seven dwarfs dwell,
Snow White is still alive and well,
And none is so fair as she."

When she heard that, all her blood rushed to her heart with fear, for she saw plainly that Snow White was again alive. "But now," she said, "I will think of something that shall put an end to you," and by the help of witchcraft, which she understood, she made a poisonous comb.

Then she disguised herself and took the shape of another old woman. So she went over the seven mountains to the seven dwarfs, knocked at the door, and cried, "Good things to sell, cheap, cheap!"

Snow White looked out and said, "Go away; I cannot let anyone come in."

"I suppose you can look," said the old woman, and pulled the poisonous comb out and held it up. It pleased the girl so well that she let herself be beguiled, and opened the door.

When they had made a bargain the old woman said, "Now I will comb you properly for once." Poor Snow White had no suspicion, and let the old woman do as she pleased, but hardly had she put the comb in her hair than the poison in it took effect, and the girl fell down senseless. "You paragon of beauty," said the wicked woman, "you are done for now," and she went away.

But fortunately it was almost evening, when the seven dwarfs came home. When they saw Snow White lying as if dead upon the ground they at once suspected the stepmother, and they looked and found the poisoned comb. Scarcely had they taken it out when Snow White came to herself, and told them what had happened. Then they warned her once more to be upon her guard and to open the door to no one.

The Queen, at home, went in front of the glass and said–

"Looking glass, Looking glass, on the wall,
Who in this land is the fairest of all?"

Then it answered as before–

"Oh, Queen, you are fairest of all I see,
But over the hills, where the seven dwarfs dwell,
Snow White is still alive and well,
And none is so fair as she."

When she heard the glass speak thus she trembled and shook with rage. "Snow White shall die," she cried, "even if it costs me my life!"

Thereupon she went into a quite secret, lonely room, where no one ever came, and there she made a very poisonous apple. Outside it looked pretty, white with a red cheek, so that everyone who saw it longed for it; but whoever ate a piece of it must surely die.

When the apple was ready she painted her face, and dressed herself up as a country woman, and so she went over the seven mountains to the seven dwarfs. She knocked at the door. Snow White put her head out of the window and said, "I cannot let any one in; the seven dwarfs have forbidden me."

"It is all the same to me," answered the woman, "I shall soon get rid of my apples. There, I will give you one."

"No," said Snow White, "I dare not take anything."

"Are you afraid of poison?" said the old woman. "Look, I will cut the apple in two pieces; you eat the red cheek, and I will eat the white." The apple was so cunningly made that only the red cheek was poisoned. Snow White longed for the fine apple, and when she saw that the woman ate part of it she could resist no longer, and stretched out her hand and took the poisonous half. But hardly had she a bit of it in her mouth than she fell down dead.

Then the queen looked at her with a dreadful look, and laughed aloud and said, "White as snow, red as blood, black as ebony-wood! This time the dwarfs cannot wake you up again." And when she asked of the looking glass at home–

"Looking glass, Looking glass, on the wall,
 Who in this land is the fairest of all?"

It answered at last–

"Oh, Queen, in this land you are fairest of all."

Then her envious heart had rest, so far as an envious heart can have rest.

The dwarfs, when they came home in the evening, found Snow White lying upon the ground; she breathed no longer and was dead. They lifted her up, looked to see whether they could find anything poisonous, unlaced her, combed her hair, washed her with water and wine, but it was all of no use; the poor child was dead, and remained dead. They laid her upon a bier, and all seven of them sat round it and wept for her, and wept three days long.

Then they were going to bury her, but she still looked as if she were living, and still had her pretty red cheeks. They said, "We could not bury her in the dark ground," and they had a transparent coffin of glass made, so that she could be seen from all sides, and they laid her in it, and wrote her name upon it in golden letters, and that she was a princess. Then they put the coffin out upon the mountain, and one of them always stayed by it and watched it. And birds came too, and wept for Snow White; first an owl, then a raven, and last a dove.

And now Snow White lay a long, long time in the coffin, and she did not change, but looked as if she were asleep; for she was as white as snow, as red as blood, and her hair was as black as ebony.

It happened, however, that a prince came into the forest, and went to the dwarfs' house to spend the night. He saw the coffin on the mountain, and the beautiful Snow White within it, and read what was written upon it in golden letters.

Then he said to the dwarfs, "Let me have the coffin, I will give you whatever you want for it."

But the dwarfs answered, "We will not part with it for all the gold in the world."

Then he said, "Let me have it as a gift, for I cannot live without seeing Snow White. I will honor and prize her as my dearest possession." As he spoke in this way the good dwarfs took pity upon him, and gave him the coffin.

And now the prince had it carried away by his servants on their shoulders. And it happened that they stumbled over a tree stump, and with the shock the poisonous piece of apple that Snow White had bitten off came out of her throat. And before long she opened her eyes, lifted up the lid of the coffin, sat up, and was once more alive.

"Oh, heavens, where am I?" she cried.

The prince, full of joy, said, "You are with me," and told her what had happened, and said, "I love you more than everything in the world; come with me to my father's palace, you shall be my wife."

And Snow White was willing, and went with him, and their wedding was held with great show and splendor. But Snow White's wicked stepmother was also bidden to the feast. When she had arrayed herself in beautiful clothes she went before the looking glass, and said–

"Looking glass, Looking glass, on the wall,
Who in this land is the fairest of all?"

The glass answered–

"Oh, Queen, of all here the fairest are you,
But the young Queen is fairer by far as I trow."

Then the wicked woman uttered a curse, and was so wretched, so utterly wretched, that she knew not what to do. At first she would not go to the wedding at all, but she had no peace, and must go to see the young queen. And when she went in she knew Snow White; and she stood still with rage and fear, and could not stir. But iron slippers had already been put upon the fire, and they were brought in with tongs, and set before her. Then she was forced to put on the red-hot shoes, and dance until she dropped down dead.

Brothers Grimm

Notes on the Story

Snow White

The Grimms were told this tale by the Hassenpflug sisters in their hometown of Kassel, and, like "Cinderella," "Snow White" is a tale that appears across the globe, from Ireland to Asia Minor to Africa. Variants of the magic mirror include a speaking trout (Scotland), the moon (Armenia), and the sun (Greece), and kindly robbers, bears, wild men, ogres, and dragons also fulfill the dwarfs' role.

✣

In many ways, this tale typifies the relationship between the Grimms and their stories. As in "Hansel and Gretel" (page 136), they changed the mother to stepmother, so as to soften the harshness of the tale. A comparison of the 1810 unpublished manuscript and the 1812 published edition also illustrates their alterations: while in the earlier version, Snow White is asked simply to cook for the dwarfs, the latter's list of duties includes cleaning, needlework, and bed linen duties, perhaps emphasizing the gender values that the Grimms wished their tales to instill.

The Firebird and Princess Vasilissa

Once upon a time a strong and powerful tsar ruled in a country far away. And among his servants was a young archer, and this archer had a horse—a horse of power—such a horse as belonged to the wonderful men of long ago—a great horse with a broad chest, eyes like fire, and hoofs of iron. There are no such horses nowadays. They sleep with the strong men who rode them, the bogatyrs (knights), until the time comes when Russia has need of them. Then the great horses will thunder up from under the ground, and the valiant men leap from the graves in the armor they have worn so long. The strong men will sit on those horses of power, and there will be swinging of clubs and thunder of hoofs, and the earth will be swept clean from the enemies of God and the tsar. So my grandfather used to say, and he was as much older than I, as I am older than you, little ones, and so he should know.

Well, one day long ago, in the green time of the year, the young archer rode through the forest on his horse of power. The trees were green; there were little blue flowers on the ground under the trees; the squirrels ran in the branches, and the hares in the undergrowth; but no birds sang. The young archer rode along the forest path and listened for the singing of the birds, but there was no singing.

The forest was silent, and the only noises in it were the scratching of four-footed beasts, the dropping of fir cones, and the heavy stamping of the horse of power in the soft path.

"What has happened to the birds?" said the young archer.

He had scarcely said this before he saw a big curving feather lying in the path before him. The feather was larger than a swan's, larger than an eagle's. It lay in the path, glittering like a flame; for the sun was on it, and it was a feather of pure gold. Then he knew why there was no singing in the forest. For he knew that the firebird had flown that way, and that the feather in the path before him was a feather from its burning breast.

The horse of power spoke and said–

"Leave the golden feather where it lies. If you take it, you will be sorry for it, and know the meaning of fear."

But the brave young archer sat on the horse of power and looked at the golden feather, and wondered whether to take it or not. He had no wish to learn what it was to be afraid, but he thought, "If I take it and bring it to the tsar my master, he will be pleased; and he will not send me away with empty hands, for no tsar in the world has a feather from the burning breast of the firebird." And the more he thought, the more he wanted to carry the feather to the tsar. And in the end he did not listen to the words of the horse of power. He leapt from the saddle, picked up the golden feather of the firebird, mounted his horse again, and galloped back through the green forest until he came to the palace of the tsar.

He went into the palace, and bowed before the tsar and said,

"O tsar, I have brought you a feather of the firebird."

The tsar looked gladly at the feather, and then at the young archer. "Thank you," said he; "but if you have brought me a feather of the firebird, you will be able to bring me the bird itself. I should like to see it. A feather is not a fit gift to bring to the tsar. Bring the bird itself, or, I swear by my sword, your head shall no longer sit between your shoulders!"

The young archer bowed his head and went out. Bitterly he wept, for he knew now what it was to be afraid. He went out into the courtyard, where the horse of power was waiting for him, tossing its head and stamping on the ground.

"Master," said the horse of power, "why do you weep?"

"The tsar has told me to bring him the firebird, and no man on earth can do that," said the young archer, and he bowed his head on his breast.

"I told you," said the horse of power, "that if you took the feather you would learn the meaning of fear. Well, do not be frightened yet, and do not weep. The trouble is not now; the trouble lies before you. Go to the tsar and ask him to have a hundred sacks of maize scattered over the open field, and let this be done at midnight."

The young archer went back into the palace and begged the tsar for this, and the tsar ordered that at midnight a hundred sacks of maize should be scattered in the open field.

Next morning, at the first redness in the sky, the young archer rode out on the horse of power, and came to the open field. The ground was scattered all over with maize. In the middle of the field stood a great oak with spreading boughs. The young archer leapt to the ground, took off the saddle, and let the horse of power loose to wander as he pleased about the field. Then he climbed up into the oak and hid himself among the green boughs.

The sky grew red and gold, and the sun rose. Suddenly, there was a noise in the forest round the field. The trees shook and swayed, and almost fell. There was a mighty wind. The sea piled itself into waves with crests of foam, and the firebird came flying from the other side of the world. Huge and golden, and flaming in the sun, it flew, dropped down with open wings into the field, and began to eat the maize.

"He came close up to the firebird, and then

suddenly stepped on one of its spreading fiery wings . . ."

The horse of power wandered in the field. This way he went, and that, but always he came a little nearer to the firebird. Nearer and nearer came the horse. He came close up to the firebird, and then suddenly stepped on one of its spreading fiery wings and pressed it heavily to the ground. The bird struggled, flapping mightily with its fiery wings, but it could not get away. The young archer slipped down from the tree, bound the firebird with three strong ropes, swung it on his back, saddled the horse, and rode to the palace of the tsar.

The young archer stood before the tsar, and his back was bent under the great weight of the firebird, and the broad wings of the bird hung on either side of him like fiery shields, and there was a trail of golden feathers on the floor. The young archer swung the magic bird to the foot of the throne before the tsar; and the tsar was glad, because since the beginning of the world no tsar had seen the firebird flung before him like a wild duck caught in a snare.

The tsar looked at the firebird and laughed with pride. Then he lifted his eyes and looked at the young archer, and he said–

"As you have known how to take the firebird, you will know how to bring me my bride, for whom I have long been waiting. In the land of Never, on the very edge of the world, where the red sun rises in flame from behind the sea, lives the Princess Vasilissa. I will marry none but her. Bring her to me, and I will reward you with silver and gold. But if you do not bring her, then, by my sword, your head will no longer sit between your shoulders!"

The young archer wept bitter tears, and went out into the courtyard, where the horse of power was stamping the ground with its hoofs of iron and tossing its thick mane.

"Master, why do you weep?" asked the horse of power.

"The tsar has ordered me to go to the land of Never, and to bring back the Princess Vasilissa."

"Do not weep–do not grieve. The trouble is not yet; the trouble is to come. Go to the tsar and ask him for a silver tent with a golden roof, and for all kinds of food and drink to take with us on the journey."

The young archer went in and asked the tsar for this, and the tsar gave him a silver tent with silver hangings and a gold-embroidered roof, and every kind of rich wine and the tastiest of foods.

Then the young archer mounted the horse of power and rode off to the land of Never. On and on he rode, many days and nights, and came at last to the edge of the world, where the red sun rises in flame from behind the deep blue sea.

On the shore of the sea the young archer reined in the horse of power, and the heavy hoofs of the horse sank in the sand. He shaded his eyes and looked out over the blue water, and there was the Princess Vasilissa in a little silver boat, rowing with golden oars.

The young archer rode back a little way to where the sand ended and the green world began. There he loosed the horse to wander where he pleased, and to feed on the green grass. Then on the edge of the shore, where the green grass ended and grew thin and the sand began, he set up the shining tent, with its silver hangings and its gold-embroidered roof. In the tent he set out the tasty dishes and the rich flagons of wine that the tsar had given him, and he sat himself down in the tent and began to regale himself, while he waited for the Princess Vasilissa.

The Princess Vasilissa dipped her golden oars in the blue water, and the little silver boat moved lightly through the dancing waves. She sat in the little boat and looked over the blue sea to the edge of the world, and there, between the golden sand and the green earth, she saw the tent standing, silver and gold in the sun. She dipped her oars, and came nearer to see it the better. The nearer she came the fairer seemed the tent, and at last she rowed to the shore and grounded her little boat on the golden sand, and stepped out daintily and came up to the tent. She was a little frightened, and now and again she stopped and looked back to where the silver boat lay on the sand with the blue sea beyond it. The young archer said not a word, but went on regaling himself on the pleasant dishes he had set out there in the tent.

At last the Princess Vasilissa came up to the tent and looked in. The young archer rose and bowed before her.

He said, "Good day to you, Princess! Be so kind as to come in and take bread and salt with me, and taste my foreign wines."

And the Princess Vasilissa came into the tent and sat down with the young archer, and ate sweetmeats with him, and drank his health in a golden goblet of the wine the tsar had given him. Now this wine was heavy, and the last drop from the goblet had no sooner trickled down her little slender throat than her eyes closed against her will, once, twice, and again.

"Ah me!" said the princess, "it is as if the night itself had perched on my eyelids, and yet it is but noon."

And the golden goblet dropped to the ground from her little fingers, and she leant back on a cushion and fell instantly asleep. If she had been beautiful before, she was lovelier still when she lay in that deep sleep in the shadow of the tent.

Quickly the young archer called to the horse of power. Lightly he lifted the princess in his strong young arms. Swiftly he leapt with her into the saddle. Like a feather she lay in the hollow of his left arm, and slept while the iron hoofs of the great horse thundered over the ground.

They came to the tsar's palace, and the young archer leapt from the horse of power and carried the princess into the palace. Great was the joy of the tsar; but it did not last for long.

"Go, sound the trumpets for our wedding," he said to his servants, "let all the bells be rung."

The bells rang out and the trumpets sounded, and at the noise of the horns and the ringing of the bells the Princess Vasilissa woke up and looked about her.

"What is this ringing of bells," she asked, "and this noise of trumpets? And where, oh, where is the blue sea, and my little silver boat with its golden oars?" And the princess put her hand to her eyes.

"The blue sea is far away," said the tsar, "and for your little silver boat I give you a golden throne. The trumpets sound for our wedding, and the bells are ringing for our joy."

But the princess turned her face away from the tsar; and there was no wonder in that, for he was old, and his eyes were not kind.

And she looked with love at the young archer; and there was no wonder in that either, for he was a young man fit to ride the horse of power.

The tsar was angry with the Princess Vasilissa, but his anger was as useless as his joy.

"Why, Princess," he said, "will you not marry me, and forget your blue sea and your silver boat?"

"In the middle of the deep blue sea lies a great stone," said the princess, "and under that stone is hidden my wedding dress. If I cannot wear that dress I will marry nobody at all."

Instantly the tsar turned to the young archer, who was waiting before the throne.

"Ride swiftly back," he said, "to the land of Never, where the red sun rises in flame. There—do you hear what the Princess says?—a great stone lies in the middle of the sea. Under that stone is hidden her wedding dress. Ride swiftly. Bring back that dress, or, by my sword, your head shall no longer sit between your shoulders!"

The young archer wept bitter tears, and went out into the courtyard, where the horse of power was waiting for him, champing its golden bit.

"There is no way of escaping death this time," he said.

"Master, why do you weep?" asked the horse of power.

"The tsar has ordered me to ride to the land of Never, to fetch the wedding dress of the Princess Vasilissa from the bottom of the deep blue sea. Besides, the dress is wanted for the tsar's wedding, and I love the princess myself."

"What did I tell you?" said the horse of power. "I told you that there would be trouble if you picked up the golden feather from the firebird's burning breast. Well, do not be afraid. The trouble is not yet; the trouble is to come. Up! Into the saddle with you, and away for the wedding-dress of the Princess Vasilissa!"

The young archer leapt into the saddle, and the horse of power, with his thundering hoofs, carried him swiftly through the green forests and over the bare plains, till they came to the edge of the world, to the land of Never, where the red sun rises in flame from behind the deep blue sea. There they rested, at the very edge of the sea.

The young archer looked sadly over the wide waters, but the horse of power tossed its mane and did not look at the sea, but on the shore. This way and that it looked, and saw at last a huge lobster moving slowly, sideways, along the golden sand.

Nearer and nearer came the lobster, and it was a giant among lobsters, the tsar of all the lobsters; and it moved slowly along the shore, while the horse of power moved carefully and as if by accident, until it stood between the lobster and the sea. Then when the lobster came close by, the horse of power lifted an iron hoof and set it firmly on the lobster's tail.

"You will be the death of me!" screamed the lobster–as well he might, with the heavy foot of the horse of power pressing his tail into the sand. "Let me live, and I will do whatever you ask of me."

"Very well," said the horse of power, "we will let you live," and he slowly lifted his foot. "But this is what you shall do for

us. In the middle of the blue sea lies a great stone, and under that stone is hidden the wedding dress of the Princess Vasilissa. Bring it here."

The lobster groaned with the pain in his tail. Then he cried out in a voice that could be heard all over the deep blue sea. And the sea was disturbed, and from all sides lobsters in their thousands made their way toward the bank. And the huge lobster that was the oldest of them all, and the tsar of all the lobsters that live between the rising and the setting of the sun, gave them the order and sent them back into the sea. And the young archer sat on the horse of power and waited.

After a little time the sea was disturbed again, and the lobsters in their thousands came to the shore, and with them they brought a golden casket in which was the wedding dress of the Princess Vasilissa. They had taken it from under the great stone that lay in the middle of the sea.

The tsar of all the lobsters raised himself painfully on his bruised tail and gave the casket into the hands of the young archer, and instantly the horse of power turned himself about and galloped back to the palace of the tsar, far, far away, at the other side of the green forests and beyond the treeless plains.

The young archer went into the palace and gave the casket into the hands of the princess, and looked at her with sadness in his eyes, and she looked at him with love. Then she went away into an inner chamber, and came back in her wedding dress, fairer than the spring itself. Great was the joy of the tsar. The wedding feast was made ready, and the bells rang, and flags waved above the palace.

The tsar held out his hand to the princess, and looked at her with his old eyes. But she would not take his hand.

"No," she said, "I will marry nobody until the man who brought me here has done penance in boiling water."

Instantly the tsar turned to his servants and ordered them to make a great fire, and to fill a great cauldron with water and set it on the fire, and, when the water should be at its hottest, to take the young archer and throw him into it, to do penance for having taken the Princess Vasilissa away from the land of Never. There was no gratitude in the mind of that tsar.

Swiftly the servants brought wood and made a mighty fire, and on it they laid a huge cauldron of water, and built the fire round the walls of the cauldron. The fire burned hot and the water steamed. The fire burned hotter, and the water bubbled and seethed. They made ready to take the young archer, to throw him into the cauldron.

"Oh misery!" thought the young archer. "Why did I ever take the golden feather that had fallen from the firebird's burning breast? Why did I not listen to the wise words of the horse of power?"

And he remembered the horse of power, and he begged the tsar, "O lord tsar, I do not complain. I shall presently die in the heat of the water on the fire. Suffer me, before I die, once more to see my horse."

"Let him see his horse," said the princess.

"Very well," says the tsar. "Say good-bye to your horse, for you will not ride him again. But let your farewells be short, for we are waiting."

The young archer crossed the courtyard and came to the horse of power, who was scraping the ground with his iron hoofs.

"Farewell, my horse of power," said the young archer. "I should have listened to your words of wisdom, for now the end is come, and we shall never more see the green trees pass above us and the ground disappear beneath us, as we race the wind between the earth and the sky."

"Why so?" said the horse of power.

"The tsar has ordered that I am to be boiled to death–thrown into that cauldron that is seething on the great fire."

"Fear not," said the horse of power, "for the Princess Vasilissa has made him do this, and the end of these things is better than I thought. Go back, and when they are ready to throw you in the cauldron, run boldly and leap into the boiling water."

The young archer went back across the courtyard, and the servants made ready to throw him into the cauldron.

"Are you sure that the water is boiling?" said the Princess Vasilissa.

"It bubbles and seethes," said the servants.

"Let me see for myself," said the princess, and she went to the fire and waved her hand above the cauldron. And some say there was something in her hand, and some say there was not.

"It is boiling," said she, and the servants laid hands on the young archer; but he threw them from him, and ran and leapt boldly before them all into the very middle of the cauldron.

Twice he sank below the surface, borne round with the bubbles and foam of the boiling water. Then he leapt from the cauldron and stood before the tsar and the princess. He had become so beautiful a youth that all who saw cried aloud in wonder.

"This is a miracle," said the tsar. And the tsar looked at the beautiful young archer, and thought of himself–of his age, of his bent back, and his gray beard, and his toothless gums. "I, too, will become beautiful," thought he, and he rose from his throne and clambered into the cauldron, and was boiled to death in a moment.

And the end of the story? They buried the tsar, and made the young archer tsar in his place. He married the Princess Vasilissa, and lived many years with her in love and good fellowship. And he built a golden stable for the horse of power, and never forgot what he owed to him.

Alexander Afanasyev

Notes on the Story

The Firebird and Princess Vasilissa

Alexander Afanasyev (1826–1871) is widely regarded as one of the world's most significant folklorists. Contemporaneous with the Brothers Grimm and other nineteenth-century collectors, Afanasyev may be said to have surpassed them all in both range and rigor. His first collection, *Russian Fairy Tales*, contained an extensive 640 stories. He also annotated and classified his tales, and his system is still used in Russia today. During his life, his work was subject to criticism and censorship from tsarist Russia, particularly for celebrating the wit of the peasants, and highlighting the abuses and corruption of the clergy and nobility.

In 1910, the Russian composer Igor Stravinsky made this story of the firebird and the brave archer into a ballet. The firebird itself soars through the pages of much Russian folklore, often leading the brave and dauntless young hero in the direction of his true love.

The Three Billy Goats Gruff

Once on a time there were three billy goats, who were to go up to the hillside to make themselves fat, and the name of all three was "Gruff."

On the way up was a bridge over a burn that they had to cross; and under the bridge lived a great ugly troll, with eyes as big as saucers, and a nose as long as a poker.

So first of all came the youngest billy goat Gruff to cross the bridge.

"Trip, trap! Trip, trap!" went the bridge.

"Who's that tripping over my bridge?" roared the troll.

"Oh! It is only I, the tiniest billy goat Gruff; and I'm going up to the hillside to make myself fat," said the billy goat, with such a small voice.

"Now, I'm coming to gobble you up," said the troll.

"Oh, no! Please don't take me. I'm too little, that I am," said the billy goat. "Wait a bit till the second billy goat Gruff comes, he's much bigger."

"Well! Be off with you," said the troll.

A little while after came the second billy goat Gruff to cross the bridge.

"Trip, trap! Trip, trap! Trip, trap!" went the bridge.

"Who's that tripping over my bridge?" roared the troll.

"Oh! It's the second billy goat Gruff, and I'm going up to the hillside to make myself fat," said the billy goat, who hadn't such a small voice.

"Now, I'm coming to gobble you up," said the troll.

"Oh, no! Don't take me, wait a little till the big billy goat Gruff comes, he's much bigger."

"Very well! Be off with you," said the troll.

But just then up came the big billy goat Gruff.

"Trip, trap! Trip, trap! Trip, trap!" went the bridge, for the billy goat was so heavy that the bridge creaked and groaned under him.

"Who's that tramping over my bridge?" roared the troll.

"It's I! The big billy goat Gruff," said the billy goat, who had an ugly hoarse voice of his own.

"Now, I'm coming to gobble you up," roared the troll.

"Well, come along! I've got two spears,
And I'll poke your eyeballs out at your ears;
I've got besides two curling stones,
And I'll crush you to bits, body and bones."

That was what the big billy goat said; and so he flew at the troll and poked his eyes out with his horns, and crushed him to bits, body and bones, and tossed him out into the burn, and after that he went up to the hillside. There the billy goats got so fat that they were scarce able to walk home again. And if the fat hasn't fallen off them, why they're still fat, and so–

Snip, snap, snout,
This tale's told out.

Asbjørnsen and Moe

Notes on the Story

The Three Billy Goats Gruff

Student friends and folklore enthusiasts, Peter Christen Asbjørnsen (1812–1885) and Jørgen Moe (1813–1882) were inspired to compile tales from their own country, Norway, by the Grimms' German collections. Unlike the Grimms, however, they were dedicated to keeping the language and style as close as they could to that of the storytellers. Although they were criticized for their "raw" Norwegian style (Danish was the literary language of the time), their story collections were fundamental to the development of modern written Norwegian.

This exuberant, childish tale of the indomitable and greedy goats is very different to the more serious "East of the Sun and West of the Moon" (page 195), and exemplifies the rich diversity of tale type to be found in their collections. Much beloved of children, it is an example of a trickster story in which the heroes escape being devoured by the swiftness of their tongues.

East of the Sun and West of the Moon

Once upon a time there was a poor husbandman who had so many children that he hadn't much of either food or clothing to give them. Pretty children they all were, but the prettiest was the youngest daughter, who was so lovely there was no end to her loveliness.

So one day, 'twas on a Thursday evening late at the fall of the year, the weather was so wild and rough outside, and it was so cruelly dark, and rain fell and wind blew, till the walls of the cottage shook again. There they all sat round the fire, busy with this thing and that. But just then, all at once something gave three taps on the windowpane. Then the father went out to see what was the matter; and, when he got out of doors, what should he see but a great big white bear.

"Good evening to you!" said the white bear.

"The same to you!" said the man.

"Will you give me your youngest daughter? If you will, I'll make you as rich as you are now poor," said the bear.

Well, the man would not be at all sorry to be so rich; but still he thought he must have a bit of a talk with his daughter first. So he went in and told them how there was a great white bear waiting outside, who had given his word to make them so rich if he could only have the youngest daughter.

The lassie said "No!" outright. Nothing could get her to say anything else. So the man went out and settled it with the white bear that he should come again the next Thursday evening and get an answer. Meantime he talked his daughter over, and kept on telling her of all the riches they would get, and how well off she would be herself. And so, at last, she thought better of it, and washed and mended her rags, made herself as smart as she could, and was ready to start. I can't say her packing gave her much trouble.

Next Thursday evening came the white bear to fetch her, and she got upon his back with her bundle, and off they went. So, when they had gone a bit of the way, the white bear said:

"Are you afraid?"

"No," she wasn't.

"Well! Mind and hold tight by my shaggy coat, and then there's nothing to fear," said the bear.

So she rode a long, long way, till they came to a great steep hill. There, on the face of it, the white bear gave a knock, and a door opened, and they came into a castle where there were many rooms all lit up; rooms gleaming with silver and gold. And there, too, was a table ready laid, and it was all as grand as grand could be. Then the white bear gave her a silver bell; and when she wanted anything, she was only to ring it, and she would get it at once.

Well, after she had eaten and drunk, and evening wore on, she got sleepy after her journey, and thought she would like to go to bed, so she rang the bell; and she had scarce taken hold of it before she came into a chamber where there was a bed made, as fair and white as any one would wish to sleep in, with silken pillows and curtains and gold fringe. All that was in the room was gold or silver. But when she had gone to bed and put out the light, a man came and laid himself alongside her. That was the white bear, who threw off his beast shape at night; but she never saw him, for he always came after she had put out the light, and before the day dawned he was up and off again. So things went on happily for a while, but at last she began to get silent and sorrowful; for there she went about all day alone, and she longed to go home to see her father and mother and brothers and sisters. So one day, when the white bear asked what it was that she lacked, she said it was so dull and lonely there, and how she longed to go home to see her father and mother and brothers and sisters, and that was why she was so sad and sorrowful, because she couldn't get to them.

"Well, well!" said the bear, "perhaps there's a cure for all this. But you must promise me one thing, not to talk alone with your mother, but only when the rest are by to hear; for she'll take you by the hand and try to lead you into a room alone to talk. But you must mind and not do that, else you'll bring bad luck on both of us."

So one Sunday, the white bear came and said now they could set off to see her father and mother. Well, off they started, she sitting on his back; and they went far and long. At last they came to a grand house, and there her brothers and sisters were running about out of doors at play, and everything was so pretty, 'twas a joy to see.

"This is where your father and mother live now," said the white bear. "But, you must not forget what I told you, else you'll make us both unlucky."

No! Bless her, she'd not forget; and when she had reached the house, the white bear turned right about and left her.

Then, when she went in to see her father and mother, there was such joy, there was no end to it. None of them thought they could thank her enough for all she had done for them. Now, they had everything they wished, as good as good could be, and they all wanted to know how she got on where she lived.

Well, she said, it was very good to live where she did; she had all she wished. What she said beside I don't know, but I don't think any of

"'Now mind,' said the white bear, 'if you have listened to your

mother's advice, you have brought bad luck on both of us . . .'"

them had the right end of the stick, or that they got much out of her. But so, in the afternoon, after they had done dinner, all happened as the white bear had said. Her mother wanted to talk with her alone in her bedroom; but she minded what the white bear had said, and wouldn't go upstairs.

"Oh! What we have to talk about will keep!" she said, and put her mother off. But, somehow or other, her mother got round her at last, and she had to tell her the whole story. So she said, how every night when she had gone to bed a man came and lay down beside her as soon as she had put out the light; and how she never saw him, because he was always up and away before the morning dawned. And how she went about woeful and sorrowing, for she thought she should so like to see him. And how all day long she walked about there alone; and how dull and dreary and lonesome it was.

"My!" said her mother. "It may well be a troll you slept with! But now I'll teach you a lesson how to set eyes on him. I'll give you a bit of candle, which you can carry home in your bosom; just light that while he is asleep, but take care not to drop the tallow on him."

Yes! She took the candle and hid it in her bosom, and as night drew on, the white bear came and fetched her away.

But when they had gone a bit of the way, the white bear asked if all hadn't happened as he had said.

Well, she couldn't say it hadn't.

"Now, mind," said the white bear, "if you have listened to your mother's advice, you have brought bad luck on us both, and then, all that has passed between us will be as nothing."

"No," she said, "I haven't listened to my mother's advice."

So when she reached home, and had gone to bed, it was the old story over again. There came a man and lay down beside her; but at dead of night, when she heard he slept, she got up and struck a light, lit the candle, and let the light shine on him, and so she saw that he was the loveliest prince anyone ever set eyes on, and she fell so deep in love with him on the spot, that she thought she couldn't live if she didn't give him a kiss there and then. And so she did; but as she kissed him, she dropped three hot drops of tallow on his shirt, and he woke up.

"What have you done?" he cried. "Now you have made us both unlucky, for had you held out only this one year, I had been freed. For I have a stepmother who has bewitched me, so that I am a white bear by day, and a man by night. But now all ties are snapped between us; now I must set off from you to her. She lives in a castle which stands east of the sun and west of the moon, and there, too, is a princess, with a nose three ells long, and she's the wife I must have now."

She wept and took it ill, but there was no help for it; go he must.

Then she asked if she could go with him.

"No, you cannot."

"Tell me the way, then," she said, "and I'll search you out; that surely I may get leave to do."

"Yes, you may do that," he said; "but there is no way to that place. It lies east of the sun and west of the moon, and thither you'll never find your way."

So next morning, when she woke up, both prince and castle were gone, and then she lay on a little green patch, in the midst of the gloomy thick wood, and by her side lay the same bundle of rags she had brought with her from her old home.

So when she had rubbed the sleep out of her eyes, and wept till she was tired, she set out on her way, and walked many, many days, till she came to a lofty crag. Under it sat an old hag, and played with a gold apple which she tossed about. Here the lassie asked if she knew the way to the prince, who lived with his stepmother in the castle, that lay east of the sun and west of the moon, and who was to marry the princess with a nose three ells long.

"How did you come to know about him?" asked the old hag. "But maybe you are the lassie who ought to have had him?"

"Yes, I am."

"So, so; it's you, is it?" said the old hag. "Well, all I know about him is, that he lives in the castle that lies east of the sun and west of the moon, and thither you'll come, late or never; but still you may have the loan of my horse, and on him you can ride to my next neighbor. Maybe she'll be able to tell you. And when you get there, just give the horse a switch under the left ear, and beg him to be off home; and, stay, this gold apple you may take with you."

So she got upon the horse, and rode a long, long time, till she came to another crag, under which sat another old hag, with a gold carding-comb. Here the lassie asked if she knew the way to the castle that lay east of the sun and west of the moon, and she answered, like the first old hag, that she knew nothing about it, except it was east of the sun and west of the moon.

"And thither you'll come, late or never, but you shall have the loan of my horse to my next neighbor; maybe she'll tell you all about it. And when you get there, just switch the horse under the left ear, and beg him to be off home."

And this old hag gave her the golden carding-comb; it might be she'd find some use for it, she said. So the lassie got up on the horse, and rode a far, far, way, and had a weary time. And so at last she came to another great crag, under which sat another old hag, spinning with a golden spinning wheel. Her, too, she asked if she knew the way to the prince, and where the castle was that lay east of the sun and west of the moon. So it was the same thing over again.

"Maybe it's you who ought to have had the prince?" said the old hag.

"Yes, it is."

But she, too, didn't know the way a bit better than the other two. "East of the sun and west of the moon it was," she knew–that was all.

"And thither you'll come, late or never; but I'll lend you my horse, and then I think you'd best ride to the East Wind and ask him; maybe he knows those parts, and can blow you thither. But when you get to him, you need only give the horse a switch under the left ear, and he'll trot home by himself."

And so, too, she gave her the gold spinning wheel. "Maybe you'll find a use for it," said the old hag.

Then on she rode many, many days, a weary time, before she got to the East Wind's house, but at last she did reach it, and then she asked the East Wind if he could tell her the way to the prince who dwelt east of the sun and west of the moon. Yes, the East Wind had often heard tell of it, the prince and the castle, but he couldn't tell the way, for he had never blown so far.

"But, if you will, I'll go with you to my brother the West Wind, maybe he knows, for he's much stronger. So, if you will just get on my back, I'll carry you thither."

Yes, she got on his back, and I should just think they went briskly along.

So when they got there, they went into the West Wind's house, and the East Wind said the lassie he had brought was the one who ought to have had the prince who lived in the castle east of the sun and west of the moon; and so she had set out to seek him, and how he had come with her, and would be glad to know if the West Wind knew how to get to the castle.

"Nay," said the West Wind, "so far I've never blown; but if you will, I'll go with you to our brother the South Wind, for he's much stronger than either of us, and he has flapped his wings far and wide. Maybe he'll tell you. You can get on my back, and I'll carry you to him."

Yes! She got on his back, and so they travelled to the South Wind, and weren't so very long on the way, I should think.

When they got there, the West Wind asked him if he could tell her the way to the castle that lay east of the sun and west of the moon, for it was she who ought to have had the prince who lived there.

"You don't say so! That's she, is it?" said the South Wind. "Well, I have blustered about in most places in my time, but so far have I never blown; but if you will, I'll take you to my brother the North Wind. He is the oldest and strongest of the whole lot of us, and if he doesn't know where it is, you'll never find anyone in the world to tell you. You can get on my back, and I'll carry you thither."

Yes! She got on his back, and away he went from his house at a fine rate. And this time, too, she wasn't long on her way.

So when they got to the North Wind's house, he was so wild and cross, cold puffs came from him a long way off.

"Blast you both, what do you want?" he roared out to them ever so far off, so that it struck them with an icy shiver.

"Well," said the South Wind, "you needn't be so foul-mouthed, for here I am, your brother, the South Wind, and here is the lassie who ought to have had the prince who dwells in the castle that lies east of the sun and west of the moon, and now she wants to ask you if you ever were there, and can tell her the way, for she would be so glad to find him again."

"Yes, I know well enough where it is," said the North Wind. "Once in my life I blew an aspen leaf thither, but, I was so tired, I couldn't blow a puff for ever so many days after. But if you really wish to go thither, and aren't afraid to come along with me, I'll take you on my back and see if I can blow you thither."

Yes! With all her heart; she must and would get thither if it were possible in any way; and as for fear, however madly he went, she wouldn't be at all afraid.

"Very well, then," said the North Wind, "but you must sleep here tonight, for we must have the whole day before us, if we're to get thither at all."

Early next morning the North Wind woke her, and puffed himself up, and blew himself out, and made himself so stout and big, 'twas gruesome to look at him; and so off they went high up through the air, as if they would never stop till they got to the world's end.

Down here below there was such a storm; it threw down long tracts of wood and many houses, and when it swept over the great sea, ships foundered by the hundreds.

So they tore on and on–no one can believe how far they went–and all the while they still went over the sea, and the North Wind got more and more weary, and so out of breath he could scarce bring out a puff, and his wings drooped and drooped, till at last he sunk so low that the crests of the waves dashed over his heels.

"Are you afraid?" said the North Wind.

"No!" she wasn't.

But they weren't very far from land; and the North Wind had still so much strength left in him that he managed to throw her up on the shore under the windows of the castle which lay east of the sun and west of the moon; but then he was so weak and worn out, he had to stay there and rest many days before he could get home again.

Next morning the lassie sat down under the castle window, and began to play with the gold apple; and the first person she saw was the long-nose who was to have the prince.

"What do you want for your gold apple, you lassie?" said the long-nose, and threw up the window.

"It's not for sale, for gold or money," said the lassie.

"If it's not for sale for gold or money, what is it that you will sell it for? You may name your own price," said the princess.

"Well! If I may get to the prince, who lives here, and be with him tonight, you shall have it," said the lassie whom the North Wind had brought.

Yes! She might; that could be done. So the princess got the gold apple; but when the lassie came up to the prince's bedroom at night he was fast asleep. She called him and shook him, and between whiles she wept sore; but for all she could do, she couldn't wake him up. Next morning, as soon as day broke, came the princess with the long nose, and drove her out again.

So in the daytime she sat down under the castle windows and began to card with her carding-comb, and the same thing happened. The princess asked what she wanted for it; and she said it wasn't for sale for gold or money, but if she might get leave to go up to the prince and be with him that night, the princess should have it. But when she went up she found him fast asleep again, and for all she called, and all she shook, and wept, and prayed, she couldn't get life into him. And as soon as the first gray peep of day came, then came the princess with the long nose, and chased her out again.

So, in the daytime, the lassie sat down outside under the castle window, and began to spin with her golden spinning wheel, and that, too, the princess with the long nose wanted to have. So she threw up the window and asked what she wanted for it. The lassie said, as she had said twice before, it wasn't for sale for gold or money; but if she might go up to the prince who was there, and be with him alone that night, she might have it.

Yes! She might do that and welcome. But now you must know there were some Christian folk who had been carried off thither, and as they sat in their room, which was next the prince, they had heard how a woman had been in there, and wept and prayed, and called to him two nights running, and they told that to the prince.

That evening, when the princess came with her sleepy drink, the prince made as if he drank, but threw it over his shoulder, for he could guess it was a sleepy drink. So, when the lassie came in, she found the prince wide-awake; and then she told him the whole story how she had come thither.

"Ah," said the prince, "you've just come in the very nick of time, for tomorrow is to be our wedding day; but now I won't have the long-nose, and you are the only woman in the world who can set me free. I'll say I want to see what my wife is fit for, and beg her to wash the shirt which has the three spots of tallow on it. She'll say yes, for she doesn't know 'tis you who put them there; but that's a work only for Christian folk, and not for such a pack of trolls, and so I'll say that I won't have any other for my bride than the woman who can wash them out, and ask you to do it."

So there was great joy and love between them all that night. But next day, when the wedding was to be, the prince said: "First of all, I'd like to see what my bride is fit for."

"Yes!" said the stepmother, with all her heart.

"Well," said the prince, "I've got a fine shirt which I'd like for my wedding shirt, but somehow or other it has got three spots of tallow on it, which I must have washed out; and I have sworn never to take any other bride than the woman who's able to do that. If she can't, she's not worth having."

Well, that was no great thing they said, so they agreed, and she with the long-nose began to wash away as hard as she could, but the more she rubbed and scrubbed, the bigger the spots grew.

"Ah!" said the old hag, her mother, "you can't wash; let me try."

But she hadn't long taken the shirt in hand before it got far worse than ever, and with all her rubbing, and wringing, and scrubbing, the spots grew bigger and blacker, and the darker and uglier was the shirt.

Then all the other trolls began to wash, but the longer it lasted, the blacker and uglier the shirt grew, till at last it was as black all over as if it had been up the chimney.

"Ah!" said the prince, "you're none of you worth a straw; you can't wash. Why there, outside, sits a beggar lassie, I'll be bound she knows how to wash better than the whole lot of you. Come in, lassie!" he shouted.

Well, in she came.

"Can you wash this shirt clean, lassie you?" said he.

"I don't know," she said, "but I think I can."

And almost before she had taken it and dipped it in the water, it was as white as driven snow, and whiter still.

"Yes; you are the lassie for me," said the prince.

At that the old hag flew into such a rage, she burst on the spot, and the princess with the long nose after her, and the whole pack of trolls after her–at least I've never heard a word about them since.

As for the prince and princess, they set free all the poor Christian folk who had been carried off and shut up there. And they took with them all the silver and gold, and flitted away as far as they could from the castle that lay east of the sun and west of the moon.

Asbjørnsen and Moe

Notes on the Story

East of the Sun and West of the Moon

Like "The Pig King" (page 22), "Beauty and the Beast" (page 102), and "The Snake Prince" (page 316), Asbjørnsen and Moe's "East of the Sun and West of the Moon" is an example of the beastly bridegroom type. The age of these tales is indicated by Apuleius' second-century story of "Cupid and Psyche" (see Notes on the Story, page 31). Indeed, "East of the Sun" is particularly close to the classical tale, in which the god Cupid marries the beautiful Psyche, who loses him the instant she sees him, and undergoes torments before she can become his deified wife.

✣

This Norwegian version with its wild, white bear husband is particularly popular with contemporary storytellers, perhaps because of its feisty and steadfast heroine, and the potency of its message as an exploration of our relationship to the wondrous wild world.

THE NETTLE SPINNER

Once upon a time there lived at Quesnoy, in Flanders, a great lord whose name was Burchard, but whom the country people called Burchard the Wolf. Now Burchard had such a wicked, cruel heart, that it was whispered how he used to harness his peasants to the plough, and force them by blows from his whip to till his land with naked feet.

His wife, on the other hand, was always tender and pitiful to the poor and miserable.

Every time that she heard of another misdeed of her husband's she secretly went to repair the evil, which caused her name to be blessed throughout the whole countryside. This countess was adored as much as the count was hated.

One day when the count was out hunting he passed the door of a lonely cottage, where he saw a beautiful girl spinning hemp.

"What is your name?" he asked her.

"Renelde, my lord."

"You must get tired of staying in such a lonely place."

"I am accustomed to it, my lord, and I never get tired of it."

"That may be so; but come to the castle, and I will make you lady's maid to the countess."

"I cannot do that, my lord. I have to look after my grandmother, who is very helpless."

"Come to the castle, I tell you. I shall expect you this evening," and he went on his way.

But Renelde, who was betrothed to a young woodcutter called Guilbert, had no intention of obeying the count, and she had, besides, to take care of her grandmother.

Three days later the count again passed by.

"Why didn't you come?" he asked the pretty spinner.

"I told you, my lord, that I have to look after my grandmother."

"Come tomorrow, and I will make you lady-in-waiting to the countess," and he went on his way.

This offer produced no more effect than the other, and Renelde did not go to the castle.

"If you will only come," said the count to her when next he rode by, "I will send away the countess, and will marry you."

But two years before, when Renelde's mother was dying of a long illness, the countess had not forgotten them, but had given help when they sorely needed it. So even if the count had really wished to marry Renelde, she would always have refused.

Some weeks passed before Burchard appeared again. Renelde hoped she had got rid of him, when one day he stopped at the door, his duck gun under his arm and his game bag on his shoulder. This time Renelde was spinning not hemp, but flax.

"What are you spinning?" he asked in a rough voice.

"My wedding shift, my lord."

"You are going to be married, then?"

"Yes, my lord, by your leave." For at that time no peasant could marry without the leave of his master.

"I will give you leave on one condition. Do you see those tall nettles that grow on the tombs in the churchyard? Go and gather them, and spin them into two fine shifts. One shall be your bridal shift, and the other shall be my shroud. For you shall be married the day that I am laid in my grave." And the count turned away with a mocking laugh.

Renelde trembled. Never in all Locquignol had such a thing been heard of as the spinning of nettles. And besides, the count seemed made of iron and was very proud of his strength, often boasting that he should live to be a hundred.

Every evening, when his work was done, Guilbert came to visit his future bride. This evening he came as usual, and Renelde told him what Burchard had said.

"Would you like me to watch for the Wolf, and split his skull with a blow from my ax?"

"No," replied Renelde, "there must be no blood on my bridal bouquet. And then we must not hurt the count. Remember how good the countess was to my mother."

An old, old woman now spoke: she was the mother of Renelde's grandmother, and was more than ninety years old. All day long she sat in her chair, nodding her head and never saying a word.

"My children," she said, "all the years that I have lived in the world, I have never heard of a shift spun from nettles. But what God commands, man can do. Why should not Renelde try it?"

Renelde did try, and to her great surprise the nettles when crushed and prepared gave a good thread, soft and light and firm. Very soon she had spun the first shift, which was for her own wedding. She wove and cut it out at once, hoping that the count would not force her to begin the other. Just as she had finished sewing it, Burchard the Wolf passed by.

"Well," said he, "how are the shifts getting on?"

"Here, my lord, is my wedding garment," answered Renelde, showing him the shift, which was the finest and whitest ever seen.

The count grew pale, but he replied roughly, "Very good. Now begin the other."

The spinner set to work. As the count returned to the castle, a cold shiver passed over him, and he felt, as the saying is, that someone was walking over his grave. He tried to eat his supper, but could not; he went to bed shaking with fever. But he did not sleep, and in the morning could not manage to rise.

This sudden illness, which every instant became worse, made him very uneasy. No doubt Renelde's spinning wheel knew all about it. Was it not necessary that his body, as well as his shroud, should be ready for the burial?

The first thing Burchard did was to send to Renelde and to stop her wheel.

Renelde obeyed, and that evening Guilbert asked her: "Has the count given his consent to our marriage?"

"No," said Renelde.

"Continue your work, sweetheart. It is the only way of gaining it. You know he told you so himself."

The following morning, as soon as she had put the house in order, the girl sat down to spin. Two hours after there arrived some soldiers, and when they saw her spinning they seized her, tied her arms and legs, and carried her to the bank of the river, which was swollen by the late rains. When they reached the bank they flung her in, and watched her

"'Well,' said he, 'how are the shifts getting on?'

'Here, my lord, is my wedding garment,' answered Renelde . . ."

sink, after which they left her. But Renelde rose to the surface, and though she could not swim she struggled to land. Directly she got home she sat down and began to spin.

Again came the two soldiers to the cottage and seized the girl, carried her to the riverbank, tied a stone to her neck and flung her into the water.

The moment their backs were turned the stone untied itself. Renelde waded the ford, returned to the hut, and sat down to spin.

This time the count resolved to go to Locquignol himself; but, as he was very weak and unable to walk, he had himself borne in a litter. And still the spinner spun.

When he saw her he fired a shot at her, as he would have fired at a wild beast. The bullet rebounded without harming the spinner, who still spun on.

Burchard fell into such a violent rage that it nearly killed him. He broke the wheel into a thousand pieces, and then fell fainting on the ground. He was carried back to the castle, unconscious.

The next day the wheel was mended, and the spinner sat down to spin. Feeling that while she was spinning he was dying, the count ordered that her hands should be tied, and that they should not lose sight of her for one instant.

But the guards fell asleep, the bonds loosed themselves, and the spinner spun on.

Burchard had every nettle rooted up for three leagues round. Scarcely had they been torn from the soil when they sowed themselves afresh, and grew as you were looking at them.

They sprung up even in the well-trodden floor of the cottage, and as fast as they were uprooted the distaff gathered to itself a supply of nettles, crushed, prepared, and ready for spinning.

And every day Burchard grew worse, and watched his end approaching.

Moved by pity for her husband, the countess at last found out the cause of his illness, and entreated him to allow himself to be cured. But the count in his pride refused more than ever to give his consent to the marriage.

So the lady resolved to go without his knowledge to pray for mercy from the spinner, and in the name of Renelde's dead mother she besought her to spin no more. Renelde gave her promise, but in the evening Guilbert arrived at the cottage. Seeing that the cloth was no farther advanced than it was the evening before, he inquired the reason. Renelde confessed that the countess had begged her not to let her husband die.

"Will he consent to our marriage?"

"No."

"Let him die then."

"But what will the countess say?"

"The countess will understand that it is not your fault; the count alone is guilty of his own death."

"Let us wait a little. Perhaps his heart may be softened."

So they waited for one month, for two, for six, for a year. The spinner spun no more. The count had ceased to persecute her, but he still refused his consent to the marriage. Guilbert became impatient.

The poor girl loved him with her whole soul, and she was more unhappy than she had been before, when Burchard was only tormenting her body.

"Let us be done with it," said Guilbert.

"Wait a little still," pleaded Renelde.

But the young man grew weary. He came more rarely to Locquignol, and very soon he did not come at all. Renelde felt as if her heart would break, but she held firm. One day she met the count. She clasped her hands as if in prayer, and cried: "My lord, have mercy!"

Burchard the Wolf turned away his head and passed on.

She might have humbled his pride had she gone to her spinning wheel again, but she did nothing of the sort.

Not long after she learnt that Guilbert had left the country. He did not even come to say goodbye to her, but, all the same, she knew the day and hour of his departure, and hid herself on the road to see him once more.

When she came in she put her silent wheel into a corner, and cried for three days and three nights.

So another year went by. Then the count fell ill, and the countess supposed that Renelde, weary of waiting, had begun her spinning anew; but when she came to the cottage to see, she found the wheel silent.

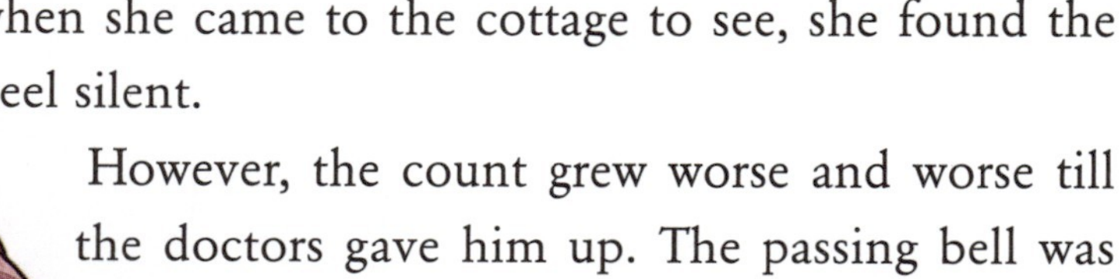

However, the count grew worse and worse till the doctors gave him up. The passing bell was rung, and he lay expecting death to come for him. But death was not so near as the doctors thought, and still he lingered. He seemed in a desperate condition, but he got neither better nor worse. He could neither live nor die; he suffered horribly, and called loudly on death to put an end to his pains.

In this extremity he remembered what he had told the little spinner long ago. If death was so slow in coming, it was because he was not ready to follow him, having no shroud for his burial.

He sent to fetch Renelde, placed her by his bedside, and ordered her at once to go on spinning his shroud.

Hardly had the spinner begun to work when the count began to feel his pains grow less.

Then at last his heart melted; he was sorry for all the evil he had done out of pride, and implored Renelde to forgive him. So Renelde forgave him, and went on spinning night and day.

When the thread of the nettles was spun she wove it with her shuttle, and then cut the shroud and began to sew it.

And as before, when she sewed the count felt his pains grow less, and the life sinking within him, and when the needle made the last stitch he gave his last sigh.

At the same hour Guilbert returned to the country, and, as he had never ceased to love Renelde, he married her eight days later.

He had lost two years of happiness, but comforted himself with thinking that his wife was a clever spinner, and, what was much more rare, a brave and good woman.

Charles Deulin

Notes on the Story

The Nettle Spinner

Charles Deulin (1827–1877) was born in the French/Flemish Escaut region. Although he moved to Paris to work as a journalist, he also wrote stories about the folklore of his native region. Inspired by the popularity of these he began to further explore and collect regional tales, and in his lifetime published three collections.

"The Nettle Spinner," a Flemish tale, was translated by Andrew Lang and published in his *Red Fairy Book* in 1890. It is a powerful and haunting story, which reminds us both of the helplessness of the peasants enduring the whims of their masters and, at the same time, the almost uncanny power which was attributed to traditional crafts. It is worth noting that spinning and storytelling have a long relationship, as the image of the spinning Fates in classical mythology exemplifies. As the English writer Marina Warner has put it: "spinning a tale, weaving a plot: the metaphors illuminate the relation."

Jack and the Beanstalk

There was once upon a time a poor widow who had an only son named Jack, and a cow named Milky-White. And all they had to live on was the milk the cow gave every morning, which they carried to the market and sold. But one morning Milky-White gave no milk, and they didn't know what to do.

"What shall we do, what shall we do?" said the widow, wringing her hands.

"Cheer up, mother, I'll go and get work somewhere," said Jack.

"We've tried that before, and nobody would take you," said his mother. "We must sell Milky-White and with the money start a shop, or something."

"All right, mother," said Jack. "It's market day today, and I'll soon sell Milky-White, and then we'll see what we can do."

So he took the cow's halter in his hand, and off he started. He hadn't gone far when he met a funny-looking old man, who said to him, "Good morning, Jack."

"Good morning to you," said Jack, and wondered how he knew his name.

"Well, Jack, and where are you off to?" asked the man.

"I'm going to market to sell our cow there."

"Oh, you look the proper sort of chap to sell cows," said the man. "I wonder if you know how many beans make five."

"Two in each hand and one in your mouth," said Jack, as sharp as a needle.

"Right you are," said the man, "and here they are, the very beans themselves," he went on, pulling out of his pocket a number of strange-looking beans. "As you are so sharp," said he, "I don't mind doing a swap with you–your cow for these beans."

"Go along," said Jack. "Wouldn't you like it?"

"Ah! You don't know what these beans are," said the man. "If you plant them overnight, by morning they grow right up to the sky."

"Really?" said Jack. "You don't say so."

"Yes, that is so. And if it doesn't turn out to be true you can have your cow back."

"Right," said Jack, and hands him over Milky-White's halter and pockets the beans.

Back goes Jack home, and as he hadn't gone very far it wasn't dusk by the time he got to his door.

"What, back already, Jack?" said his mother. "I see you haven't got Milky-White, so you've sold her. How much did you get for her?"

"You'll never guess, mother," said Jack.

"No, you don't say so. Good boy! Five pounds? Ten? Fifteen? No, it can't be twenty."

"I told you, you couldn't guess. What do you say to these beans? They're magical. Plant them overnight and–"

"What!" said Jack's mother. "Have you been such a fool, such a dolt, such an idiot, as to give away my Milky-White, the best milker in the parish, and prime beef to boot, for a set of paltry beans? Take that! Take that! Take that! And as for your precious beans, here they go out of the window, and now off with you to bed! Not a sup shall you drink, and not a bit shall you swallow this very night."

So Jack went upstairs to his little room in the attic, and sad and sorry he was, to be sure, as much for his mother's sake as for the loss of his supper. At last he dropped off to sleep. When he woke up, the room looked so funny. The sun was shining into part of it, and yet all the rest was quite dark and shady. So Jack jumped up and dressed himself and went to the window. And what do you think he saw? Why, the beans his mother had thrown out of the window into the garden had sprung up into a big beanstalk, which went up and up and up till it reached the sky. So the man spoke the truth after all.

The beanstalk grew up quite close past Jack's window, so all he had to do was to open it and give a jump onto the beanstalk, which ran up just like a big ladder. So Jack climbed, and he climbed, and he climbed, and he climbed, and he climbed, and he climbed, and he climbed till at last he reached the sky. And when he got there he found a long, broad road going as straight as a dart. So he walked along, and he walked along, and he walked along till he came to a great big tall house, and on the doorstep there was a great big tall woman.

"Good morning, ma'am," said Jack, quite polite-like. "Could you be so kind as to give me some breakfast?" For he hadn't had anything to eat, you know, the night before, and was as hungry as a hunter.

"It's breakfast you want, is it?" said the great big tall woman. "It's breakfast you'll be if you don't move off from here. My man is an ogre and there's nothing he likes better than boys broiled on toast. You'd better be moving on or he'll soon be coming."

"Oh! Please, ma'am, do give me something to eat, ma'am. I've had nothing to eat since yesterday morning, really and truly, ma'am," said Jack. "I may as well be broiled as die of hunger."

Well, the ogre's wife wasn't such a bad sort after all. So she took Jack into the kitchen, and gave him a hunk of bread and cheese and a jug of milk. But Jack hadn't half finished these when thump! Thump! Thump! The whole house began to tremble with the noise of someone coming.

"Goodness gracious me! It's my old man," said the ogre's wife. "What on earth shall I do? Come along quick and jump in here." And she bundled Jack into the oven just as the ogre came in.

He was a big one, to be sure. At his belt he had three calves strung up by the heels, and he unhooked them and threw them down on the table and said, "Here, wife, broil me a couple of these for breakfast. Ah! What's this I smell?

> Fee-fi-fo-fum,
> I smell the blood of an Englishman,
> Be he alive, or be he dead,
> I'll grind his bones to make my bread."

"Nonsense, dear," said his wife. "You're dreaming. Or perhaps you smell the scraps of that little boy you liked so much for yesterday's dinner. Here, you go and have a wash and tidy up, and by the time you come back your breakfast will be ready for you."

So off the ogre went, and Jack was just going to jump out of the oven and run away when the woman told him not. "Wait till he's asleep," said she, "he always has a snooze after breakfast."

Well, the ogre had his breakfast, and after that he went to a big chest and took out a couple of bags of gold, and down he sat and counted till at last his head began to nod and he began to snore till the whole house shook again. Then Jack crept out on tiptoe from his oven, and as he was passing the ogre, he took one of the bags of gold under his arm, and off he ran till he came to the beanstalk, and then he threw down the bag of gold, which, of course, fell into his mother's garden, and then he climbed down, and climbed down, till at last he got home, and told his mother and showed her the gold, and said, "Well, mother, wasn't I right about the beans? They are really magical, you see."

So they lived on the bag of gold for some time, but at last they came to the end of it, and Jack made up his mind to try his luck once more up at the top of the beanstalk. So one fine morning he rose up early, and got onto the beanstalk, and he climbed, and he climbed, and he climbed, and he climbed, and he climbed, and he climbed till at last he came out onto the road again and up to the great big tall house he had been to before. There, sure enough, was the great big tall woman a-standing on the doorstep.

"Good morning, ma'am," said Jack, as bold as brass, "could you be so good as to give me something to eat?"

"Go away, my boy," said the big tall woman, "or else my man will eat you for breakfast. But aren't you the youngster who came here once before? Do you know, that day my man missed one of his bags of gold."

"That's strange, ma'am," said Jack, "I daresay I could tell you something about that, but I'm so hungry I can't speak till I've eaten."

Well, the big tall woman was that curious that she took him in and gave him something to eat. But he had scarcely begun munching it as slowly as he could when thump, thump! They heard the giant's footsteps, and his wife hid Jack away in the oven.

All happened as it did before. In came the ogre as he did before, said, "Fee-fi-fo-fum," and had his breakfast of three broiled oxen.

Then he said, "Wife, bring me the hen that lays the golden eggs." So she brought it, and the ogre said, "Lay," and it laid an egg all of gold. And then the ogre began to nod his head, and to snore till the house shook.

Then Jack crept out of the oven on tiptoe and caught hold of the golden hen, and was off before you could say "Jack Robinson." But this time the hen gave a cackle, which woke the ogre, and just as Jack got out of the house he heard him calling, "Wife, what have you done with my golden hen?"

And the wife said, "Why, my dear?"

But that was all Jack heard, for he rushed off to the beanstalk and climbed down like a house on fire. And when he got home he showed his mother the wonderful hen, and said, "Lay" to it; and it laid a golden egg every time he said, "Lay."

"Down climbed Jack,

and after him climbed the ogre."

Well, Jack was not content, and it wasn't very long before he determined to have another try at his luck up there at the top of the beanstalk. So one fine morning he got up early and went up to the beanstalk, and he climbed, and he climbed, and he climbed, and he climbed till he got to the top.

But this time he knew better than to go straight to the ogre's house. And when he got near it, he waited behind a bush till he saw the ogre's wife come out with a pail to get some water, and then he crept into the house and got into the copper. He hadn't been there long when he heard thump, thump, thump, as before, and in came the ogre and his wife.

"Fee-fi-fo-fum, I smell the blood of an Englishman," cried out the ogre. "I smell him, wife, I smell him."

"Do you, my dearie?" said the ogre's wife. "Then, if it's that little rogue that stole your gold and the hen that laid the golden eggs he's sure to have got into the oven." And they both rushed to the oven.

But Jack wasn't there, luckily, and the ogre's wife said, "There you are again with your fee-fi-fo-fum. Why, of course, it's the laddie you caught last night that I've broiled for your breakfast. How forgetful I am, and how careless you are not to tell the difference between a live 'un and a dead 'un after all these years."

So the ogre sat down to the breakfast and ate it, but every now and then he would mutter, "Well, I could have sworn–" and he'd get up and search the pantry and the cupboards and everything, only, luckily, he didn't think of the copper.

After breakfast was over, the ogre called out, "Wife, wife, bring me my golden harp."

So she brought it and put it on the table before him. Then he said, "Sing!" and the golden harp sang most beautifully. And it went on singing till the ogre fell asleep, and commenced to snore like thunder. Then Jack lifted up the copper lid very quietly and got down like a mouse and crept on hands and knees till he came to the table, when up he crawled, caught hold of the golden harp and dashed with it toward the door.

But the harp called out quite loud, "Master! Master!" and the ogre woke up just in time to see Jack running off with his harp.

Jack ran as fast as he could, and the ogre came rushing after, and would soon have caught him, only Jack had a start and dodged him a bit and knew where he was going. When he got to the beanstalk the ogre was not more than twenty yards away when suddenly he saw Jack disappear like, and when he came to the end of the road he saw Jack underneath climbing down for dear life. Well, the ogre didn't like trusting himself to such a ladder, and he stood and waited, so Jack got another start.

But just then the harp cried out, "Master! Master!" and the ogre swung himself down onto the beanstalk, which shook with his weight. Down climbed Jack, and after him climbed the ogre.

By this time Jack had climbed down and climbed down and climbed down till he was very nearly home. So he called out, "Mother! Mother! Bring me an ax, bring me an ax." And his mother came rushing out with the ax in her hand, but when she came to the beanstalk she stood stock still with fright, for there she saw the ogre just coming down with his legs just through the clouds.

But Jack jumped down and got hold of the ax and gave a chop at the beanstalk, which cut it almost half in two. The ogre felt the beanstalk shake and quiver, so he stopped to see what was the matter. Then Jack gave another chop with the ax, and the beanstalk was cut in two and began to topple over. Then the ogre fell down and broke his crown, and the beanstalk came toppling after.

Then Jack showed his mother his golden harp, and what with showing that and selling the golden eggs, Jack and his mother became very rich, and he married a great princess, and they lived happily ever after.

Joseph Jacobs

Notes on the Story

Jack and the Beanstalk

"Who says that English folk have no fairy tales of their own?" wrote Joseph Jacobs (1854–1916) in the preface to his *English Fairy Tales*. Although he was born not in England but Australia, Jacobs published two collections of English folklore, as well as Indian, Celtic, and European fairy tales. Influenced by the Grimms, Jacobs, who addressed his tales to children and folklorists alike, was criticized for his substantial edits. In response, he likened himself to "any other story-teller" who makes the tale his own.

Jacobs certainly respected his audience, as exemplified in "Jack and the Beanstalk." An earlier version of 1807 had inserted a good fairy into this traditional trickster tale, to inform Jack that the ogre had killed his own father, and to translate Jack's thieving and ogre-murder into righteous vengeance. Jacobs deleted the fairy, and dismissed the idea that the tale might encourage theft in children, writing, "I have had greater confidence in my young friends."

Childe Rowland

"Childe Rowland and his brothers twain
Were playing at the ball,
And there was their sister Burd Ellen
In the midst, among them all.

Childe Rowland kicked it with his foot
And caught it with his knee;
At last as he plunged among them all
O'er the church he made it flee.

Burd Ellen round about the aisle
To seek the ball is gone,
But long they waited, and longer still,
And she came not back again.

They sought her east, they sought her west,
They sought her up and down,
And woe were the hearts of those brethren,
For she was not to be found."

So at last her eldest brother went to the Warlock Merlin and told him all about the case, and asked him if he knew where Burd Ellen was.

"The fair Burd Ellen," said the Warlock Merlin, "must have been carried off by the fairies, because she went round the church 'widdershins'–the opposite way to the sun. She is now in the Dark Tower of the King of Elfland; it would take the boldest knight in Christendom to bring her back."

"If it is possible to bring her back," said her brother, "I'll do it, or perish in the attempt."

"Possible it is," said the Warlock Merlin, "but woe to the man or mother's son that attempts it, if he is not well taught beforehand what he is to do."

The eldest brother of Burd Ellen was not to be put off, by any fear of danger, from attempting to get her back, so he begged the Warlock Merlin to tell him what he should do, and what he should not do, in going to seek his sister. And after he had been taught, and had repeated his lesson, he set out for Elfland.

But long they waited, and longer still,
With doubt and muckle pain,
But woe were the hearts of his brethren,
For he came not back again.

Then the second brother got sick and tired of waiting, and he went to the Warlock Merlin and asked him the same as his brother. So he set out to find Burd Ellen.

But long they waited, and longer still,
With muckle doubt and pain,
And woe were his mother's and brother's heart,
For he came not back again.

And when they had waited and waited a good long time, Childe Rowland, the youngest of Burd Ellen's brothers, wished to go, and went to his mother, the good queen, to ask her to let him go. But she would not at first, for he was the last of her children she now had, and if he was lost, all would be lost. But he begged, and he begged, till at last the good queen let him go, and gave him his father's good brand that never struck in vain. And as she girt it round his waist, she said the spell that would give it victory.

So Childe Rowland said goodbye to the good queen, his mother, and went to the cave of the Warlock Merlin.

"Once more, and but once more," he said to the Warlock, "tell how man or mother's son may rescue Burd Ellen and her brothers twain."

"Well, my son," said the Warlock Merlin, "there are but two things, simple they may seem, but hard they are to do. One thing to do, and one thing not to do. And the thing to do is this: after you have entered the land of Fairy, whoever speaks to you, till you meet the Burd Ellen, you must out with your father's brand and off with their head. And what you've not to do is this: bite no bit, and drink no drop, however hungry or thirsty you be; drink a drop, or bite a bit, while in Elfland you be and never will you see Middle Earth again."

So Childe Rowland said the two things over and over again, till he knew them by heart, and he thanked the Warlock Merlin and went on his way. And he went along, and along, and along, and still further along, till he came to the horse-herd of the King of Elfland feeding his horses. These he knew by their fiery eyes, and knew that he was at last in the land of Fairy.

"Can you tell me," said Childe Rowland to the horse-herd, "where the King of Elfland's Dark Tower is?"

"I cannot tell you," said the horse-herd, "but go on a little further and you will come to the cow-herd, and he, maybe, can tell you."

Then, without a word more, Childe Rowland drew the good brand that never struck in vain, and off went the horse-herd's head, and Childe Rowland went on further, till he came to the cow-herd, and asked him the same question.

"I can't tell you," said he, "but go on a little farther, and you will come to the hen-wife, and she is sure to know." Then Childe Rowland out with his good brand, that never struck in vain, and off went the cow-herd's head. And he went on a little further, till he came to an old woman in a gray cloak, and he asked her if she knew where the Dark Tower of the King of Elfland was.

"Go on a little further," said the hen-wife, "till you come to a round green hill, surrounded with terrace-rings, from the bottom to the top; go round it three times, widdershins, and each time say:

'Open, door! Open, door!
And let me come in.'

And the third time the door will open, and you may go in."

And Childe Rowland was just going on, when he remembered what he had to do; so he out with the good brand, that never struck in vain, and off went the hen-wife's head.

Then he went on, and on, and on, till he came to the round green hill with the terrace-rings from top to bottom, and he went round it three times, widdershins, saying each time:

"Open, door! Open, door!
And let me come in."

And the third time the door did open, and he went in, and it closed with a click, and Childe Rowland was left in the dark.

It was not exactly dark, but a kind of twilight or gloaming. There were neither windows nor candles, and he could not make out where the twilight came from, if not through the walls and roof. These were rough arches made of a transparent rock, encrusted with sheep silver and rock spar, and other bright stones. But though it was rock, the air was quite warm, as it always is in Elfland. So he went through this passage till at last he came to two wide and high folding doors that stood ajar. And when he opened them, there he saw a most wonderful and glorious sight. A large and spacious hall, so large that it seemed to be as long, and as broad, as the green hill itself. The roof was supported by fine pillars, so large and lofty, that the pillars of a cathedral were as nothing to them. They were all of gold and silver, with fretted work, and between them and around them, wreaths of flowers, composed of what do you think? Why, of diamonds and emeralds, and all manner of precious stones. And the very keystones of the arches had for ornaments clusters of diamonds and rubies and pearls, and other precious stones. And all these arches met in the middle of the roof, and just there, hung by a gold chain, an immense lamp made out of one big pearl hollowed out and quite transparent. And in the middle of this was a big, huge carbuncle, which kept spinning round and round, and this was what gave light by its rays to the whole hall, which seemed as if the setting sun was shining on it.

The hall was furnished in a manner equally grand, and at one end of it was a glorious couch of velvet, silk, and gold, and there sat Burd Ellen, combing her golden hair with a silver comb. And when she saw Childe Rowland she stood up and said:

"God pity you, poor luckless fool,
What have you here to do?

Hear you this, my youngest brother,
Why didn't you bide at home?
Had you a hundred thousand lives
You couldn't spare any a one.

But sit you down; but woe, O, woe,
That ever you were born,
For come the King of Elfland in,
Your fortune is forlorn."

Then they sat down together, and Childe Rowland told her all that he had done, and she told him how their two brothers had reached the Dark Tower, but had been enchanted by the King of Elfland, and lay there entombed as if dead. And then after they had talked a little longer Childe Rowland began to feel hungry from his long travels, and told his sister Burd Ellen how hungry he was and asked for some food, forgetting all about the Warlock Merlin's warning.

Burd Ellen looked at Childe Rowland sadly, and shook her head, but she was under a spell, and could not warn him. So she rose up, and went out, and soon brought back a golden basin full of bread and milk. Childe Rowland was just going to raise it to his lips, when he looked at his sister and remembered why he had come all that way. So he dashed the bowl to the ground, and said: "Not a sup will I swallow, nor a bit will I bite, till Burd Ellen is set free."

"'Fee-fi-fo-fum,

I smell the blood of a Christian man . . .'"

Just at that moment they heard the noise of someone approaching, and a loud voice was heard saying:

"Fee-fi-fo-fum,
I smell the blood of a Christian man,
Be he dead, be he living, with my brand,
I'll dash his brains from his brain-pan."

And then the folding doors of the hall were burst open, and the King of Elfland rushed in.

"Strike then, Bogle, if you dare," shouted out Childe Rowland, and rushed to meet him with his good brand that never yet did fail. They fought, and they fought, and they fought, till Childe Rowland beat the King of Elfland down on to his knees, and caused him to yield and beg for mercy.

"I grant you mercy," said Childe Rowland, "release my sister from your spells and raise my brothers to life, and let us all go free, and you shall be spared."

"I agree," said the Elfin king, and rising up he went to a chest from which he took a phial filled with a blood-red liquor. With this he anointed the ears, eyelids, nostrils, lips, and fingertips of the two brothers, and they sprang at once into life, and declared that their souls had been away, but had now returned. The Elfin king then said some words to Burd Ellen, and she was disenchanted, and they all four passed out of the hall, through the long passage, and turned their backs on the Dark Tower, never to return again. And they reached home, and the good queen, their mother, and Burd Ellen never went round a church widdershins again.

Joseph Jacobs

Notes on the Story

CHILDE ROWLAND

Jacobs borrowed the tale "Childe Rowland" from the collections of the Scotsman Robert Jamieson, who heard it from "a tailor in his youth." Its combination of verse and prose suggest origins in Scottish ballads. "Childe Rowland" contains many fairy-tale familiarities, including the injunction not to eat fairy food, as well as the success of the youngest son where his siblings have failed. However, it also contains shocking elements, particularly the killing of those who aid Rowland upon the way. While the hen-wife, cow-herd, and horse-herd may be interpreted as incarnations of the Elfland king who must be eliminated, their seemingly undeserved deaths act as a startling exception to the folkloric law of reciprocity between hero and guide.

While the tale itself is not well known, reference to the questing knight and his dark tower was made by Shakespeare in *King Lear,* and the powerful image has since inspired authors from Robert Browning to Louis MacNeice to Stephen King.

Connla and the Fairy Maiden

Connla of the Fiery Hair was son of Conn of the Hundred Fights. One day as he stood by the side of his father on the height of Usna, he saw a maiden clad in strange attire coming toward him.

"Whence come you, maiden?" said Connla.

"I come from the Plains of the Ever Living," she said, "there where there is neither death nor sin. There we keep holiday always, nor need we help from any in our joy. And in all our pleasure we have no strife. And because we have our homes in the round green hills, men call us the Hill Folk."

The king and all with him wondered much to hear a voice when they saw no one. For save Connla alone, none saw the Fairy Maiden.

"To whom are you talking, my son?" said Conn the king.

Then the maiden answered, "Connla speaks to a young, fair maid, whom neither death nor old age awaits. I love Connla, and now I call him away to the Plain of Pleasure, Moy Mell, where Boadag is king for ever, nor has there been complaint or sorrow in that land since he has held the kingship. Oh, come with me, Connla of the Fiery Hair, ruddy as the dawn with your tawny skin. A fairy crown awaits you to grace thy comely face and royal form. Come, and never shall your comeliness fade, nor your youth, till the last awful Day of Judgment."

The king in fear at what the maiden said, which he heard though he could not see her, called aloud to his Druid, Coran by name.

"Oh, Coran of the many spells," he said, "and of the cunning magic, I call upon your aid. A task is upon me too great for all my skill and wit, greater than any laid upon me since I seized the kingship. A maiden unseen has met us, and by her power would take from me my dear, my comely son. If you help not, he will be taken from your king by woman's wiles and witchery."

Then Coran the Druid stood forth and chanted his spells toward the spot where the maiden's voice had been heard. And none heard her voice again, nor could Connla see her longer. Only as she vanished before the Druid's mighty spell, she threw an apple to Connla.

For a whole month from that day Connla would take nothing, either to eat or to drink, save only from that apple. But as he ate it grew again and always kept whole. And all the while there grew within him a mighty yearning and longing after the maiden he had seen.

But when the last day of the month of waiting came, Connla stood by the side of the king his father on the Plain of Arcomin, and again he saw the maiden come toward him, and again she spoke to him.

"'Tis a glorious place, truly, that Connla holds among short-lived mortals awaiting the day of death. But now the folk of life, the ever-living ones, beg and bid you come to Moy Mell, the Plain of Pleasure, for they have learnt to know you, seeing you in your home among your dear ones."

When Conn the king heard the maiden's voice he called to his men aloud and said: "Summon swift my Druid Coran, for I see she has again this day the power of speech."

Then the maiden said, "Oh, mighty Conn, fighter of a hundred fights, the Druid's power is little loved; it has little honor in the mighty land, peopled with so many of the upright. When the Law will come, it will do away with the Druid's magic spells that come from the lips of the false black demon."

"Connla of the Fiery Hair rushed away from them

and sprang into the curragh . . ."

Then Conn the king observed that since the maiden came, Connla his son spoke to none that spoke to him. So Conn of the Hundred Fights said to him, "Is it to your mind what the woman says, my son?"

"'Tis hard upon me," then said Connla, "I love my own folk above all things; but yet, but yet a longing seizes me for the maiden."

When the maiden heard this, she answered and said: "The ocean is not so strong as the waves of your longing. Come with me in my curragh, the gleaming, and straight-gliding crystal canoe. Soon we can reach Boadag's realm. I see the bright sun sink; yet far as it is, we can reach it before dark. There is, too, another land worthy of your journey, a land joyous to all that seek it. Only wives and maidens dwell there. If you will, we can seek it and live there alone together in joy."

When the maiden ceased to speak, Connla of the Fiery Hair rushed away from them and sprang into the curragh, the gleaming, straight-gliding crystal canoe. And then they all, king and court, saw it glide away over the bright sea toward the setting sun. Away and away, till eye could see it no longer, and Connla and the Fairy Maiden went their way on the sea, and were no more seen, nor did any know where they came.

Joseph Jacobs

Notes on the Story

Connla and the Fairy Maiden

Published in Jacobs' *Celtic Fairy Tales*, this is an old Irish tale of love between fairy and mortal man. Jacobs, who dates it to the life of the historical King Conn during the second century, argues that it is "the earliest fairy tale of modern Europe."

Tales of love between fairy and mortal are numerous. In some, such as the ballad of "Tam Lin," the human is rescued by his mortal lover. In others, the human lives blissfully in fairy land, and tragedy only occurs on his return to the mortal realm. This is the case in the tale of Oisin, in which three years pass as three centuries, and when Oisin's feet touch the mortal ground he is assailed with decrepit age (see also "Rip Van Winkle," page 251). However, no conclusion is given here, and for all we know, Connla lives with the Fairy Maiden upon the Plain of Pleasure "till the last awful Day of Judgment."

Brewery of Eggshells

Twt y Cymrws is a certain shepherd's cottage in Treneglwys. It is so called because of the strange strife that occurred there. In this cottage there once lived a man and his wife, and they had twins whom the woman nursed tenderly. One day she was called away to the house of a neighbor at some distance. She did not much like going and leaving her little ones all alone in a solitary house, especially as she had heard tell of the good folk haunting the neighborhood.

Well, she went and came back as soon as she could, but on her way back she was frightened to see some old elves of the blue petticoat crossing her path though it was midday. She rushed home, but found her two little ones in the cradle and everything seemed as it was before.

But after a time the good people began to suspect that something was wrong, for the twins didn't grow at all.

The man said: "They're not ours."

The woman said: "Whose else should they be?"

And so arose the great strife so that the neighbors named the cottage after it. It made the woman very sad, so one evening she made up her mind to go and see the Wise Man of Llanidloes, for he knew everything and would advise her what to do.

So she went to Llanidloes and told the case to the Wise Man. Now there was soon to be a harvest of rye and oats, so the Wise Man said to her, "When you are getting dinner for the reapers, clear out the shell of a hen's egg and boil some potage in it, and then take it to the door as if you meant it as a dinner for the reapers. Then listen if the twins say anything. If you hear them speaking of things beyond the understanding of children, go back and take them up and throw them into the waters of Lake Elvyn. But if you don't hear anything remarkable, do them no injury."

So when the day of the harvest came the woman did all that the Wise Man ordered, and put the eggshell on the fire and took it off and carried it to the door, and there she stood and listened. Then she heard one of the children say to the other:

"Acorn before oak I knew,
An egg before a hen,
But I never heard of an eggshell brew
A dinner for harvest men."

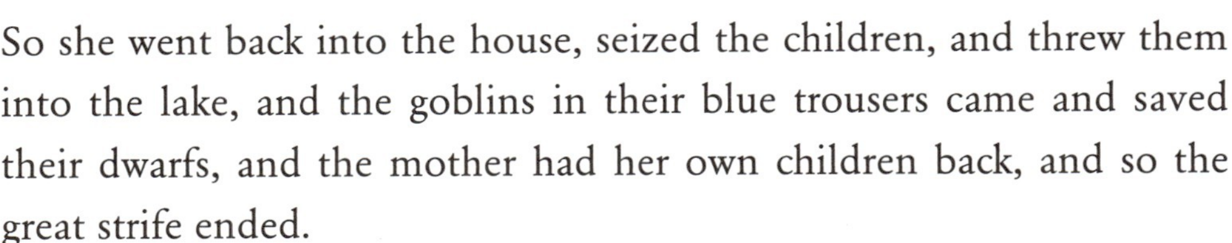

So she went back into the house, seized the children, and threw them into the lake, and the goblins in their blue trousers came and saved their dwarfs, and the mother had her own children back, and so the great strife ended.

Joseph Jacobs

Notes on the Story

Brewery of Eggshells

"Brewery of Eggshells" was published in Jacobs' collection called *Celtic Fairy Tales*. Representing an ancient and pervasive belief that infants were in danger from the "other folk," changeling tales such as this appear across the world. This is a comparatively gentle tale in which the imposter infants are tricked into revealing themselves by the uncanny nature of their speech; a similar version involves tricking a changeling into laughing at water boiled in a shell, representing the power of laughter to diffuse uncanny powers. Other versions suggest far more violent attentions to the troublesome child and make for unsettling reading.

Perhaps fictionalized responses to the complexities of alienation that may develop between parent and child, changeling tales have been variously interpreted, from justifications of child abuse to admonitions to neglectful parents to pay attention to their children, in case they are stolen away.

Dinewan the Emu and Goomblegubbon the Bustard

Dinewan the emu, being the largest bird, was acknowledged as king by the other birds. The Goomblegubbons, the bustards, were jealous of the Dinewans. Goomblegubbon, the mother, was particularly jealous of the Dinewan mother. She would watch with envy the high flight of the Dinewans, and their swift running. And she always fancied that the Dinewan mother flaunted her superiority in her face, for whenever Dinewan alighted near Goomblegubbon, after a long, high flight, she would flap her big wings and begin booing in her pride, not the loud booing of the male bird, but a little, triumphant, satisfied booing noise of her own, which never failed to irritate Goomblegubbon when she heard it.

Goomblegubbon used to wonder how she could put an end to Dinewan's supremacy. She decided that she would only be able to do so by injuring her wings and checking her power of flight. But how was she to do this? She knew she would gain nothing by having a quarrel with Dinewan and fighting her, for no Goomblegubbon would stand any chance against a Dinewan. There was evidently nothing to be gained by an open fight. She would have to effect her end by cunning.

One day, when Goomblegubbon saw in the distance Dinewan coming toward her, she squatted down and doubled in her wings in

"'But you have wings,' said Dinewan.

'No, I have no wings.'"

such a way as to look as if she had none. After Dinewan had been talking to her for some time, Goomblegubbon said: "Why do you not imitate me and do without wings? Every bird flies. The Dinewans, to be the king of birds, should do without wings. When all the birds see that I can do without wings, they will think I am the cleverest bird and they will make a Goomblegubbon king."

"But you have wings," said Dinewan.

"No, I have no wings." And indeed she looked as if her words were true, so well were her wings hidden, as she squatted in the grass. Dinewan went away after awhile, and thought much of what she had heard. She talked it all over with her mate, who was as disturbed as she was. They made up their minds that it would never do to let the Goomblegubbons reign in their stead, even if they had to lose their wings to save their kingship.

At length they decided on the sacrifice of their wings. The Dinewan mother showed the example by persuading her mate to cut off hers with a combo or stone tomahawk, and then she did the same to his. As soon as the operations were over, the Dinewan mother lost no time in letting Goomblegubbon know what they had done. She ran swiftly down to the plain on which she had left Goomblegubbon, and, finding her still squatting there, she said: "See, I have followed your example. I have now no wings. They are cut off."

"Ha! Ha! Ha!" laughed Goomblegubbon, jumping up and dancing round with joy at the success of her plot. She spread out her wings, flapped them, and said: "I have taken you in, old stumpy wings. I have my wings yet. You are fine birds, you Dinewans, to be chosen kings, when you are so easily taken in. Ha! Ha! Ha!" And, laughing derisively, Goomblegubbon flapped her wings right in front of Dinewan, who rushed toward her to chastise her treachery. But Goomblegubbon flew away, and, alas, the now wingless Dinewan could not follow her.

Brooding over her wrongs, Dinewan walked away, vowing she would be revenged. But how? That was the question which she and her mate failed to answer for some time. At length the Dinewan mother thought of a plan and prepared at once to execute it. She hid all her young Dinewans but two, under a big salt bush. Then she walked off to the Goomblegubbons' plain with the two young ones following her. As she walked off the Morilla Ridge, where her home was, on to the plain, she saw Goomblegubbon out feeding with her twelve young ones.

After exchanging a few remarks in a friendly manner with Goomblegubbon, she said to her, "Why do you not imitate me and only have two children? Twelve are too many to feed. If you keep so many they will never grow into big birds like the Dinewans. The food that would make big birds of two would only starve twelve."

Goomblegubbon said nothing, but she thought it might be so. It was impossible to deny that the young Dinewans were much bigger than the young Goomblegubbons, and, discontentedly, Goomblegubbon walked away, wondering whether the smallness of her young ones was owing to the number of them being so much greater than that of the Dinewans. It would be grand, she thought, to grow as big as the Dinewans. But she remembered the trick she had played on Dinewan, and she thought that perhaps she was being fooled in her turn. She looked back to where the Dinewans fed, and as she saw how much bigger the two young ones were than any of hers, once more mad envy of Dinewan possessed her. She determined she would not be outdone. Rather would she kill all her young ones but two.

She said, "The Dinewans shall not be the king birds of the plains. The Goomblegubbons shall replace them. They shall grow as big as the Dinewans, and shall keep their wings and fly, which now the Dinewans cannot do."

And straightaway Goomblegubbon killed all her young ones but two. Then back she came to where the Dinewans were still feeding.

When Dinewan saw her coming and noticed she had only two young ones with her, she called out: "Where are all your young ones?"

Goomblegubbon answered, "I have killed them, and have only two left. Those will have plenty to eat now, and will soon grow as big as your young ones."

"You cruel mother to kill your children. You greedy mother. Why, I have twelve children and I find food for them all. I would not kill one for anything, not even if by so doing I could get back my wings. There is plenty for all. Look at the emu bush how it covers itself with berries to feed my big family. See how the grasshoppers come hopping round, so that we can catch them and fatten on them."

"But you have only two children."

"I have twelve. I will go and bring them to show you." Dinewan ran off to her salt bush where she had hidden her ten young ones. Soon she was to be seen coming back. Running with her neck stretched forward, her head thrown back with pride, and the feathers of her boobootella swinging as she ran, booming out the while her queer throat noise, the Dinewan song of joy, the pretty, soft-looking little ones with their zebra-striped skins, running beside her whistling their baby Dinewan note.

When Dinewan reached the place where Goomblegubbon was, she stopped her booing and said in a solemn tone, "Now you see my words are true, I have twelve young ones, as I said. You can gaze at my loved ones and think of your poor murdered children. And while you do so, I will tell you the fate of your descendants for ever. By trickery and deceit you lost the Dinewans their wings, and now for evermore, as long as a Dinewan has no wings, so long shall a Goomblegubbon lay only two eggs and have only two young ones. We are quits now. You have your wings and I my children."

And ever since that time a Dinewan, or emu, has had no wings, and a Goomblegubbon, or bustard of the plains, has laid only two eggs in a season.

Mrs. K. L. Parker

Notes on the Story

Dinewan the Emu and Goomblegubbon the Bustard

In 1897, Mrs. K. L. Parker published a book called *Australian Legendary Tales* that contained thirty stories from the Aboriginal dreamtime tradition. Dreamtime tales are animist stories, explaining how the world became the way it is. The tales in *Australian Legendary Tales* come from the Narran or Noongahburrah tribe, although Parker was familiar with many Aboriginal tribes, all of which have dreamtime tales. Through her story collections, Parker wanted to help preserve the folklore and customs that she believed were at risk due to the arrival of colonists in Australia.

The tale of Dinewan and Goomblegubbon describes how the emu became flightless and how the bustards, or bush turkeys, came to have only two eggs in the nest at one time. Unlike Aesop's fables, which use animals to transmit moral lessons, the dreamtime tales are more like creation myths or pourquoi (why) tales. Similar tales can be found in Rudyard Kipling's *Just So Stories*, published in 1902.

Rip Van Winkle

The story of Rip Van Winkle is the best known of American legends. Rip was a real person, and the Van Winkles were a considerable family in their day. An idle, good-natured, happy-go-lucky fellow, he lived, presumably, in the village of Catskill, and began his long sleep in 1769. His wife was a shrew, and to escape her abuse Rip often took his dog and gun and roamed away to the Catskills, nine miles westward, where he lounged or hunted, as the humor seized him. It was on a September evening, during a jaunt on South Mountain, that he met a stubby, silent man, of goodly girth, his round head topped with a steeple hat, the skirts of his belted coat and flaps of his petticoat trousers meeting at the tops of heavy boots, and the face–ugh!–green and ghastly, with unmoving eyes that glimmered in the twilight like phosphorus. The dwarf carried a keg, and on receiving an indication in a sign, that he would like Rip to relieve him of it, that cheerful vagabond shouldered it and marched on up the mountain.

At nightfall they emerged on a little plateau where a score of men in the garb of long ago, with faces like that of Rip's guide, and equally still and speechless, were playing bowls with great solemnity, the balls sometimes rolling over the plateau's edge and rumbling down the rocks with a boom like thunder. A cloaked and snowy-bearded figure, watching aloof, turned like the others, and gazed uncomfortably at

the visitor who now came blundering in among them. Rip was at first for making off, but the sinister glare in the circle of eyes took the run out of his legs, and he was not displeased when they signed to him to tap the keg and join in a draught of the ripest schnapps that ever he had tasted—and he knew the flavor of every brand in Catskill. While these strange men grew no more genial with the passing of the flagons, Rip was pervaded by a satisfying glow; then, overcome by sleepiness and resting his head on a stone, he stretched his tired legs out and fell to dreaming.

Morning. Sunlight and leaf shadow were dappled over the earth when he awoke, and rising stiffly from his bed, with pains in his bones, he reached for his gun. The already venerable implement was so far gone with rot and rust that it fell to pieces in his hand, and looking down at the fragments of it, he saw that his clothes were dropping from his body in rags and mold, while a white beard flowed over his breast. Puzzled and alarmed, shaking his head ruefully as he recalled the silent carouse, he hobbled down the mountain as fast as he could because of the grip of the rheumatism on his knees and elbows, and entered his native village. What! Was this Catskill? Was this the place that he left yesterday? Had all these houses sprung up overnight, and these streets been pushed across the meadows in a day? The people, too: where were his friends? The children who had romped with him, the rotund drinkers whom he had left cooling their hot noses in pewter pots at the tavern door, the dogs that used to bark a welcome, recognizing in him a kindred spirit of vagrancy: where were they?

And his wife, whose athletic arm and agile tongue had half disposed him to linger in the mountains, how happened it that she was not awaiting him at the gate? But gate there was none in the familiar place: an unfenced yard of weeds and ruined foundation wall were there. Rip's home was gone. The idlers jeered at his bent, lean form, his snarl of beard and hair, his disreputable dress, his look of grieved

"He met a stubby, silent man, of goodly girth,

his round head topped with a steeple hat . . ."

astonishment. He stopped, instinctively, at the tavern, for he knew that place in spite of its new sign: an officer in blue regimentals and a cocked hat replacing the crimson George III of his recollection, and labeled "General Washington." There was a quick gathering of ne'er-do-wells, of tavern-haunters and gaping apprentices, about him, and though their faces were strange and their manners rude, he made bold to ask if they knew such and such of his friends.

"Nick Vedder? He's dead and gone these eighteen years."

"Brom Dutcher? He joined the army and was killed at Stony Point."

"Van Brummel? He, too, went to the war, and is in Congress now."

"And Rip Van Winkle?"

"Yes, he's here. That's him yonder."

And to Rip's utter confusion he saw before him a counterpart of himself, as young, lazy, ragged, and easy-natured as he remembered himself to be, yesterday—or, was it yesterday?

"That's young Rip," continued his informer. "His father was Rip Van Winkle, too, but he went to the mountains twenty years ago and never came back. He probably fell over a cliff, or was carried off by Indians, or eaten by bears."

Twenty years ago! Truly, it was so. Rip had slept for twenty years without awaking. He had left a peaceful colonial village; he returned to a bustling republican town. How he eventually found, among the oldest inhabitants, some who admitted that they knew him; how he found a comfortable home with his married daughter and the son who took after him so kindly; how he recovered from the effect of the tidings that his wife had died of apoplexy, in a quarrel; how he resumed his seat at the tavern tap and smoked long pipes and told long yarns for the rest of his days, were matters of record up to the beginning of this century.

And a strange story Rip had to tell, for he had served as cup-bearer to the dead crew of the Half Moon. He had quaffed a cup of Hollands with no other than Henry Hudson himself. Some say that Hudson's spirit made its home amid these hills, that it may look into the lovely valley that he discovered; but others hold that every twenty years he and his men assemble for a revel in the mountains that so charmed them when first seen swelling against the western heavens. And the liquor they drink on this night has the bane of throwing any mortal who lips it into a slumber whence nothing can arouse him until the day dawns when the crew shall meet again. As you climb the east front of the mountains by the old carriage road, you pass, halfway up the height, the stone that Rip Van Winkle slept on, and may see that it is slightly hollowed by his form. The ghostly revelers are due in the Catskills in 1909, and let all tourists who are among the mountains in September of that year beware of accepting liquor from strangers.

Charles M. Skinner

Notes on the Story

Rip Van Winkle

The American writer Charles M. Skinner (1852–1907) published one of the first collections of North American folklore, *Myths and Legends of Our Own Land* (1896). His stories came from many regions of the United States, showcasing American folklore as its own genre and style.

"Rip Van Winkle" was first published as a short story by Washington Irving in 1819, but has its roots in the Greek tale of Epimenides (Erasmus, 1496) and the German folktale of "Peter Klaus." Irving made the tale truly American by placing it in the Catskill Mountains, describing the Dutch immigrants of the area, and referencing the American Revolution. Rip's magical sleep is part of a belief that years pass differently in fairyland, causing the protagonist to lose track of time. An example is the legend of Herla, King of the Britons, who attended the dwarf king's daughter's wedding and arrived home two hundred years later.

THE CULPRIT FAY

The wood-tick's drum summons the elves at the noon of night on Crow Nest top, and, clambering out of their flower-cup beds and hammocks of cobweb, they fly to the meeting, not to frolic about the grass or banquet at the mushroom table, but to hear sentence passed on the fay who, forgetting his vow of chastity, has loved an earthly maid.

From his throne under a canopy of tulip petals, borne on pillars of shell, the king commands silence, and with severe eye but softened voice he tells the culprit that, while he has scorned the royal decree, he has saved himself from the extreme penalty, of imprisonment in walnut shells and cobweb dungeons, by loving a maid who is gentle and pure. So it shall be enough if he will go down to the Hudson and seize a drop from the bow of mist that a sturgeon leaves when he makes his leap; and after, to kindle his darkened flame-wood lamp at a meteor spark.

The fairy bows, and without a word slowly descends the rocky steep, for his wing is soiled and has lost its power. But once at the river, he tugs with all his might at a mussel shell till he has it afloat. Then, leaping in, he paddles out with a strong grass-blade till he comes to the spot where the sturgeon swims, though the water sprites plague him and toss his boat, and the fish and the leeches butt and drag. But, suddenly, the sturgeon shoots from the water, and ere the arch of mist that he tracks through the air has vanished, the sprite has caught a drop of the spray in a tiny blossom, and in this he cleans his wings.

The water-goblins torment him no longer. They push his boat to the shore, where, alighting, he kisses his hand, then, even as a bubble, he flies back to the mountain top, dons his acorn helmet, his corselet of bee-hide, his shield of ladybug shell, and grasping his lance, tipped with wasp sting, he bestrides his firefly steed and off he goes like a flash. The world spreads out and then grows small, but he flies straight on. The ice-ghosts leer from the topmost clouds, and the mists surge round, but he shakes his lance and pipes his call, and at last he comes to the Milky Way, where the sky-sylphs lead him to their queen, who lies in a palace with a ceiling of stars, its dome held up by northern lights and the curtains made of the morning's flush. Her mantle is twilight purple, tied with threads of gold from the eastern dawn, and her face is as fair as the silver moon.

She begs the fay to stay with her and taste forever the joys of heaven, but the knightly elf keeps down the beating of his heart, for he remembers a face on earth that is fairer than hers, and he begs to go. With a sigh she fits him a carriage of cloud, with the firefly steed chained on behind, and he hurries away to the northern sky whence the meteor comes, with roar and whirl, and as it passes it bursts into flame. He lights his lamp at a glowing spark, then wheels away to the fairy-land. His king and his brothers hail him stoutly, with song and shout, and feast and dance, and the revel is kept till the eastern sky has a ruddy streak. Then the cock crows shrill and the fays are gone.

Charles M. Skinner

Notes on the Story

The Culprit Fay

Skinner's tale of "The Culprit Fay" is a prose retelling of a poem by the same name written by Joseph Rodman Drake in 1819. Like "Rip Van Winkle" (page 251), this tale takes place by the Hudson River, home to the sturgeon from which the culprit fay must collect the mist in order to be pardoned. Drake's biography states that he wrote the poem after a friend remarked it would be a challenge to have a fairy poem with no human characters to aid the story.

✣

Skinner had a keen interest in nature and the environment, which is evidenced in many of the local legends and myths he published. The Hudson River especially entranced him, as shown by the large number of tales from that region contained in *Myths and Legends of Our Own Land*. "I love my Hudson," Skinner wrote in 1906, "and am much in its company; it solaces many whose unkind fate holds them to town."

Were-Wolves of Detroit

Long the shores of Detroit were vexed by the Snake God of Belle Isle and his children, the witches, for the latter sold enchantments and were the terror of good people. Jacques Morand, the trader, was in love with Genevieve Parent, but she disliked him and wished only to serve the church. Courting having proved of no avail, he resolved on force when she had decided to enter a convent, and he went to one of the witches, who served as the devil's agent, to sell his soul. The witch accepted the slight commodity and paid for it with a grant of power to change from a man's form to that of a were-wolf, or *loup garou*, that he might the easier bear away his victim. Incautiously, he followed her to Grosse Pointe, where an image of the Virgin had been set up, and as Genevieve dropped at the feet of the statue to implore aid, the wolf, as he leaped to her side, was suddenly turned to stone.

Harder was the fate of another maiden, Archange Simonet, for she was seized by a were-wolf at this place and hurried away while dancing at her own wedding. The bridegroom devoted his life to the search for her, and finally lost his reason, but he prosecuted the hunt so vengefully and shrewdly that he always found assistance. One of the neighbors cut off the wolf's tail with a silver bullet, the appendage being for many years preserved by the Indians. The lover finally came upon the creature and chased it to the shore, where its footprint is still seen in one of the boulders, but it leaped into the water and disappeared. In his crazy fancy, the lover declared that it had jumped down the throat of a catfish, and that is why the French Canadians have a prejudice against catfish as an article of diet.

The man-wolf dared as much for gain as for love. On the night that Jean Chiquot got the Indians drunk and bore off their beaver-skins, the wood witches, known as "the white women," fell upon him and tore a part of his treasure from him, while a were-wolf pounced so hard on his back that he lost more. He drove the creatures to a little distance, but was glad to be safe inside of the fort again, though the officers laughed at him and called him a coward.

When they went back over the route with him they were astonished to find the grass scorched where the women had fled before him, and little springs in the turf showed where they had been swallowed up. Sulphur-water was bubbling from the spot where the wolf dived into the earth when the trader's rosary fell out of his jacket. Belle Fontaine (Beautiful Spring), the spot was called, long afterward.

Charles M. Skinner

Notes on the Story

Were-Wolves of Detroit

American tales are often a fusion of stories from many cultures, as demonstrated here in Skinner's were-wolf tales. Detroit, formerly a French settlement and in constant trade with French Canada, had the influence of both the indigenous Native American tales and French beliefs imported from Europe. The *loup garou* is a similar creature to the wolf that stalks Perrault's Little Red Riding Hood (page 72), though the were-wolf is considered to be a human man under a spell and not an anthropomorphic wolf.

The wolf has a quality akin to the devil in these tales—he is turned to stone by the image of the Virgin and repelled by the rosary of Jean Chiquot. The were-wolf is also defeated by the holiness of the silver bullet, a belief that may come from the legend of Jean Chastel, who killed the Beast of Gévaudan in 1767 with a bullet made from a silver communion chalice.

The Nain Rouge

Among all the impish offspring of the Stone God, wizards and witches, that made Detroit feared by the early settlers, none were more dreaded than the Nain Rouge (Red Dwarf), or Demon of the Strait, for it appeared only when there was to be trouble. In that it delighted. It was a shambling, red-faced creature, with a cold, glittering eye, and teeth protruding from a grinning mouth. Cadillac, founder of Detroit, having struck at it, presently lost his dominion and his fortunes. It was seen scampering along the shore on the night before the attack on Bloody Run, when the brook that afterward bore this name turned red with the blood of soldiers. People saw it in the smoky streets when the city was burned in 1805, and on the morning of Hull's surrender it was found grinning in the fog. It rubbed its bony knuckles expectantly when David Fisher paddled across the strait to see his love, Soulange Gaudet, in the only boat he could find—a wheelbarrow, namely—but was sobered when David made a safe landing.

It chuckled when the youthful bloods set off on Christmas day to race the frozen strait for the hand of buffer Beauvais's daughter Claire, but when her lover's horse, a wiry Indian nag, came pacing in it fled before their happiness. It was twice seen on the roof of the stable where that sour-faced, evil-eyed old mumbler, Jean Beaugrand, kept his horse, Sans Souci—a beast that, spite of its hundred years or more, could and did leap every wall in Detroit, even the twelve-foot stockade of the fort, to steal corn and watermelons, and that had been seen in the same

"It was a shambling, red-faced creature, with a cold, glittering eye,

and teeth protruding from a grinning mouth."

barn, sitting at a table, playing seven-up with his master, and drinking a liquor that looked like melted brass. The dwarf whispered at the sleeping ear of the old chief who slew Friar Constantine, chaplain of the fort, in anger at the teachings that had parted a white lover from his daughter and led her to drown herself–a killing that the red man afterward confessed, because he could no longer endure the tolling of a mass bell in his ears and the friar's voice in the wind.

The Nain Rouge it was who claimed half of the old mill, on Presque Isle, that the sick and irritable Josette swore that she would leave to the devil when her brother Jean pestered her to make her will in his favor, giving him complete ownership. On the night of her death, the mill was wrecked by a thunderbolt, and a red-faced imp was often seen among the ruins, trying to patch the machinery so as to grind the devil's grist. It directed the dance of black cats in the mill at Pont Rouge, after the widow's curse had fallen on Louis Robert, her brother-in-law. This man, succeeding her husband as director of the property, had developed such miserly traits that she and her children were literally starved to death, but her dying curse threw such ill luck on the place and set afloat such evil report about it that he took himself away.

The Nain Rouge may have been the Lutin (hobgoblin) that took Jacques L'Esperance's ponies from the stable at Grosse Pointe, and, leaving no tracks in sand or snow, rode them through the air all night, restoring them at dawn quivering with fatigue, covered with foam, bloody with the lash of a thorn-bush. It stopped that exercise on the night that Jacques hurled a font of holy water at it, but to keep it away the people of Grosse Pointe still mark their houses with the sign of a cross.

It was lurking in the wood on the day that Captain Dalzell went against Pontiac, only to perish in an ambush, to the secret relief of his superior, Major Gladwyn, for the major hoped to win the betrothed of Dalzell. But, when the girl heard that her lover had been killed at

Bloody Run, and his head had been carried on a pike, she sank to the ground never to rise again in health, and in a few days she had followed the victims of the massacre.

There was a suspicion that the Nain Rouge had power to change his shape for one not less offensive. The brothers Tremblay had no luck in fishing through the straits and lakes until one of them agreed to share his catch with St. Patrick, the saint's half to be sold at the church door for the benefit of the poor, and for buying masses to relieve souls in purgatory. His brother doubted if this benefit would last, and feared that they might be lured into the water and turned into fish, for had not St. Patrick eaten pork chops on a Friday, after dipping them into holy water and turning them into trout? But his good brother kept on and prospered and the bad one kept on grumbling.

Now, at Grosse Isle was a strange thing called the rolling muff, that all were afraid of, since to meet it was a warning of trouble; but, like the *feu follet* (will-o'-the-wisp), it could be driven off by holding a cross toward it or by asking it on what day of the month came Christmas. The worse of the Tremblays encountered this creature and it filled him with dismay. When he returned his neighbors observed an odor—not of sanctity—on his garments, and their view of the matter was that he had met a skunk. The graceless man felt convinced, however, that he had received a devil's baptism from the Nain Rouge, and St. Patrick had no stauncher allies than both the Tremblays, after that.

Charles M. Skinner

Notes on the Story

The Nain Rouge

The terror of the Nain Rouge does not begin and end with Skinner's tales—first accounts of such a "red dwarf" are found in Normandy, France where it is sometimes called *lutin*, a type of hobgoblin.

✣

The folklore of the Nain Rouge was probably brought to Detroit when it was a French settlement, though creatures like this one can be found all across Europe. Use of the Nain Rouge to explain calamities faced by Detroit and its people makes him a particularly local threat whose legacy is still ongoing. Sightings have been recorded regularly since the nineteenth century. An annual parade—the Marche du Nain Rouge—celebrates release from the Nain Rouge's grasp by observing positives that have happened in the city, though those who attend wear costumes so that the Nain Rouge cannot recognize them if he is ever able to manifest once more and seek revenge.

Nineteenth-Century Literary Fairy Tales

Another type of fairy tale which emerged in the nineteenth century was the original literary fairy tale. Many successful fiction writers tried their hand at creating short fairy tales, including Oscar Wilde, George MacDonald, and Robert Louis Stevenson. These stories used the familiar conventions, themes, and motifs of fairy tales, but also kept the style of the author. Arguably, some of the most famous stories from this era of fairy tales came from the Danish author Hans Christian Andersen. His tales were so popular that they took their place in the canon of the fairy-tale genre despite many of them being Andersen's own inventions.

The Tinderbox

A soldier came marching along the high road: left, right–left, right. He had his knapsack on his back, and a sword at his side; he had been to the wars, and was now returning home.

As he walked on, he met a very frightful-looking old witch in the road. Her underlip hung quite down on her breast, and she stopped and said, "Good evening, soldier; you have a very fine sword, and a large knapsack, and you are a real soldier; so you shall have as much money as ever you like."

"Thank you, old witch," said the soldier.

"Do you see that large tree?" asked the witch, pointing to a tree that stood beside them. "Well, it is quite hollow inside, and you must climb to the top, when you will see a hole, through which you can let yourself down into the tree to a great depth. I will tie a rope round your body, so that I can pull you up again when you call out to me."

"But what am I to do, down there in the tree?" asked the soldier.

"Get money," she replied, "for you must know that when you reach the ground under the tree, you will find yourself in a large hall, lighted up by three hundred lamps; you will then see three doors, which can be easily opened, for the keys are in all the locks. On entering the first of the chambers, to which these doors lead, you will see a large chest, standing in the middle of the floor, and upon it a dog seated, with a pair of eyes as large as teacups. But you need not be at all afraid of him; I will give you my blue-checked apron, which you must spread upon the floor, and then boldly seize hold of the dog, and place him upon it. You can then open the chest, and take from it as many pence as you please, they are only copper pence; but if you would rather have silver money, you must go into the second chamber. Here you will find another dog, with eyes as big as mill wheels; but do not let that trouble you. Place him upon my apron, and then take what money you please. If, however, you like gold best, enter the third chamber, where there is another chest full of it. The dog who sits on this chest is very dreadful; each of his eyes is as big as the Round Tower, but do not mind him. If he also is placed upon my apron, he cannot hurt you, and you may take from the chest what gold you will."

"This is not a bad story," said the soldier, "but what am I to give you, you old witch? For, of course, you do not mean to tell me all this for nothing."

"No," said the witch, "but I do not ask for a single penny. Only promise to bring me an old tinderbox, which my grandmother left behind the last time she went down there."

"Very well; I promise. Now tie the rope round my body."

"Here it is," replied the witch, "and here is my blue-checked apron."

As soon as the rope was tied, the soldier climbed up the tree, and let himself down through the hollow to the ground beneath; and here he found, as the witch had told him, a large hall, in which many hundred lamps were all burning. Then he opened the first door. "Ah!" there sat the dog, with the eyes as large as teacups, staring at him.

"You're a pretty fellow," said the soldier, seizing him, and placing him on the witch's apron, while he filled his pockets from the chest with as many pieces as they would hold. Then he closed the lid, seated the dog upon it again, and walked into another chamber. And, sure enough, there sat the dog with eyes as big as mill wheels.

"You had better not look at me in that way," said the soldier, "you will make your eyes water." And then he seated him also upon the apron, and opened the chest. But when he saw what a quantity of silver money it contained, he very quickly threw away all the coppers he had taken, and filled his pockets and his knapsack with nothing but silver.

Then he went into the third room, and there the dog was really hideous; his eyes were truly as big as the Round Tower, and they turned round and round in his head like wheels.

"Good morning," said the soldier, touching his cap, for he had never seen such a dog in his life. But after looking at him more closely, he thought he had been civil enough, so he placed him on the floor, and opened the chest. Preserve us! What a lot of gold! He could buy the whole of Copenhagen with it, and all the sugar pigs from the cake-women, all the tin soldiers, whips, and rocking horses in the world! That was money indeed! So the soldier now threw away all the silver money he had taken, and filled his pockets and his knapsack with gold instead; and not only his pockets and his knapsack, but even his cap and boots, so that he could scarcely walk.

He was really rich now; so he replaced the dog on the chest, closed the door, and called up through the tree, "Now pull me out, you old witch."

"Have you got the tinderbox?" asked the witch.

"Oh, to be sure!" said the soldier. "I had quite forgotten it." And he went back to fetch it. Then the witch hauled him up out of the tree, and he stood again in the high road, with his pockets, his knapsack, his cap, and his boots full of gold.

"What are you going to do with the tinderbox?" asked the soldier.

"That is nothing to you," replied the witch, "you have the money, now give me the tinderbox."

"I tell you what," said the soldier, "if you don't tell me what you are going to do with it, I will draw my sword and cut off your head."

"No!" said the witch.

So the soldier cut off her head, and there she lay on the ground. Then he tied up all his money in her apron and slung it on his back like a bundle, put the tinderbox in his pocket, and walked off to the nearest town. It was a very nice town, and he put up at the best inn, and ordered a dinner of all his favorite dishes, for now he was rich and had plenty of money.

The servant, who cleaned his boots, thought they certainly were a shabby pair to be worn by such a rich gentleman, for he had not yet bought new ones. The next day, however, he bought some good clothes and proper boots, so that the soldier soon became known as a fine gentleman, and the people visited him, and told him all the wonders that were to be seen in the town, and of the king's beautiful daughter, the princess.

"Where can I see her?" asked the soldier.

"She is not to be seen at all," they said. "She lives in a large copper castle, surrounded by walls and towers. No one but the king himself can pass in or out, for there has been a prophecy that she will marry a common soldier, and the king cannot bear to think of such a marriage."

"I should like very much to see her," thought the soldier; but he could not obtain permission to do so. However, he passed a very pleasant time; went to the theatre, drove in the king's garden, and gave a great deal of money to the poor, which was very good of him. He remembered what it had been in olden times to be without a shilling. Now he was rich, had fine clothes, and many friends, who all declared he was a fine fellow and a real gentleman, and all this gratified him exceedingly. But his money would not last forever; and as he spent and gave away a great deal daily, and received none, he found himself at last with only two shillings left. So he was obliged to leave his elegant rooms, and live in a little garret under the roof, where he had to clean his own boots, and even mend them with a large needle. None of his friends came to see him; there were too many stairs to mount up. One dark evening, he had not even a penny to buy a candle; then all at once he remembered that there was a piece of candle stuck in the tinderbox, which he had brought from the old tree, into which the witch had helped him.

He found the tinderbox, but no sooner had he struck a few sparks from the flint and steel, than the door flew open and the dog with eyes as big as teacups, whom he had seen while down in the tree, stood before him, and said, "What orders, master?"

"Heavens!" said the soldier, "this is a nice kind of tinderbox, if it brings me all I wish for."

"Bring me some money," said he to the dog.

He was gone in a moment, and presently returned, carrying a large bag of coppers in his mouth. The soldier very soon discovered after this the value of the tinderbox. If he struck the flint once, the dog who sat on the chest of copper money made his appearance; if twice, the dog came from the chest of silver; and if three times, the dog with eyes as big as the Round Tower, who watched over the gold. The soldier now had plenty of money; he returned to his elegant rooms, and reappeared in his fine clothes, so that his friends knew him again directly, and made as much of him as before.

After a while he began to think it was very strange that no one could get a look at the princess. "Everyone says she is very beautiful," thought he to himself, "but what is the use of that if she is to be shut up in a copper castle with all the towers? Can't I somehow get to see her? Hang on, where's my tinderbox?" Then he struck a light, and in a moment the dog with eyes as big as teacups stood before him.

"It is midnight," said the soldier, "yet I should very much like to see the princess, if only for a moment."

The dog disappeared instantly, and before the soldier could even look round, he returned with the princess. She was lying on the dog's back, asleep, and looked so lovely, that everyone who saw her would know she was a real princess. The soldier could not help kissing her, true soldier as he was. Then the dog ran back with the princess. But in the morning, while at breakfast with the king and queen, she told them what a singular dream she had had during the night, of a dog and a soldier, that she had ridden on the dog's back, and been kissed by the soldier.

"That is a very pretty story, indeed," said the queen. So the next night one of the old ladies of the court was set to watch by the princess's bed, to discover whether it really was a dream, or what else it might be.

The soldier longed very much to see the princess once more, so he sent for the dog again in the night to fetch her, and to run with her as fast as ever he could. But the old lady put on galoshes, and ran after him as quickly as he did, and found that he carried the princess into a large house. She thought it would help her to remember the place if she made a large cross on the door with a piece of chalk. Then she went home to bed, and the dog presently returned with the princess. But when he saw that a cross had been made on the door of the house where the soldier lived, he took another piece of chalk and made crosses on all the doors in the town, so that the lady-in-waiting might not be able to find out the right door.

Early the next morning the king and queen accompanied the lady and all the officers of the household, to see where the princess had been.

"Here it is," said the king, when they came to the first door with a cross on it.

"No, my dear husband, it must be that one," said the queen, pointing to a second door having a cross also.

"And here is one, and there is another!" they all exclaimed; for there were crosses on all the doors in every direction.

So they felt it would be useless to search any farther. But the queen was a very clever woman; she could do a great deal more than merely ride in a carriage. She took her large gold scissors, cut a piece of silk into squares, and made a neat little bag. This bag she filled with buckwheat flour, and tied it round the princess's neck; and then she cut a small hole in the bag, so that the flour might be scattered on the ground as the princess went along. During the night, the dog came again and carried the princess on his back, and ran with her to the soldier, who loved her very much, and wished that he had been a prince, so that he might have her for a wife. The dog did not observe how the flour ran out of the bag all the way from the castle wall to the soldier's house, and even up to the window, where he had climbed with the princess.

Therefore in the morning, the king and queen found out where their daughter had been, and the soldier was taken up and put in prison. Oh, how dark and dreary it was as he sat there, and the people said to him, "Tomorrow you will be hanged." It was not very pleasant news, and besides, he had left the tinderbox at the inn.

In the morning he could see through the iron grating of the little window how the people were hastening out of the town to see him hanged; he heard the drums beating, and saw the soldiers marching. Every one ran out to look at them, and a shoemaker's boy, with a leather apron and slippers on, galloped by so fast, that one of his slippers flew off and struck against the wall where the soldier sat looking through the iron grating.

"Hey, you boy, don't be in such a hurry," cried the soldier to him. "There will be nothing to see till I come; but if you will run to the house where I have been living, and bring me my tinderbox, you shall have four shillings, but you must be quick about it."

"'Help me now, that I may not be hanged,' . . .

And the dogs fell upon the judges . . ."

The shoemaker's boy liked the idea of getting four shillings, so he ran very fast and fetched the tinderbox, and gave it to the soldier. And now we'll see what happened. Outside the town a large gallows had been erected, round which stood the soldiers and several thousand people. The king and the queen sat on splendid thrones opposite to the judges and the whole council. The soldier already stood on the ladder; but as they were about to place the rope around his neck, he said that a harmless request was often granted to a poor criminal before he suffered death. He wished very much to smoke a pipe, as it would be the last pipe he should ever smoke in the world. The king could not refuse this request, so the soldier took his tinderbox, and struck fire, once, twice, thrice–and there in a moment stood all the dogs–the one with eyes as big as teacups, the one with eyes as large as mill-wheels, and the third, with eyes as big as the Round Tower. "Help me now, that I may not be hanged," cried the soldier.

And the dogs fell upon the judges and all the councilors; seized one by the legs, and another by the nose, and tossed them many feet high in the air, so that they fell down and were dashed to pieces.

"Not me!" said the king. But the largest dog seized him, as well as the queen, and threw them after the others. Then the soldiers and all the people were afraid, and cried, "Good soldier, you shall be our king, and you shall marry the beautiful princess."

So they placed the soldier in the king's carriage, and the three dogs ran on in front and cried, "Hurrah!" And the little boys whistled through their fingers, and the soldiers presented arms. The princess came out of the copper castle, and became queen, which certainly pleased her! The wedding festivities lasted a whole week, and the dogs sat at the table, staring with their big eyes.

Hans Christian Andersen

Notes on the Story

THE TINDERBOX

Hans Christian Andersen (1805–1875) was a Danish fairy-tale author and collector, perhaps best known for his tale "The Little Mermaid." He also composed the tales "The Snow Queen," "The Little Match Girl," "The Emperor's New Clothes," and others. Andersen primarily wrote original fairy tales. However, like "The Tinderbox," some of his stories were inspired by Danish folktales that Andersen had read or heard during his childhood. Andersen gave the tale his own characteristic style intermingled with classic folktale motifs and details. Like the Grimms' tale "The Blue Light," the hero is a hardened soldier, returning from service, atypical to the common youthful hero.

✣

"The Tinderbox" also resembles the tale of "Aladdin and the Wonderful Lamp" (see page 84), with the tinderbox as the magic lamp and the wondrous dogs the genie. Andersen was familiar with "Aladdin"; indeed, he identified with the character, believing that his talent, like the genie, could raise him from his plain appearance and the poor origins in which he was born.

"'That is the wife for me,' he thought,

'but she is too grand, and lives in a castle . . .'"

The Brave Tin Soldier

There were once five-and-twenty tin soldiers, who were all brothers, for they had been made out of the same old tin spoon. They shouldered arms and looked straight before them, and wore a splendid uniform, red and blue. The first thing in the world they ever heard were the words, "Tin soldiers!" uttered by a little boy, who clapped his hands with delight when the lid of the box, in which they lay, was taken off. They were given him for a birthday present, and he stood at the table to set them up. The soldiers were all exactly alike, excepting one, who had only one leg; he had been left to the last, and then there was not enough of the melted tin to finish him. But there he stood, able to stand as firmly on one leg as the others did on two; and this is what made him the remarkable one.

The table on which the tin soldiers stood was covered with other toys, but the most eye-catching was a pretty little paper castle. Through the small windows the rooms could be seen. In front of the castle, a number of little trees surrounded a piece of looking glass, which was intended to represent a transparent lake. Swans, made of wax, swam on the lake, and were reflected in it. All this was very pretty, but the prettiest of all was a tiny little lady, who stood at the open door of the castle. She, also, was made of paper, and she wore a dress of clear muslin, with a narrow blue ribbon over her shoulders just like a scarf. In front of these was fixed a glittering tinsel rose, as large as her whole face.

The little lady was a dancer, and she stretched out both her arms, and raised one of her legs so high that the tin soldier could not see it at all, and he thought that she, like himself, had only one leg.

"That is the wife for me," he thought, "but she is too grand, and lives in a castle, while I have only a box to live in, five-and-twenty of us altogether, that is no place for her. Still I must try and make her acquaintance." Then he laid himself at full length on the table behind a snuffbox that stood upon it, so that he could peep at the little delicate lady, who continued to stand on one leg without losing her balance. When evening came, the other tin soldiers were all placed in the box, and the people of the house went to bed. Then the toys began to have their own games together, to pay visits, to have sham fights, and to give balls. The tin soldiers rattled in their box; they wanted to get out and join the amusements, but they could not open the lid. The nutcracker turned somersaults, and the slate pencil scribbled over the slate. There was such a noise that the canary woke up and began to chatter, and in verse, too. Only the tin soldier and the dancer remained in their places. She stood on tiptoe, with her legs stretched out, as firmly as he did on his one leg. He never took his eyes from her for even a moment. The clock struck twelve, and, with a bounce, up sprang the lid of the snuffbox; but, instead of snuff, there jumped up a little black goblin; for the snuffbox was a toy puzzle.

"Tin soldier," said the goblin, "don't wish for what does not belong to you."

But the tin soldier pretended not to hear.

"Very well; wait till tomorrow, then," said the goblin.

When the children came in the next morning, they placed the tin soldier in the window. Now, whether it was the goblin who did it, or the draught, is not known, but the window flew open, and out fell the tin soldier, heels over head, from the third story, into the street beneath. It was a terrible fall; for he came head downward, his helmet and his bayonet stuck in between the flagstones, and his one leg up in the air. The servant maid and the little boy went downstairs directly to look for him; but he was nowhere to be seen, although once they nearly trod upon him. If he had called out, "Here I am," it would have been all right, but he was too proud to cry out for help while he wore a uniform.

Presently it began to rain, and the drops fell faster and faster, till there was a heavy shower. When it was over, two boys happened to pass by, and one of them said, "Look, there is a tin soldier. He ought to have a boat to sail in."

So they made a boat out of a newspaper, and placed the tin soldier in it, and sent him sailing down the gutter, while the two boys ran by the side of it, and clapped their hands. Good gracious, what large waves arose in that gutter! And how fast the stream rolled on! For the rain had been very heavy. The paper boat rocked up and down, and turned itself round, sometimes so quickly that the tin soldier trembled. Yet he remained firm, his countenance did not change; he looked straight before him, and shouldered his musket. Suddenly the boat shot under a bridge, which formed a part of a drain, and then it was as dark as the tin soldier's box.

"Where am I going now?" thought he. "This is the black goblin's fault, I am sure. Ah, well, if the little lady were only here with me in the boat, I should not care for any darkness."

Suddenly there appeared a great water rat, who lived in the drain.

"Have you a passport?" asked the rat. "Give it to me at once."

But the tin soldier remained silent and held his musket tighter than ever. The boat sailed on and the rat followed it. How he did gnash his teeth and cry out to the bits of wood and straw, "Stop him, stop him; he has not paid toll, and has not shown his pass."

But the stream rushed on stronger and stronger. The tin soldier could already see daylight shining where the arch ended. Then he heard a roaring sound quite terrible enough to frighten the bravest man. At the end of the tunnel the drain fell into a large canal over a steep place, which made it as dangerous for him as a waterfall would be to us. He was too close to it to stop, so the boat rushed on, and the poor tin soldier could only hold himself as stiffly as possible, without moving an eyelid, to show that he was not afraid. The boat whirled round three or four times, and then filled with water to the very edge; nothing could save it from sinking. He now stood up to his neck in water, while deeper and deeper sank the boat, and the paper became soft and loose with the wet, till at last the water closed over the soldier's head. He thought of the elegant little dancer whom he should never see again, and the words of the song sounded in his ears–

"Farewell, warrior! ever brave,
Going forward to your grave."

Then the paper boat fell to pieces, and the soldier sank into the water and immediately afterward was swallowed up by a great fish. Oh how dark it was inside the fish! A great deal darker than in the tunnel, and narrower too, but the tin soldier continued firm, and lay at full length, shouldering his musket. The fish swam to and fro, making the most wonderful movements, but at last he became quite still.

After a while, a flash of lightning seemed to pass through him, and then the daylight approached, and a voice cried out, "I declare here is the tin soldier."

The fish had been caught, taken to the market, and sold to the cook, who took him into the kitchen and cut him open with a large knife. She picked up the soldier and held him by the waist between her finger and thumb, and carried him into the room. They were all anxious to see this wonderful soldier who had traveled about inside a fish; but he was not at all proud. They placed him on the table, and–how many curious things do happen in the world—there he was in the very same room from whose window he had fallen, there were the same children, the same toys standing on the table, and the pretty castle with the elegant little dancer at the door; she still balanced herself on one leg, and held up the other, so she was as firm as himself. It touched the tin soldier so much to see her that he almost wept tin tears, but he kept them back. He only looked at her and they both remained silent.

Presently one of the little boys took up the tin soldier, and threw him into the stove. He had no reason for doing so, therefore it must have been the fault of the black goblin who lived in the snuffbox. The flames lit up the tin soldier as he stood; the heat was very terrible, but whether it proceeded from the real fire or from the fire of love he could not tell. Then he could see that the bright colors were faded from his uniform, but whether they had been washed off during his journey or from the effects of his sorrow, no one could say. He looked at the little lady, and she looked at him. He felt himself melting away, but he still remained firm with his gun on his shoulder. Suddenly the door of the room flew open and the draught of air caught up the little dancer, she fluttered like a sylph right into the stove by the side of the tin soldier, and was instantly in flames and was gone. The tin soldier melted down into a lump, and the next morning, when the maidservant took the ashes out of the stove, she found him in the shape of a little tin heart. But of the little dancer nothing remained but the tinsel rose, which was burnt black as a cinder.

Hans Christian Andersen

Notes on the Story

The Brave Tin Soldier

The imaginative stories of toys and other inanimate objects coming to life are found in many cultures, past and present, from Ovid's *Pygmalion* to Tchaikovsky's *The Nutcracker* ballet to the modern-day Disney/Pixar films in the *Toy Story* series. Andersen himself frequently used anthropomorphized objects to give a sense of everyday magic to his tales—stories such as "The Darning Needle," "Five Peas in a Pod," or "The Pen and the Inkstand" contain speaking objects that give a parable-like quality to the tales, teaching a moral through their behavior. Like the tin soldier's failed romance, Andersen explored complex human experiences through needles, pens, and dolls.

Aside from the animated toys, "The Brave Tin Soldier" also stands out from other classical fairy tales with its tragic ending. Andersen's tales were not always concerned with the happy-ever-after, something that has been attributed to dissatisfaction in his own life (especially in matters of the heart, like the poor one-legged soldier).

Sir Worm Wymble

One snowy evening in the depth of winter, Kirsty had promised to tell us the tale of the armed knight who lay in stone upon the tomb in the church. She seated herself on one side of the fire with Davie on her lap, and we moved our chairs as near her as we could, with Turkey, as the valiant man of the party, farthest from the center of safety, namely Kirsty, who was at the same time to be the source of all the delightful horror. I may as well say that I do not believe Kirsty's tale had the remotest historical connection with Sir Worm Wymble, if that was anything like the name of the dead knight. It was an old Highland legend, which she adorned with the flowers of her own Celtic fancy, and swathed around the form so familiar to us all.

"There is a pot in the Highlands," began Kirsty, "not far from our house, at the bottom of a little glen. It is not very big, but fearfully deep; so deep that they do say there is no bottom to it."

"An iron pot, Kirsty?" asked Allister.

"No, goosey," answered Kirsty. "A pot means a great hole full of water—black, black, and deep, deep."

"Oh!" remarked Allister, and was silent.

"Well, in this pot there lived a kelpie."

"What's a kelpie, Kirsty?" interposed Allister, who in general asked all the necessary questions and at least as many unnecessary.

"A kelpie is an awful creature that eats people."

"But what is it like, Kirsty?"

"It's something like a horse, with a head like a cow."

"How big is it? As big as Hawkie?"

"Bigger than Hawkie; bigger than the biggest ox you ever saw."

"Has it a great mouth?"

"Yes, a terrible mouth."

"With teeth?"

"Not many, but dreadfully big ones."

"Oh!"

"Well, there was a shepherd many years ago, who lived not far from the pot. He was a knowing man, and understood all about kelpies, and brownies, and fairies. And he put a branch of the rowan tree (mountain ash), with the red berries in it, over the door of his cottage, so that the kelpie could never come in.

"Now, the shepherd had a very beautiful daughter–so beautiful that the kelpie wanted very much to eat her. I suppose he had lifted up his head out of the pot some day and seen her go past, but he could not come out of the pot except after the sun was down."

"Why?" asked Allister.

"I don't know. It was the nature of the beast. His eyes couldn't bear the light, I suppose; but he could see in the dark quite well. One night the girl woke suddenly, and saw his great head looking in at her window."

"But how could she see him when it was dark?" asked Allister.

"His eyes were flashing so that they lighted up all his head," explained Kirsty to Allister.

"But he couldn't get in!"

"No, he couldn't get in. He was only looking in, and thinking how he should like to eat her. So in the morning she told her father. And her father was very frightened, and told her she must never be out one moment after the sun was down. And for a long time the girl was very careful. And she had need to be; for the creature never made any noise, but came up as quiet as a shadow.

"One afternoon, however, she had gone to meet her lover a little way down the glen; and they stayed talking so long, about one thing and another, that the sun was almost set before she remembered. She said goodnight at once, and ran for home. Now she could not reach home without passing the pot, and just as she passed the pot, she saw the last sparkle of the sun as he went down."

"I should think she ran!" remarked our mouthpiece, Allister.

"She did run," said Kirsty, "and had just got past the awful black pot, which was terrible enough day or night without such a beast in it, when–"

"But there was the beast in it," said Allister.

"When," Kirsty went on without heeding him, "she heard a great whish of water behind her. That was the water tumbling off the beast's back as he came up from the bottom. If she ran before, she flew now. And the worst of it was that she couldn't hear him behind her, so as to tell whereabouts he was. He might be just opening his mouth to take her every moment. At last she reached the door, which her father, who had gone out to look for her, had set wide open that she might run in at once; but all the breath was out of her body, and she fell down flat just as she got inside."

Here Allister jumped from his seat, clapping his hands and crying–

"Then the kelpie didn't eat her!–Kirsty! Kirsty!"

"No. But as she fell, one foot was left outside the threshold, so that the rowan branch could not take care of it. And the beast laid hold of the foot with his great mouth, to drag her out of the cottage and eat her at his leisure."

Here Allister's face was a picture to behold! His hair was almost standing on end, his mouth was open, and his face as white as paper.

"Make haste, Kirsty," said Turkey, "or Allister will go in a fit."

"But her shoe came off in his mouth, and she drew in her foot and was safe."

Allister's hair subsided. He drew a deep breath, and sat down again. But Turkey must have been a very wise or a very unimaginative Turkey, for here he broke in with–

"I don't believe a word of it, Kirsty."

"What!' said Kirsty, "don't believe it!"

"No. She lost her shoe in the mud. It was some wild duck she heard in the pot, and there was no beast after her. She never saw it, you know."

"She saw it look in at her window."

"Yes, yes. That was in the middle of the night. I've seen as much myself when I woke up in the middle of the night. I took a rat for a tiger once."

Kirsty was looking angry, and her knitting needles were going even faster than when she approached the climax of the shoe.

"Hold your tongue, Turkey," I said, "and let us hear the rest of the story."

But Kirsty kept her eyes on her knitting, and did not resume.

"Is that all, Kirsty?" said Allister.

Still Kirsty returned no answer. She needed all her force to overcome the anger she was busy stifling. For it would never do for one in her position to lose her temper because of the unbelieving criticism of a herd-boy. After a few moments she began again as if she had never stopped and no remarks had been made, only her voice trembled a little at first.

"Her father came home soon after, in great distress, and there he found her lying just within the door. He saw at once how it was, and his anger was kindled against her lover more than the beast. Not that he had any objection to her going to meet him; for although he was a gentleman and his daughter only a shepherd's daughter, they were both of the blood of the MacLeods."

This was Kirsty's own clan. And indeed I have since discovered that the original legend on which her story was founded belongs to the island of Raasay, from which she came.

"But why was he angry with the gentleman?" asked Allister.

"Because he liked her company better than he loved herself," said Kirsty. "At least that was what the shepherd said, and that he ought to have seen her safe home. But he didn't know that MacLeod's father had threatened to kill him if ever he spoke to the girl again."

"But," said Allister, "I thought it was about Sir Worm Wymble–not Mr. MacLeod."

"Sure, boy, and am I not going to tell you how he got the new name of him?" returned Kirsty, with an eagerness that showed her fear lest the spirit of inquiry should spread. "He wasn't Sir Worm Wymble then. His name was . . . " Here she paused a moment, and looked full at Allister. "His name was Allister–Allister MacLeod."

"Allister!" exclaimed my brother, repeating the name as an incredible coincidence.

"Yes, Allister," said Kirsty. "There's been many an Allister, and not all of them MacLeods, that did what they ought to do, and didn't know what fear was. And you'll be another, my bonnie Allister, I hope," she added, stroking the boy's hair.

Allister's face flushed with pleasure. It was long before he asked another question.

"Well, as I say," resumed Kirsty, "the father of her was very angry, and said she should never go and meet Allister again. But the girl said she ought to go once and let him know why she could not come any more; for she had no complaint to make of Allister. And she had agreed to meet him on a certain day the week after; and there was no post-office in those parts. And so she did meet him, and told him all about it. And Allister said nothing much then. But next day he came striding up to the cottage, at dinnertime, with his claymore at one side, his dirk at the other, and his little skene dubh (black knife) in his stocking. And he was grand to see–such a big strong gentleman! And he came striding up to the cottage where the shepherd was sitting at his dinner.

'Angus MacQueen,' said he, 'I understand the kelpie in the pot has been rude to your Nelly. I am going to kill him.'

'How will you do that, sir?' said Angus, quite curtly, for he was the girl's father.

'Here's a claymore I could put in a peck,' said Allister, meaning it was such good steel that he could bend it round till the hilt met the point without breaking; 'and here's a shield made out of the hide of old Raasay's black bull; and here's a dirk made of a foot and a half of an old Andrew Ferrara (a famous sword-maker); and here's a skene dubh that I'll drive through your door, Mr. Angus. And so we're fitted, I hope.'

'Not at all,' said Angus, who as I told you was a wise man and knowing; 'not one bit,' said Angus. 'The kelpie's hide is thicker than three bull-hides, and none of your weapons would do more than mark it.'

'What am I to do then, Angus, for kill him I will somehow?'

'I'll tell you what to do; but it needs a brave man to do that.'

'And do you think I'm not brave enough for that, Angus?'

'I know one thing you are not brave enough for.'

'And what's that?' asked Allister, and his face grew red, only he did not want to anger Nelly's father.

'You're not brave enough to marry my girl in the face of the clan,' said Angus. 'If my Nelly's good enough to talk to in the glen, she's good enough to lead into the hall before the ladies and gentlemen.'

"He came striding up to the cottage . . . with his claymore at one side,

his dirk at the other, and his little skene dubh in his stocking."

Then Allister's face grew redder still, but not with anger, and he held down his head before the old man, but only for a few moments. When he lifted it again, it was pale, not with fear but with resolution, for he had made up his mind like a gentleman.

'Mr. Angus MacQueen,' he said, 'will you give me your daughter to be my wife?'

'If you kill the kelpie, I will,' answered Angus; for he knew that the man who could do that would be worthy of his Nelly.

"But what if the kelpie ate him?" suggested Allister.

"Then he'd have to go without the girl," said Kirsty, coolly. "But," she resumed, "there's always some way of doing a difficult thing; and Allister, the gentleman, had Angus, the shepherd, to teach him.

"So Angus took Allister down to the pot, and there they began. They tumbled great stones together, and set them up in two rows at a little distance from each other, making a lane between the rows big enough for the kelpie to walk in. If the kelpie heard them, he could not see them, and they took care to get into the cottage before it was dark, for they could not finish their preparations in one day. And they sat up all night, and saw the huge head of the beast looking in now at one window, now at another, all night long.

"As soon as the sun was up, they set to work again, and finished the two rows of stones all the way from the pot to the top of the little hill on which the cottage stood. Then they tied a cross of rowan-tree twigs on every stone, so that once the beast was in the avenue of stones he could only get out at the end. And this was Nelly's part of the job. Next they gathered a quantity of furze and brushwood and peat, and piled it in the end of the avenue next the cottage. Then Angus went and killed a little pig, and dressed it ready for cooking."

'Now you go down to my brother Hamish,' he said to Mr. MacLeod; 'for he's a carpenter, you know, and you must ask him to lend you his longest wimble.'

'What's a wimble?' asked little Allister.

'A wimble is a long tool, like a great gimlet, with a cross handle, with which you turn it like a screw.' And Allister ran and fetched it, and got back only half an hour before the sun went down. Then they put Nelly into the cottage, and shut the door. But I ought to have told you that they had built up a great heap of stones behind the brushwood, and now they lighted the brushwood, and put down the pig to roast by the fire, and laid the wimble in the fire halfway up to the handle. Then they laid themselves down behind the heap of stones, and waited.

"By the time the sun was out of sight, the smell of the roasting pig had got down the avenue to the side of the pot, just where the kelpie always got out. He smelt it the moment he put up his head, and he thought it smelt so nice that he would go and see where it was. The moment he got out he was between the stones, but he never thought of that, for it was the straight way to the pig. So up the avenue he came, and as it was dark, and his big soft web feet made no noise, the men could not see him until he came into the light of the fire.

'There he is!' said Allister.

'Hush!' said Angus, 'he can hear well enough.'

"So the beast came on. Now Angus had meant that he should be busy with the pig before Allister should attack him; but Allister thought it was a pity he should have the pig, and he put out his hand and got hold of the wimble, and drew it gently out of the fire. And the wimble was so hot that it was as white as the whitest moon you ever saw. The pig was so hot also that the brute was afraid to touch it, and before ever he put his nose to it Allister had thrust the wimble into his hide, behind the left shoulder, and was boring away with all his might. The kelpie gave a hideous roar, and turned away to run from the wimble. But he could not get over the row of crossed stones, and he had to turn right round in the narrow space before he could run. Allister, however, could run as well as the kelpie, and he hung on to the handle of the wimble, giving it another turn at every chance as the beast went floundering on; so that before he reached his pot the wimble had reached his heart, and the kelpie fell dead on the edge of the pot.

"Then they went home, and when the pig was properly done they had it for supper. And Angus gave Nelly to Allister, and they were married, and lived happily ever after."

"But didn't Allister's father kill him?"

"No. He thought better of it, and didn't. He was very angry for a while, but he got over it in time. And Allister became a great man, and because of what he had done, he was called Allister MacLeod no more, but Sir Worm Wymble. And when he died," concluded Kirsty, "he was buried under the tomb in your father's church. And if you look close enough, you'll find a wimble carved on the stone, but I'm afraid it's worn out by this time."

George MacDonald

Notes on the Story

Sir Worm Wymble

A Scottish minister influenced by Novalis (page 127), George MacDonald (1824–1905) was a Victorian author who had a significant influence on Lewis Carroll, C. S. Lewis, and J. R. R. Tolkien, and thus on the evolution of fantasy literature today. MacDonald stated that he wrote "not for children, but for the child-like, whether they be of five, or fifty, or seventy-five." Indeed, the childlike capacity for wonder was, for him, central both to the motivation of fantasy and real life.

MacDonald is best known for his light-hearted and yet complex stories, *The Princess and the Goblin*, *The Princess and Curdie*, and "The Light Princess," in which a princess is cursed by lack of gravity. Many of his fairy tales appear as oral stories in novels, such as "Sir Worm Wymble," which is a chapter in *Ranald Bannerman's Boyhood* (1871). This is a largely autobiographical tale of a boy from the Scottish Highlands and the stories with which he grew up.

The Selfish Giant

Every afternoon, as they were coming from school, the children used to go and play in the Giant's garden. It was a large lovely garden, with soft green grass. Here and there over the grass stood beautiful flowers like stars, and there were twelve peach trees that in the springtime broke out into delicate blossoms of pink and pearl, and in the autumn bore rich fruit. The birds sat on the trees and sang so sweetly that the children used to stop their games in order to listen to them. "How happy we are here!" they cried to each other.

One day the Giant came back. He had been to visit his friend the Cornish Ogre, and had stayed with him for seven years. After the seven years were over he had said all that he had to say, for his conversation was limited, and he determined to return to his own castle. When he arrived he saw the children playing in the garden.

"What are you doing here?" he cried in a very gruff voice, and the children ran away.

"My own garden is my own garden," said the Giant; "any one can understand that, and I will allow nobody to play in it but myself." So he built a high wall all round it, and put up a notice board.

Trespassers Will Be Prosecuted

He was a very selfish giant. So, the poor children had now nowhere to play. They tried to play on the road, but the road was very dusty and full of hard stones, and they did not like it. They used to wander round the high wall when their lessons were over, and talk about the beautiful garden inside.

"How happy we were there," they said to each other.

Then the Spring came, and all over the country there were little blossoms and little birds. Only in the garden of the Selfish Giant it was still winter. The birds did not care to sing in it as there were no children, and the trees forgot to blossom. Once a beautiful flower put its head out from the grass, but when it saw the notice board it was so sorry for the children that it slipped back into the ground again, and went off to sleep. The only people who were pleased were the Snow and the Frost.

"Spring has forgotten this garden," they cried, "so we will live here all the year round."

The Snow covered up the grass with her great white cloak, and the Frost painted all the trees silver. Then they invited the North Wind to stay with them, and he came. He was wrapped in furs, and he roared all day about the garden, and blew the chimneypots down.

"This is a delightful spot," he said, "we must ask the Hail on a visit."

So the Hail came. Every day for three hours he rattled on the roof of the castle till he broke most of the slates, and then he ran round and round the garden as fast as he could go. He was dressed in gray, and his breath was like ice.

"I cannot understand why the Spring is so late in coming," said the Selfish Giant, as he sat at the window and looked out at his cold white garden; "I hope there will be a change in the weather."

But the Spring never came, nor the Summer. The Autumn gave golden fruit to every garden, but to the Giant's garden she gave none. "He is too selfish," she said. So it was always winter there, and the

North Wind, and the Hail, and the Frost, and the Snow danced about through the trees.

One morning the Giant was lying awake in bed when he heard some lovely music. It sounded so sweet to his ears that he thought it must be the king's musicians passing by. It was really only a little linnet singing outside his window, but it was so long since he had heard a bird sing in his garden that it seemed to him to be the most beautiful music in the world. Then the Hail stopped dancing over his head, and the North Wind ceased roaring, and a delicious perfume came to him through the open casement.

"I believe the Spring has come at last," said the Giant; and he jumped out of bed and looked out.

What did he see?

He saw a most wonderful sight. Through a little hole in the wall the children had crept in, and they were sitting in the branches of the trees. In every tree that he could see there was a little child. And the trees were so glad to have the children back again that they had covered themselves with blossoms, and were waving their arms gently above the children's heads. The birds were flying about and twittering with delight, and the flowers were looking up through the green grass and laughing. It was a lovely scene, only in one corner it was still winter. It was the farthest corner of the garden, and in it was standing a little boy. He was so small that he could not reach up to the branches of the tree, and he was wandering all round it, crying bitterly. The poor tree was still quite covered with frost and snow, and the North Wind was blowing and roaring above it. "Climb up! little boy," said the Tree, and it bent its branches down as low as it could; but the boy was too tiny.

And the Giant's heart melted as he looked out. "How selfish I have been!" he said; "now I know why the Spring would not come here. I will put that poor little boy on the top of the tree, and then I will knock

"The trees were so glad to have the children back again

that they had covered themselves with blossoms . . ."

down the wall, and my garden shall be the children's playground for ever and ever." He was really very sorry for what he had done.

So he crept downstairs and opened the front door quite softly, and went out into the garden. But when the children saw him they were so frightened that they all ran away, and the garden became winter again. Only the little boy did not run, for his eyes were so full of tears that he did not see the Giant coming. And the Giant stole up behind him and took him gently in his hand, and put him up into the tree. And the tree broke at once into blossom, and the birds came and sang on it, and the little boy stretched out his two arms and flung them round the Giant's neck, and kissed him. And the other children, when they saw that the Giant was not wicked any longer, came running back, and with them came the Spring.

"It is your garden now, little children," said the Giant, and he took a great ax and knocked down the wall. And when the people were going to market at twelve o'clock they found the Giant playing with the children in the most beautiful garden they had ever seen.

All day long they played, and in the evening they came to the Giant to bid him goodbye.

"But where is your little companion?" he said: "the boy I put into the tree." The Giant loved him the best because he had kissed him.

"We don't know," answered the children, "he has gone away."

"You must tell him to be sure and come here tomorrow," said the Giant. But the children said that they did not know where he lived, and had never seen him before; and the Giant felt very sad.

Every afternoon, when school was over, the children came and played with the Giant. But the little boy whom the Giant loved was never seen again. The Giant was very kind to all the children, yet he longed for his first little friend, and often spoke of him. "How I would like to see him!" he used to say.

Years went over, and the Giant grew very old and feeble. He could not play about any more, so he sat in a huge armchair, and watched the children at their games, and admired his garden. “I have many beautiful flowers,” he said; “but the children are the most beautiful flowers of all.”

One winter morning he looked out of his window as he was dressing. He did not hate the Winter now, for he knew that it was merely the Spring asleep, and that the flowers were resting.

Suddenly he rubbed his eyes in wonder, and looked and looked. It certainly was a marvelous sight. In the farthest corner of the garden was a tree quite covered with lovely white blossoms. Its branches were all golden, and silver fruit hung down from them, and underneath it stood the little boy he had loved.

Downstairs ran the Giant in great joy, and out into the garden. He hastened across the grass, and came near to the child. And when he came quite close his face grew red with anger, and he said, “Who hath dared to wound thee?” For on the palms of the child’s hands were the prints of two nails, and the prints of two nails were on the little feet.

“Who hath dared to wound thee?” cried the Giant, “tell me, that I may take my big sword and slay him.”

“Nay!” answered the child. “But these are the wounds of Love.”

“Who art thou?” said the Giant, and a strange awe fell on him, and he knelt before the little child.

And the child smiled on the Giant, and said to him, “You let me play once in your garden, today you shall come with me to my garden, which is Paradise.”

And when the children ran in that afternoon, they found the Giant lying dead under the tree, all covered with white blossoms.

Oscar Wilde

Notes on the Story

THE SELFISH GIANT

Known for his plays of satirical wit, Irishman Oscar Wilde (1854–1900) is one of Britain's most famous fairy-tale authors. He published *The Happy Prince and Other Tales* in 1888, which included "The Selfish Giant," just as his fame began to climb, and a later collection of fairy tales called *House of Pomegranates* in 1891. Like many before him, Wilde used the fairy-tale form to criticize hypocrisy and reflect on the outrages of social injustice. Similar to Hans Christian Andersen's, his tales are often tragic, ending not with love but with death.

As in George MacDonald's tales, Wilde's fairy stories have a mystical and spiritual element to them. In "The Selfish Giant," it is a Christ-like figure who redeems the lonely giant and brings the return of spring to the winter-bound garden. Here the tone of the tale is optimistic. In others, such as "The Happy Prince," the self-sacrifice offered by the hero appears to have no impact on the foolish hypocrisy that continues to structure a cruel and unjust society.

The Touchstone

The king was a man that stood well before the world; his smile was sweet as clover, but his soul within was as little as a pea. He had two sons; and the younger son was a boy after his heart, but the elder was one whom he feared. It befell one morning that the drum sounded in the dun (fort) before it was yet day; and the king rode with his two sons, and a brave array behind them. They rode two hours, and came to the foot of a brown mountain that was very steep.

"Where do we ride?" asked the elder son.

"Across this brown mountain," said the king, and smiled to himself.

"My father knows what he is doing," said the younger son. And they rode two hours more, and came to the sides of a black river that was wondrous deep.

"And where do we ride?" asked the elder son.

"Over this black river," said the king, and smiled to himself.

"My father knows what he is doing," said the younger son. And they rode all that day, and about the time of the sun setting they came to the side of a lake, where was a great dun.

"It is here we ride," said the king, "to a king's house, and a priest's, and a house where you will learn much."

At the gates of the dun, the king who was a priest met them; and he was a grave man, and beside him stood his daughter, and she was as fair as the morn, and one that smiled and looked down.

"These are my two sons," said the first king.

"And here is my daughter," said the king who was a priest.

"She is a wonderful fine maid," said the first king, "and I like her manner of smiling."

"They are wonderful well-grown lads," said the second, "and I like their gravity."

And then the two kings looked at each other, and said, "The thing may come about."

And in the meanwhile the two lads looked upon the maid, and the one grew pale and the other red; and the maid looked upon the ground, smiling.

"Here is the maid that I shall marry," said the elder. "For I think she smiled upon me."

But the younger plucked his father by the sleeve. "Father," said he, "a word in your ear. If I find favor in your sight, might not I wed this maid, for I think she smiles upon me?"

"A word in yours," said the king his father. "Waiting is good hunting, and when the teeth are shut the tongue is at home."

Now they were come into the dun, and feasted; and this was a great house, so that the lads were astonished; and the king that was a priest sat at the end of the board and was silent, so that the lads were filled with reverence; and the maid served them smiling with downcast eyes, so that their hearts were enlarged.

Before it was day, the elder son arose, and he found the maid at her weaving, for she was a diligent girl.

"Maid," quoth he, "I would fain marry you."

"You must speak with my father," said she, and she looked upon the ground smiling, and became like the rose.

"Her heart is with me," said the elder son, and he went down to the lake and sang.

A little after came the younger son. "Maid," quoth he, "if our fathers were agreed, I would like well to marry you."

"You can speak to my father," said she; and looked upon the ground, and smiled and grew like the rose.

"She is a dutiful daughter," said the younger son, "she will make an obedient wife." And then he thought, "What shall I do?" and he remembered the king her father was a priest; so he went into the temple, and sacrificed a weasel and a hare.

Presently the news got about; and the two lads and the first king were called into the presence of the king who was a priest, where he sat upon the high seat.

"Little I have of wealth," said the king who was a priest, "and little of power. For we live here among the shadow of things, and the heart is sick of seeing them. And we stay here in the wind like raiment drying, and the heart is weary of the wind. But one thing I love, and that is truth; and for one thing will I give my daughter, and that is the trial stone. For in the light of that stone the seeming goes, and the being shows, and all things besides are worthless. Therefore, lads, if ye would wed my daughter, out foot, and bring me the stone of touch, for that is the price of her."

"A word in your ear," said the younger son to his father. "I think we do very well without this stone."

"A word in yours," said the father. "I am of your way of thinking; but when the teeth are shut the tongue is at home." And he smiled to the king that was a priest.

But the elder son got to his feet, and called the king that was a priest by the name of father. "For whether I marry the maid or no, I will call you by that word for the love of your wisdom; and even now I will ride forth and search the world for the stone of touch." So he said farewell, and rode into the world.

"I think I will go, too," said the younger son, "if I can have your leave. For my heart goes out to the maid."

"You will ride home with me," said his father.

So they rode home, and when they came to the dun, the king had his son into his treasury. "Here," said he, "is the touchstone which shows truth; for there is no truth but plain truth; and if you will look in this, you will see yourself as you are."

And the younger son looked in it, and saw his face as it were the face of a beardless youth, and he was well enough pleased; for the thing was a piece of a mirror.

"Here is no such great thing to make a work about," said he, "but if it will get me the maid I shall never complain. But what a fool is my brother to ride into the world, and the thing all the while at home!"

So they rode back to the other dun, and showed the mirror to the king that was a priest; and when he had looked in it, and seen himself like a king, and his house like a king's house, and all things like themselves, he cried out and blessed God.

"For now I know," said he, "there is no truth but the plain truth; and I am a king indeed, although my heart misgave me." And he pulled down his temple, and built a new one; and then the younger son was married to the maid.

In the meantime the elder son rode into the world to find the touchstone of the trial of truth; and whenever he came to a place of habitation, he would ask the men if they had heard of it. And in every place the men answered: "Not only have we heard of it, but we alone, of all men, possess the thing itself, and it hangs in the side of our chimney to this day."

Then would the elder son be glad, and beg for a sight of it. And sometimes it would be a piece of mirror, that showed the seeming of things; and then he would say, "This can never be, for there should be more than seeming." And sometimes it would be a lump of coal, which showed nothing; and then he would say, "This can never be, for at least there is the seeming." And sometimes it would be a touchstone indeed, beautiful in hue, adorned with polishing, the light inhabiting its sides;

"And the younger son looked in it, and saw his face as it were

the face of a beardless youth, and he was well enough pleased . . ."

and when he found this, he would beg the thing, and the persons of that place would give it him, for all men were very generous of that gift. So that at the last he had his wallet full of them, and they chinked together when he rode; and when he halted by the side of the way he would take them out and try them, till his head turned like the sails upon a windmill.

"A curse upon this business!" said the elder son, "for I perceive no end to it. Here I have the red, and here the blue and the green; and to me they seem all excellent, and yet shame each other. A curse on the trade! If it were not for the king that is a priest and whom I have called my father, and if it were not for the fair maid of the dun that makes my mouth to sing and my heart enlarge, I would even tumble them all into the salt sea, and go home and be a king like other folk."

But he was like the hunter that has seen a stag upon a mountain, so that the night may fall, and the fire be kindled, and the lights shine in his house; but desire of that stag is single in his heart.

Now after many years the elder son came upon the sides of the salt sea; and it was night, and a savage place, and the clamor of the sea was loud. There he was aware of a house, and a man that sat there by the light of a candle, for he had no fire. Now the elder son came in to him, and the man gave him water to drink, for he had no bread; and wagged his head when he was spoken to, for he had no words.

"Have you the touchstone of truth?" asked the elder son, and when the man had wagged his head, "I might have known that," cried the elder son. "I have here a wallet full of them!" And with that he laughed, although his heart was weary. And with that the man laughed too, and with the fuff of his laughter the candle went out.

"Sleep," said the man, "for now I think you have come far enough; and your quest is ended, and my candle is out."

Now when the morning came, the man gave him a clear pebble in his hand, and it had no beauty and no color;

and the elder son looked upon it scornfully and shook his head; and he went away, for it seemed a small affair to him.

All that day he rode, and his mind was quiet, and the desire of the chase allayed.

"How if this poor pebble be the touchstone, after all?" said he. And he got down from his horse, and emptied forth his wallet by the side of the way. Now, in the light of each other, all the touchstones lost their hue and fire, and withered like stars at morning. But in the light of the pebble, their beauty remained; only the pebble was the most bright. And the elder son smote upon his brow.

"How if this be the truth?" he cried, "that all are a little true?" And he took the pebble, and turned its light upon the heavens, and they deepened about him like the pit. And he turned it on the hills, and the hills were cold and rugged, but life ran in their sides so that his own life bounded. And he turned it on the dust, and he beheld the dust with joy and terror; and then he turned it on himself, and kneeled down and prayed.

"Now, thanks be to God," said the elder son, "I have found the touchstone; and now I may ride home to the king and to the maid of the dun that makes my mouth to sing and my heart enlarge."

Now when he came to the dun, he saw children playing by the gate where the king had met him in the old days; and this stayed his pleasure, for he thought in his heart, "It is here my children should be playing." And when he came into the hall, there was his brother on the high seat and the maid beside him; and at that his anger rose, for he thought in his heart, "It is I that should be sitting there, and the maid beside me."

"Who are you?" said his brother. "And what make you in the dun?"

"I am your elder brother," he replied. "And I am come to marry the maid, for I have brought the touchstone of truth."

Then the younger brother laughed aloud. "Why," said he, "I found the touchstone years ago, and married the maid, and there are our children playing at the gate."

Now at this the elder brother grew as gray as the dawn. "I pray you have dealt justly," said he, "for I perceive my life is lost."

"Justly?" quoth the younger brother. "It becomes you ill, that are a restless man and a runagate, to doubt my justice, or the king my father's, that are sedentary folk and known in the land."

"Nay," said the elder brother, "you have all else, have patience also; and suffer me to say the world is full of touchstones, and it appears not easily which is true."

"I have no shame of mine," said the younger brother. "There it is, and look in it."

So the elder brother looked in the mirror, and he was sore amazed; for he was an old man, and his hair was white upon his head; and he sat down in the hall and wept aloud.

"Now," said the younger brother, "see what a fool's part you have played, that ran over all the world to seek what was lying in our father's treasury, and came back an old man for the dogs to bark at, and without chick or child. And I that was dutiful and wise sit here crowned with virtues and pleasures, and happy in the light of my hearth."

"Methinks you have a cruel tongue," said the elder brother; and he pulled out the clear pebble and turned its light on his brother; and behold the man was lying, his soul was shrunk into the smallness of a pea, and his heart was a bag of little fears like scorpions, and love was dead in his bosom. And at that the elder brother cried out aloud, and turned the light of the pebble on the maid. And, lo! She was but a mask of a woman, and within she was quite dead, and she smiled as a clock ticks, and knew not wherefore.

"Oh, well," said the elder brother, "I perceive there is both good and bad. So fare ye all as well as ye may in the dun; but I will go forth into the world with my pebble in my pocket."

Robert Louis Stevenson

Notes on the Story

THE TOUCHSTONE

Best known for *Treasure Island* and *Strange Case of Dr. Jekyll and Mr. Hyde*, Scottish author Robert Louis Stevenson (1850–1894) also wrote literary fairy tales and fables based on the folklore of the Scottish Highlands, Europe, and the South Pacific. This Celtic-style tale was serialized in 1895, and then published posthumously in a collection of fables appended to *Dr. Jekyll and Mr. Hyde*. Stevenson may have aimed it to be part of a volume of *Märchen* (fairy tales) he was creating, but this never came about.

A "touchstone" is a piece of jasper or quartz used to test the quality of precious metals. The idea of looking through the stone to see the truth of things can perhaps be associated with the art of fantasy itself. Early reviewers associated Stevenson's fables with this concept of a touchstone, "which reduces falsehoods to their natural ugliness, and illuminates the severe outlines of unpalatable truth" (R. H. Hutton).

Twentieth-Century Folktale Collections

Many of the late nineteenth-century folktale collectors continued their efforts into the twentieth century. Amongst collectors, there was a movement toward a more global approach. Many Western folklorists traveled to other countries to gather tales, or looked to indigenous tribes to learn about culture through folklore. Comparisons of tales across cultures showed some plots and motifs were common internationally. Anthologies such as Andrew Lang's popular *Fairy Books* compiled traditional stories from multiple countries and eras. In today's age of adaptation, these fairy stories and folktales collected in the twentieth century, both local and international, continue to inspire authors, filmmakers, and artists to reimagine them in new media forms.

The Snake Prince

Once upon a time there lived by herself, in a city, an old woman who was desperately poor. One day she found that she had only a handful of flour left in the house, and no money to buy more, nor hope of earning it. Carrying her little brass pot, very sadly she made her way down to the river to bathe and to obtain some water, thinking afterward to come home and to make herself an unleavened cake with the flour she had left; and after that she did not know what was to become of her.

While she was bathing, she left her little brass pot on the riverbank covered with a cloth, to keep the inside nice and clean. But, when she came up out of the river and took the cloth off to fill the pot with water, she saw inside it the glittering folds of a deadly snake. At once she popped the cloth again into the mouth of the pot and held it there; and then she said to herself: "Ah, kind death! I will take you home to my house, and there I will shake you out of my pot and you shall bite me and I will die, and then all my troubles will be ended."

With these sad thoughts in her mind, the poor old woman hurried home, holding her cloth carefully in the mouth of the pot. And when she got home she shut all the doors and windows, and took away the cloth, and turned the pot upside down upon her hearthstone. What was her surprise to find that, instead of the deadly snake that she expected to see fall out of it, there fell out with a rattle and a clang a most magnificent necklace of flashing jewels!

For a few minutes she could hardly think or speak, but stood staring. And then with trembling hands she picked the necklace up, and folding it in the corner of her veil, she hurried off to the king's hall of public audience.

"A petition, O King!" she said. "A petition for your private ear alone!"

And when her prayer had been granted, and she found herself alone with the king, she shook out her veil at his feet, and there fell from it in glittering coils the splendid necklace.

As soon as the king saw it he was filled with amazement and delight, and the more he looked at it the more he felt that he must possess it at once. So he gave the old woman five hundred silver pieces for it, and put it straightaway into his pocket. Away she went full of happiness; for the money that the king had given her was enough to keep her for the rest of her life.

As soon as he could leave his business, the king hurried off and showed his wife his prize, with which she was as pleased as he, if not more so. And, as soon as they had finished admiring the wonderful necklace, they locked it up in the great chest where the queen's jewelry was kept, the key of which hung always round the king's neck.

A short while afterward, a neighboring king sent a message to say that a most lovely girl baby had been born to him; and he invited his neighbors to come to a great feast in honor of the occasion. The queen told her husband that of course they must be present at the banquet, and she would wear the new necklace that he had given her. They had only a short time to prepare for the journey, and at the last moment the king went to the jewel chest to take out the necklace for his wife to wear, but he could see no necklace at all, only, in its place, a fat little baby boy crowing and shouting. The king was so astonished that he nearly fell backward, but presently he found his voice, and called for his wife so loudly that she came running, thinking that the necklace must at least have been stolen.

"Look here! Look!" cried the king, "haven't we always longed for a son? And now heaven has sent us one!"

"What do you mean?" cried the queen. "Are you mad?"

"Mad? No, I hope not," shouted the king, dancing in excitement round the open chest. "Come here, and look! Look what we've got instead of that necklace!"

Just then the baby let out a great crow of joy, as though he would like to jump up and dance with the king; and the queen gave a cry of surprise, and ran up and looked into the chest.

"Oh!" she gasped, as she looked at the baby, "What a darling! Where could he have come from?"

"I'm sure I can't say," said the king. "All I know is that we locked up a necklace in the chest, and when I unlocked it just now there was no necklace, but a baby, and as fine a baby as ever was seen."

By this time the queen had the baby in her arms.

"Oh, the blessed one!" she cried, "fairer ornament for the bosom of a queen than any necklace that ever was wrought. Write," she continued, "write to our neighbor and say that we cannot come to his feast, for we have a feast of our own, and a baby of our own! Oh, happy day!"

So the visit was given up; and, in honor of the new baby, the bells of the city, and its guns, and its trumpets, and its people, small and great, had hardly any rest for a week; there was such a ringing, and banging, and blaring, and such fireworks, and feasting, and rejoicing, and merry-making, as had never been seen before.

A few years went by; and, as the king's boy baby and his neighbor's girl baby grew and throve, the two kings arranged that as soon as they were old enough they should marry. And so, with much signing of papers and agreements, and wagging of wise heads, and stroking of gray beards, the compact was made, and signed, and sealed, and lay waiting for its fulfillment. And this too came to pass; for, as soon as the prince and princess were eighteen years of age, the kings agreed that it was time for the wedding; and the young prince journeyed away to the neighboring kingdom for his bride, and was there married to her with great and renewed rejoicings.

Now, I must tell you that the old woman who had sold the king the necklace had been called in by him to be the nurse of the young prince; and although she loved her charge dearly, and was a most faithful servant, she could not help talking just a little, and so, by-and-by, it began to be rumored that there was some magic about the young prince's birth; and the rumor of course had come in due time to the ears of the parents of the princess.

So now that she was going to be the wife of the prince, her mother (who was curious, as many other people are) said to her daughter on the eve of the ceremony: "Remember that the first thing you must do is to find out what this story is about the prince. And in order to do it, you must not speak a word to him, whatever he says, until he asks you why you are silent. Then you must ask him what the truth is about his magic birth; and until he tells you, you must not speak to him again."

And the princess promised faithfully that she would follow her mother's advice.

Therefore, when they were married, and the prince spoke to his bride, she did not answer him. He could not think what was the matter, but even about her old home she would not utter a word. At last he asked why she would not speak; and then she said: "Tell me the secret of your birth."

Then the prince was very sad and displeased, and although she pressed him sorely he would not tell her, but always reply: "If I tell you, you will repent that ever you asked me."

For several months they lived together; and it was not such a happy time for either as it ought to have been, for the secret was still a secret, and lay between them like a cloud between the sun and the earth, making what should be fair, dull and sad.

At length the prince could bear it no longer; so he said to his wife one day: "At midnight I will tell you my secret if you still wish it; but you will repent it all your life." However, the princess was overjoyed that she had succeeded, and paid no attention to his warnings.

That night the prince ordered horses to be ready for the princess and himself a little before midnight. He placed her on one, and mounted the other himself, and they rode together down to the river to the place where the old woman had first found the snake in her brass pot. There the prince drew rein and said sadly: "Do you still insist that I should tell you my secret?"

And the princess answered, "Yes."

"If I do," answered the prince, "remember that you will regret it all your life."

But the princess only replied, "Tell me!"

"Then," said the prince, "know that I am the son of the king of a far country, but by enchantment I was turned into a snake."

The word "snake" was hardly out of his lips when he disappeared, and the princess heard a rustle and saw a ripple on the water; and in the faint moonlight she beheld a snake swimming into the river. Soon it disappeared and she was left alone. In vain she waited with beating heart for something to happen, and for the prince to come back to her. Nothing happened and no one came; only the wind mourned through the trees on the riverbank, and the night birds cried, and a jackal howled in the distance, and the river flowed black and silent beneath her.

In the morning they found her, weeping and disheveled, on the riverbank; but no word could they learn from her or from anyone as to the fate of her husband. At her wish they built on the riverbank a little house of black stone; and there she lived in mourning, with a few servants and guards to watch over her.

A long, long time passed by, and still the princess lived in mourning for her prince, and saw no one, and went nowhere away from her house on the riverbank and the garden that surrounded it. One morning, when she woke up, she found a stain of fresh mud upon the carpet. She sent for the guards, who watched outside the house day and night, and asked them who had entered her room while she was asleep. They declared that no one could have entered; for they kept such careful watch that not even a bird could fly in without their knowledge; but none of them could explain the stain of mud. The next morning, again, the princess found another stain of wet mud, and she questioned everyone most carefully; but none could say how the mud came there. The third night the princess determined to lie awake herself and watch; and, for fear that she might fall asleep, she cut her finger with a penknife and rubbed salt into the cut, that the pain of it might keep her from sleeping. So she lay awake, and at midnight she saw a snake come wriggling along the ground with some mud from the river in its mouth; and when it came near the bed, it reared up its head and dropped its muddy head on the bedclothes. She was very frightened, but tried to control her fear, and called out:

"Who are you, and what do you here?"

And the snake answered: "I am the prince, your husband, and I am come to visit you."

Then the princess began to weep; and the snake continued: "Alas! Did I not say that if I told you my secret you would repent it? And have you not repented?"

"Oh, indeed!" cried the poor princess, "I have repented it, and shall repent it all my life! Is there nothing I can do?"

And the snake answered: "Yes, there is one thing, if you dared to do it."

"Only tell me," said the princess, "and I will do anything!"

"Then," replied the snake, "on a certain night you must put a large bowl of milk and sugar in each of the four corners of this room. All the snakes in the river will come out to drink the milk, and the one that leads the way will be the queen of the snakes. You must stand in her way at the door, and say: "Oh, Queen of Snakes, Queen of Snakes, give me back my husband!" and perhaps she will do it. But if you are frightened, and do not stop her, you will never see me again." And he glided away.

On the night of which the snake had told her, the princess got four large bowls of milk and sugar, and put one in each corner of the room, and stood in the doorway waiting. At midnight there was a great hissing and rustling from the direction of the river, and presently the ground appeared to be alive with horrible writhing forms of snakes, whose eyes glittered and forked tongues quivered as they moved on in the direction of the princess's house. Foremost among them was a huge, repulsive, scaly creature that led the dreadful procession. The guards were so terrified that they all ran away; but the princess stood in the doorway, as white as death, and with her hands clasped tight together for fear she should scream or faint, and fail to do her part.

As they came closer and saw her in the way, all the snakes raised their horrid heads and swayed them to and fro, and looked at her with wicked, beady eyes, while their breath seemed to poison the very air. Still the princess stood firm, and, when the leading snake was within a few feet of her, she cried: "Oh, Queen of Snakes, Queen of Snakes, give me back my husband!"

Then all the rustling, writhing crowd of snakes seemed to whisper to one another, "Her husband? Her husband?"

But the queen of snakes moved on until her head was almost in the princess's face, and her little eyes seemed to flash fire. And still the

"'Oh, Queen of Snakes, Queen of Snakes,

give me back my husband!'"

princess stood in the doorway and never moved, but cried again: "Oh, Queen of Snakes, Queen of Snakes, give me back my husband!"

Then the queen of snakes replied: "Tomorrow you shall have him–tomorrow!"

When she heard these words and knew that she had conquered, the princess staggered to her bed and fainted. As in a dream, she saw that her room was full of snakes, all jostling and squabbling over the bowls of milk until it was finished. And then they went away.

In the morning the princess was up early, and took off the mourning dress that she had worn for five whole years, and put on gay and beautiful clothes. And she swept the house and cleaned it, and adorned it with garlands and nosegays of sweet flowers and ferns, and prepared it as though she were making ready for her wedding. And when night fell, she lit up the woods and gardens with lanterns, and spread a table as for a feast, and lit in the house a thousand wax candles. Then she waited for her husband, not knowing in what shape he would appear. And at midnight there came striding from the river the prince, laughing, but with tears in his eyes; and she ran to meet him, and threw herself into his arms, crying and laughing too.

So the prince came home; and the next day they two went back to the palace, and the old king wept with joy to see them. And the bells, so long silent, were set a-ringing again, and the guns firing, and the trumpets blaring, and there was fresh feasting and rejoicing.

And the old woman who had been the prince's nurse became nurse to the prince's children–at least she was called so; though she was far too old to do anything for them but love them. Yet she still thought that she was useful, and knew that she was happy. And happy, indeed, were the prince and princess, who in due time became king and queen, and lived and ruled long and prosperously.

Andrew Lang

Notes on the Story

THE SNAKE PRINCE

Between 1889 and 1913 Andrew Lang (1844–1912) published his twelve "Fairy Books of Many Colors." Lang was a Scottish folklorist who gathered tales from across the world, collating them together for the aim of "pleasing children." Alongside Mrs. Lang, who helped to translate and adapt the tales for the child audience, Lang published some of the best-known English versions of folktales from other countries.

✣

"The Snake Prince," a Punjabi tale from India, is reminiscent of many other tales of the animal bridegroom type. Like "The Pig King" (page 22) and "Beauty and the Beast" (page 102), it contrasts a repulsive animal with a handsome and kind prince. The snake in Punjabi tradition is both feared and worshipped, sometimes by offering milk and sugar as in the tale. Like "East of the Sun and West of the Moon" (page 195), "The Snake Prince" requires the heroine to act with bravery to save her beloved.

The Lion and the Crane

The Bodhisatta was at one time born in the region of Himavanta as a white crane; now Brahmadatta was at that time reigning in Benares. Now it chanced that as a lion was eating meat a bone stuck in his throat. The throat became swollen, he could not take food, and his suffering was terrible. The crane seeing him, as he was perched on a tree looking for food, asked, "What ails you, friend?" The lion told him why.

"I could free you from that bone, friend, but dare not enter your mouth for fear you might eat me."

"Don't be afraid, friend, I'll not eat you; only save my life."

"Very well," said the crane, and caused the lion to lie down on his left side. But thinking to himself, "Who knows what this fellow will do," he placed a small stick upright between his two jaws that he could not close his mouth, and inserting his head inside his mouth struck one end of the bone with his beak. Whereupon the bone dropped and fell out. As soon as he had caused the bone to fall, he got out of the lion's mouth, striking the stick with his beak so that it fell out, and then settled on a branch. The lion got well, and one day was eating a buffalo he had killed. The crane, thinking, "I will sound him," settled on a branch just over him, and in conversation spoke this first verse:

"A service have we done you
To the best of our ability,
King of the Beasts! Your Majesty!
What return shall we get from you?"

In reply the Lion spoke the second verse:

"As I feed on blood,
And always hunt for prey,
'Tis much that you are still alive
Having once been between my teeth."

Then in reply the crane said the two other verses:

"Ungrateful, doing no good,
Not doing as he would be done by,
In him there is no gratitude,
To serve him is useless."

"His friendship is not won
By the clearest good deed.
Better softly withdraw from him,
Neither envying nor abusing."

And having thus spoken, the crane flew away.

And when the great Teacher, Gautama the Buddha, told this tale, he used to add: "Now at that time the lion was Devadatta the Traitor, but the white crane was I myself."

Joseph Jacobs

Notes on the Story

The Lion and the Crane

Joseph Jacobs, whose English and Celtic fairy tales appear earlier in this collection (see pages 219–244), sought tales not only from the British Isles but also from across the world. His collection *Indian Fairy Tales* was published in 1912 and he believed many of Europe's fables and fairy tales had roots in older tales from India.

The story of the lion and the white crane is a type of animal fable from a collection of Buddhist tales called Jātakas, or Buddha birth-stories (c. 241 BCE). Beast fables, which generally relate a moral or allegory through anthropomorphic animals, are most commonly associated with Aesop, a slave in Greece who wrote down many of the best-known fables. Jacobs noted several Jātakas that had parallels in Aesop, but also many more that did not, demonstrating that the Jātakas were their own genre in the Buddhist tradition. However, he felt this tale was a typical example of the way fables originated in India and moved westward.

A Lesson For Kings

Once upon a time, when Brahmadatta was reigning in Benares, the future Buddha returned to life as his son and heir. And when the day came for choosing a name, they called him Prince Brahmadatta. He grew up in due course; and when he was sixteen years old, went to Takkasila, and became accomplished in all arts. And after his father died he ascended the throne, and ruled the kingdom with righteousness and equity. He gave judgments without partiality, hatred, ignorance, or fear. Since he thus reigned with justice, with justice also his ministers administered the law. Lawsuits being thus decided with justice, there were none who brought false cases. And as these ceased, the noise and tumult of litigation ceased in the king's court. Though the judges sat all day in the court, they had to leave without any one coming for justice. It came to this, that the Hall of Justice would have to be closed!

Then the future Buddha thought, "It cannot be from my reigning with righteousness that none come for judgment; the bustle has ceased, and the Hall of Justice will have to be closed. I must, therefore, now examine into my own faults; and if I find that anything is wrong in me, put that away, and practice only virtue."

Thenceforth, he sought for some one to tell him his faults, but among those around him he found no one who would tell him of any fault, but heard only his own praise.

"'Take your chariot out of the way,

O charioteer!'"

Then he thought, "It is from fear of me that these men speak only good things, and not evil things," and he sought among those people who lived outside the palace. And finding no faultfinder there, he sought among those who lived outside the city, in the suburbs, at the four gates. And there, too, finding no one to find fault, and hearing only his own praise, he determined to search the country places.

So he made over the kingdom to his ministers, and mounted his chariot; and taking only his charioteer, left the city in disguise. And searching the country through, up to the very boundary, he found no faultfinder, and heard only of his own virtue; and so he turned back from the outermost boundary, and returned by the high road toward the city.

Now at that time the king of Kosala, Mallika by name, was also ruling his kingdom with righteousness; and when seeking for some fault in himself, he also found no faultfinder in the palace, but only heard of his own virtue! So seeking in country places, he too came to that very spot. And these two came face to face in a low cart track with precipitous sides, where there was no space for a chariot to get out of the way!

Then the charioteer of Mallika the king said to the charioteer of the king of Benares, "Take your chariot out of the way!"

But he said, "Take your chariot out of the way, O charioteer! In this chariot sits the lord over the kingdom of Benares, the great King Brahmadatta."

Yet the other replied, "In this chariot, O charioteer, sits the lord over the kingdom of Kosala, the great King Mallika. Take your carriage out of the way, and make room for the chariot of our king!"

Then the charioteer of the king of Benares thought, "They say then that he too is a king! What is now to be done?" After some consideration, he said to himself, "I know a way. I'll find out how old he is, and then I'll let the chariot of the younger be got out of the way, and so make room for the elder."

And when he had arrived at that conclusion, he asked that charioteer what the age of the King of Kosala was. But on inquiry he found that the ages of both were equal. Then he inquired about the extent of his kingdom, and about his army, and his wealth, and his renown, and about the country he lived in, and his caste and tribe and family. And he found that both were lords of a kingdom three hundred leagues in extent; and that in respect of army and wealth and renown, and the countries in which they lived, and their caste and their tribe and their family, they were just on a par!

Then he thought, "I will make way for the most righteous." And he asked, "What kind of righteousness has this king of yours?"

Then the charioteer of the King of Kosala, proclaiming his king's wickedness as goodness, uttered the first stanza:

"The strong he overthrows by strength,
The mild by mildness, does Mallika;
The good he conquers by goodness,
And the wicked by wickedness too.
Such is the nature of this king!
Move out of the way, O charioteer!"

But the charioteer of the king of Benares asked him, "Well, have you told all the virtues of your king?"

"Yes," said the other.

"If these are his virtues, where are then his faults?" replied he.

The other said, "Well, they shall be faults, if you like! But pray, then, what is the kind of goodness your king has?"

And then the charioteer of the king of Benares called unto him to hearken, and uttered the second stanza:

"Anger he conquers by calmness,
And by goodness the wicked;
The stingy he conquers by gifts,
And by truth the speaker of lies.
Such is the nature of this king!
Move out of the way, O charioteer!"

And when he had thus spoken, both Mallika the king and his charioteer alighted from their chariot. And they took out the horses, and removed their chariot, and made way for the king of Benares!

Joseph Jacobs

Notes on the Story

A Lesson for Kings

"A Lesson for Kings" is a Jātaka, or Buddha birth-story, like "The Lion and the Crane" (page 326), although "A Lesson for Kings" is not an animal fable. The encounter between Brahmadatta, the future Buddha, and Mallika is a religious parable for the Buddha's teachings. Jacobs considered this to be one of the earliest existing moral allegories. When Brahmadatta's charioteer recites the second stanza, he is referring to verse 223 in the *Dhammapada* (one of the Buddhist scriptures), which describes the "Four Forms of Victories." This peaceful way of treating others shows that calm patience, good deeds, generosity, and honesty make a mightier king.

Jacobs called the Jātakas the "Indian Grimm," and saw them as one of the oldest folktale collections in the world. The Jātakas' religious significance was one of the driving factors for followers of the Buddha to record them. Later European versions of similar tales were not always as explicitly religious, although they often retained the moral messages.

Why the Fish Laughed

Once upon a time as a certain fisherwoman passed by a palace crying her fish, the queen appeared at one of the windows and beckoned her to come near and show what she had. At that moment a very big fish jumped about in the bottom of the basket.

"Is it a he or a she?" inquired the queen. "I wish to purchase a she fish."

On hearing this, the fish laughed aloud.

"It's a he," replied the fisherwoman, and proceeded on her rounds.

The queen returned to her room in a great rage; and on coming to see her in the evening, the king noticed that something had disturbed her.

"Are you indisposed?" he said.

"No; but I am very much annoyed at the strange behavior of a fish. A woman brought me one today, and on my inquiring whether it was a male or female, the fish laughed most rudely."

"A fish laugh! Impossible! You must be dreaming."

"I am not a fool. I speak of what I have seen with my own eyes and have heard with my own ears."

"Passing strange! Be it so. I will inquire concerning it."

On the morrow the king repeated to his vizier what his wife had told him, and bade him investigate the matter, and be ready with a satisfactory answer within six months, on pain of death. The vizier promised to do his best, though he felt almost certain of failure. For five months he labored indefatigably to find a reason for the laughter of the fish. He sought everywhere and from every one. The wise and learned, and they who were skilled in magic and in all manner of trickery, were consulted. Nobody, however, could explain the matter; and so he returned broken-hearted to his house, and began to arrange his affairs in prospect of certain death, for he had had sufficient experience of the king to know that His Majesty would not go back from his threat. Amongst other things, he advised his son to travel for a time, until the king's anger should have somewhat cooled.

The young fellow, who was both clever and handsome, started off wherever fate might lead him. He had been gone some days, when he fell in with an old farmer, who also was on a journey to a certain village. Finding the old man very pleasant, he asked him if he might accompany him, professing to be on a visit to the same place. The old farmer agreed, and they walked along together. The day was hot, and the way was long and weary.

"Don't you think it would be pleasanter if you and I sometimes gave one another a lift?" said the youth.

"What a fool the man is!" thought the old farmer.

Presently they passed through a field of corn ready for the sickle, and looking like a sea of gold as it waved to and fro in the breeze.

"Is this eaten or not?" said the young man.

Not understanding his meaning, the old man replied, "I don't know."

After a little while the two travelers arrived at a big village, where the young man gave his companion a clasp knife, and said, "Take this, friend, and get two horses with it; but mind and bring it back, for it is very precious."

The old man, looking half amused and half angry, pushed back the knife, muttering something to the effect that his friend was either a fool himself or else trying to play the fool with him.

The young man pretended not to notice his reply, and remained almost silent till they reached the city, a short distance outside which was the old farmer's house. They walked about the bazaar and went to the mosque, but nobody saluted them or invited them to come in and rest.

"What a large cemetery!" exclaimed the young man.

"What does the man mean," thought the old farmer, "calling this largely populated city a cemetery?"

On leaving the city their way led through a cemetery where a few people were praying beside a grave and distributing chapattis and kulchas to passers-by, in the name of their beloved dead. They beckoned to the two travelers and gave them as much as they would.

"What a splendid city this is!" said the young man.

"Now, the man must surely be demented!" thought the old farmer. "I wonder what he will do next? He will be calling the land water, and the water land; and be speaking of light where there is darkness, and of darkness when it is light." However, he kept his thoughts to himself.

Presently they had to wade through a stream that ran along the edge of the cemetery. The water was rather deep, so the old farmer took off his shoes and pajamas and crossed over; but the young man waded through it with his shoes and pajamas on.

"Well! I never did see such a perfect fool, both in word and in deed," said the old man to himself.

However, he liked the fellow; and thinking that he would amuse his wife and daughter, he invited him to come and stay at his house as long as he had occasion to remain in the village.

"Thank you very much," the young man replied; "but let me first inquire, if you please, whether the beam of your house is strong."

The old farmer left him in despair, and entered his house laughing.

"There is a man in yonder field," he said, after returning their greetings. "He has come the greater part of the way with me, and I wanted him to put up here as long as he had to stay in this village.

But the fellow is such a fool that I cannot make anything out of him. He wants to know if the beam of this house is all right. The man must be mad!" and saying this, he burst into a fit of laughter.

"Father," said the farmer's daughter, who was a very sharp and wise girl, "this man, whosoever he is, is no fool, as you deem him. He only wishes to know if you can afford to entertain him."

"Oh! Of course," replied the farmer. "I see. Well perhaps you can help me to solve some of his other mysteries. While we were walking together he asked whether he should carry me or I should carry him, as he thought that would be a pleasanter mode of proceeding."

"Most assuredly," said the girl, "he meant that one of you should tell a story to beguile the time."

"Oh yes. Well, we were passing through a cornfield, when he asked me whether it was eaten or not."

"And didn't you know the meaning of this, father? He simply wished to know if the man was in debt or not; because, if the owner of the field was in debt, then the produce of the field was as good as eaten to him; that is, it would have to go to his creditors."

"Yes, yes, yes, of course! Then, on entering a certain village, he bade me take his clasp knife and get two horses with it, and bring back the knife again to him."

"Are not two stout sticks as good as two horses for helping one along on the road? He only asked you to cut a couple of sticks and be careful not to lose his knife."

"I see," said the farmer. "While we were walking over the city we did not see anybody that we knew, and not a soul gave us a scrap of anything to eat, till we were passing the cemetery; but there some people called to us and put into our hands some chapattis and kulchas; so my companion called the city a cemetery, and the cemetery a city."

"This also is to be understood, father, if one thinks of the city as the place where everything is to be obtained, and of inhospitable people as worse than the dead. The city, though crowded with people, was as if dead, as far as you were concerned; while, in the cemetery, which is crowded with the dead, you were saluted by kind friends and provided with bread."

"True, true!" said the astonished farmer. "Then, just now, when we were crossing the stream, he waded through it without taking off his shoes and pajamas."

"I admire his wisdom," replied the girl. "I have often thought how stupid people were to venture into that swiftly flowing stream and over those sharp stones with bare feet. The slightest stumble and they would fall, and be wetted from head to foot. This friend of yours is a most wise man. I should like to see him and speak to him."

"Very well," said the farmer, "I will go and find him, and bring him in."

"Tell him, father, that our beams are strong enough, and then he will come in. I'll send on ahead a present to the man, to show him that we can afford to have him for our guest."

Accordingly she called a servant and sent him to the young man with a present of a basin of ghee, twelve chapattis, and a jar of milk, and the following message: "O friend, the moon is full; twelve months make a year, and the sea is overflowing with water."

Halfway the bearer of this present and message met his little son, who, seeing what was in the basket, begged his father to give him some of the food. His father foolishly complied. Presently he saw the young man, and gave him the rest of the present and the message.

"Give your mistress my salaam," he replied, "and tell her that the moon is new, and that I can only find eleven months in the year, and the sea is by no means full."

Not understanding the meaning of these words, the servant repeated them word for word, as he had heard them, to his mistress; and thus his theft was discovered, and he was severely punished. After a little while the young man appeared with the old farmer. Great attention was shown to him, and he was treated in every way as if he were the son of a great man, although his humble host knew nothing of his origin. At length he told them everything: about the laughing of the fish, his father's threatened execution, and his own banishment, and asked their advice as to what he should do.

"The laughing of the fish," said the girl, "which seems to have been the cause of all this trouble, indicates that there is a man in the palace who is plotting against the king's life."

"Joy, joy!" exclaimed the vizier's son. "There is yet time for me to return and save my father from an ignominious and unjust death, and the king from danger."

The following day he hastened back to his own country, taking with him the farmer's daughter. Immediately on arrival he ran to the palace and informed his father of what he had heard. The poor vizier, now almost dead from the expectation of death, was at once carried to the king, to whom he repeated the news that his son had just brought.

"Never!" said the king.

"But it must be so, Your Majesty," replied the vizier; "and in order to prove the truth of what I have heard, I pray you to call together all the maids in your palace, and order them to jump over a pit, which must be dug. We'll soon find out whether there is any man there."

The king had the pit dug, and commanded all the maids belonging to the palace to try to jump it. All of them tried, but only one succeeded. That one was found to be a man!

Thus was the queen satisfied, and the faithful old vizier saved.

Afterward, as soon as could be, the vizier's son married the old farmer's daughter; and a most happy marriage it was.

Joseph Jacobs

"'O friend, the moon is full; twelve months make a year,

and the sea is overflowing with water.'"

Notes on the Story

Why the Fish Laughed

Jacobs published not only a selection of the Jātakas, but many other types of Indian folktales. This Kashmiri tale, "Why the Fish Laughed," is a riddling tale or a brainteaser, which poses seemingly impossible questions or tasks to the characters. The solutions usually involve clever responses that play with the literal and figurative meanings of the challenges or questions. The vizier's son uses "puzzling language" to devise who is clever enough to answer the riddle of the fish; but only the farmer's daughter can interpret it.

The motif of a clever daughter or little girl who is smarter than her father and bests the aristocracy is also found in many other riddling tales. For example, the Grimms' "The Farmer's Clever Daughter" and a similar Russian tale collected by Alexander Afanasyev, "The Wise Little Girl," both contain a daughter whose wisdom protects her father and ultimately leads to her marrying a king or tsar.

The Pigeon and the Crow

Once upon a time the Bodhisatta was a pigeon, and lived in a nest-basket, which a rich man's cook had hung up in the kitchen, in order to earn merit by it. A greedy crow, flying near, saw all sorts of delicate food lying about in the kitchen, and fell a-hungering after it. "How in the world can I get some?" thought he. At last he hit upon a plan.

When the pigeon went to search for food, behind him, following, following, came the crow.

"What do you want, Mr. Crow? You and I don't feed alike."

"Ah, but I like you and your ways! Let me be your friend, and let us feed together."

The pigeon agreed, and they went on in company. The crow pretended to feed along with the pigeon, but ever and anon he would turn back, peck to bits some heap of cow dung, and eat a fat worm. When he had got a bellyful of them, up he flies, as pert as you like:

"Hullo, Mr. Pigeon, what a time you take over your meal! One ought to draw the line somewhere. Let's be going home before it is too late." And so they did.

The cook saw that his pigeon had brought a friend, and hung up another basket for him.

A few days afterward there was a great purchase of fish, which came to the rich man's kitchen. How the crow longed for some! So there he lay, from early morn, groaning and making a great noise. Said the pigeon to the crow:

"Come, Sir Crow, and get your breakfast!"

"Oh dear! Oh dear! I have such a fit of indigestion!" said he.

"Nonsense! Crows never have indigestion," said the pigeon. "If you eat a lamp-wick, that stays in your stomach a little while; but anything else is digested in a trice, as soon as you eat it. Now do what I tell you; don't behave in this way just for seeing a little fish."

"Why do you say that, master? I have indigestion."

"Well, be careful," said the pigeon, and flew away.

The cook prepared all the dishes, and then stood at the kitchen door, wiping the sweat off his body. "Now's my time!" thought Mr. Crow, and alighted on a dish containing some dainty food. Click! The cook heard it, and looked round. Ah! He caught the crow, and plucked all the feathers out of his head, all but one tuft; he powdered ginger and cumin, mixed it up with buttermilk, and rubbed it well all over the bird's body.

"That's for spoiling my master's dinner and making me throw it away!" said he, and threw him into his basket. Oh, how it hurt!

By and by the pigeon came in, and saw the crow lying there, making a great noise. He made great game of him, and repeated a verse of poetry:

"Who is this tufted crane I see
Lying where he's no right to be?
Come out! My friend, the crow is near,
And he may do you harm, I fear!"

To this the crow answered with another:

"No tufted crane am I–no, no!
I'm nothing but a greedy crow.
I would not do as I was told,
So now I'm plucked, as you behold."

And the pigeon rejoined with a third verse:

"You'll come to grief again, I know–
It is your nature to do so;
If people make a dish of meat,
'Tis not for little birds to eat."

Then the pigeon flew away, saying: "I can't live with this creature any longer." And the crow lay there groaning till he died.

Joseph Jacobs

Notes on the Story

The Pigeon and the Crow

This tale is another Jātaka, once again using the beast fable to illustrate tenets of the Buddhist belief system. Jacobs ended his collection of *Indian Fairy Tales* with this fable, stating in his notes that this tale demonstrated the effective representation of animals in the Jātakas, and how "terribly moral" they were. This lesson against greed was important; so much so that it is repeated four times in the full set of the Jātakas.

A particular quality of the Jātakas is that many of the stories begin in a frame narrative, like the fairy tales written by Straparola and Basile. The tales usually started with a "story of the present" before moving to a moral tale of the Buddha's previous incarnation. This version, abridged by Jacobs for his collection, substituted the frame for the familiar "once upon a time" in order to move the reader from the Buddha's present to past life.

The Boy Who Wanted More Cheese

Klaas Van Bommel was a Dutch boy, twelve years old, who lived where cows were plentiful. He was over five feet high, weighed a hundred pounds, and had rosy cheeks. His appetite was always good and his mother declared his stomach had no bottom. His hair was of a color halfway between a carrot and a sweet potato. It was as thick as reeds in a swamp and was cut level, from under one ear to another.

Klaas stood in a pair of timber shoes, which made an awful rattle when he ran fast to catch a rabbit, or scuffed slowly along to school over the brick road of his village. In summer Klaas was dressed in a rough, blue linen blouse. In winter he wore woolen breeches as wide as coffee bags. They were called bell trousers, and in shape were like a couple of cowbells turned upward. These were buttoned on to a thick warm jacket. Until he was five years old, Klaas was dressed like his sisters. Then, on his birthday, he had boy's clothes, with two pockets in them, of which he was proud enough.

Klaas was a farmer's boy. He had rye bread and fresh milk for breakfast. At dinnertime, beside cheese and bread, he was given a plate heaped with boiled potatoes. Into these he first plunged a fork and then dipped each round, white ball into a bowl of hot melted butter.

Very quickly then did potato and butter disappear "down the red lane." At supper, he had bread and skim milk, left after the cream had been taken off, with a saucer, to make butter. Twice a week the children enjoyed a bowl of bonnyclabber or curds, with a little brown sugar sprinkled on the top. But at every meal, there was cheese, usually in thin slices, which the boy thought not thick enough. When Klaas went to bed, he usually fell asleep as soon as his shock of yellow hair touched the pillow. In summertime, he slept till the birds began to sing, at dawn. In winter, when the bed felt warm and Jack Frost was lively, he often heard the cows talking, in their way, before he jumped out of his bag of straw, which served for a mattress. The Van Bommels were not rich, but everything was shining clean.

There was always plenty to eat at the Van Bommels' house. Stacks of rye bread, a yard long and thicker than a man's arm, stood on end in the corner of the cool, stone-lined basement. The loaves of dough were put in the oven once a week. Baking time was a great event at the Van Bommels' and no menfolk were allowed in the kitchen on that day, unless they were called in to help. As for the milk-pails and pans, filled or emptied, scrubbed or set in the sun every day to dry, and the cheeses, piled up in the pantry, they seemed sometimes enough to feed a small army.

But Klaas always wanted more cheese. In other ways, he was a good boy, obedient at home, always ready to work on the cow farm, and diligent in school. But at the table, he never had enough. Sometimes his father laughed and asked him if he had a well, or a cave, under his jacket.

Klaas had three younger sisters, Trintjé, Anneké, and Saartjé; which is Dutch for Kate, Annie, and Sallie. These, their fond mother, who loved them dearly, called her "orange blossoms"; but when at dinner, Klaas would keep on, dipping his potatoes into the hot butter, while others were all through, his mother would laugh and call him her Buttercup. But always Klaas wanted more cheese. When unusually greedy, she twitted him as a boy "worse than Butter-and-Eggs"; that is, as troublesome as the yellow and white plant, called toadflax, is to the farmer–very pretty, but nothing but a weed.

One summer's evening, after a good scolding, which he deserved well, Klaas moped and, almost crying, went to bed in bad humor. He had teased each one of his sisters to give him her bit of cheese, and this, added to his own slice, made his stomach feel as heavy as lead.

Klaas's bed was up in the garret. When the house was first built, one of the red tiles of the roof had been taken out and another one, made of glass, was put in its place. In the morning, this gave the boy light to put on his clothes. At night, in fair weather, it supplied air to his room.

A gentle breeze was blowing from the pinewoods on the sandy slope, not far away. So Klaas climbed up on the stool to sniff the sweet piney odors. He thought he saw lights dancing under the tree. One beam seemed to approach his roof hole, and, coming nearer, played round the chimney. Then it passed to and fro in front of him. It seemed to whisper in his ear as it moved by. It looked very much as if a hundred fireflies had united their cold light into one lamp. Then Klaas thought that the strange beams bore the shape of a lovely girl, but he only laughed at himself at the idea. Pretty soon, however, he thought the whisper became a voice. Again, he laughed so heartily that he forgot his moping and the scolding his mother had given him. In fact, his eyes twinkled with delight, when the voice gave this invitation:

"There's plenty of cheese. Come with us."

To make sure of it, the sleepy boy now rubbed his eyes and cocked his ears. Again, the light-bearer spoke to him: "Come."

Could it be? He had heard old people tell of the ladies of the wood that whispered and warned travelers. In fact, he himself had often seen the "fairies' ring" in the pinewoods. To this, the flame-lady was inviting him.

Again and again the moving, cold light circled round the red tile roof, which the moon, then rising and peeping over the chimneys, seemed to turn into silver plates. As the disc rose higher in the sky, he could hardly see the moving light that had looked like a lady; but the voice, no longer a whisper, as at first, was now even plainer:

"There's plenty of cheese. Come with us."

"I'll see what it is, anyhow," said Klaas, as he drew on his thick woolen stockings and prepared to go downstairs and out, without waking a soul. At the door, he stepped into his wooden shoes. Just then the cat purred and rubbed up against his shins. He jumped, for he was scared; but looking down, for a moment, he saw the two balls of yellow fire in her head and knew what they were. Then he sped to the pinewoods and toward the fairy ring.

What an odd sight! At first Klaas thought it was a circle of big fireflies. Then he saw clearly that there were dozens of pretty creatures, hardly as large as dolls, but as lively as crickets. They were as full of light, as if lamps had wings. Hand in hand, they flitted and danced around the ring of grass, as if this was fun.

Hardly had Klaas got over his first surprise, than of a sudden he felt himself surrounded by the fairies. Some of the strongest among them had left the main party in the circle and come to him. He felt himself pulled by their dainty fingers. One of them, the loveliest of all, whispered in his ear:

"Come, you must dance with us."

Then a dozen of the pretty creatures murmured in chorus:

"Plenty of cheese here. Plenty of cheese here. Come, come!"

Upon this, the heels of Klaas seemed as light as a feather. In a moment, with both hands clasped in those of the fairies, he was dancing in high glee. It was as much fun as if he were at the kermiss (festival), with a row of boys and girls, hand in hand, swinging along the streets, as Dutch maids and youths do, during kermiss week.

Klaas had not time to look hard at the fairies, for he was too full of the fun. He danced and danced, all night and until the sky in the east began to turn, first gray and then rosy. Then he tumbled down, tired out, and fell asleep. His head lay on the inner curve of the fairy ring, with his feet in the center.

Klaas felt very happy, for he had no sense of being tired, and he did not know he was asleep. He thought his fairy partners, who had danced with him, were now waiting on him to bring him cheeses. With a golden knife, they sliced them off and fed him out of their own hands. How good it tasted! He thought now he could, and would, eat all the cheese he had longed for all his life. There was no mother to scold him, or father to shake his finger at him. How delightful!

But by and by, he wanted to stop eating and rest a while. His jaws were tired. His stomach seemed to be loaded with cannon balls. He gasped for breath.

But the fairies would not let him stop, for Dutch fairies never get tired. Flying out of the sky—from the north, south, east, and west—they came, bringing cheeses. These they dropped down around him, until the piles of the round masses threatened first to enclose him as with a wall, and then to overtop him. There were the red balls from Edam, the pink and yellow spheres from Gouda, and the gray loaf-shaped ones from Leyden. Down through the vista of sand, in the pinewoods, he looked, and oh, horrors! There were the tallest and strongest of the fairies rolling along the huge, round, flat cheeses from Friesland! Any one of these was as big as a cartwheel, and would feed a regiment. The fairies trundled the heavy discs along, as if they were playing with hoops. They shouted hilariously, as, with a pine stick, they beat them forward like boys at play. Farm cheese, factory cheese, Alkmaar cheese, and, to crown all, cheese from Limburg—which Klaas never could bear,

"Dutch fairies never get tired. Flying out of the sky–from the north,

south, east, and west–they came, bringing cheeses."

because of its strong odor. Soon the cakes and balls were heaped so high around him that the boy, as he looked up, felt like a frog in a well. He groaned when he thought the high cheese walls were tottering to fall on him. Then he screamed, but the fairies thought he was making music. They, not being human, do not know how a boy feels.

At last, with a thick slice in one hand and a big hunk in the other, he could eat no more cheese; though the fairies, led by their queen, standing on one side, or hovering over his head, still urged him to take more.

At this moment, while afraid that he would burst, Klaas saw the pile of cheeses, as big as a house, topple over. The heavy mass fell inward upon him. With a scream of terror, he thought himself crushed as flat as a Friesland cheese.

But he wasn't! Waking up and rubbing his eyes, he saw the red sun rising on the sand dunes. Birds were singing and the cocks were crowing all around him, in chorus, as if saluting him. Just then also the village clock chimed out the hour. He felt his clothes. They were wet with dew. He sat up to look around. There were no fairies, but in his mouth was a bunch of grass, which he had been chewing lustily.

Klaas never would tell the story of his night with the fairies, nor has he yet settled the question whether they left him because the cheese-house of his dream had fallen, or because daylight had come.

William Elliot Griffis

Notes on the Story

The Boy Who Wanted More Cheese

William Elliot Griffis (1843–1928) was an American pastor and author who published extensively on many topics. He had an interest in fairylands from many cultures, and published volumes of Japanese, Chinese, Korean, Belgian, Swiss, Welsh, and Dutch tales (like this one). Indeed, Griffis' interest in the Netherlands did not stop at fairy tales; he also published many books on the Netherlands and Dutch Americans.

This didactic tale cautions the listener not to be a glutton, demonstrating that there can be too much of a good thing. Unusually for a fairy tale, there are many specifics, from the clothes Klaas wears to the regional cheeses the fairies bring him. Though the fairies teach him a lesson, they seem to straddle the borderline between merry indulgence and bad intentions. The ambiguity of the fairies' objective is a common theme in encounters with them, as in "Connla and the Fairy Maiden" (page 237), "Rip Van Winkle" (page 251), and "Whanawhana of the Bush" (page 363).

YUKI-ONNA

Mosaku, an old man, and Minokichi, his apprentice, were two woodcutters, who lived in Musachi Province. Every day they went to a forest; on the way, there was a wide river to cross, and a ferryboat. One cold evening, on their way home, a great snowstorm overtook them. They reached the ferry, and found that the ferryman had left. So the woodcutters took shelter in the ferryman's hut, thinking themselves lucky to find any shelter at all.

The woodcutters fastened the door, and lay down to rest. The old man quickly fell asleep, but Minokichi lay awake listening to the awful wind, and the lashing of the snow against the door. But at last, he too fell asleep. He was awakened by a shower of snow in his face. A woman, all in white, was bending above Mosaku, and blowing her breath upon him, which was like a bright white smoke. She then turned to Minokichi and stooped over him. He tried to cry out, but could not utter a sound. The white woman crouched over him, until her face almost touched him; and he saw that she was very beautiful, though her eyes made him afraid.

She smiled, and whispered, "I intended to treat you like the other man. But I feel some pity for you, because you are so young and handsome, and I will not hurt you now. But, if you ever tell anybody about what you have seen this night, I shall know it; and then I will kill you. Remember what I say!"

With these words, she turned and left. Minokichi sprang up, and looked out. But the woman was nowhere to be seen. He called to Mosaku, but the old man did not answer. He put out his hand and touched Mosaku's face, and found that it was ice. Mosaku was dead!

One evening, the following winter, Minokichi met a pretty girl called O-Yuki. She was going to Yedo to find work as a servant. He was charmed by this girl. He asked her whether she was yet betrothed; and she answered, laughingly, that she was free. Minokichi asked O-Yuki to rest at his house and to delay her journey to Yedo. And so, Yuki never went to Yedo at all. She remained in the house, as an "honorable daughter-in-law."

O-Yuki proved a very good wife. She bore Minokichi ten children, boys and girls, all handsome children and with very fair skin.

One night, O-Yuki was sewing by the light of a paper lamp and Minokichi, watching her, said: "To see you there, reminds me of a strange thing that happened when I was a lad. I saw somebody as beautiful and white as you are now–indeed, she was very like you."

O-Yuki responded: "Tell me about her; where did you see her?"

Then Minokichi told her about the terrible night in the ferryman's hut, and about the white woman that had stooped above him, smiling and whispering; and about the silent death of old Mosaku.

And he said: "Asleep or awake, that was the only time that I saw a being as beautiful as you. Of course, she was not a human being; and I was very much afraid, but she was so white. Indeed, I have never been sure whether it was a dream that I saw, or the Woman of the Snow."

O-Yuki bowed above Minokichi where he sat, and shrieked into his face: "It was I! Yuki! I said that I would kill you if you ever said one word about it! But for those children asleep there, I would kill you now!"

Even as she screamed, her voice became thin, like a crying of wind; then she melted into a bright white mist that spired to the roof beams, and shuddered away through the smoke-hold. Never again was she seen.

Lafcadio Hearn

Notes on the Story

YUKI-ONNA

"Yuki-Onna" is a Japanese tale, and only one of the many chilling stories about the risks of meeting the snow spirit called Yuki-Onna. This version has been abridged from a story in a collection by Lafcadio Hearn (1850–1904), *Kwaidan: Stories and Studies of Strange Things* (1904). Hearn was an American journalist and translator, who moved to Japan in 1890. He was so captivated by its culture that he made it his home and married a Japanese woman, taking the name Koizumo Yakomo.

✣

Yuki-Onna is a legendary figure in Japanese mythology. She is found across Japan, a feminine embodiment of the dangerous winter. She appears during snowstorms, to travelers lost in the snow, or to parents whose children have gone missing in winter. She is sometimes considered the spirit of someone who perished in the snow, similar to the European beliefs of the will-o'-the-wisp, where the light of a fairy or unbaptized soul leads travelers deep into the woods, or White Lady tales, where a ghost who died after a romantic tragedy foretells death to her observers.

The Adventures of Juan

Juan was always getting into trouble. He was a lazy boy, and more than that, he did not have good sense. When he tried to do things, he made such dreadful mistakes that he might better not have tried.

His family grew very impatient with him, scolding and beating him whenever he did anything wrong. One day his mother, who was almost discouraged with him, gave him a bolo and sent him to the forest, for she thought he could at least cut firewood. Juan walked leisurely along, contemplating some means of escape. At last he came to a tree that seemed easy to cut, and then he drew his long knife and prepared to work.

Now it happened that this was a magic tree and it said to Juan: "If you do not cut me I will give you a goat that shakes silver from its whiskers."

This pleased Juan wonderfully, both because he was curious to see the goat, and because he would not have to chop the wood. He agreed at once to spare the tree, whereupon the bark separated and a goat stepped out. Juan commanded it to shake its whiskers, and when the money began to drop he was so delighted that he took the animal and started home to show his treasure to his mother.

On the way he met a friend who was more cunning than Juan, and when he heard of the boy's rich goat he decided to rob him. Knowing

"'If you do not cut me,

I will give you a goat that shakes silver from its whiskers.'"

Juan's fondness for tuba, he persuaded him to drink, and while he was drunk, the friend substituted another goat for the magic one. As soon as he was sober again, Juan hastened home with the goat and told his people of the wonderful tree, but when he commanded the animal to shake its whiskers, no money fell out. The family, believing it to be another of Juan's tricks, beat and scolded the poor boy.

He went back to the tree and threatened to cut it down for lying to him, but the tree said: "No, do not cut me down and I will give you a net which you may cast on dry ground, or even in the tree tops, and it will return full of fish."

So Juan spared the tree and started home with his precious net, but on the way he met the same friend who again persuaded him to drink tuba. While he was drunk, the friend replaced the magic net with a common one, so that when Juan reached home and tried to show his power, he was again the subject of ridicule.

Once more Juan went to his tree, this time determined to cut it down. But the offer of a magic pot, always full of rice and spoons, which provided whatever he wished to eat with his rice, dissuaded him, and he started home, happier than ever. Before reaching home, however, he met with the same fate as before, and his folks, who were becoming tired of his pranks, beat him harder than ever.

Thoroughly angered, Juan sought the tree a fourth time and was on the point of cutting it down when once more it arrested his attention. After some discussion, he consented to accept a stick to which he had only to say, "Boombye, Boomba," and it would beat and kill anything he wished.

When he met his friend on this trip, he was asked what he had and he replied: "Oh, it is only a stick, but if I say 'Boombye, Boomba' it will beat you to death."

At the sound of the magic words the stick leaped from his hands and began beating his friend until he cried:

"Oh, stop it and I will give back everything that I stole from you." Juan ordered the stick to stop, and then he compelled the man to lead the goat and to carry the net and the jar and spoons to his home.

There Juan commanded the goat, and it shook its whiskers until his mother and brothers had all the silver they could carry. Then they ate from the magic jar and spoons until they were filled. And this time Juan was not scolded. After they had finished Juan said: "You have beaten me and scolded me all my life, and now you are glad to accept my good things. I am going to show you something else: 'Boombye, Boomba.'" Immediately the stick leaped out and beat them all until they begged for mercy and promised that Juan should ever after be head of the house.

From that time Juan was rich and powerful, but he never went anywhere without his stick. One night, when some thieves came to his house, he would have been robbed and killed had it not been for the magic words "Boombye, Boomba," which caused the death of all the robbers.

Some time after this he married a beautiful princess, and because of the kindness of the magic tree they always lived happily.

Mabel Cook Cole

Notes on the Story

The Adventures of Juan

Mabel Cook Cole (1880–1977) was an American anthropologist who lived for four years with indigenous tribes of the Philippines, publishing *Philippine Folk Tales* in 1916. While the tales vary from myth to fable in style, Cole collected this story from the Tagalog, a people who had had some contact with Western culture, and thus their fabric of indigenous stories also shares the cultural inheritance of the fairy tale.

This tale of a boy who gains, loses, and regains treasures is found across Europe, from Norway to the Czech Republic. It is typical of tale types that begin with a lazy or foolish child (often with a particularly common name such as a Hans, Jack, or Juan) who eventually makes good. The "normality" of his name perhaps represents him as an everyman figure, the aspect of all of us who is both "nothing special," and, at the same time, the hero, trickster, and figure of transformative power.

Whanawhana of the Bush

Once upon a time, not so very long ago, said my old *tohunga* (spiritual leader) friend, two ancestors of my *hapu* (clan) lived over yonder on the western side of the Waipa River, on the narrow levels at the foot of the Hakarimata Range. They were husband and wife; the man was Ruarangi, the wife, a young handsome woman, was Tawhai-tu. Their home was a carved house called "Uru-tomokia." Their cultivation where they grew their kumara and potatoes was at the edge of the forest; in fact it was partly surrounded by forest, and the tall rimu and rata stretched their arms over the fringes of the garden plots, for the Maori liked the protection of the high timber for their crops; it saved them many a frost.

Into this cultivation one day went the wife Tawhai-tu to dig potatoes for the evening meal. She filled a large basket with the potatoes, and then she sought a flax-bush wherefrom to make a kawe or sling to fasten her heavy basket upon her shoulders for the journey to the hamlet of thatched huts, where she and her husband dwelt. She could find no flax, therefore she plucked some of the long, tough leaves of the wharawhara, growing in a low tree fork, and these leaves she split and knotted for shoulder straps.

Now, as Tawhai-tu went about her work, a strange man who crouched within some low, thick bushes at the forest edge watched her all the time. He was a man of wild aspect, with long hair that fell upon

"He was a Patu-paiarehe, *that is to say a fairy–*

he was not a man of the Maori people."

his shoulders and was confined at the back with a cord of mountain flax, and the curious thing about his hair was that it was of a reddish or rather coppery tinge, with a glint of dull fire in it. He was a *Patu-paiarehe*, that is to say a fairy—he was not a man of the Maori people. His home was the bush, and in it he hunted his food. This day he hunted not food but women, for he sought a wife, and it was his fancy to seek for one among the tribes of the Maori. So, he stalked the outskirts of Maori settlements for such straggling females that might suit his taste. And here before him was the most desirable one he had ever set eyes upon. For Tawhai-tu was a beauty, as she sat there unconscious that she was almost within hand-grasp of a *Patu-paiarehe*. Her well-rounded charms of breast and hip and limb set the man of the mountains on fire for possession of her.

As silently as a night owl stealing upon a nestling in a hollow tree, so silently the fairy hunter crept up behind the young woman. He sprang upon her, silenced her before she had time to scream, and *aue*! while still dazed from the sudden capture, she found herself in the depths of the gloomy bush, being borne swiftly through the forest in the wild man's long powerful arms.

Now an even more terrifying thing happened. The fairy with his beautiful burden had gained the summit of a small hill in the forest; its top was clear, in a circle as if artificially formed. This circle Tawhai-tu knew, for all she had heard, must be a meeting-place of the fairies, and therefore *tapu* (sacred). She knew by now, also, that her captor was a *Patu-paiarehe*—he was not of this Maori world.

The red-haired fairy sat his captive on the ground and in a high, thin voice he recited an incantation, and in a moment the hilltop was enveloped in a thick mist. He seized the young woman again, and in another moment she felt herself mounting into the air, sustained by the fairy's arms. All about her were the mists of the mountains. The pair mounted higher and higher, and at last they came to rest upon the higher peak of the ranges, and Tawhai-tu knew now that she must be in the most secret fastnesses of the *Patu-paiarehe* tribe, on the summit of Mount Pirongia.

She found herself surrounded by strange forest folk, with fair hair of the ruddy tint called *uru-kehu*. Their garments were but dangling forest leaves. Their habitations were living trees, the mamaku fern-tree and the nikau palm, arranged in the form of small round houses. Into one of these bowers the fairy lover bore Tawhai-tu and now she knew what it was to become the wife of a *Patu-paiarehe*.

In the morning, while she lay in a deep sleep made heavy by the incantations of the fairy, she was borne away again through the clouds. She awoke, and there she was, lying upon the fairy mound in the bush—and before her stood her husband Ruarangi.

The pair pressed noses and wept as they took each other's hands, and Ruarangi told how in his grief and alarm at his wife's vanishing he had sought her in the forest, fearing greatly that she had been stolen by a *Patu-paiarehe*.

"Alas! It is even so!" said Tawhai-tu, and she told the strange tale of her abduction and her flight through the air and her night in the fairy citadel. She told that her captor's name was Whanawhana—this he had told her when they reposed together. He was the supreme chief of the fairy tribe on Pirongia Mountain, and the name of the forested peak upon which he dwelt was Hihikiwi. Moreover, he had cast a most

powerful spell upon her, and the effect of this was that although she would be returned to her husband in the daytime, by night she must become again the bride of the fairy.

The husband and the wife returned to their home, but as the evening approached the thick fogs and mists rolled down from the mountains and all in a moment Tawhai-tu vanished from Ruarangi's gaze. The *Patu-paiarehe* had carried her off again.

In the morning Tawhai-tu was returned to her husband in the same miraculous manner.

"Alas!" she said. "I have slept once more with the *Patu-paiarehe*! His spell is upon me–my will is as the water of yonder river before his incantations and his fairy *mana*."

And that evening again Ruarangi found himself powerless to hold his wife with him; she vanished in a breath with the cloudy coming of her fairy lord; and as before, in the morning, she stood weeping on the threshold of the house on the Waipa bank.

The husband and the wife now resolved to call the *tohunga* of the tribe to their aid. Ruarangi had watched with spear and stone club to slay the *Patu-paiarehe*, but to what avail are mortal weapons against a fairy chief? He must be fought with charms and potent ceremonies; mere bravery, and muscle, and spear, and club are useless.

The *tohunga* devised his occult schemes and gave directions to Ruarangi and his wife.

"Build quickly," he said, "a small hut of sapling and fern-tree fronds, and lay across the doorway a heavy timber for a *paepaepoto* (threshold)."

The shelter was soon built, and then the magician ordered that the timbers of the hut and the threshold should be coated thickly with the red ocher called *kokowai*. (This is hæmatite earth, mixed with shark oil.)

"And paint your bodies also with the *kokowai*, and smear your garments with it, for it is a thing dreaded by all the fairy tribe."

And this was done, and the odor of the oil-mixed ocher hung heavy on the air.

"Now," the *tohunga* said to the young woman, "kindle an earth-oven in front of the hut and when it is heated pour water upon it and place food in it so that the steam of the cooking will safeguard you from the *Patu-paiarehe*, for the fairy tribe greatly fear the steam that rises from cooking-ovens." And this was done.

As the sun went down to its cave over the high shoulder of the Hakarimata Range, and the river mists came curling up to mingle with the mists of the mountain, Ruarangi and his wife Tawhai-tu sat within the red-painted threshold of their hut, holding tightly to each other's hands, and repeating the charms that the *tohunga* had taught them. Without stood the *tohunga* himself, naked but for a kilt of green flax-leaves, reciting his spells to drive away the fairies. The earth-oven had been opened, and its steam enveloped all the front of the whare.

In a moment there appeared the fairy chief Whanawhana. With him came three of his fellow-chiefs of the bush; their names were Te Rangi-pouri, Tapu-te-uru, and Ripiro-aiti. They came to stretch forth their hands and seize Whanawhana's Maori wife and bear her off through the clouds to Hihikiwi Peak. But the steam of cooking affrighted them, and they smelled also the odor of the oil and ocher with which everything was plentifully daubed, and they heard the rhythmic mutterings of the priest. So they stood at a distance, and stretching out their arms they sang in chorus a *waiata*, a chant of lamentation, and Whanawhana cried aloud for the Maori wife whom he had lost. His spell was powerless now; the *tohunga* had snatched the woman from his grasp. Bitterly he lamented for the desirable Tawhai-tu, and when his chant of sorrow was ended, he and his companions vanished from the Maoris' sight. They melted into the clouds and the forest; and never again did they trouble Ruarangi and his wife. But the song that Whanawhana the *Patu-paiarehe* chanted as he stood there outside the sacred circle of incantation was well remembered by those who heard it–it was from it that they learned the names of his fellow-fairies–and it is known among all of us today. And this, my friend, is the song–

But I need not chant it to my readers. Sufficient is it that I have the words of this true fairy lament, and have done them into English, though in the alien dress they lose the subtle sound and color of the bush. As for Ruarangi and Tawhai-tu, they are no myth; their descendants live on the banks of the Waipa to this day.

"You may know them," says wise old Te Pou, "by the peculiar tinge of the hair in some of the families; it is what we call *uru-kehu*, because it is distinctly red or copper-colored; indeed it glistens like gold in the sun."

James Cowan

Notes on the Story

Whanawhana of the Bush

"Whanawhana of the Bush" is a tale from the Maori of New Zealand. The Maori believe that the demigod Maui fished the land of New Zealand out of the sea as they arrived in voyaging canoes. James Cowan (1870–1943), a New Zealander, was a historian and ethnographer, who collected Maori folklore and was fluent in the Maori language.

The *Patu-paiarehe* fairies of New Zealand are supernatural forest creatures, often human-sized. They guard sacred places and only come out at night Another tale of the *Patu-paiarehe* describes how the Maori learned to make fishnets from the fairies, which gave them sustenance from the sea. This demonstrates the simultaneously helpful and harmful nature of the fairies, as is the case the world over. Although in this tale, Whanawhana's desire is not reciprocated, love between fairies and mortals can carry a similar ambiguity, as in the case of "Connla and the Fairy Maiden" (see page 237).

Mochomo

Once there was a mochomo, a chieftain of the ants, who was driving a mule train of little mochomos. One night it turned very cold and snowed, and the snow killed every one of his train of mules.

"I shall go to the king of the snow," said Mochomo. "He has killed all of my mules!" He went to the house of the king of the snow, saying, "I am angry. Your snow killed my mule train! If you are a brave man you will fight me!"

"Oh, no," said the king of the snow, "I am not brave. I am very soft and weak. There is a man who is stronger than I am and he is the sun. When the sun shines on me I disappear."

"Well, I will go to see the sun then," shouted Mochomo. And he strode off. To the sun he said, "The snow has killed all my train of

mules. You are braver than the snow, so I am going to fight you, since you are so strong."

"Oh, no," said the sun, "there is one who is stronger than I. That is the clouds. I have no strength when they cover me."

So Mochomo went to the king of the clouds, offering to fight him.

The king of the clouds said, "The strongest of all is the wind. It blows me wherever it wills."

"Then I shall have to fight the wind. Where does he live?" asked Mochomo.

"Down there in that blacksmith shop," said the king of the clouds.

Mochomo went down to the blacksmith shop and strode up to the bellows.

"I am very angry. The snow killed all of my mules. Since you are the strongest and bravest, I am going to fight you!" he shouted.

The bellows made no answer. Then suddenly they blew very hard, blowing the angry Mochomo, chief of the ants, far away.

Ruth Warner Giddings

Notes on the Story

MOCHOMO

"Mochomo" is a tale that comes from the Yaqui people, a Cahitan-speaking tribe native to Sonora, Mexico. The history of the Yaqui people is entwined with Spanish conquest and Jesuit conversion, which intermingled indigenous beliefs with European traditions. Ruth Warner Giddings, a scholar from the University of Arizona, collected stories from Yaqui narrators, which she compiled alongside notes on Yaqui history into the book *Yaqui Myths and Legends* (1959).

✣

The tale of "Mochomo" is an accumulative or chain tale, in which each component builds on the last. Longer versions of this story include further elements in the chain, including a wall, mouse, cat, dog, stick, fire, water, ox, and, ultimately, God. Versions of this kind of story can be found in Spain, France, and Portugal. The Europeans who came to the Americas possibly brought the tale with them, as similar tales can now also be found in New Mexico, California, and Brazil.

The Trickster's Great Fall and His Revenge

Once while the buzzard was soaring away through the air he saw Manabozho walking along. He flew a little toward the ground, with his wings outspread, and heard Manabozho say to him, "Buzzard, you must be very happy up there, where you can soar through the air and see what is transpiring in the world beneath. Take me on your back so that I may ascend with you and see how it appears down here from where you live."

The buzzard came down, and said, "Manabozho, get on my back and I will take you up into the sky to let you see how the world appears from my abode."

Manabozho approached the buzzard, but seeing how smooth his back appeared said, "Buzzard, I am frightened you will let me slide from your back, so you must be careful not to sweep around too rapidly, that I may retain my place upon your back."

The buzzard told Manabozho that he would be careful, although the bird was determined to play a trick on him if possible. Manabozho mounted the buzzard and held on to his feathers as well as he could. The buzzard took a short run, leaped from the ground, spread his wings and rose into the air. Manabozho felt rather timid as the buzzard swept through the air, and as he circled around his body leaned so much that Manabozho could scarcely retain his position, and he was afraid of slipping off. Presently, as Manabozho was looking down upon the broad earth below, the buzzard made a sharp curve to one side so that his body leaned more than ever. Manabozho, losing his grasp, slipped off and dropped to earth like an arrow. He struck the ground with such force as to knock him senseless. The buzzard returned to his place in the sky, but hovered around to see what would become of Manabozho.

Manabozho lay a long time like one dead. When he recovered he saw something close to and apparently staring him in the face. He could not at first recognize it, but when he put his hands against the object he found that it was his own buttocks, because he had been all doubled up. He arose and prepared to go on his way, when he espied the buzzard above him, laughing at his own trickery.

Manabozho looked up and then said, "Buzzard, you have played a trick on me by letting me fall, but as I am more powerful than you, I shall revenge myself."

The buzzard then replied, "No, Manabozho, you will not do anything of the kind, because you cannot deceive me. I shall watch you."

Manabozho kept on, and the buzzard, not noticing anything peculiar in the movements of Manabozho, flew on his way through the air. Manabozho then decided to transform himself into a dead deer, because he knew the buzzard had chosen to subsist on dead animals and fish.

Manabozho then went to a place visible from a great distance and from many directions, where he laid himself down and changed himself into the carcass of a deer. Soon the various birds and beasts and crawling things that subsist on such food began to congregate about the dead deer. The buzzard saw the birds flying toward the place where the body lay, and joined them. He flew around several times to see if it was Manabozho trying to deceive him, then thought to himself, "No, that is not Manabozho; it is truly a dead deer."

He then approached the body and began to pick a hole into the fleshy part of the thigh. Deeper and deeper into the flesh the buzzard picked until his head and neck was buried each time he reached in to pluck the fat from the intestines. Without warning, while the buzzard had his head completely hidden in the carcass of the deer, the deer jumped up and pinched together his flesh, thus firmly grasping the head and neck of the buzzard.

Then Manabozho said, "Aha! Buzzard, I did catch you after all, as I told you I would. Now pull out your head."

The buzzard with great difficulty withdrew his head from the cavity in which it had been enclosed, but the feathers were all pulled off, leaving his scalp and neck covered with nothing but red skin.

Then Manabozho said to the bird, "Thus do I punish you for your deceitfulness; henceforth you will go through the world without feathers on your head and neck, and you shall always stink because of the food you will be obliged to eat."

That is why the buzzard is such a bad-smelling fellow, and why his head and neck are featherless.

The Menominee Tribe, collected by Stith Thompson

"'No, that is not Manabozho;

it is truly a dead deer.'"

Notes on the Story

The Trickster's Great Fall and His Revenge

Stith Thompson (1885–1976) was an American folklorist who contributed much to the study of the genre. He translated and enlarged the Aarne-Thompson Tale Type Index, a tool that organized folktales into types across cultures. Thompson also further developed the Motif Index, a catalog of common occurrences in folktales and fairy tales. He published *Tales of the North American Indians* in 1929, the first comprehensive collection of Native American folklore.

This tale comes from the Menominee Tribe in Wisconsin in the Northern United States. The trickster character, Manobhozo, is recurrent in Menominee myths, and often crosses the boundary between animal and human by transforming back and forth from one to the other. The trickster, found across the world in folklore, is sometimes reprehensible, acting with the basest of human flaws. But tricksters also improved the world or made it the way it is. Like "Dinewan and Goomblegubbon" (page 245), this tale explains why an animal (the buzzard) looks the way it does.

The Offended Rolling Stone

Coyote was going along, and as he had not had anything to eat for some time he was very hungry. In the evening he went to a high hill and sat down. Early the next morning he started again. He came to a big, round stone. He took out his knife and said: "Grandfather, this knife I give to you as a present. I want you to help me to get something to eat."

Coyote went over a hill, and there in the bottom was a village of people. He went into the village and he could see meat hanging on poles everywhere in the camp. He went into one of the tepees and the people in the tepee roasted a piece of meat for him. Just as he was about to taste of the meat he thought of his knife and said:

"Why did I give my knife to that stone? I should have kept it and then I should have been able to cut the meat without having to pull it with my hands."

"'Grandchildren, there is a person running after me.'

The bullbats then said: 'Enter our lodge and remain there.'"

He asked to be excused and went out. He went to where the stone was. He said: "Grandfather, I will have to take back this knife, for I have found a village of people with plenty of meat."

He went over the hills and into the bottom, but there was no village there. Coyote went back and returned the knife to the stone. He went back over the hills and there saw the village and he entered one of the tepees. They placed before him some meat. He began to chew the meat. He thought of his knife.

He went back to the stone, and as he took the knife the stone said: "Why do you take the knife away from me? I am now going to kill you."

Then the stone ran after the Coyote. Coyote ran and came to a den of bears. He told the bears that a person was running after him and he asked them to help him. The bears said that they were not afraid of anything. They asked what the thing was, and he said it was the stone. The bears said: "Keep on running. We cannot do anything with the stone." The stone was close to Coyote when he came up to another den of mountain lions. They also told Coyote to pass on, as they could not do anything for him. After a while Coyote came to a buffalo standing all alone, but when the buffalo found out that it was the stone running after Coyote he told him to pass on. At last Coyote came to a place where the bullbats (nighthawks) stayed.

Coyote said: "Grandchildren, there is a person running after me."

The bullbats then said: "Enter our lodge and remain there."

When the stone came rolling up it said: "Where is that person who came here?" The bullbats did not reply and the stone became angry.

Then the bullbats said to the stone: "He is here and we are going to protect him."

The bullbats flew up and then down, and they expelled flatus on the stone. Every time they did this a piece broke off from the stone. The largest bullbat came down and expelled flatus right on the center and broke the stone into pieces. Then the coyote was told to come out and go on his way.

Coyote started off, and when he got over the hills he turned around and yelled at the bullbats and said: "All you big-nosed funny things, how you did behave to that stone."

The bullbats heard it and did not pay any attention, but he kept on making fun of them. Then the bullbats flew up in a group, and came down, and with their wings they got the stone together again and started it rolling, and said: "Go and kill that fellow."

The stone then ran after Coyote, and Coyote tried to get away, but he could not. At last, he gave up. He jumped over a steep bank and the stone was right behind him. As Coyote struck the bottom, the stone fell on him and killed him. This is why we used to find dead coyotes in the hills and valleys.

The Pawnee Nation, collected by Stith Thompson

Notes on the Story

The Offended Rolling Stone

The Pawnee Nation resides in the Midwestern United States. The religion of the Pawnees is based around cosmology, *Atius Tirawa* (the Father Above), and the personification of the moon, sun, and stars. This personification of gods and demigods also relates to the way Coyote as the trickster is portrayed in his frequent appearances in Pawnee folklore. He is not necessarily a talking coyote; rather, Coyote is one of the American Indian First People, or shapeshifting beings who lived in mythic times prior to the existence of humans. Coyote also exists in many other Native American tribal traditions across the United States.

This story has a moral message relating to Coyote's mistake in taking back what he had gifted to the stone. The true entertainment comes in how the trickster uses his wiles to attempt to come out on top, although in this story, he is ultimately punished for his misbehavior.

Orpheus

The Sun lived on the other side of the sky vault, but her daughter lived in the middle of the sky, directly above the earth, and every day as the Sun was climbing along the sky arch to the west she used to stop at her daughter's house for dinner.

Now, the Sun hated the people on the earth, because they could never look straight at her without screwing up their faces. She said to her brother, the Moon, "My grandchildren are ugly; they grin all over their faces when they look at me." But the Moon said, "I like my younger brothers; I think they are very handsome," because they always smiled pleasantly when they saw him in the sky at night, for his rays were milder.

The Sun was jealous and planned to kill all the people; so every day when she got near her daughter's house she sent down such sultry rays that there was a great fever and the people died by hundreds, until everyone had lost some friend and there was fear that no one would be left. They went for help to the Little Men, who said the only way to save themselves was to kill the Sun.

The Little Men made medicine and changed two men into snakes, the Spreading-adder and the Copperhead, and sent them to watch near the door of the daughter of the Sun to bite the old Sun when she came next day. They went together and hid near the house until the Sun came, but when the Spreading-adder was about to spring, the bright light blinded him and he could only spit out yellow slime, as he does to this day when he tries to bite. She called him a nasty thing and went by into the house, and the Copperhead crawled off without trying to do anything.

So the people still died from the heat, and they went to the Little Men a second time for help. The Little Men made medicine again and changed one man into a great Uktena (horned serpent) and another into the Rattlesnake and sent them to watch near the house and kill the old Sun when she came for dinner. They made the Uktena very large, with horns on his head, and everyone thought he would be sure to do the work, but the Rattlesnake was so quick and eager that he got ahead and coiled up just outside the house, and when the Sun's daughter opened the door to look out for her mother, he sprang up and bit her and she fell dead in the doorway. He forgot to wait for the old Sun, but went back to the people, and the Uktena was so very angry that he went back, too. Since then we pray to the Rattlesnake and do not kill him, because he is kind and never tries to bite if we do not disturb him.

The Uktena grew angrier all the time and very dangerous, so that if he even looked at a man, that man's family would die. After a long time the people held a council and decided that he was too dangerous to be with them, so they sent him up to Galunlati, and he is there now. The Spreading-adder, the Copperhead, the Rattlesnake, and the Uktena were all men.

When the Sun found her daughter dead, she went into the house and grieved, and the people did not die any more, but now the world was dark all the time, because the Sun would not come out. They went again to the Little Men, and these told them that if they wanted the Sun to come out again they must bring back her daughter from Tsusginai, the Ghost Country, in Usunhiyi, the Darkening Land in the west. They chose seven men to go, and gave each a sourwood rod a handbreadth long. The Little Men told them they must take a box with them, and when they got to Tsusginai they would find all the ghosts at a dance. They must stand outside the circle, and when the young woman passed in the dance they must strike her with the rods and she would fall to the ground. Then they must put her into the box and bring her back to her mother, but they must be very sure not to open the box, even a little way, until they were home again.

They took the rods and a box and traveled seven days to the west until they came to the Darkening Land. There were a great many people there, and they were having a dance just as if they were at home in the settlements. The young woman was in the outside circle, and as she swung around to where the seven men were standing, one struck her with his rod and she turned her head and saw him. As she came around the second time another touched her with his rod, and then another and another, until at the seventh round she fell out of the ring, and they put her into the box and closed the lid fast. The other ghosts seemed never to notice what had happened.

They took up the box and started home toward the east. In a little while the girl came to life again and begged to be let out of the box, but they made no answer and went on. Soon she called again and she said she was hungry, but still they made no answer and went on. After another while she spoke again, and called for a drink, and pleaded so that it was very hard to listen to her, but the men who carried the box said nothing and still went on. When at last they were very near home,

"The Sun . . . cried, 'My daughter, my daughter,'

and wept until her tears made a flood upon the earth . . ."

she called again and begged them to raise the lid just a little, because she was smothering. They were afraid she was really dying now, so they lifted the lid a little to give her air, but as they did so there was a fluttering sound inside and something flew past them into the thicket and they heard a redbird cry, "Kwish! Kwish! Kwish!" in the bushes. They shut down the lid and went on again to the settlements, but when they got there and opened the box it was empty.

So we know the redbird is the daughter of the Sun, and if the men had kept the box closed, as the Little Men told them to do, they would have brought her home safely, and we could bring back our other friends also from the Ghost Country, but now when they die we can never bring them back.

The Sun had been glad when they started to the Ghost Country, but when they came back without her daughter she grieved and cried, "My daughter, my daughter," and wept until her tears made a flood upon the earth, and the people were afraid the world would be drowned. They held another council, and sent their handsomest young men and women to amuse her so that she would stop crying. They danced before the Sun and sang their best songs, but for a long time she kept her face covered and paid no attention, until at last the drummer suddenly changed the song, when she lifted up her face, and was so pleased at the sight that she forgot her grief and smiled.

The Cherokee Nation, collected by Stith Thompson

Notes on the Story

Orpheus

This tale comes from the Cherokee Nation, a Native American tribe from the Southeastern United States. The tale explains the origins of the various types of snakes found in the area: the copperhead, the spreading-adder, and the rattlesnake. The angry Uktena who is sent to Galunlati is a horned serpent from American Indian lore, and his banishment in the story explains why he no longer exists in the real world.

The second part of the tale, in which the Sun's daughter is rescued from death and becomes a redbird, echoes the story of Orpheus and Eurydice from Greek mythology. The contact between the European settlers and the Cherokee Nation generated a trade of culture that may have influenced a similar myth that the Cherokees already had. However, Thompson most likely named this story "Orpheus" when he created his anthology of Native American tales and noticed the similarity between the two myths.

The Son-in-Law Tests

Wemicus (the animal-trickster) had a son-in-law who was a man. This man's wife, the daughter of Wemicus, had had a great many husbands, because Wemicus had put them to so many different tests that they had all been killed except this one. He, however, had succeeded in outwitting Wemicus in every scheme that he tried on him. Wemicus and this man hunted beaver in the spring of the year by driving them all day with dogs.

The man's wife warned him before they started out to hunt, saying, "Look out for my father; he might burn your moccasins in camp. That's what he did to my other husbands."

That night in camp Wemicus said, "I didn't tell you the name of this lake. It is called 'Burnt Moccasins Lake.'"

When the man heard this, he thought that Wemicus was up to some sort of mischief and was going to burn his moccasins. Their moccasins were hanging up before a fire to dry and, while Wemicus was not looking, the man changed the places of Wemicus' moccasins and his own, and then went to sleep. Soon the man awoke and saw Wemicus get up and throw his own moccasins into the fire.

Wemicus then said, "Say! Something is burning; it is your moccasins."

Then the man answered, "No, not mine, but yours." So Wemicus had no moccasins, and the ground was covered with snow. After this had happened the man slept with his moccasins on.

The next morning the man started on and left Wemicus there with no shoes. Wemicus started to work. He got a big boulder, made a fire, and placed the boulder in it until it became red hot. He then wrapped his feet with spruce boughs and pushed the boulder ahead of him in order to melt the snow. In this way he managed to walk on the boughs.

Then he began to sing, "Spruce is warm, spruce is warm." When the man reached home he told his wife what had happened.

"I hope Wemicus will die," she said.

A little while after this they heard Wemicus coming along singing, "Spruce is warm, spruce is warm." He came into the wigwam and as he was the head man, they were obliged to get his meal ready.

The ice was getting bad by this time, so they stayed in camp awhile. Soon Wemicus told his son-in-law, "We'd better go sliding."

He then went to a hill where there were some very poisonous snakes. The wife warned her husband of these snakes and gave him a split stick holding a magic tobacco, which she told him to hold in front of him so that the snakes would not hurt him. Then the two men went sliding.

At the top of the hill Wemicus said, "Follow me," for he intended to pass close by the snakes' lair. So when they slid, Wemicus passed safely and the man held his stick with the tobacco in it in front of him, thus preventing the snakes from biting him. The man then told Wemicus that he enjoyed the sliding.

The following day Wemicus said to his son-in-law, "We had better go to another place."

When she heard this, the wife told her husband that, as it was getting summer, Wemicus had in his head many poisonous lizards instead of lice.

She said, "He will tell you to pick lice from his head and crack them in your teeth. But take low-bush cranberries and crack them instead."

So the man took cranberries along with him. Wemicus took his son-in-law to a valley with a great ravine in it. He said, "I wonder if anybody can jump across this?"

"Wemicus, looking up, saw his son-in-law,

but mistook him for a gull."

"Surely," said the young man, "I can." Then the young man said, "Closer," and the ravine narrowed and he jumped across easily.

When Wemicus tried, the young man said, "Widen," and Wemicus fell into the ravine. But it did not kill him, and when he made his way to the top again, he said, "You have beaten me." Then they went on.

They came to a place of hot sand and Wemicus said, "You must look for lice in my head."

"All right father," replied the son-in-law. So Wemicus lay down and the man started to pick the lice. He took the cranberries from inside his shirt and each time he pretended to catch a louse, he cracked a cranberry and threw it on the ground, and so Wemicus got fooled a second time.

Then they went home and Wemicus said to his son-in-law, "There are a whole lot of eggs on that rocky island where the gulls are. We will go get the eggs, come back, and have an egg supper." As Wemicus was the head man, his son-in-law had to obey him.

So they started out in their canoe and soon came to the rocky island. Wemicus stayed in the canoe and told the man to go ashore and to bring the eggs back with him and fill the canoe. When the man reached the shore, Wemicus told him to go farther back on the island, saying, "That's where the former husbands got their eggs, there are their bones."

He then started the canoe off in the water by singing, without using his paddle. Then Wemicus told the gulls to eat the man, saying to them, "I give you him to eat."

The gulls started to fly about the man, but the man had his paddle with him and he killed one of the gulls with it. He then took the gulls' wings and fastened them on himself, filled his shirt with eggs, and started flying over the lake by the aid of the wings.

When he reached the middle of the lake, he saw Wemicus going along and singing to himself. Wemicus, looking up, saw his son-in-law, but mistook him for a gull. The man flew back to camp and told his wife to cook the eggs, and he told his children to play with the wings.

When Wemicus reached the camp, he saw the children playing with the wings and said, "Where did you get those wings?"

"From father," was the reply.

"Your father? Why the gulls ate him!" Then he went to the wigwam and there he saw the man smoking. Then Wemicus thought it very strange how the man could have gotten home, but no one told him how it had been done. Thought he, "I must try another scheme to do away with him."

One day Wemicus said to his son-in-law, "We'd better make two canoes of birch-bark, one for you and one for me. We'd better get bark."

So they started off for birch-bark. They cut a tree almost through and Wemicus said to his son-in-law, "You sit on that side and I'll sit on this." He wanted the tree to fall on him and kill him.

Wemicus said, "You say, 'Fall on my father-in-law,' and I'll say, 'Fall on my son-in-law,' and whoever says it too slowly or makes a mistake will be the one on whom it will fall."

But Wemicus made the first mistake, and the tree fell on him and crushed him. However, Wemicus was a *manitu* (spirit) and was not hurt. They went home with the bark and made the two canoes. After they were made, Wemicus said to his son-in-law, "Well, we'll have a race in our two canoes, a sailing race."

Wemicus made a big bark sail, but the man did not make any, as he was afraid of capsizing. They started the race. Wemicus went very fast and the man called after him, "Oh, you are beating me."

He kept on fooling and encouraging Wemicus, until the wind upset Wemicus's canoe and that was the end of Wemicus. When the man sailed over the spot where Wemicus had upset, he saw a big pike there, into which Wemicus had been transformed when the canoe upset. This is the origin of the pike.

The Temagami First Nation, collected by Stith Thompson

Notes on the Story

The Son-in-Law Tests

The Temagami First Nation are located in Canada, they primarily live on Bear Island in Lake Temagami. This tale features a trickster character, like Manobhozo in "The Trickster's Great Fall and his Revenge" (page 374) and Coyote in "The Offended Rolling Stone" (page 379). Thompson saw "The Son-in-Law Tests" as noteworthy, since it is simultaneously a trickster tale and a hero tale. In Native American folklore, hero tales follow a man who must escape multiple times from death.

✣

The threat from a father-in-law is similar to European fairy tales in which a suitor must overcome tests to marry a princess. The wife or future wife often helps him to defeat her father's tests (this is less likely if the princess sets the test, as in "Fair Goldilocks," see page 55). Suitor tests speak to the desire in most cultures to see that one's children will marry someone worthy. They also explore the difficulties of relating to one's mother- or father-in-law after marriage.

BIBLIOGRAPHY

Andersen, Hans Christian. *Hans Andersen's Fairy Tales*. Translated by Mrs. Henry H. B. Paull; illustrated by Wilhelm Petersen and Lorenz Frolich. London: Frederick Warne & Co., 1872, 1883.

Andersen, Hans Christian. *The Fairy Tales of Hans Christian Andersen*. Edited by Noel Daniel. Cologne: Taschen, 2013.

Appleton, Dr. Naomi. *Jātaka Stories in Theravada Buddhism: Narrating the Bodhisatta Path*. Farnham: Ashgate Publishing, Ltd., 2013.

Asbjørnsen, Peter Christen and Jørgen Moe. *East of the Sun and West of the Moon: Old Tales from the North*. Translated by George Webbe Dasent. Edinburgh: David Douglass, 1888.

Basile, Giambattista. *Stories from the Pentamerone*. Edited by E. F. Strange; illustrated by Warwick Goble. London: Macmillan & Co., 1911.

Basile, Giambattista. *The Tale of Tales, or Entertainment for Little Ones*. Translated by Nancy L. Canepa. Detroit: Wayne State University Press, 2007.

Bealle, John. "Another Look at Charles M. Skinner." *Western Folklore* 53, no. 2 (1994): 99–123.

Bright, William. *A Coyote Reader*. Berkeley: University of California Press, 1993.

Buddhaghoṣa, and Thomas William Rhys Davids. *Buddhist Birth-Stories (Jātaka Tales)*. New Delhi: Asian Educational Services, 1999.

Cole, Mabel Cook. *Philippine Folk Tales*; illustrations by Fay-Cooper Cole. Chicago: A. C. McClurg & Co., 1916.

Cowan, James. *Fairy Folk Tales of the Maori*. Auckland: Whitcomb and Tombs Ltd., 1925.

Cox, Marian Roalfe. *Cinderella; Three Hundred and Forty-Five Variants of Cinderella, Catskin, and Cap o'Rushes, Abstracted and Tabulated, with a Discussion of Mediaeval Analogues, and Notes*. London: The Folklore Society, 1893.

D'Aulnoy, Mme. *The Fairy Tales of Madame d'Aulnoy, Newly Done into English*. Translated by Annie Macdonell and Miss Lee. London: Lawrence and Bullen, 1892.

Drake, Joseph Rodman. *The Culprit Fay: And Other Poems*. New York: G. Dearborn, 1835.

Dundas, Marjorie. *Riddling Tales from Around the World*. Jackson: University Press of Mississippi, 2002.

Espinosa, Aurelio M. "Comparative Notes on New-Mexican and Mexican Spanish Folk-Tales." *The Journal of American Folklore* 27, no. 104 (1914): 211–31.

Francis, H. T. and E. J. Thomas. *Jātaka Tales*. Cambridge: Cambridge University Press, 2014.

Giddings, Ruth Warner. *Yaqui Myths and Legends*. Chicago: University of Arizona, 1959.

Gray, William. *Death and Fantasy: Essays on Philip Pullman, C. S. Lewis, George MacDonald and R. L. Stevenson*. Newcastle upon Tyne: Cambridge Scholars Publishing, 2009.

Gray, William. *Fantasy, Art and Life: Essays on George MacDonald, Robert Louis Stevenson and Other Fantasy Writers*. Newcastle upon Tyne: Cambridge Scholars Publishing, 2011.

Gray, William. "The Incomplete Fairy Tales of Robert Louis Stevenson." *Journal of Stevenson Studies* 2 (2005): 98–109.

Grimm, Jacob and Wilhelm Grimm. *The Annotated Brothers Grimm*. Edited by Maria Tatar and A. S. Byatt. Bicentennial Edition. New York: W. W. Norton & Company, 2012.

Grimm, Jacob and Wilhelm Grimm. *Household Tales*. Translated by Margaret Hunt. London: George Bell, 1884, 1892.

Grinnell, George Bird. "Pawnee Mythology." *The Journal of American Folklore* 6, no. 21 (1893): 113–30.

Haase, Donald. *The Greenwood Encyclopedia of Folktales and Fairy Tales*. 3 vols. Westport: Greenwood Publishing Group, 2007.

Hadland Davis, Frederick. *Myths and Legends of Japan*. Illustrated by Evelyn Paul. New York: T. Y. Crowell Co., 1912.

Hahn, Daniel. *The Oxford Companion to Children's Literature*. Oxford: Oxford University Press, 2015.

Hennard Dutheil de la Rochère, Martine. "Updating the Politics of Experience: Angela Carter's Translation of Charles Perrault's 'Le Petit Chaperon Rouge.'" *Palimpsestes. Revue de Traduction*, no. 22 (October 9, 2009): 187–204.

Hermansson, Casie. *Bluebeard: A Reader's Guide to the English Tradition*. Jackson: University Press of Mississippi, 2009.

Holbek, Bengt. "Hans Christian Andersen's Use of Folktales." *Merveilles et Contes* 4, no. 2 (1990): 220–32.

Jacobs, Joseph. *Celtic Fairy Tales*. London: David Nutt, 1892.

Jacobs, Joseph. *English Fairy Tales*. London: David Nutt, 1890.

Jacobs, Joseph. *English Fairy Tales: And, More English Fairy Tales*. Edited by John Dickson Batten. Santa Barbara: ABC-CLIO, 2002.

Jacobs, Joseph. *Indian Fairy Tales*, illustrated by John D. Batten. London: David Nutt, 1892.

Johnson, Rossiter and John Howard Brown. *The Twentieth Century Biographical Dictionary of Notable Americans*. Boston: The Biographical Society, 1904.

Knowles, James Hinton. *Folk-Tales of Kashmir*. London: K. Paul, Trench, Trübner & Co. Ltd., 1893.

Krenner, Walther G. von and Ken Jeremiah. *Creatures Real and Imaginary in Chinese and Japanese Art: An Identification Guide*. Jefferson: McFarland, 2015.

Kuznets, Lois R. *When Toys Come Alive: Narratives of Animation, Metamorphosis, and Development*. New Haven: Yale University Press, 1994.

Lang, Andrew. *The Arabian Nights Entertainments*. London: Longmans, Green & Co., 1898.

Lang, Andrew. *The Olive Fairy Book*. London: Longmans, Green & Co., 1907.

Le Prince de Beaumont, Marie. *Beauty and the Beast: A Tale for the Entertainment of Juvenile Readers*. Glasgow: J. Lumsden and Son, 1756.

MacDonald, George. *Ranald Bannerman's Boyhood*. London: Strahan & Co., 1871.

Martin, Peggy. *Stith Thompson: His Life and His Role in Folklore Scholarship : With a Bibliography*. Bloomington: Indian University Folklore Publications Group, 1976.

Metge, Joan. *Rautahi: The Maori of New Zealand*. Abingdon: Psychology Press, 2004.

Perrault, Charles. *Old Time Stories*. New York: Dodd, Mead, 1921.

Ransome, Arthur. *Old Peter's Russian Tales*. London and Edinburgh: T. C. & E. C. Jack, Ltd, 1916.

Silva, Sara Graça da and Jamshid J. Tehrani. "Comparative Phylogenetic Analyses Uncover the Ancient Roots of Indo-European Folktales." *Royal Society Open Science* 3, no. 1 (January 1, 2016): 150645.

Skinner, Charles M. *Myths And Legends Of Our Own Land*. Philadelphia: J. B. Lippincott Company, 1896.

Smith, Richard Gordon. *Ancient Tales and Folklore of Japan*. London: A. & C. Black, 1908.

Steiger, Brad. *The Werewolf Book: The Encyclopedia of Shape-Shifting Beings*. Canton: Visible Ink Press, 2011.

Stevenson, Robert Louis. *Short Stories IV: Fables. Island Nights' Entertainments*, edited by Professor William Gray. New Edinburgh Edition of the Works of Robert Louis Stevenson. Edinburgh: Edinburgh University Press, 2017.

Straparola, Giovanni Francesco. *The facetious nights of Straparola*. London: Privately printed for members of the Society of Bibliophiles, 1901.

Tatar, Maria. *The Annotated Classic Fairy Tales*. 1st ed. London: Norton, 2002.

Tatar, Maria. *The Hard Facts of the Grimms' Fairy Tales*. Guildford: Princeton University Press, 1987.

Thompson, Stith. *Tales of the North American Indians*. Bloomington: Indiana University Press, 1929.

Thompson, Stith. *The Folktale*. Berkeley: University of California Press, 1977.

Turner, Kay. *Transgressive Tales: Queering the Grimms*. Detroit: Wayne State University Press, 2012.

Warner, Marina. *From the Beast to the Blonde: On Fairy Tales and Their Tellers*. London: Vintage, 1995.

Watts, Linda S. *Encyclopedia of American Folklore*. New York: Infobase Publishing, 2006.

Wilde, Oscar. *The Happy Prince and Other Tales*. Illustrated by Walter Crane and G. P. Jacomb-Hood. London: David Nutt, 1888.

Young, Philip. "Fallen from Time: The Mythic Rip Van Winkle." *The Kenyon Review* 22, no. 4 (1960): 547–73.

Zipes, Jack. *Fairy Tales and the Art of Subversion*. New York: Routledge, 2012.

Zipes, Jack. *Hans Christian Andersen: The Misunderstood Storyteller*. New York: Routledge, 2014.

Zipes, Jack. *The Oxford Companion to Fairy Tales*. Oxford: Oxford University Press, 2015.

Fairy Tale Online Resources

https://archive.org

http://classics-illustrated.com

http://hca.gilead.org

www.endicott-studio.com

www.gutenberg.org

www.sacred-texts.com

www.surlalunefairytales.com

www.worldoftales.com

Index

Acknowledgments

The publishers would like to thank
Professor William Gray, Lorna Gray, Dr. Joanna Gilar,
Heather Robbins, and Rose Williamson for their
contributions to this book, and Fausto Bianchi
for his inspired illustrations.

Silhouette source images © Shutterstock: agrino; Aleks Melnik; AnastasiaSonne; Anastasiia Golovkova; AnastasijaD; ashva; basel101658; Benguhan; blambca; briddy; Cat Design; Cattallina; chronicler; Cienpies Design; Darq; De-V; debra hughes; derGriza; Designer things; Dn Br; Edvard Molnar; eladora; Ellika; elmm; ESZA Design; eva_mask; foodonwhite; Fun Way Illustration; grmarc; grynold; Heitor Barbosa; Hibrida; HuHu; Jacky Brown; jkerrigan; John Erickson; Kalcutta; KatarinaF; Kazakova Maryia; Kjolak; kostins; KravOK; Ksanawo; Leone_V; lilac; Liubou Yasiukovich; majivecka; Martial Red; mashakotcur; Maxi_m; McVectors; Miceking; Mike H; mirabile; Mischoko; Morgunova Tetiana; Naddya; nahariyani; Nataliia Sydorova; nenad vojnovic; Nowik Sylwia; Ola-ola; Oleg7799; Olesia Misty; Olga Lebedeva; paprika; patrimonio designs ltd; Potapov Alexander; Reshetnyova Oxana; sababa66; sabri deniz kizil; Santi0103; Seamartini Graphics; Seita; Shpak Anton; silm; Snez; StellaL; StockSmartStart; SuslO; tachyglossus; tantrik71; The Polovinkin; Tronin Andrei; URRRA; Valadzionak Volha; Vasmila; Vector Draco; Vector FX; vectorbomb; Vitaly Ilyasov; Voropaev Vasiliy; whiteisthecolor; ylq; yod67; Yoko Design; Yunna; Yurchenko Yulia; yyang; Zimniy.